Bride of the Barrier Master

3

Kureha

YEN ON

NEW YORK

Bride of the Barrier Master 3

KUREHA

Translation by Linda Liu ◆ Cover art by Bodax

KEKKAISHI NO ICHIRINKA Vol.3
©Kureha 2023
First published in Japan in 2023 by KADOKAWA CORPORATION, Tokyo.
English translation rights arranged with KADOKAWA CORPORATION, Tokyo, through TUTTLE-MORI AGENCY, INC., Tokyo.

English translation © 2024 by Yen Press, LLC

Yen On
150 West 30th Street, 19th Floor
New York, NY 10001

Visit us at yenpress.com
facebook.com/yenpress
twitter.com/yenpress
yenpress.tumblr.com
instagram.com/yenpress

First Yen On Edition: June 2024
Edited by Yen On Editorial: Leilah Labossiere
Designed by Yen Press Design: Madelaine Norman

Yen On is an imprint of Yen Press, LLC.
The Yen On name and logo are trademarks of Yen Press, LLC.

Library of Congress Cataloging-in-Publication Data
Names: Kureha (Light novel author), author. | Liu, Linda (Translator), translator.
Title: Bride of the barrier master / Kureha ; translation by Linda Liu.
Other titles: Kekkaishi no ichirinka. English
Description: First Yen On edition. | New York : Yen On, 2023–
Identifiers: LCCN 2022043316 | ISBN 9781975360528 (v. 1 ; trade paperback) |
   ISBN 9781975370336 (v. 2 ; trade paperback) | ISBN 9781975389116 (v. 3 ; trade paperback)
Subjects: LCGFT: Fantasy fiction. | Romance fiction. | Light novels.
Classification: LCC PZ7.1.K85 Br 2023 | DDC [Fic]—dc23
LC record available at https://lccn.loc.gov/2022043316

ISBNs: 978-1-9753-8911-6 (paperback)
        978-1-9753-8912-3 (ebook)

10 9 8 7 6 5 4 3 2 1

LSC-C

Printed in the United States of America

Contents

Prologue

On a mountain deep within Japan's borders—dimly lit despite the sun shining high above—among the scores of trees growing wild, a momentous event was underway: the Association of Practitioners' exam to advance from the Fourth Color rank to the Fifth.

The objective of this exam was to exterminate the shades residing on the mountain.

As befitting the Fifth Color advancement exam, the shades were no small fries.

After several practitioners had tried but failed to destroy them, a barrier had been placed around the mountain to seal the shades in and prevent further casualties. The Fifth Color practitioners were about to be summoned to handle the extermination, but then the exam hopeful had appeared, and thus the mountain had been co-opted as the stage for the exam.

The challenger was Yukizasa Sankourou, a young man with an icy gaze and hair as light as snow. He was slim and tall, with refined facial features like a model. He was only twenty years old, and yet he had already been nominated as the next Sankourou clan lord.

Yukizasa had entered the mountain ages ago.

As a candidate for the Fifth Color, he was far from weak. The fact that the extermination had taken so long was a testament to the formidability of the shades. The practitioners maintaining the barrier saw the trouble he was having and grew concerned about Yukizasa. However, he came down the mountain at regular intervals to report on his progress, so the exam was technically still underway. That said, if he took much longer, he would be unlikely to pass—a fact that he knew very well.

Fifth Color practitioners, the highest ranked in the profession, were the final bastion. Anyone who could not take down shades the level of those on the mountain could not be permitted to assume the prestigious title.

In fact, Fifth Color practitioners often had to face shades far stronger than the ones Yukizasa was fighting. The rank would mean little if it was easily achievable.

As such, Obsidian practitioners were both respected and feared.

Yukizasa fought on, first advancing, then forced to fall back, and at last, he prevailed. He descended the mountain with wounds all over his body.

The practitioners maintaining the barrier welcomed him back, calling out, "Good work."

"I have successfully exterminated the horde," Yukizasa announced.

His proclamation set the crowd buzzing. "That's great news! Congratulations!" one person shouted.

He had banished the shades single-handedly. In other words, he had passed the exam.

One practitioner presented Yukizasa with his reward: an obsidian pendant.

He took it with a confident smile. He removed the lapis one he had been wearing and hung the obsidian one around his neck instead.

The pendant was shiny and jet-black. It settled around his collar as if it had always been there.

"I've finally done it," Yukizasa said. "It may have taken me a little longer than it took Saku, but I've caught up." He failed to fully suppress his satisfied grin.

It was during that moment of triumph that one of the practitioners hesitantly approached him and said, "Sir, while you have been occupied here, Lord Ichinomiya has succeeded the Ichinomiya clan and is now the clan lord."

"What? Are you serious?" Yukizasa asked in shock.

"Yes, sir."

"But he's not married. What does he plan to do about the barrier around the pillar?"

"It is said that he has already taken a bride and completed the barrier's transfer."

"What?" Yukizasa exclaimed, forgetting his exhaustion momentarily. That was how unbelievable the news was. "He's married? You've got to be kidding me. To the daughter of which family exactly?"

After a bit of thinking, his expression brightened with understanding. "Come to think of it, there's a chick in one of Ichinomiya's branch families with a human shikigami, isn't there? The Ichise family. The son is the youngest practitioner to obtain the Lapis rank, and she's his younger sister. I've heard she's quite accomplished. It must be her." He nodded, satisfied that he'd solved the mystery.

Loath to contradict him, the other practitioner said awkwardly, "The lady in question is likely not the younger sister you are thinking of, but the other one, I believe."

Yukizasa furrowed his brow. "Huh? What are you talking about?"

"Lord Ichinomiya did indeed marry one of the Ichise daughters. However, his wife is not the one widely regarded as exceptional but the one infamous for being her sister's scraps."

Not following, Yukizasa tilted his head in puzzlement. "Is that a joke?"

Chapter 1

In the Ichise family's halls, from whence both Hana and Hazuki had gone, their parents remained, sequestered in their room and obviously irritated. The residence's servants—not wishing to become scapegoats for their master and mistress's wrath—had started to avoid the room, and thus, the vicinity was cloaked in silence.

Unbeknownst to the two, word that Hazuki had left the house had already spread; the servants circulated the story in whispers.

"Miss Hazuki has finally flown the coop, it seems."

"Really? But who could blame her? Should've seen it coming, honestly."

"What the Master and Mistress put her through was more like abuse than an educational regimen. Of course she would grow to hate it. If only they had doted on her more, instead of pushing her the way they did."

"Shhh! We'll get in trouble if they overhear."

Oblivious to the conversations the servants were having, the twins' father was pacing around the master bedroom, unable to sit still. Their mother was biting her nails and trying to regain her composure. When

Hana—that ungrateful whelp—had suddenly shown her face at the house, they had assumed she'd been kicked out of the Ichinomiya residence. But instead, she had gone and dragged Hazuki away with her.

Until now, Hazuki had obeyed their wishes—had been a daughter they could be proud of. For her to reject the marriage they had labored to arrange for her... Outrageous! They were incensed over this rebellion by the daughter who had never once gone against them and were adamant that Hana's bad influence was the cause.

It would have been one thing if they were worried for Hazuki, even if only slightly, but there wasn't a shadow of a thought for their daughter in their hearts. They were merely agitated and in disbelief that she had defied them.

Apparently, Hazuki had ended up in the Ichinomiya main residence.

As for how they knew, they had received a call from the Ichinomiya clan lord's mother, Mio, informing them that Hazuki would live in the Ichinomiya residence from that day forward. The matter-of-fact report left no room for refusal. Immediately after stating her business, she had hung up, as if to say the Ichise parents' opinions were unnecessary.

Mio's dismissive attitude further fueled their indignation.

"Hazuki must have been deceived by Hana. That must be it. There is no other reason she would defy us," the Ichise patriarch spat.

"Yes, exactly," the mother agreed.

The two egotistical parents did not yield to anything so trivial as self-reflection. The thought that they could be at fault didn't so much as cross their minds, though it was clear to even the servants why Hazuki had left.

"That wretched Hana! How much more of a nuisance does she intend to be to this family? I knew we should have given her up for adoption. We let her stay since Hazuki was so against it, and this is how she repays us? What a worthless daughter!" the father cursed.

The twins' parents directed their rage at Hana.

"Let us complain to the clan!" the mother suggested. "She is the wife of the clan lord. We can accuse her of abusing her authority. Hazuki belongs to the Ichise family, after all."

"Ah, however…," he mumbled, "this is the main family we are dealing with. We cannot incur their ire…" The zeal he had shown earlier was nowhere to be seen.

Her eyes narrowed with fury. "Darling! You cannot afford to be so spineless. Hazuki will be snatched away from us!"

"I know that!" His ferocious roar reverberated around the room.

"Pardon me," came a voice from outside.

The speaker was Hana and Hazuki's older brother, Yanagi. He had been absent from the house for the past several days due to work. He came in and immediately sat down next to the sliding doors.

Talented enough to have become the youngest person to achieve the Lapis rank, Yanagi should have been the shining hope of his parents, who dreamed of restoring their family name to its former glory. However, compared to their fervor toward Hazuki, their treatment of him was frigid.

To be blunt, had they truly wanted to climb the ranks, the best course of action would have been to yield the head of the family position to Yanagi sooner rather than later. It was well-known that the clan lord, Saku, favored him and often relied on him for work.

But the Ichise elder didn't do that. He was still occupying the seat.

At the moment, he was looking at Yanagi with eyes so cold, it was hard to believe he could be looking at his own child. "Yanagi," he said dismissively. "We're busy. Why have you come?"

"It appears that Hazuki has left the house," Yanagi said.

He merely meant to verify the situation, but his calm demeanor grated on his father's nerves.

"So what?! Are you saying it's *my* fault?" his father shouted. He gnashed his teeth in rage.

"...I am only asking to confirm," Yanagi said.

Suddenly, his father was struck by a realization. "That's it. Yanagi! You visit the main residence regularly, do you not? You are in good standing with Lord Ichinomiya, as well. Go and persuade Hazuki. Bring her back no matter what!" he demanded.

Yanagi looked at his father, who was fully convinced of his plan's genius, with placid eyes that showed no confusion nor turbulence. "I cannot."

"Why not?! That's an order. You only need to do what I say!"

The haughty declaration could hardly be thought of as words from a father. Nevertheless, Yanagi was unshaken, tranquil like the deep waters of the ocean. "Hazuki left of her own volition."

"Hana is to blame!"

"Hazuki is no longer a child. Besides, Lord Ichinomiya has now become her guardian. He took her in under her own wishes. What can one insignificant branch family do?"

Insignificant...like the fallen Ichise family was implied.

"You are free to come and go through the main residence. Drag her here by force and be done with it!" his father yelled.

Does he understand how cowardly a move that would be? No. His ignorance is precisely why he can spit such pathetic words.

"Do you mean to anger the main family by doing so? As a servant of the Ichinomiya clan, I must decline. Even if I were not, making an enemy out of the Ichinomiyas would be a foolish decision. I suggest you reconsider," Yanagi said, calmly selecting his words of warning even when faced with his father's open wrath.

However, the words that were meant to prevent his father from giving in to irrational impulses only fanned the flames.

"You have always been like this. Your younger sister is gone, and yet you are as expressionless as ever," his father accused. "Behind your mask, you sneer at us. Mock us! Do you feel superior to have been chosen by your grandfather? But how unfortunate for you. The head of the Ichise family is me! Not Father, not you, but me!"

Finished with his tirade, he panted while glaring daggers at Yanagi.

Yanagi's mother was flustered by the turn of events but made no attempt to rein in her husband. It was no secret to anyone in the household that it was next to impossible to placate him when he was so worked up.

Accomplished though Yanagi might be, he was despised by his father. Or envied, perhaps it was more accurate to say.

Hana's existence had kept such feelings at bay, but before the twins had been born, Yanagi's father had always watched him with callous eyes. His mother had not intervened then, either.

In his heart, the only things Yanagi felt toward his parents were exhaustion and resignation.

His father was tormented by an inferiority complex to this day.

"It does not matter how you feel about me," Yanagi said. "However, do not interfere with Hazuki and Hana any further."

"Interfere?! I am their father! It is my ri—!" He cut himself off, caving under the pressure of Yanagi's gaze.

Yanagi had not moved from his seat nor done anything in particular, but his daggerlike stare subdued his father. "The girls will decide their own paths. If you intend to disturb them, you will have to go through me."

His father turned bright red, trembling. He opened and closed his mouth several times without a sound. Finally, he managed to spit out the words lodged in his throat, his anger exploding out of him. "Wh-who do you think you are?!"

Yanagi looked at his father with a chilly glare. There was no filial affection to be found in his eyes.

But the same could be said for the father.

"Refrain from dragging those girls into your inferiority complex," Yanagi said.

"What did you say?!" his father shouted.

"Your shikigami is an insect…," Yanagi said, watching his father with a still and focused gaze. His father flinched. The young man stood and said, "I don't need to go on, do I? You know best of all, I'm sure. Neither Hana nor Hazuki are here any longer to feed your speck of pride, so miniscule that a light breeze would blow it away. Best you consider carefully what to do going forward before you act. For the sake of your beloved Ichise name as well."

After saying his piece, he turned to leave.

"D-don't mess with me! Stop right there, Yanagi! Stop!" his father yelled.

He ignored his father and exited the room. Through the closed sliding doors came a *thud*; his father must have thrown something. Yanagi didn't care.

The time when he concerned himself with his father's moods the way Hazuki did had long passed. Let him be as angry as he liked. It had nothing to do with Yanagi.

There was only one thing he was worried about.

"I hope those two won't pick up his bad habits…," Yanagi said, thinking of his runaway sisters.

◆

Hazuki walked down the hallway of the main Ichinomiya residence, where she would be living from then on. She was unable to settle down.

Her anxiety was perfectly understandable given that the only two times she had previously visited the house were for Saku's succession ceremony and his and Hana's wedding.

"Are you okay, Hazuki?" Hana asked, trying to ease her sister's tension by engaging her in conversation.

"I-I'm fine," Hazuki replied.

"There's no need to be so stiff. You're going to be living here now. If you don't loosen up, you're going to wear yourself out."

Hana, for her part, felt not a single drop of nerves—a while had passed since she had come to live at the residence. Granted, she hadn't been anxious at the beginning, either.

So what if no one in the household wanted her around? That had been her stance. In any case, her impudence was precisely what Saku liked about her and was perhaps why her strength had been acknowledged by the Ichinomiyas faster than she had expected. Crucially, she had won the approval of Mio, who ran the estate when Saku was away.

Were Hana still just a good-for-nothing, she would have been treated very differently around the household, and she probably wouldn't have been able to be as carefree as she was at the moment. Nonetheless, even in such circumstances, no doubt she would have carried on doing whatever she wanted anyway.

Though the twins had been formed from the same split cell, asking the sensitive Hazuki to behave the way Hana did was a tall order.

Hazuki furrowed her brows in worry. "Don't say such unreasonable things. Where do you think we are? This is the main residence, you know."

To Hazuki, it was a sacred place one rarely had the chance to set foot in. Distinguished and revered—the kind of place that made one feel small.

"Not to mention…," Hazuki continued, looking in front of her timidly.

Her gaze was on Saku, who was striding ahead of the girls with his arms crossed. He exuded a confidence befitting the master of the house.

An *excess* of confidence, one could say.

"You're worried about Saku? He won't be around most of the time because of work, so don't worry about him," Hana said. "He acts like a big shot, but his mental age is below ours, for sure. It'll be fine."

Hazuki gawked at Hana—who was laughing cheerfully—with eyes as wide as saucers, shocked at her sister's rude remarks toward the clan head. "H-Hana! He's going to hear you!" she exclaimed, worried that Hana, who didn't have a prudent bone in her body, would receive a tongue-lashing from Saku.

Hana was still chuckling, perfectly unbothered.

A vein pulsed on Saku's temple.

"He can rage all he likes. I'm not afraid," Hana drawled.

While she was laughing it up, Saku unleashed a karate chop to her head. Bull's-eye.

He hadn't put much power into the blow, but the important thing was that he had done it at all.

"What gives?! This is a violence-free zone!" Hana said.

"Violence-free? That's rich coming from you," Saku retorted.

Hana regularly let her fists do the talking.

But Saku was no different.

"You're such a jerk!" she yelled, then pouted.

He grabbed her face in one hand, squeezing her cheeks. Seeing her lips pursed like an octopus, his lips curved in a terrifying grin.

"Who do you think made it possible for your sister to escape that house, huh?" Saku demanded.

"Ip fwas thwanks to my cwoperation, wasn't ip?" Hana protested incoherently.

"I agreed to be her guardian, but arranging for her to live here was a bonus."

"Scrooge!"

"Complain if you want. I'll just throw her out." He smiled smugly.

Despite Hana's rude remarks, she was actually grateful he had agreed to take Hazuki in.

However, his taunts grated on her.

She shook off the hand gripping her face and kicked him hard in the shins.

"That hurts!" he howled.

She sniffed haughtily and ignored Saku in favor of grabbing Hazuki's hand instead. "Come on, Hazuki. Let's go introduce you to my mother-in-law. She's much scarier than Saku when she's angry, so we must not tempt fate."

"Wha— But…," Hazuki stuttered.

She looked at Saku worriedly, but Hana was pulling her forward without regard for her concerns. Saku sighed and shook his head in exasperation. Seeing that, Hazuki reluctantly followed Hana.

Their destination was the room where Hana and the family usually ate. It was noon, and Mio was already seated for lunch.

Hana had explained the situation to Mio beforehand and had stated her wish for the Ichinomiyas to bring Hazuki into the fold. Mio had phoned the Ichises, but the details of her conversation were a mystery to Hana. At the time, Mio had only said to her coolly, "One must follow the proper channels."

Though she had seemed angry on the surface, she was a tsundere, so she might have actually called to keep Hana and Hazuki's parents in line.

Refusing to simply say what one was thinking was classic tsundere.

However, there was no way that Hazuki, who was meeting Mio for the first time, would see through the matriarch's frosty exterior to the softy hiding underneath.

Hana could sense her twin quaking beneath Mio's sharp, appraising gaze. She directed Hazuki to sit in front of Mio and announced, "Mother, this is my elder twin sister, Hazuki. Please look after her from now on."

Pinned by Mio's glare, Hazuki flinched, but everything was business as usual.

"I remember. Originally, I was staunchly against taking in a girl from a branch family—one who is not even a prospective wife—but Saku was adamant, so what is there to do?" Mio said. "If you are to live in the Ichinomiya household, you are to obey the rules and conduct yourself with respectability."

Hazuki stiffly replied, "Y-yes, ma'am. Thank you for your hospitality." She bowed deeply.

Mio's words did not exactly ring of welcome. Hana and Saku, who were aware of her difficult nature, watched her with weary expressions.

Just then, Towa came in with tea and said what the two were thinking. "Miss Mio, you said you were opposed, but were you not the one to take the initiative to arrange a room for Miss Hazuki? Knowing the young lady's situation and finding it appalling, you were quite irate at their parents, I believe."

"Towa!" Mio snapped admonishingly, her face red.

A longtime servant of the household, Towa could be called, in a sense, the shadow don of the Ichinomiya family. She cackled. "Ho-ho-ho. I am merely stating the facts. What was it you said? 'No matter if it is for the family, to disparage the child's own will is unthinkable,' I recall. These ears of mine heard you quite clearly. How outraged you were."

Mio averted her gaze in embarrassment.

Hazuki looked shocked by the exchange, while Hana and Saku stifled their laughter.

"Saku! Hana! Sit," Mio commanded, shifting targets to find another outlet for her irritation. "We cannot dine while you stand!"

It was taking all Hana had to stop herself from bursting into laughter. "Yes, ma'am...," she managed to get out.

Saku, exasperated by his family's antics, took a seat at the head of the table, and Hana sat next to him.

"Over here, Hazuki," Hana said, patting the seat next to hers. Hazuki hesitantly obeyed. "We all eat together in this room. That includes you."

"Wh— Everyone? Lord Ichinomiya, as well?" Hazuki asked.

"When he has time."

"Is that so...?"

It was only natural that Hazuki was surprised.

In the Ichise house, everyone made excuses to take their meals separately. Their life was far removed from the ideal happy, harmonious family.

Their brother, Yanagi, was often away from the house for work, so they hardly ever saw him. No wonder it came as a shock to Hazuki that Saku, who was surely just as busy, made time for his family.

Hana knew that Hazuki might find it disturbing at first, but she would soon grow used to it. When she did, the food she ate alone would start to taste bland and lackluster.

On another subject, Nozomu had yet to arrive.

"By the way, Saku," Hana said, "did you tell Nozomu about Hazuki?"

"Nope. Mother told him," Saku answered.

However, Mio said, "I did not. I assumed Hana would."

The people gathered all made identical *Oops?* faces.

That was when Nozomu entered the room. His eyes fell on Hazuki sitting smack-dab in front of him, in *his* seat. After a beat, he yelled, "What the hell?!" pointing a finger straight at her. "Why—*why* is Hazuki here?!"

"I'll be living here from today onward," Hazuki answered, somewhat apologetically.

"This is the first I've heard of it!" he protested.

Nozomu looked to Saku and Mio, and finally Hana for an explanation. Apparently, all three had thought someone else would inform Nozomu, and in the end, no one had.

Badly shaken, he demanded, "What is going on?!"

Saku tried to pacify him. "Calm down, Nozomu. It's as Hazuki said. I'm going to be her legal guardian from now on, and she'll be living with us," he said. "Hazuki, I'll leave you to explain the details. I'm sure there are parts of the story you do and don't want to tell. Besides, you're already classmates, so you're the best suited for the job."

"I understand," Hazuki replied. She turned back to face Nozomu and smiled. "I'll tell you everything later. Let's get along."

Nozomu blushed fiercely and said, "S-sure."

He couldn't look her in the eye, but he kept darting glances at her, unable to help himself. Even after they started eating, he was as meek as a lamb, a drastic difference from his usual attitude toward Hana.

Bothered by his behavior, Hana asked, "Are the two of you close?"

"What?! D-don't say stupid things out of the blue!" Nozomu said.

"What're you so worked up about?"

"I'm not!"

But it was clear to everyone that he was extremely agitated.

Hana couldn't hide her sly grin as she asked again, "Well? Are you close or not?"

"We are," Hazuki said. "We've always been in the same class. He could even be the one I get along with the best. Right?"

She smiled at Nozomu, and he nodded dutifully.

He was usually quick to jump down Hana's throat. Hana and Hazuki had the same face, but there was a wide gulf between his treatment of them...

"That's perfect. The room arranged for Hazuki is close to yours, Nozomu," Mio said.

Nozomu gaped at her. "If I may ask, why? Hana and Hazuki are sisters. Would it not be better for them to be close to each other?"

His tone was courteous. Saku was the same way when he spoke to Mio, which spoke to her importance in the household's hierarchy.

"Hana's room is next to Saku's. Sisters they may be, but allocating a room next to the clan lord and his wife to a branch family member is out of the question. If you are on friendly terms, all the more reason for your rooms to be close, no? It will be more convenient for her to ask you for help."

Besides, even though Hana and Hazuki had lived together before, they had not been, strictly speaking, under the same roof. Hana had been in an annex while Hazuki had been in the main house. To be frank, it would have been difficult for them to suddenly become attached at the hip. In fact, in a contest of who had spent the most time together with Hazuki, the winner might have been Nozomu.

The location of Hazuki's room may have been chosen to illuminate the difference in her and Hana's standing—the former a daughter of a low-ranking branch family and the latter the bride of the clan lord. However, in the end, having her room close to Nozomu worked in her favor.

Hana felt a twinge of sadness that Hazuki seemed to have a closer relationship with Nozomu, but if it benefited Hazuki, she had no right to interfere.

"I appreciate your help," Hazuki said to Mio. "And thanks, Nozomu."

Finally free from the Ichises, she was on cloud nine, and the bright smile that lit her face was like a flower in bloom.

"H-h-h-happy to be of service!" Nozomu stuttered.

Struck by Hazuki's smile up close, his manner veered sharply into suspicious territory. Their interaction was like that of a dewy-eyed couple who had just started dating.

Even Mio looked like she was nursing some theories about the pair's conversation, but if she was, she kept them to herself.

Hana watched them with a mischievous and unnerving grin.

Saku, with a bowl in one hand, cautioned her calmly, "Don't stick your nose where it doesn't belong."

"I know, I know. I just want to have a little fun," she said.

"Well, don't."

He, too, looked like he had an inkling about Nozomu's behavior.

The only one who was oblivious was Hazuki.

Hana had learned something new about Hazuki: Her grades were excellent, but she was clueless about love.

◆

It was the first school day since Hazuki had moved into the Ichinomiya residence.

First thing in the morning, they were already fighting.

Well, to be precise, it was Hana and Nozomu.

The reason was insignificant—they were arguing over whose car Hazuki would ride in to go to school—but the two combatants were deadly serious.

"Hazuki is coming with me!" Nozomu shouted.

"What are you talking about? She's *my* sister, so she's coming with me," Hana snapped. Having finally made up with Hazuki, she wanted to make up for lost time and was loath to yield any of their time together.

However, Nozomu gave as good as he got, refusing to back down. "There are things me and Hazuki have to discuss."

"It doesn't have to be right *now.* Your rooms are close anyway. You have plenty of time to talk."

"Says the one who's been camping out in her room since the day she came."

Nozomu wasn't wrong. Now that Hana had realized the motives behind Hazuki's previous behavior, she was feeling apologetic. She had been fussing over her sister, diligently bringing her tea and snacks, visiting her room regularly to check in, and hovering around her anxiously.

Hazuki seemed a little fatigued by Hana's actions, but whether Hana had noticed was a different story.

Nozomu, for his part, had been unable to relax knowing that he was living under the same roof as Hazuki—next to her room, of all things. When he had gone to pay Hazuki a visit, he had run into Hana, and the situation had quickly gotten out of hand.

Mio had put an end to their fight. She had scolded them both, saying, "Hazuki won't be able to settle in with you two bothering her!" and had thrown them out of Hazuki's room.

The day after that incident, Hana and Nozomu were once again fighting over a right they both refused to give up.

"Like you're one to talk! You tried to sneak back into her room after I left yesterday, didn't you?" Hana accused. Then, dropping her voice so Hazuki wouldn't hear, she whispered, "Any wicked thoughts you want to confess?"

"As if! Stupid!!" he yelled.

Hazuki hadn't heard what Hana said and was startled by Nozomu's reaction, but Hana was enjoying herself, the way one does when playing with a newfound toy.

"Besides," Hana continued, "if the two of you show up at school in the morning together, rumors are bound to spread. Ohhh, is that your goal? To have the public decide for you?"

Nozomu became visibly agitated under Hana's accusatory gaze. "No!" he cried.

"Ew, gross. Did I guess right? I have to warn Hazuki."

Hana was having the time of her life teasing him. Had Saku been there, he might have stopped her, but alas, he had already left the house.

"I'm telling you, you're wrong!" Nozomu protested.

"Then it shouldn't be a problem if Hazuki rides with me." She turned to her sister and quickly snatched up her hand. "Let's go, Hazuki."

Nozomu panicked. "Wait!"

"No way," Hana said. "Come on, Hazuki. Climb aboard."

"S-sure," Hazuki said.

She was bothered by the pair's fight, but she got into the car as directed. Hana got in as well.

However, immediately after—surprise, surprise—Nozomu opened the back seat door on the opposite side and climbed in without asking.

So even though normally Nozomu staunchly refused to ride in the same car as Hana, all three of them ended up sitting together, with Hazuki sandwiched in the middle.

Nozomu sniffed haughtily and turned away, sitting with his arms crossed and projecting an air of arrogance. However, the tips of his ears were red with embarrassment. Adorable.

"Wow, you want to come with your big sis to school that badly? You spoiled baby," Hana teased. Of course, she was saying it knowing full well that the one he wanted to ride with was not herself but Hazuki.

Nozomu was shaking, but denying it would be as good as admitting he wanted to be with Hazuki, and he wouldn't do that.

"Mwah-ha-ha, how delightful," Hana said and cackled.

"Master, that's not very nice," Azuha admonished quietly from her perch in Hana's hair.

Hazuki twitched and looked at Azuha. "Your butterfly spoke…"

Butterflies and all other insect shikigami were the lowest on the pyramid. They were weak creatures with only the bare minimum power and shouldn't have had the ability to understand speech or to communicate their thoughts. No wonder Hazuki was surprised.

Actually, Hazuki should have seen the two speak during the assault on their school. Granted, she wouldn't have had time to waste on such details, and she had probably already forgotten.

"Yeah," Hana said. "This is your first proper meeting, I guess."

The twins knew of each other's shikigami, but because their living situation had drastically changed after their first summoning attempt, they hadn't had the chance to interact with the shikigami in private.

The first and only time Hana had spoken with Hazuki's shikigami, Hiragi, was when he had accompanied Sae to ask Hana to help his master.

That was a testament to the gulf that had existed between them ever since they turned ten years old.

The distance, along with everything else, had been their parents' fault.

"Introduce yourself, Azuha," Hana said.

The butterfly fluttered off Hana's hair and flew to hover in front of Hazuki's eyes. "I'm Azuha," she said in a lisping child's voice.

Hazuki followed suit and said, "I'm Hazuki…"

Hana snickered.

"Has she always been able to talk?" Hazuki asked.

"Nope. My powers awakened when I was fifteen. That was when she became able to speak," explained Hana.

"You have other ones, too, right? Two human shikigami and a dog…"

"Aoi, Miyabi, and Arashi. I'll introduce them to you later."

Azuha was Hana's only companion for the day. The others were house-sitting.

She was accompanied by different shikigami depending on the day. At times, Azuha stayed behind to guard the house. Other times, all her shikigami went with her.

However, unlike Azuha, who was visible all the time, Aoi and Miyabi stayed hidden even when they were at Hana's side. Only practitioners of Saku's level were able to detect them. For that reason, they had been convenient bodyguards, but now that Hana had given up playing the role of a good-for-nothing, it didn't matter who she took.

Incidentally, Arashi, an inugami deity, could make himself invisible, but he often chose to manifest himself. Apparently, it was easier to use his powers that way.

The particulars were an enigma to humans, but as far as Hana was concerned, Arashi could do as he liked. He was a god with a generous heart. He had once become a cursed tatarigami spirit, his altruism warped by others' pain. He would never hurt another without reason. Hana had faith in that.

Their school was not far from the Ichinomiya residence, and they soon arrived. Hana and Nozomu, who were sitting by the doors, got out first. The other students, surprised to see the two come to school together, stared at them wide-eyed. Nonetheless, it was hardly a secret that they lived together, so it was not so big a shock.

However, Hazuki's appearance caused ripples in the crowd. The students whispered among each other.

"What? Why is Hazuki with them?"

"They *are* twins. What's the fuss?"

"But I've never once seen them together before."

"You're right about that."

Hana and Hazuki went to and from school separately. On top of that, they never did anything together in school, either. For the pair of them to come in the same car was unimaginable. Not to mention that Hana was now the wife of the Ichinomiya clan lord, a position which naturally drew people's attention. There wasn't a bigger commotion only because they were, in fact, twins.

Had Nozomu and Hazuki come to school alone together, rumors would have started to fly about their relationship for sure. Hana glared at the featherbrained Nozomu, who had so enjoyed the fact that he got to ride with Hazuki even if he had needed to force his way in.

Did he properly receive the message she was sending with her eyes?

Nozomu went on ahead into the school, looking somewhat shamefaced.

Hazuki was being interrogated by a group of students that had surrounded her. It was unclear whether they were her friends or groupies.

"Hazuki! Why did you come with them?"

"Even Nozomu was with you."

"What the hell is going on?"

Hana was pissed at the jerks who were so quick to barge into someone else's private affairs, but Hazuki smiled and fielded their inquiries with tactful answers.

"Just what you would expect from a star student," Hana commented in appreciation of Hazuki's crowd-wrangling skills, and she set off for her own classroom.

There was no point in her sticking with Hazuki since they were in different classes anyway. Hazuki would surely resolve the situation gracefully.

When Hana got to her own class, Suzu immediately came up to her.

"Morning, Hana," Suzu said. "I heard the news. You came to school with your sister, right? First time, isn't it? For you two to commute together all chummy."

"I think this every time, but your information network is fast. Where are you getting your intel from?" Hana questioned.

She had come to the classroom directly without making any pit stops, yet Suzu had already heard the news.

"It's nothing like that. The newspaper club posted about it," Suzu said dismissively.

"What are you talking about?" Hana asked.

"You don't know about their account?"

"Nope."

"They post on social media about the latest rumors. They wrote about you and your sister arriving together just a minute ago. See?"

Suzu held out her phone for Hana to see.

The newspaper club's post featured a picture of none other than the two of them standing outside the car with the caption, WHAT'S THE HOT GOSS ON THE TWINS?! THE ICHINOMIYA LORD'S WIFE AND HER TWIN GET OUT OF THE SAME CAR!

"They're practically paparazzi, sneaking around like that. When in the world...?" Rather than being angry that her photo had been taken without her permission, she was more exasperated.

"They post about all the goings-on around the school. I bet most of the students follow them. I'm shocked you didn't know," Suzu said.

"...I wonder if I would win if I sued them on the grounds that they infringed on my image rights," Hana said.

She scrolled through their post history. Was that a post about her and Saku's wedding? They had even uploaded a photo of Hana dressed as a bride.

Not to mention, the post was from the day of the ceremony.

She had the urge to shake them down and demand where they had gotten the photo.

If even information about her wedding had been leaked so easily, no wonder word had already gotten out about the three of them coming to school together.

Hana remembered the commotion from earlier. She had plenty to say to the newspaper club, but she swallowed her words. For the time being, she decided to follow the account.

The silver lining—if there was one—was that the club had yet to dig up the news that Hazuki had left the Ichise household, but it was only a matter of time...

Whatever happens, happens, she thought, composing herself.

Just then, their teacher walked into the room.

That day, Hana had bigger worries than Hazuki.

The moment she had been anxiously waiting for had finally come.

The teacher announced, "I'm going to hand back your tests."

Exam season had followed hot on the heels of the Skull of Nirvana incident, and they were finally getting their grades back. Some rejoiced. Some lamented. Every person reacted to the news in their own way, but surely there was no one who was more nervous than Hana. Everything was riding on these results.

"—Next. Hana Ichise... Ah, I mean, Hana Ichinomiya," the teacher said.

"Here!" she said.

She leaped up to retrieve her exams, too preoccupied to spare a thought for the teacher who *still* couldn't remember to use her married name.

With her exams in hand, she returned to her seat and took a deep breath before looking at her score.

What she saw had her clutching her hair and chanting desperately under her breath, "Damn. Damn. Damn. Damn."

The boy in the seat next to her looked creeped out, but she didn't have the luxury to worry about him. Her grades took over her thoughts. Azuha fluttered around her with worry.

Suzu walked up to Hana's desk cheerily and peeked at her friend's answer sheets. Suzu's face split into a delighted grin. "I knew it. *F*s across the board. Last-minute cramming won't do you any good, but at least you tried. There's always next time."

Hana didn't know if Suzu was trying to comfort or insult her, but Suzu seemed to think she was helping and patted Hana on the shoulder kindly.

However, "next time" wouldn't be good enough.

"...I'm screwed. I can't show my face after this. How is it possible I didn't manage to pass at least one or two tests after all that studying?" Hana groused.

"A little bit of studying won't do you any good. It has to be a habit," Suzu said.

After hearing Suzu's very sound advice, Hana made up her mind. "I'll make sure this never sees the light of day!"

"How?"

"By burning my tests and destroying the evidence."

"That sounds dangerous."

"The Ichinomiya grounds are massive. A campfire or two is nothing."

Hana wasn't wrong per se, but Suzu frowned, nonetheless. "Be a good girl and apologize to Lord Ichinomiya. Wouldn't that be best?"

Hana's face paled. "Do you know what would happen to me if I did that? I get chills just thinking about it..." She balled up her tests and shoved them into her desk. "This is the worst..."

She was wrong. The worst was yet to come. It was lying in wait at the Ichinomiya residence.

That night, Hana, Hazuki, Saku, and Nozomu ate together. Mio would be home later than usual.

Hana had already completely forgotten about her test scores, but over dinner, Saku asked her, "How did you do on your exams?"

Her face instantly stiffened. "H-how do you know about that?" she spluttered, choking on her words.

"Nozomu showed me his results earlier."

Hana glared at Nozomu.

"Hmph. It's the first time I've done better than Hazuki," he said, beaming with pride.

His expression rubbed her the wrong way. She stared daggers at him. "Who cares? Bet you lost to Kiriya anyway," she said.

"Ugh," he groaned, unable to say anything else. Hana's words had dealt him a huge blow.

Kiriya, one half of the Nijouin twins, had demonstrated his intelligence soon after transferring, overtaking Hazuki in a heartbeat.

Nozomu had been over the moon at having beaten Hazuki, but given his reaction, he must have scored lower than Kiriya.

Talk about easy to read.

"Shut up!" Nozomu yelled. "Hazuki used to always be number one. Beating her is still an amazing feat!"

"Hazuki is mentally worn out from having to deal with that shitty old man of ours. Gloating over a win against an exhausted girl, aren't you ashamed to call yourself an Ichinomiya?" Hana sneered.

"………" Nozomu wilted. He couldn't argue. "Is it a crime to be a little happy that I did better than Hazuki? I just wanted to show Saku… I didn't have any other intentions… I didn't mean to kick her while she was down. Is that what she thinks? Do I seem like an inhuman bastard to her now?" he muttered.

"Nozomu, I don't mind," Hazuki said kindly, but Nozomu didn't seem to have heard.

Hana hadn't expected to land a critical hit, but that was exactly what she had done.

Saku, sitting beside her, reached over and flicked her hard on the forehead.

"Ow!" she cried, glaring at him.

He smiled and held out his hand. "So? Where are your exam scores?"

Hana clicked her tongue without thinking. She thought she had successfully diverted the conversation onto Nozomu. How persistent.

"You studied so hard. Surely, you must have passed all your exams, right?" Saku said.

This was bad.

Hana tried to laugh it off. "Ha…ha-ha-ha…" She couldn't meet Saku's gaze.

Saku's eyes narrowed and he called out, "Tsubaki."

A shikigami with dog ears manifested in a heartbeat. "Here, Master!" Tsubaki said brightly.

She was clothed in her usual maid costume, and her hair was in pigtails.

"Go to Hana's room and find her tests," he ordered.

"Aye-aye, sir!" she said.

"W-wait. Y-you can't!" Hana protested.

She leaped up to chase after Tsubaki, but Saku grabbed her arm in a viselike grip.

"Let go, Saku," she said.

"Give it up."

"Please, I'm begging you," she said, yanking her arm desperately.

Her demeanor made it painfully obvious how she had done.

Tsubaki returned shortly. In her hand were Hana's crumpled exam papers…

Hana's shoulders slumped. "I'm done for…"

She buried her face in her hands, averting her eyes from her problems and running away from reality.

The papers crackled loudly in the otherwise silent room as Saku smoothed them out. Hana peeked and saw him grimacing.

"Are you kidding me?" he said. It was unclear from his expression whether he was angry or just tired.

Saku let out a long sigh and passed the papers to Nozomu and Hazuki.

"Nooo! What're you doing?!" Hana cried.

What was he thinking, showing her grades to those two?

As Nozomu and Hazuki leafed through the exams, their eyes grew wider and wider in astonishment. They looked up at Hana with identical expressions. Even Tsubaki was looking at her with pity in her eyes.

"You're doomed...," Nozomu said.

"Hana...," Hazuki said.

Nozomu's blunt honesty. Hazuki's compassionate reticence. Both reactions gutted Hana. For a moment, she was struck with regret that she hadn't studied more diligently, but she regained her peace of mind by heaping the blame on her parents' terrible child-rearing instead.

"I didn't think your results would be *this* bad," Saku said wearily.

Normally, Hana would be quick to argue, but she couldn't muster the energy.

Then he added, "It is what it is. Nozomu, Hazuki, help her with her studies."

"What?!" she cried, displeased.

At the same time, Nozomu stabbed a finger at Hana and argued back loudly, "I don't have the confidence to teach someone as stupid as her, even if you're the one asking."

Hana was offended. "Aren't you taking it too far?! Sure, my grades aren't anything to celebrate, but I still worked my ass off!"

"Coulda fooled me! Why don't you take a leaf out of Hazuki's book? Are you really twins?!"

"Well, *excuse* me! Being twins has nothing to do with being smart!"

Hazuki watched helplessly as Hana and Nozomu shouted at each other.

Saku karate-chopped them both on the head. He had adjusted the power behind the blow to match the severity of the crime, so it hurt more than usual. Obviously, he saw Hana's test results as a problem.

"Quiet," Saku said. "Nozomu, teaching Hana will be tough, but the Ichinomiyas will become laughingstocks if the lady of the clan is failing all her classes. You're the only one I can count on."

"Me...?" Nozomu muttered.

"Yeah."

No one who idolized their brother the way Nozomu did could be unhappy when said beloved brother came to them for help.

Nozomu's attitude flipped on its head. "Got it." He then declared to Hana, "Me and Hazuki are going to make you work like a dog until you're fit to call yourself Lady Ichinomiya. You better be grateful."

"You gotta be kidding me," Hana whined, displeasure rolling off her in waves.

"Behave and do as you're told if you don't want me showing your tests to my mother," Saku threatened.

"Bully!" she cried.

"Better than my mother finding out, no?"

"Ugh."

That was true. There was no denying that.

"Have the two of them teach you, all right?" Saku said.

Hana's shoulders drooped in defeat. "Fine..."

With the conversation closed, they returned to their seats.

Saku changed the topic. He said in a formal tone, "I have news to share with...all of you, but it's most relevant to you, Hana."

"What is it?" Hana replied.

"After the Skull of Nirvana assaulted your school, there have been discussions within the Association about whether more effort should be put toward raising the practical skills of the students."

"Yeah, that was a rough day."

During the incident, a barrier had been used to seal up the school, and the shades had rampaged in the enclosed space. The majority of the students had panicked when faced with the shades and could do nothing but scream for help. Only a handful of students and teachers had been of any use. The purpose of the school was to train practitioners, but the reality was bleak.

Hazuki and the other Class A students had fought hard, but had Hana not been there, even breaking through the barrier might have been impossible. Hana's shikigami, Aoi and Miyabi, had saved many students as well. There was no doubt that it was only thanks to Hana that the disaster had been resolved as quickly as it had.

Saku continued his explanation. "Ideally, such an incident will not occur a second time. However, to prepare for such a worst-case scenario, many in the Association are of the opinion that it is necessary to level up the students' fighting ability. As a result, the curriculum will be revised on the basis that hands-on battle experience is a must."

"How is it going to change?" Hana asked.

"Up until now, primarily only Class A has been summoned to fight, but going forward, Classes B and C will be asked to participate in normal battles as well in order for them to build experience."

"No waaay," she grumbled, her tone thoroughly annoyed.

However, she didn't complain any more than that. She, too, understood the need for the training.

She sighed involuntarily. "Haaah. I guess there's no other way."

Hana thought back on the way her classmates had run around like chickens with their heads cut off, completely abandoning the will to fight. Yes, the attack had come out of the blue, but her classmates had been *too* helpless in front of the shades. She agreed with Saku that it was crucial for everyone to gain real battle experience.

She was unhappy to be dragged into the plan, but there was nothing for her to say.

To be a practitioner meant risking your life. Unlike Class A, Classes B and C had almost no experience on the battlefield. It would benefit them in the future to have their eyes opened to the dangers of the job.

The Association had to plan for what-ifs. Their judgment was sound. Hana was not guaranteed to be around during every emergency, and Association practitioners were not always available to help.

"Will Class A's curriculum be changing as well?" Hazuki asked.

Her class had plenty of hands-on experience and was often exposed to danger. She must have been worried that her class would be called into even riskier situations.

Nozomu waited for Saku's answer with a solemn expression, too.

"For the most part, Class A will continue to operate as it has," Saku replied. "You third-years, in particular, are already fighting in your fair share of battles. However, you might have more practicals from now on."

"I see," Hazuki said. She seemed relieved to hear that Class A wouldn't change much.

In contrast, this was a dire situation for Hana, who spent most of her classes sleeping. "Maybe I'll start ditching class," she mused. "I can sleep in the nurse's office."

"Take your classes seriously! This is exactly why you failed your tests!" Nozomu snapped.

"Bwah-ha-ha-ha," she laughed heartily. "Tsk, tsk, tsk. I'm much more useful in a fight than a certain someone who was immediately decimated in the fight he picked himself."

Nozomu had challenged her to a duel right after she had married Saku. They had fought with their shikigami, and Azuha had crushed him.

He instantly caught onto what she was alluding to, and his face flushed with embarrassment. "That was different! I was off my game. There's no way Guren would lose so easily! I was just going easy on you!"

She cackled. "Heh-heh-heh. If that's the case, I'm happy to give you a chance to take revenge. Azuha's going to KO you right away anyway."

"I *said* I'm different now! I'll show you!"

"Looks like you're dying to embarrass yourself in front of Hazuki. Let's take this outside," Hana suggested.

"Fine by me!"

The two stomped out of the room. Confused, Hazuki looked over at Saku. He hadn't moved an inch and was calmly sipping his tea.

"Shouldn't you stop them?" she asked.

"Leave them be. Hana has perfect control of her power, so it'll be fine," he replied.

"You take it for granted she's going to win."

Saku smirked. "Of course. She's the woman I picked as my bride."

His smile confirmed the deep faith he had in Hana.

◆

The duel held outside in the darkening twilight ended, as predicted, in Hana's overwhelming victory.

"Wah-ha-ha-ha! I hope you now understand how awesome your honored sister is," Hana taunted Nozomu. He was lying collapsed on the ground, frustration pouring off him. "I worked up a sweat. Time for a bath and then straight to bed." She pranced off in a jolly mood to retire for the night.

At school the next day, the teacher made an announcement about the curriculum changes Saku had mentioned.

There were quite a few students in Class C, and the Association wanted them all to gain hands-on experience, too. It would be foolish to throw them straight onto a real battlefield, so instead, they would have mock battles during class. Once the students acclimated to the classes, they would then be dispatched to fight actual shades. That was the goal.

As the Class C students listened to the details of the plan, their expressions clouded over. A few complained openly and loudly.

"Why now?"

"It's impossible for us."

"Yeah, there's no way."

Up until now, the closest they had been to battle was as rear support. It must have been terrifying to suddenly be told that they had to fight.

However, it had been the Association's decision, and as fledgling practitioners, the students weren't allowed to argue. Ultimately, a large portion of the class would end up working for the Association after graduation.

As the final nail in the coffin, to remind the students of their place, the teacher declared that the plan had been approved by the lords of the five clans. Every one of the students was born to low-ranking practitioner families, so they couldn't possibly revolt. Defying the five clan lords meant making an enemy of the entire country.

The bellyachers suddenly forgot their objections and quietly sat back in their seats. While some students continued to look sullen, no one complained any further.

Hana glanced over at Suzu, who looked anxious more than upset. She smiled bitterly, already worn out by the situation.

Actually, Hana was better at practical classes than lectures, and getting to move around was a good thing, not that she didn't have any desire to play hooky. However, when she remembered the assault on the school, she thought that she should take the classes seriously, no matter how confident she was that she could handle the shades. At the very least, she wanted to be strong enough to protect her best friend, who was dead set on becoming a rear support practitioner after graduation...

Hana used to think of a practitioner's job as not her problem, but after marrying Saku, she had been tossed into the deep end, and she had experienced over and over how dangerous the practitioner's world was.

Suzu was not a strong practitioner.

Hana could no longer say that Suzu would be safe in the rear with any confidence, not after the school—which was supposed to be secure—had been attacked.

The prospect of Suzu being injured shattered Hana's devil-may-care attitude. If Suzu were hurt, it would be too late for regrets. So if Suzu was attending the classes, Hana was going to be right by her side.

Hana had been wondering when the new curriculum would go into effect. Apparently, the answer was "immediately." The first session was going to be that very day.

The class was held on the PE field. The students' task was to conjure a barrier to extinguish a shade. That was as basic as it got.

In fact, that much was no different from what Class C already practiced during their usual classes. The difference was that they would be facing *real* shades.

Previously, it had been deemed too dangerous to let the Class C washouts face actual shades, so the students had never undertaken such a trial before. Thus, when their teacher summoned a mob of shades bound in barriers as if it was the most natural thing in the world, pandemonium ensued.

To Hana, the shades were the smallest of small fries, worthless vermin she could destroy instantly. They were nothing to shriek about. The racket her classmates were making demonstrated as clear as day how weak they were. Her mixed emotions could be read on her face.

Suzu was one of the screamers. She squealed as she clung to Hana's arm.

Hana had decided she would stick around until Suzu could hold her own, but faced with the long road ahead of her, she suddenly wanted to renege on her vow.

As Hana stared into the abyss that was her future, the teacher explained the directions. "Quiet. Settle down. Today, you will each be trapping one shade in a barrier and exterminating it."

Grumbles along the lines of "No freaking way" and "I don't want to" could be heard from the crowd.

But the teacher showed no mercy. He grabbed one boy and threw him into a dome-like barrier with one of the freed shades.

The boy was half in tears as he banged on the barrier from the inside, screaming, "*Gyaaah!* Let me out!" However, he was trapped.

"That barrier was created with a Nijouin-crafted talisman. Once it's up, you're stuck inside until the shade is destroyed," boasted a girl with a bob haircut styled in loose waves.

It was Kikyou. She was a candidate to be the next-generation head of the Nijouin clan, but she often gave the impression of being meek and anxious.

Her twin, Kiriya, was standing next to her. They had similar facial features, but he had short black hair and a clean, refreshing image.

Why were the two Class A students present? Well, no one could deny that Class C didn't have enough experience. Therefore, for the exercise, they had been paired together with Class A, who were seasoned junior practitioners.

"I have a question," Hana said.

"What is it?" Kikyou asked.

"The two of you transferred here to take back the talismans that the Skull of Nirvana stole, right?"

"That's right."

"Then why are you still here?"

Kikyou flinched. "What an awful thing to ask! Are you saying I'm a bother?! Aren't we best friends now?!"

For a moment, Hana wanted to applaud Kikyou's ability to summon tears at the drop of a hat, but if she were to do so, the other girl might *actually* start crying.

"But I mean, there's no reason for you to be here, right? Why not go back?" Hana asked.

Kikyou grabbed Hana's arm and squeezed it tightly. "How can you say that? Of course I have a reason! I want to be with my best friend! You! After everything we've been through to become friends, there's no way I would let you go," she said beseechingly.

Suzu, who was clinging onto Hana's other arm, was pissed off by Kikyou's rant. "Hana's best friend is me and only me. Don't go calling yourself her best friend without permission!"

"It won't kill you to share once in a while!" Kikyou yelled.

"I refuse."

Hana wished they wouldn't fight while she was stuck in between them. "*Ha-ha...*," she laughed dryly. That was the best she could do.

She turned to Kiriya instead. "I get why Kikyou's still around, but are you okay with being here? Didn't you have friends back on the other campus?"

The twins went around together like they were a set. Even so, there was no need for Kiriya to put up with Kikyou's selfishness to this extent. He didn't need to attend the same school as her.

However, Kiriya replied, "...Nah, I don't care. There's no one I'm particularly close to back at our old school, and Kikyou looks like she's enjoying herself here."

That in and of itself was upsetting to hear.

What kind of school life did the twins have in Obsidian High School Campus Two?

Kiriya had said before that their classmates had avoided Kikyou because she was next in line to lead the Nijouin clan. Maybe it had been the same for Kiriya.

Best not to pry.

While their group stood around, talking and arguing, the male student who had been tossed into the barrier earlier managed to kill the shade and escape the barrier. He was covered in wounds. The moment he was out, he sat down heavily on the ground.

Class C showered him with praise for his valiant fighting. On the opposite end of the spectrum, the students in Class A were muttering things like "You can't be serious..." and "Killing a weakling like that is nothing. What're they getting so excited about?" They had been stunned by the battle and, needless to say, not in a good way. They were shocked by how weak Class C was. The difference between the two classes was glaringly obvious.

Now that one person had successfully dealt with a shade, another student from Class C was suddenly raring to go and volunteered to be next.

Given how motivated he was despite his fear, Hana started to think there might be some hope for her classmates after all.

That lasted only until he opened his mouth. "I will be your opponent, shade." He followed it up with his barrier incantation. "Seal my enemy who intends me harm."

Hana was dumbstruck. Sure, he had created a barrier and trapped the shade, but his incantation was too convoluted.

Who exactly are you ordering to seal the shade? Hana wanted to ask. *You're the one putting the barrier up.*

He passed the baton to the next student, who said...

"The time has come to free my left eye from its bonds. Suffer thee my arcane technique!"

Another long-winded and completely incomprehensible incantation. Class A gaped in disbelief.

For the first time, Hana felt embarrassed to be in Class C. She didn't want to be grouped with those guys.

"Um, Class C's incantations are rather...unique, don't you think, Hana?" Kikyou said, picking her words carefully.

Hana would have preferred if she just said what she was thinking.

"They're victims of a deadly illness. Do them a favor and don't say anything," Hana said.

Yes, they were victims of Cringey Tween Syndrome.

When Hana paid closer attention, she realized that the classmates waiting for their turn were already practicing their incantations.

Unlike the short and easy-to-say phrases picked by the Class A students, the incantations thrown around by Class C were all lengthy tongue twisters, further proof that the illness was in its late stages.

The incantations used differed from person to person. Practitioners chose words that helped them picture the intended effect. Needlessly long phrases only ate up time, so most practitioners picked punchy phrases.

In which case, what was the deal with these overly complex and cryptic chants?

The incantations smacked of indifference. It seemed like they had been selected with no intention of using them in an actual fight. Even the teacher seemed to despair.

The students would be attacked long before they managed to finish speaking. All they were doing was giving the shades an opening. The bottom-feeder shades used in class were one thing, but shades that were any stronger would be major problems.

Hana's group watched the other students, Suzu and Kikyou arguing all the while, and then Suzu's turn rolled around.

She stepped up to the stage and yelled, "Pancake! Pancake! Red bean and jelly!"

The words she had picked were certainly short and memorable. The tension drained from Hana's body at the very Suzu-like incantation.

Hana, for her part, had taken hers straight from the textbook with zero deviations.

Suzu often whined at her, saying, "Your incantation is borrrrrring," but being interesting was not a requirement. Simple was best.

Her incantation was used by many practitioners in modern times. It had been proven to be effective and easy to use. It should have been irreproachable, but it was unsatisfactory in Suzu's eyes.

Hana was called up after Suzu, and she defeated her shade in the blink of an eye. In contrast, even such low-ranking shades proved to be high hurdles for her classmates, and it took a long time for everyone to take their turn.

After Class C finished, Hazuki stepped up to demonstrate her technique as one of the top scorers in Class A. She took on the remaining shades all at once and eliminated them instantly.

As she watched her classmates cheer for Hazuki, it once again dawned on Hana that they had a long road ahead of them.

◆

Hana, Kikyou, Kiriya, and Suzu ended up eating lunch together.

They sat at an open table in the cafeteria, setting down the lunches they had ordered (Hana had picked the fried chicken lunch set).

Suzu propped her head on one hand and poked at a carrot in her curry with her spoon. "Ugh. We have to duel with our shikigami in the afternoon. What a drag," she said with a bleak look in her eyes.

The squirrel shikigami riding on her shoulder looked equally sullen. Like master, like shikigami. The two were exactly alike in personality.

"No use complaining, not after that attack on the school," Hana said. "We need to learn to protect ourselves. There's no guarantee there won't be a next time. It was a miracle no one died last time."

A blunder could end up costing more than one or two lives. Both the students and teachers understood the potential consequences. That was precisely why everyone was going along with the curriculum change.

Suzu was as aware of the dangers as anyone else. Her expression darkened. "I know, I know," she said.

She had been in their classroom when the school had been invaded. She had been fine thanks to Hana dispatching Aoi to help, but the hallways had swarmed with shades, and she remembered how terrifying it had been.

Hana observed Suzu's reaction as she said sternly, "Suzu, working for the Association of Practitioners means putting yourself in harm's way. Being in the rear doesn't mean you'll be safe. If you can't fight shades, you shouldn't join the Association."

"...Yeah," Suzu muttered.

Had Hana's warning found its mark? It was obvious to anyone Suzu was dejected.

Suzu started eating quietly, and Hana turned to Kikyou and Kiriya instead. "How have your classes changed?"

"It's hard to say they've changed, per se," Kikyou replied. "Since we're the most trained, we're going to be having joint classes with Classes B and C and the other grades and demonstrating the right way to do things. On top of that, apparently we'll be fighting outside the school even more than we are already." She let out an annoyed sigh. "We have a battle outside today, too, so we have to stay behind after classes are over…"

"That's rough," Hana said. She was grateful from the bottom of her heart that she wasn't in Class A.

"See here—me and Kiriya are Nijouins! Our clan specializes in crafting talismans to use against shades, not fighting," Kikyou protested loudly.

Kiriya tried to rein her in. "There, there. Calm down."

But that wasn't enough to soothe her, and she demanded, "Don't you agree with me?!"

"Ummm… I don't care either way…," he said. "I like getting to move around."

"Traitor! I thought you were my ally!"

"But it's the truth."

Kikyou's face was filled with rage. On the other hand, Kiriya's poker face made it impossible to tell what he was thinking. Nevertheless, it was obvious that the two were close.

Deep down, Hana used to be envious of their relationship, but ever since she reconciled with Hazuki, whenever she saw the two of them together, she felt all warm inside.

Chapter 2

Hana returned to the Ichinomiya residence to find Nozomu waiting for her, legs planted firmly and arms crossed. Hazuki was with him.

"You're late," he said. "Get ready for Hazuki and me to fill up that empty brain of yours."

Hana instinctively turned to flee, but sadly, she was apprehended and dragged to supplementary study hell.

"Come ooon," Hana whined. "Didn't you have to stay after school? That's what Kikyou said."

For that reason, she had assumed Hazuki and Nozomu wouldn't be home yet.

"Not everyone. We were put into groups. We'll be accompanying the Association practitioners while they work, but only a few of us at a time," Hazuki answered.

Hana's eyes widened. "What? Isn't that dangerous?"

Class A had been in real battles before, but they were only summoned when the shades were too weak to dispatch professionals to deal with.

To shadow a practitioner meant that the students would be exposed to jobs with actual risk involved.

"Practitioners have to deal with low-ranking shades, too, you know," Hazuki replied. "I can't say it'll be perfectly safe, but we'll have pros with us, so I think it should be fine. However, they won't be able to watch all of us at the same time, hence the groups."

"I see."

Strictly speaking, the third-years would be graduating in less than a year, and more than half of the class would join the Association as practitioners anyway. You could say they were just getting a head start.

Newbies didn't jump immediately into active duty. They first underwent a training period where they shadowed veterans and learned on the job. That was exactly what Class A would be doing.

"Looks like the Association is taking that incident seriously," Hana remarked.

Nozomu sniffed and said arrogantly, "Of course. It's the first time Obsidian High has been exposed to such a threat."

Their school was composed of five campuses. It had been established to cultivate the next generation of practitioners, so naturally, it was a tempting target for anyone with a grudge against the five clans. Accordingly, the campuses were all heavily guarded—though not to the degree of the Association headquarters—and in the past, the school's rigid security had repelled enemies several times over.

The difference was, while the school had been attacked before, the situation had never escalated to the point where lives had been at risk, so the Association and the clans were currently in a frenzy.

"You have more urgent things to worry about, like failing your classes! Get a move on," Nozomu ordered.

"Seriouslyyy?" Hana moaned.

As Hana was dragged through the house by Nozomu, Arashi padded alongside her. He was as enchantingly fluffy as always, and she wanted nothing more than to dive face-first into his fur. Behind him were Aoi and Miyabi. Perhaps they had come to welcome her home.

"You're back, Hana," Arashi said.

"Arashiii. Help meee," she begged.

"What's wrong?"

Azuha flew off her perch on Hana's head and fluttered over to Arashi. "Master's grades were very bad, so they're going to study together. Master doesn't want to. That's why she's trying to run away."

Arashi thought for a moment before falling into line behind Hana. "In that case, I will lend a hand and supervise as well."

This should have been where he listened to his master's wishes and helped her escape, but Arashi was a straitlaced and gentle god, so he chose the option that would best serve her in the future.

They went to the room where they normally ate. Hana sat down to start her remedial session, flanked by Nozomu and Hazuki on either side.

"Ughhh... Maaan," she moaned as Nozomu placed a worksheet in front of her, one that he had written himself, no less.

Undoubtedly, the fact that his beloved older brother had asked him for help had fired Nozomu up, and the result of his mania was this worksheet.

As she started to answer the questions, Hana complained mentally, *Way to go overboard.*

Every time she finished a question, she would hear Hazuki murmur "Wait" or "What?" and Nozomu sigh tiredly. Their reactions chipped away at her motivation.

"If I got something wrong, just tell me," she whined.

Nozomu gawked at her. "I knew you were stupid, but not *this* stupid," he yelled.

"That's taking it too far. Give me a break. These questions cover more than the stuff we learn at school. There are ones about the five clans and practitioners, too," Hana argued.

"That's exactly what's wrong with you. The answers should be obvious to anyone raised in a practitioner household, not to mention it's all information that should have been beaten into any Obsidian High student. What have you been doing in class?!"

"Sleeping." She shamelessly gave him a thumbs-up as if to say, *What else?*

"You dumbass."

She pursed her lips sullenly. "Says *you.*"

He rolled up his workbook and smacked her on the head. It made a satisfying *thwap.*

"If you're not stupid, who is? You know the names of the clans at least—thank god—but you don't know anything about their backgrounds."

"I get along perfectly fine without that info. I'm gonna join a normal company instead of working my butt off as a practitioner, so all this studying is useless to me."

Hana had hardly any knowledge of what was considered standard for a practitioner child to know, which went to show how badly she wanted to distance herself from that world.

"But, Hana, aren't there things you should know now that you're the lady of the Ichinomiya clan?" Hazuki argued. "You have to learn all of this so that people won't make fun of you."

That was where their opinions differed.

Hana rebutted, "Saku and I are gonna get divorced sooner or later anyway, so it's moot."

Saku had threatened her about her ignorance using Mio's name, but if they were going to get divorced, she didn't need to know anything.

If she were to mention the divorce, however, he would flatly refuse, and it would put him in a bad mood, so she usually kept that train of thought to herself. The point was, she didn't see any reason to study.

Hazuki was stunned. "What? What are you talking about? You're going to get divorced?"

"Are you insane?! What could you possibly not like about my brother?!" Nozomu demanded.

At school, Hana and Saku's relationship was seen as the romance of the century. Since she wasn't allowed to reveal the details, she could neither confirm nor deny the rumors. However, this was Hazuki and Nozomu she was talking to. As long as she didn't say anything about the pillars, she should be able to get away with explaining the situation.

"It's a contractual arrangement," Hana said.

The other two looked at her with blank faces.

She explained further. "Ummm, I can't say anything specific, but Saku needed a bride who's as strong as he is for the sake of the family. I wanted to get away from the Ichise house and for the Ichinomiyas to cover for me after I revealed my powers. Our interests aligned, so we got hitched."

"That's wrong," Azuha cut in. "Master was told she would get one billion yen and a house. She was blinded by greed."

"Shhh. You can't say that, Big Sis. You have to keep it a secret," Miyabi said, raising her index finger to her lips.

But Miyabi cut in too late. Not to mention she hadn't said anything helpful, either. If anything, she had made it worse.

Hana could feel Nozomu's gaze digging into her.

"You're telling me, you're married to my perfect brother, to a man without a single flaw, in name only? Does our mother know?" Nozomu asked.

"She's the former lady of the clan. She must've guessed once she found out how strong I actually am. I'm positive she knows it wasn't out of love," Hana replied.

Love had no place in a clan lord's marriage. Mio, who was the former Lady Ichinomiya and knew the secret of the pillar, should be well aware of that fact.

It was a wonder that she treated Hana as if she was her real daughter.

"Then you'll be divorcing Lord Ichinomiya? When?" Hazuki asked.

The question stumped Hana. "…About that. Saku won't agree. That's why I'm still here."

"Why not?" Hazuki was genuinely curious.

Hana was too embarrassed to admit that Saku liked her.

"I mean, you know, this and that." She desperately hoped her vague answer would be enough.

"I see. It all makes sense now, I think. I was shocked when Lord Ichinomiya came and declared he was marrying you given that you had hardly ever talked. Now I understand why," Hazuki said.

"And here you were the one telling me to hand him over," Hana teased with a smile.

Hazuki looked abashed. "Erase that from your memory."

Nozomu interrupted them, shouting, "If our mother knew, why didn't I know?!" He was furious, but at the same time, it looked like he was about to cry. "It must be because I'm too weak…"

Hana's lips quirked up with amusement. Nozomu was stubborn but surprisingly fragile. What a problem child.

"No such thing," she said. "Our arrangement concerns info only the heads of the clans are privy to, and since my mother-in-law has sharp instincts, I figured she would have guessed. That's all. I haven't told her anything myself, and I didn't plan to leave you out. If you're upset that you don't know the clan's secrets, knock Saku down from the throne. Then I'll tell you." She paused. "Actually, at that point, we'd be doomed if you didn't know."

By "we," she meant the entire country, protected as it was by the pillars.

Only the Ichinomiya clan heads and their spouses knew that the pillar was located beneath the grounds of the residence.

It was difficult for her to judge how much she could say. Maybe she could get away with telling them that both yin and yang energy—female and male energy—were needed to repair the brittle barrier. She decided to leave the rest to Saku.

"Saku will answer any questions you have. He'll tell you what he can. Go and ask him later," Hana said.

"...Fine," Nozomu said.

She was relieved that he seemed to be satisfied with that answer, if begrudgingly.

"In conclusion, there's no reason for me to study, right? I'm not going to join the Association," Hana said.

"Given how strong you are, I think the Association will scout you," Hazuki said. "They've already approached me."

Hana had assumed that the Association wouldn't overlook a student as excellent as Hazuki, and she had been right. Apparently, they had already contacted her sister.

But she had absolutely no intention of joining.

"Nope, no way. Not interested. All I want is to enter an ordinary company like a normal person and grind until I can retire."

She wanted nothing to do with the Association.

"Won't that be tough if you don't do well in your classes?" Hazuki rebutted. "You failed the tests for the standard academic classes, too."

"..." Hana didn't respond. She had no comeback.

"The companies under the Ichinomiya umbrella all require you to pass an entrance exam, too," Nozomu muttered.

Hana wanted to cry. "Oh my god, Hazuki, what am I going to do?"

All of a sudden, Hazuki found her arms full of a sobbing Hana. Her expression troubled, Hazuki said, "Study hard."

"I don't want tooooo," Hana whined.

While Hana was throwing her tantrum, in the background, the shikigami were getting to know each other.

"I'm Azuha."

"Miyabi."

"Aoi."

Opposite them was Hazuki's shikigami, Hiragi, quietly sitting on his knees in *seiza*. "I'm Hiragi. Hazuki and I will be in your care." He bowed low to the ground.

Arashi, who had been watching him with warm eyes, nuzzled his bowed head. "I'm Arashi. I am but a novice shikigami, but I hope you will treat me as the others all the same."

"All right. I'll remember your names. It's nice to meet you," Hiragi said.

He looked like a child at first glance, but he seemed much more mature than Aoi.

In fact, Hazuki had manifested him on the same day Hana had manifested Azuha, her first shikigami, so he had lived far longer than Aoi and Miyabi. He could be considered their older brother.

Of course, none of them could hold a candle to Arashi, an actual god.

They were a unique bunch, but they were getting along just fine.

◆

While Hana and the gang were having their fun, over in the sitting room, Saku was in a meeting with Hana and Hazuki's older brother, Yanagi. The twins knew nothing about his visit.

Hazuki was aware that he often dropped by the Ichinomiya residence for work. Hana had rarely ever seen Yanagi, so she hadn't even known that much until Hazuki had told her. However, he actually visited the residence far more frequently than Hazuki assumed.

His visits had continued after Hana had gotten married and, unbeknownst to Hana, they had almost bumped into each other several times.

The near misses had been *misses* not in small part because Yanagi had purposefully steered away from her before she had seen him.

He wasn't avoiding her out of dislike. If anything, he actually...

"Thank you for protecting Hana and Hazuki. I hope you will continue to take care of them going forward," Yanagi said to Saku, bowing deeply.

His expression showed not indifference, but rather the heartfelt concern of an older brother for his sisters.

Saku scanned him with an appraising gaze. "...You knew that Hana was hiding a great power, and you kept it a secret on purpose?"

"Yes," Yanagi said.

Saku raised an eyebrow at his nonchalant answer. "As I suspected. I thought it was strange that you of all people hadn't noticed. After all, you do hold the record for the youngest practitioner to reach the Lapis rank. Why didn't you inform me? I'm sure you were aware that I was seeking a powerful woman."

"I merely weighed my priorities: my younger sister versus my lord."

There was a dignity to Yanagi's calm demeanor in front of Saku.

"You chose your sister over me?" Saku asked.

"If you wish to interpret it as such."

"When did you realize?"

"When I visited her to check on her condition the day after her fifteenth birthday," Yanagi replied. "I sensed an enormous power pouring out of her. She had yet to learn to conceal it entirely, so it was immediately obvious."

Saku sighed tiredly. "You mean to say you knew from the start. Why didn't you tell Hana?"

"It didn't seem like she wanted anyone to know."

Yanagi's simple replies exasperated Saku. He knew from the start that the other man wasn't a skilled conversationalist, but even so, Yanagi was a man of *too* few words. That was surely why he was misunderstood by the younger sisters he cherished. Suddenly, Saku felt pity for him.

"Haven't I told you that your replies are too brief?" Saku said.

"I apologize."

"Instead of apologizing, tell me why you didn't say anything to Hana."

Yanagi was reluctant to explain, but Saku refused to let him off the hook. He opened his mouth slowly and with little enthusiasm. "...Hana has been repeatedly exploited by our parents. She exhausted herself for them only to be betrayed. If she would rather hide her strength than reveal it to our parents, then I wanted to honor her decision. Given the way our parents are, I knew they would drain her dry without a second thought."

"In that case, you should have protected her. Shielded her from your parents," Saku said. "Her and Hazuki both."

"That was impossible for me. My involvement would only have further incensed our parents...our father, in particular. As a result, he might have treated Hana and Hazuki even more horribly. I couldn't risk it."

As Yanagi spoke, his hands gradually balled into fists, frustration bleeding out of him. Seeing him like that, Saku didn't have the heart to reprimand him further.

Saku sighed deeply. "Christ. You siblings are all cut from the same cloth. You act so cold even though you cherish each other more than anything."

When Hana had asked Saku to become Hazuki's guardian, he had replied, "Fascinating." What had motivated such a response was the man in front of him.

In fact, before Hana had talked to him, Yanagi had requested of him the same exact thing: Help Hazuki and temporarily take her into the Ichiniomiya family. The two siblings had come to him for the same favor around the same time.

Normally, Yanagi showed no interest in his parents or his sisters and stayed away from his house as much as possible, but despite his outward behavior, he actually loved Hana and Hazuki deeply.

"Don't think I don't know about your notebook," Saku said. "The one in your inner pocket, with a picture of your sisters inside."

Yanagi raised his hand reflexively to his chest. He looked at Saku with suspicion.

Saku grinned mischievously. "I'm not the only one. Other people have noticed you looking fondly of that photo of the two little girls."

Yanagi turned away in embarrassment.

"There are rumors you have a Lolita complex, but that's not it, right? The girls are Hana and Hazuki when they were young."

"You've seen it?" asked Yanagi.

"Once. I remember because they looked identical. That's why I figured they're your sisters. Am I wrong?"

"No, that's right," Yanagi said. "It's a photo from when they were just innocent little kids, before they learned anything about the world."

He pulled the notebook from his pocket and took out the picture sandwiched in its pages.

A young Hana and Hazuki stared out at them from the photo. Yanagi was behind them, his arms around them. The twins didn't know, but it was the only photo the three of them had taken together.

The girls posed in the middle with ear-to-ear grins. Yanagi was smiling softly and kindly as well.

It was the sole photo of them from the past and Yanagi's cherished treasure; he always kept it on his person.

"I wanted to protect their smiles, but I wasn't strong enough. They became sacrifices to our parents' obsession with restoring our family's standing," Yanagi said. "The only thing I can do for them is to stay away..."

"You are so dense," Saku snapped.

Yanagi wasn't cold and unfeeling. Surely, he was the one who cared for Hana and Hazuki the most in the world. However, since he didn't show his affection on the surface, it went unnoticed by them.

He may have been their brother, but to them, he was but a remote existence. It was too pitiful.

However, the essence that made Yanagi who he was—the blend of compassion, diligence, and stubbornness—was what made Saku trust him and keep him close.

The gods willing, the day would come when Yanagi's feelings would reach his younger sisters. The two would no doubt be surprised to know that he not only carried their photo with him but did so with the utmost devotion.

"...They're an eyesore," Saku mumbled.

"Pardon?"

"Your parents. They can't be allowed to carry on as they are, don't you agree?" A wicked, crooked smile spread over Saku's face.

Yanagi replied, "Of course. I will give them a final warning and have them retire from the stage."

"I'll lend you a hand," Saku promised, the malicious grin still on his face. "It's for the sake of my beloved Hana after all."

And in the hopes of seeing the three Ichises laugh together as they did in the photo.

"I appreciate it," Yanagi said and bowed.

◆

After being thoroughly chewed out by Nozomu and Hazuki about the importance of her studies, especially if she wanted to work for an ordinary company, Hana returned to her room exhausted.

When Saku dropped by to see her, she was lying spread-eagle on the floor.

"Hey, welcome back," she said.

He gazed down at her with fascination. "Welcome back? I've been in the house the whole time."

"Oh yeah? This place is too massive to know who's here and who's not."

"This *is* the main clan residence we're talking about. It's only natural that it gets a lot of foot traffic."

Although the living quarters and visiting quarters were under the same roof, they were separate from one another. No strangers had ever come as far as Hana's room.

The grounds were big enough to fit a baseball field with ease, which gave rise to the problem that it was impossible to tell who was on the premises. Granted, the visitors were rigorously logged, so there should be no need to worry on that front, and indeed, numerous practitioners came in and out of the residence every day.

Saku was usually on the premises so that he could direct the practitioners serving the clan. Not only was he the current head of the clan, but he was also an Obsidian-rank practitioner, after all.

He did leave the grounds when his expertise was required, and there was no shortage of high-risk cases that necessitated the skills of an Obsidian practitioner.

He regularly risked his life in his line of work, but because of his composure and aloofness, most people didn't realize.

He bore responsibilities that were unimaginable for someone who was only twenty-four, but he didn't show a hint of the pressure he was under.

That was part of what made him so incredible.

If it were Hana, she would have made it widely known exactly how much she was sacrificing to help others, but Saku performed his duties without fanfare.

She knew such stoicism was beyond her, which was why, even though they argued like cats and dogs, she respected him.

"...Thanks, Saku," Hana said, still lying on the floor.

Saku smiled softly and sat down next to her. "What's gotten into you all of a sudden?"

"You helped Hazuki," she said. "You became her guardian and let her live here. Seriously, thank you. I never imagined that we would be able to talk like regular sisters again."

Hana and Hazuki had both worked hard to pretend they didn't care about each other. She hadn't tried to speak to Hazuki, nor had Hazuki spoken to her. They had merely been two strangers living in the same house. All along, she had assumed that even once she moved away from the Ichise house, the distance would never shrink.

However, her marriage to Saku had brought major changes to their relationship.

She had never imagined that Saku would consent to becoming Hazuki's legal guardian, sister or not, and the ease with which he had agreed had shocked her.

He had stepped up to bat for Hazuki. By doing so, he had not only salvaged Hana and Hazuki's relationship, but he had given Hazuki her future back when the Ichises had bled her dry.

"I can't thank you enough," Hana said.

"You don't say?"

"Yeah. I owe it all to you. I wasn't strong enough to free Hazuki from that house myself."

"...In that case, I should receive an appropriate reward."

"Huh?"

Saku smirked suggestively. The wicked expression set off alarms in her head, but before she could escape, he caught her and pinned her down.

Hana broke into a cold sweat. This was an extremely dangerous position.

"Wh-wh-what do you think you're doing?!" she demanded.

"Can't you tell by looking? I'm showing my love for my darling wife."

"Thanks, but no thanks! Get off me already!"

"I. Don't. Wanna. Don't you think it's about time for us to become a *real* couple? I know you're thinking it," he purred.

She shook her head fiercely. "Not even a little!"

But his hand was on her cheek, and she couldn't get away.

"Hana…," he murmured, way too seductively.

Hana's head went blank with panic. She couldn't run, but she wasn't mentally prepared to take that next step, either. She wished more than anything she could just faint right here and now.

No. She sensed that blacking out here would only put her in more danger.

As Hana tried to push away Saku's lips, which were rapidly nearing her face, the door to her room slid open.

"Hana, I put together some problems for you to…," Hazuki said as she walked in.

She froze when she saw Hana with Saku hovering over her.

Hana went as still as a stone, too.

A strange tension filled the room.

Hazuki snapped out of her daze. Looking uncomfortable, she started to close the door. "Sorry to bother you. Please continue with what you were doing…"

"Nooo, hold on a sec, Hazuki!" Hana cried. "You've got it all wrong."

"Does she? She said we should continue, so don't mind her, Hana," Saku said.

"Zip it, you!" she snapped.

Having recovered her spirit, Hana kicked Saku off her and scrambled to grab Hazuki as she backed out of the room.

"It's a misunderstanding. I'm serious!"

"It's hard to believe what you say given what I saw a second ago," Hazuki said. "What happened to 'contractual arrangement'? Didn't you say you were going to get divorced?"

Hana opened her mouth to argue that they *were* married by contract, but Saku interrupted her. "It might have been a formality at first, but it's different now. Hana and I are in love. Divorce is out of the question," he declared with a smug look.

Hazuki threw a dubious look at Hana. It was like she suspected *Hana* of lying.

She read the room, and it was clear that Hana was at a disadvantage.

"Hazuki, can you step out for a moment? I need to speak with Saku," Hana said.

"Sure," Hazuki agreed, and she rushed out of the room like she couldn't wait to be gone.

Once they were alone again, Hana turned a glare on Saku and growled, "Saku Ichinomiya."

Her tone made it immensely clear that she was furious. She stomped up to him and grabbed him by the collar.

"What nonsense are you spouting to Hazuki?! You're going to give her the wrong idea!"

"How is it wrong? It's the truth. I have no intention of divorcing you."

"Stop that. I don't want to hear it..."

She was worn out having the same old argument again and again.

"Then let me ask you." He fixed her with a solemn stare. "Are you really fine with leaving me?"

She flinched at the intensity of his gaze.

"You could really divorce me without any regrets?"

"I—I…" She couldn't bring herself to continue. "…"

Saku reached his hand toward the silent Hana. "I don't intend to take anyone else but you as my bride."

"—…"

A flush rose to her cheeks. He shed his serious mask for a devilish grin. In the next moment, he drew her face toward him and touched his lips to hers.

The kiss was fleeting, but it was enough to throw her off balance.

Saku chuckled. "Heh-heh, only a little longer now."

"U-until what?!"

"Until you're head over heels for me."

"Nope, nuh-uh! Never gonna happen! I'm gonna be a normal office worker and live out my golden years in peace."

"You seriously still intend to find work outside the clan?" Saku said, a trace of astonishment in his voice.

"Of course!"

There were no other options open to her.

"Why not join the Association right after you graduate? They've been nudging me about you. Obsidian rank is not a pipe dream for you, and I'm not just saying that to flatter you."

"No. Way." Being a practitioner was out of the question. "Spare me. I want to live a life free of shades and grow old in the countryside somewhere."

"The countryside… How lovely. Shall I purchase a nice plot of land? There are the shikigami to consider, too, so it'll have to be suitably spacious."

"Why does it sound like you're planning to come with me? Or am I just imagining it?"

"What are you talking about? Of course I'm going with you. I'm your husband."

"Please, no. I'm begging you," Hana moaned.

Saku sidled up to her with a wide grin on his face. "What? Do you want another kiss?"

"No thank you," she refused.

Shot down point-blank, he clicked his tongue rudely at her, but facing his irritation was a small price to pay.

Saku's kisses made her brain overload, and she ended up unable to think of anything else but him...

However, Hana sensed that admitting as much would put her in a dicey position, so she was determined to keep it a secret.

◆

Over the weekend, with no need to go to class, Hana had plans to go out with Suzu and Kikyou as a change of pace.

Hazuki saw Hana dolled up more than usual and asked, "Are you going somewhere?"

"Yeah. I'm hanging out with Suzu and Kikyou," Hana answered.

"...That's nice," she said, her reply brief. Her expression was wistful.

"Do you want to come?"

Hazuki brightened. "Really? Can I?"

Hana had extended the invitation without thinking much about it, so she was surprised by Hazuki's delighted reaction. She blinked in astonishment before saying, "Uh, yeah. If you're cool with it."

"Of course! I would love to! It's the first time I've hung out with anyone."

Hana couldn't ignore what she had just heard. "What?!" she said in outrage. "You've never gone out with friends before?"

"No. I never had the time…"

Hazuki's dispirited demeanor reminded Hana of something she had wiped from her mind.

Their parents had dictated Hazuki's schedule down to the minute, from the time she spent in school to what she did at home and even on her days off. "Free time" wasn't a concept that had existed for her, and she wouldn't have had the time to hang out with friends the way normal teenagers did.

Fury boiled up inside Hana.

"Those piece-of-shit parents—" she cursed.

She should have punched them once or twice when she left that house. The next time she saw them, she resolved to do just that without hesitating.

However, Hana was guilty, as well, for being apathetic toward Hazuki.

She would jump at the opportunity to turn back time if only it were possible.

Now there was only one thing she could do to atone.

"Let's go, Hazuki!" Hana declared. "Don't worry. Suzu and Kikyou are both good people. We're going to have so much fun, you won't know what hit you."

"Okay."

Hana waited while her sister went to her room to get ready, and the two of them set off together.

Suzu and Kikyou were already at the meeting place by the time they arrived.

It may have been the first time Hana had ever seen Kikyou without Kiriya at her side. Hana had initially been worried whether Kikyou would be able to find the place without her brother, but it seemed that she had managed.

"Morning, Hana!" Suzu said.

"Good morning," Kikyou said.

Then the two of them spotted Hazuki standing next to Hana, and they made identical expressions of surprise…

"You brought your sister with you," Suzu remarked, genuinely pleased. There was no hidden meaning behind her words.

Kikyou, on the other hand, looked bewildered. "Why is she here?"

"Didn't I mention? She's living in the Ichinomiya residence now," Hana said.

Suzu's eyes widened. "Really?"

"I see. That's why she's been coming to school with you and Nozomu," Kikyou said, satisfied by Hana's explanation.

"That's right. The newspaper club hasn't caught wind of it yet."

At least, they hadn't posted anything about it. The club was slower on the uptake than Hana had thought.

But Hazuki contradicted Hana. "Not exactly. They know about it, but Lord Ichinomiya has issued a gag order."

"Oh yeah?"

"He told me to keep quiet about my living situation as well. I wonder if he's planning something."

"Hmmm. I haven't heard anything," Hana mused. "Hold on. He should've told me sooner, before I blew the secret to these two."

If he had a plan to combat their parents, she wished he would loop her in on it. He couldn't imagine she would spill the beans, could he? She would be irritated if that was his impression of her.

"Not even the newspaper club can defy an order straight from Lord Ichinomiya," Suzu said. "Oh, and don't worry about me. I'm known for having tight lips!"

So Suzu boasted, but she was normally one to hop right on the gossip train. Hana was worried how long she could count on her friend to remain silent.

"I won't say anything outside this group, either, so please rest assured," Kikyou promised.

Hana was pretty sure she could rely on Kikyou. *Suzu would be mad if she knew,* Hana thought to herself.

"I trust you," Hana said. "Anyway, shall we get going?"

Their plan had been to stroll around the town and pop into any store that caught their eye, but that was before Hazuki had joined them.

Hana directed her gaze at her sister. The other two naturally followed suit as well.

"Do you have anywhere you want to go?" asked Hana.

"*I* have to decide?" Hazuki replied, bewildered.

"Didn't you say this was your first time hanging out with friends? Isn't there anything you want to do?"

"What?! Your first time ever?" Suzu asked.

"Yes. Oh, and please call me Hazuki."

"Okey dokey, Hazuki."

It was rare for anyone to address Hazuki so familiarly, and she seemed bashful but happy.

As the top student in their school and the master of a human shiki-gami, she was often treated as different from the other students. It was quite possible that she had no one around her willing to speak to her as a friend. Suzu's easygoing personality was a boon.

"Where to, then?" Suzu asked Hazuki.

"Um, I...," Hazuki said hesitantly. Judging by the way she was fidgeting, it seemed like she had a place in mind. Eventually, she admitted, "I want to go to an arcade."

"Is that a first for you, too?" Suzu asked.

Hazuki nodded self-consciously. Hana mentally smacked her parents several times over.

"Sounds great. Let's go," Hana said.

Suzu, who was always game for anything, pumped her fist in the air. "Aye, aye!"

The four girls found an arcade. When they entered the store with its blaring machines, Hazuki's eyes widened into saucers, and she gazed around with fascination. She was venturing into the unknown.

"Let's go try the claw machines, Hazuki," Hana suggested. "They're geared toward beginners, so you shouldn't have any problems."

"Okay," Hazuki said.

After a bit of indecision, she picked a prize to target.

"Put your coins in here," Hana instructed.

As soon as the words were out of her mouth, she was struck by a realization.

If Hazuki had never spent time with friends before, had she received any allowance from their parents?

There was a real possibility that they hadn't given her a cent, deeming it unnecessary.

Back when Hana had lived in the Ichise house, she hadn't worked a part-time job. Their parents had left her to her own devices, and she had received the money for her living expenses through Sae.

Their parents must have thought that as long as they gave her money, they were fulfilling their parental obligations.

However, it hadn't been rare for them to forget, and Sae had ended up scrambling to requisition the funds from them.

Presently, Hana received a fixed allowance from Saku. It was a relief not to have to worry about money anymore.

Hazuki, on the other hand, was basically a freeloader in the Ichinomiya household. It was hard to imagine she would go begging to Saku for pocket change.

If Hazuki didn't have any money, Hana might have just shamed her by accident.

She fumbled for her own wallet. "It's on me!"

But Hazuki stopped her. "It's okay. You don't have to do that. I have enough to pay for myself."

"What? You have money? Dumb and dumber gave you an allowance?"

Hazuki wouldn't have had time for a job, so any money she had must have come from their parents, Hana assumed. But...

"That's not it." Hazuki let out a disappointed sigh. "You really don't care at all about practitioners or your classes, do you?"

She wasn't the only one. Kikyou was wearing an identical tired expression. "There's a lot Hana doesn't know."

"If she's not skipping class, she's sleeping," Suzu added.

Both Kikyou and Suzu had just casually dissed Hana, but they weren't wrong, so she couldn't argue.

"Class A is given a bit of compensation whenever we're dispatched to deal with shades. Since we're tied up fighting until late at night for these so-called field classes, it's hard for most of us to find any part-time work. Apparently, that's why we're paid," Hazuki explained. "I didn't have any use for the money before now, so I have more saved than you're probably imagining. Don't worry about me."

Hana was relieved. "Good. I was going to ask Saku for money if you needed it, but it looks like I won't have to."

"They've already taken me into their home. I couldn't possibly ask Lord Ichinomiya for money on top of that."

"It's fine. He's the *lord* of the *Ichinomiya* clan. He has money in spades. Even Kikyou is well-off enough to have offered me three billion yen to break up with Saku."

Hana's revelation sent Kikyou into a tizzy. Hana snickered.

Reminiscing, she found herself lamenting the choice she had made. Had Saku not stopped her right as she had been about to sign the papers, she would have gotten her hands on three billion yen.

"Did you really?" Hazuki asked Kikyou with surprise in her eyes.

"Don't tell them that, Hanaaa," Kikyou whined. "I'm sorry for what I did."

"Nothing for you to be sorry about. I'm happy to sign the divorce papers right here and now if you'll give me the three billion," Hana said, teasing.

Kikyou's expression turned serious. "I think it would be better for you to stop joking about that."

"Why?"

"If you hand divorce papers to Lord Ichinomiya, he won't hesitate to use the entire might of the clan to shackle you. You shouldn't give up your life of freedom so lightly!" Kikyou seized Hana's shoulder and shook her roughly. "It's suicide to make him your enemy."

"Not even Saku would stoop so low."

"You're wrong! You're underestimating him! Believe me! He'll take you by force before you can declare a divorce!" Kikyou shouted. She delivered the terrifying threat without a trace of humor in her tone.

"No, no, no, no, no," Hana protested.

"Yes," Kikyou said. "You're too naive. Such a feat would be trivial for Lord Ichinomiya. If only you could see the way he looks at you. It's as if he's holding on to the last thread of his reason. He's dangerous! Kiriya said as much, too, that he worries about you."

How like Kiriya to say that.

"I don't want you to pity me behind my back…," Hana mumbled.

"He said watching the two of you is like watching a rabbit being hunted by a wolf."

Hana didn't know how to respond.

Hazuki added insult to injury, saying, "Lord Ichinomiya did say that he refused to get divorced. When I walked in, he had you pinned underneath him, too…"

"Not you, too, Hazuki…"

"*Eek!* You're already falling prey to his advances! Watch out, Hana. The moment you're separated from your shikigami, you're going to be gobbled up in an instant."

Oddly, it seemed that Kikyou was panicking more than Hana herself.

"Especially never let your inugami leave your side," Kikyou advised. "Not even Saku would dare to confront a god. Understood?!"

"Y-yeah. I got it…," Hana mumbled, buckling under the immense pressure Kikyou was exerting.

"As your best friend, I'll protect your chastity!"

"Nuh-uh, that won't be needed…," Hana said.

Kikyou had worked herself up into a frenzy, but that was when a new challenger stepped into the ring.

"What are you talking about?!" Suzu cried, stabbing a finger at Kikyou. "Hana and Lord Ichinomiya found their way to each other despite opposition from their families. They're Romeo and Juliet! As her *real* best friend, I won't let you interfere with their love!"

It seemed that Suzu was still laboring under a few misunderstandings.

"Do you even hear yourself? He may look like a gentleman, but he's got ulterior motives written all over him!"

"That's the mark of love."

"You're way off."

Hana stood beside her bickering friends, flabbergasted. "This is chaos…"

The two seemed content to amuse themselves without Hana.

"Hazuki, let's go see what's over there," she suggested.

"They won't mind if we leave them?"

"They're fine. They do this all the time."

Suzu and Kikyou argued day in and day out. It was unclear if they were enemies or amazing friends. In any case, their fights had never turned into anything dangerous.

Hana used to try breaking up their arguments, but they seemed to enjoy their quarrels, so recently, she had started leaving them alone.

While she was showing Hazuki her favorite arcade machines, she asked, "Are you going to join the Association after we graduate?"

"It'll probably end up that way. Like I said before, they've already approached me, and I'll be able to make the best use of Hiragi if I become a practitioner," Hazuki replied. "Besides, it seems like it would be difficult for me to live in ordinary society."

Hazuki had been made to walk the path of practitioners from the start. She didn't know anything about what was considered ordinary. No one had ever taught her. It would require immense courage to leap into a completely unfamiliar world.

In any case, there was no way the Association would ignore a practitioner with a human shikigami like Hazuki, so the answer was obvious from the get-go.

"I thought they would have tried to persuade you to join, too," Hazuki said. "You played a crucial role in resolving the attack on our school, you have two human shikigami—not to mention your inugami turned shikigami—so I was positive they would try to headhunt you."

"Not yet, they haven't. Anyway, as part of the deal I made with Saku, I requested to work at a regular company. He might be helping me keep them away."

Otherwise, considering the way Hana had brandished her power during the incident, there was no way she hadn't attracted the Association's attention. The Class A teacher had even tried to persuade her to join his class. In fact, it was downright bizarre that the Association had left her alone all this time. The natural conclusion was that someone was pulling strings in the background.

"I don't want to deal with them. It sounds like a pain. Do you think Saku will handle it for me if I ask?"

"You're really *that* staunchly against joining?"

"It'll happen when hell freezes over."

"But you're so strong."

What a waste, she seemed to want to say.

But it didn't matter what Hazuki said. Hana was determined to become a run-of-the-mill office drone. Perhaps it was time she reminded Saku of that fact. She wanted the Association to stay far away from her.

As Hana and Hazuki were talking, a man appeared in front of them out of nowhere. "Hey, you two," he called to them.

Hana looked at him with suspicion. "Us?"

The man had white hair and a face like a model. He wore a long coat that complemented his figure. With his earrings and jewelry, he looked a bit like a playboy, but his gaze was humorless and intense.

For a stranger, the way he was staring at them was downright rude.

His eyes darted between Hana and Hazuki. He lifted a hand to his chin as if he were mulling something over.

Then he asked, "Which of you is married to Saku?"

Hana was the first to respond to his question. "What?" She glared at him with distrust. What an outrageous thing to ask before even introducing himself. "Who the hell are you?" she demanded.

He turned to her and his eyes flicked up to where Azuha was resting on her hair. Struck by a thought, he snatched Azuha from her head.

Hana was greatly disturbed seeing her precious Azuha ripped violently away from her. "Stop! What are you doing?!" she yelled.

She reached out a hand to take the shikigami back, but the difference in their height was too large, so she couldn't reach.

He scoffed as if to incense her further.

Hana was quivering with rage. "Dammit. Give her back!"

"And if I refuse?" he drawled.

She gnashed her teeth in frustration. He was clearly making fun of her.

That was when Azuha released the restraints on her abilities and blasted the man with her full power.

"Shit!" he cried, shielding his eyes from the piercing light Azuha was emitting.

The shikigami took advantage of the opening to flit away, returning safely to Hana's side.

"Are you okay, Azuha?" Hana asked.

"Yes."

Relieved, Hana turned a furious glower on the rude interloper.

"Aaah. Judging from that display, you must be Saku's bride," he remarked. "The younger of the twins was rumored to be a washout, but I suppose that info is outdated?"

"It's none of your business!" Hana exploded.

Next to Hana, Hazuki found her eyes drawn to the man's chest where a familiar pendant was dangling from a cord around his neck. She grabbed Hana's arm in a panic. "Wait a minute, Hana. He has an obsidian pendant."

"Your other half seems much more composed," the man said scornfully, holding the pendant aloft as if to say, *Take a good look.* "I'm Yukizasa Sankourou. I obtained the Obsidian rank just recently."

Hazuki reacted to the name with shock. "What?!"

Hana, on the other hand, couldn't have cared less, consumed as she was by anger at the man in front of them.

Azuha was special to Hana, and she could not forgive him for treating her little one with such violence.

While she was debating how to best exact revenge, the man said, "How about you break up with Saku?"

She immediately snapped, "No one in their right mind would agree to a request like that from a stranger. Are you stupid?" She repaid his earlier mockery in kind.

A vein on his temple throbbed. "Who do you think you're mouthing off to? Bravery and recklessness aren't the same, you know. Consider your audience and pick your words accordingly."

He fixed Hana with a piercing gaze. His expression had frosted over in an instant. His eyes were cold enough to make hardened men quake.

Hazuki swallowed heavily and took a step back, but Hana advanced instead, ready to fight. She refused to be the first to look away.

"Cheeky brat," the man murmured and grabbed her arm.

She tried to shake off his hand right away, but his grip was too strong. "Let go," she growled, scowling.

The threat in her tone had no effect on her opponent.

Still, she kept her eyes locked on his, sensing that the one to avert their eyes would lose their duel. Her thoughts were ruled by her anger. Driven by her refusal to lose, she stood her ground.

A piercing "Hey!" interrupted their staring contest.

It was Kikyou. Apparently, her argument with Suzu had finished. It had taken longer than usual.

"Is that you, Yukizasa?! What are you doing to Hana?!" Kikyou cried.

The two contestants finally disengaged from their duel and turned to look at Kikyou.

Yukizasa made a face like he had just bitten into a lemon. "Here comes the crybaby. Where's your partner today?"

Kikyou flinched, and her brows drew downward. Unlike when she was fighting with Suzu, she looked afraid.

"N-none of your business. Wh-wh-what about your exam? Aren't you supposed to be in the middle of your Obsidian-rank trial? Did you skip again? I'm going to report this to your mother! Hurry up and get your hands off Hana," she shouted.

However, maybe out of fear, she was keeping her distance, so she did not make for an effective rescuer.

Nevertheless, she managed to temper Yukizasa's anger. All the motivation visibly drained from his body, and he flung Hana's arm away.

"I'm sick of this."

Hana's arm wasn't broken, but the pain from his viselike grip still lingered. She didn't want to show any weakness in front of him, so she put everything she had into pretending her arm didn't bother her.

She glowered at him, threatening him with a world of pain if he tried to come near her again.

Yukizasa turned away and disappeared into the crowd without another word.

Once he was gone, Hana rolled up her sleeves to find that his hand had left a significant bruise.

"I should have slugged him," she grumbled, her hatred of losing rearing its head.

Suzu and Hazuki approached her with worried faces.

"Hana, are you okay?" Suzu asked. Her eyes landed on Hana's arm, and she winced. "Oh my god. That's one heck of a bruise."

"Does it hurt?" Hazuki asked.

"I'm fine," Hana replied curtly. "More importantly, do you know that jerk, Kikyou?"

However, the one to answer was Suzu. "You're probably the only one here who doesn't know him."

"What? Seriously?" Hana turned to her sister. "You know him, too?"

Hazuki nodded. "I didn't recognize his face, but I realized right away after hearing his name."

"You too, Suzu?"

"Of course. I'm a Mitsui. My family falls under the Sankourou clan. I've never talked to him, but I know what he looks like at least."

"You're kidding."

In the end, Hana was the only one still in the dark.

"Please explain, Kikyou," Hana asked.

"That was Yukizasa Sankourou. As you can tell by his name, he's from one of the five great clans, the Sankourou clan. He's the son of the current clan head, and the one who has been nominated as the successor."

"So he's in the same position as you and Kiriya, then."

"No. We are merely candidates, whereas he is the confirmed successor," she said. "As long as nothing goes wrong, at least."

A man like *him* was going to be the clan lord? That seemed like poor judgment.

Hana wanted to file a complaint with whoever had made that ridiculous decision.

"The Sankourou clan specializes in defense," Hazuki added in simple terms for Hana's understanding.

Kikyou picked up the conversational thread. "Like Hazuki said, the clan excels at creating robust barriers, and a nomination by the current clan head means that Yukizasa's skills are the real deal. He was originally a Lapis-rank practitioner, and I had heard that he would be undergoing the promotion exam to claim the Obsidian rank, but that's all I know…"

Hazuki said, "Earlier, he was wearing an obsidian pendant."

Kikyou looked surprised. "That must mean he passed… I see. He must have heard about Lord Ichinomiya's marriage after returning from the testing grounds and come to see for himself who the spouse is. This is a disaster, Hana."

Kikyou's pitying gaze irritated Hana. "Is he related to Saku somehow?" she asked.

"Yes, they're old friends, though it feels a little one-sided on Yukizasa's end. He's fixated on Lord Ichinomiya. I'm sure he was dying to know who he married. Geez. Talk about having too much time on your hands."

"Yet another troublemaker crawls out of the woodwork." Hana stared meaningfully at Kikyou and sighed deeply.

"Why are you sighing while looking at me?!" Kikyou demanded, tears springing to her eyes.

Hana wanted to point to her reaction and tell her, *Exhibit A.*

◆

Because of the chaos caused by the unexpected Sankourou run-in, the girls called it a day early.

After Hana returned home, Aoi found out she had been injured and flew into a rage. He pulled his sword, having every intention of running out of the house to find that Yukizasa guy and cut him down. Miyabi calmly stepped in and quieted him with a swing of her giant squeaky hammer. Then she brought out the first aid kit, saying that taking care of Hana came first.

"Master, are you really okay?" Aoi asked.

"I'm fine, I'm fine."

"So you say, but I can't forgive him for marring your beautiful skin," Miyabi said.

"See?! You agree with me. Then let's go pay him a visit and show our *thanks*," Aoi said.

"You have a point." Miyabi's lips curved into a grim smile—her eyes weren't laughing. From her expression, it was clear that she was equally outraged by the bruise on Hana's arm.

"I told you already— No," Hana said.

"But whyyy?" Aoi whined in displeasure.

"Yukizasa is the successor of the Sankourou clan, so he must be very strong—strong enough to capture Azuha without breaking a sweat," she said. "He's on a different level. If you pick a fight with him blindly, you might end up hurt, and that would make me sad. So no, you can't go."

Of course, the one who had stood up to such a dangerous person and openly glared at him as if to say *Come at me anytime!* was none other than Hana herself. If Hazuki hadn't been by her side, she undoubtedly would have thrown at least one punch at him.

But in hindsight, thinking about it logically, her opponent had been the next head of the Sankourou clan. As the wife of the Ichinomiya clan lord, her actions might have sown the seeds of discord between the clans. It was a good thing she hadn't laid a hand on him.

Not that he had shown her the same courtesy, given the bruise on her arm… She wondered if her injury was grounds enough for her to complain to the Sankourou clan, but she decided to defer to Saku's judgment.

"Let's take care of your wound first, Master," Miyabi said.

"I'll deal with it. You may all leave," Hana said.

"But…"

"I can treat myself."

She couldn't bear for her shikigami to see the bruise, which had gradually turned a horrifying color. She didn't want to worry them.

"Go on already. Bring me a snack and tea," Hana requested. "We were going to eat lunch together, but thanks to that a-hole, we missed our meal. Oh, and bring some to Hazuki, too."

Miyabi stared solemnly at Hana for a while, but then she sighed in defeat. "I understand. We'll prepare something, so please treat yourself properly."

Hana laughed softly. "I got it already."

Miyabi and Aoi cast her one last concerned glance, then left the room. Azuha followed them.

Once she was alone, Hana sighed deeply.

"Ugh, geez, he did a number on me. Monster," she grumbled as she opened the first aid kit and started to treat her bruise.

The throbbing pain seemed to have only gotten worse as time had passed. She had put on a brave face in front of her shikigami, but it seriously hurt. No one could blame her for the dark mutterings that came pouring from her mouth.

She let out a steady stream of complaints as she cleaned her wound, but since she was limited to using one hand, she wasn't having as much success as she would have liked, and the inconvenience only fueled her irritation.

"I should have just let Miyabi do it," she muttered.

However, Hana knew that Miyabi, despite looking as beautiful and gentle as a goddess, actually had a shorter fuse than Aoi, and she hadn't been able to ask that of the shikigami.

While Hana was wrestling with the kit, Saku entered the room.

The moment she saw his face, she started airing her grievances. "Sakuuu. What's with your friends?"

"I heard. That's my bad."

"Why are you the one apologizing? It's not *your* fault."

"Because mainly, I was the reason he did it…" Then, unable to watch her struggle with the attempted treatment any longer, he said, "Give that here," and offered to take over.

Hana obeyed and handed Saku the kit, and he started to tend to her injury.

"Does it hurt?" he asked.

"Badly."

In front of Miyabi, she had been able to play it cool and say she was fine, so why had she told Saku the truth?

She didn't have to put on airs around him and could say what she was thinking without holding back. He was older than her, but they faced each other as equals.

The more she thought about it, the more curious their relationship seemed.

"Sorry," Saku said.

"Seriously, why are you apologizing?"

"Yukizasa recently found out I married and has been hounding me to get divorced. I refused, obviously. He was being extremely annoying, so I started rejecting his calls, and it seems like that only piqued his interest more."

"How does he have the gall to tell someone else to divorce?"

"He's a my-way-or-the-highway kind of guy, and he thinks you're not suitable for me. He believes we only married for the sake of the barrier. On top of that, he's irritated that I didn't tell him beforehand. But how was I supposed to contact a guy in the middle of the Obsidian-rank exam?"

Saku gently stroked Hana's bruised arm apologetically. His usual fire was nowhere to be seen.

"Anyway, it's my fault for letting him off his leash," he added.

Hana was overcome by an urge to pet his head. She withdrew her arm in alarm.

"You're friends?" she asked.

"I guess you could say that…"

"Huh? That's vague."

"He's a buddy from my rebel days."

"Rebel? Who? You?"

Considering that Saku was now the exemplary lord of the Ichinomiya clan, Hana couldn't picture him as a teenage rebel in the slightest.

"I was pretty wild in my student days."

She looked at him with surprise. "Really?"

"Shocked?"

"Yup," she replied without hesitation.

Saku chuckled. "I hated everyone and everything back then. I saw the whole world as my enemy." He sighed and paused. "Those aren't days I like remembering..."

Hana watched Saku as he told her about his past, but his eyes were focused somewhere far away.

"You said before that you understand how Nozomu feels, but I empathize with Hazuki," he admitted. "I faced expectations and pressure from everyone around me. To answer them, I pushed myself to the brink, and as a result, I broke down. For a time, not even my mother could deal with me."

His tone was light, but his words were anything but.

"Not to copy what you said, but why does everyone and their mother feel the need to compare...?"

In his expression was a trace of loneliness—and pain.

Saku was a tyrant and a narcissist. He was strong and had walked the path of a practitioner all his life without straying. That was what Hana had thought.

But he had his own woes.

It felt like this was the first time she had seen his vulnerable side.

Without thinking, Hana embraced Saku.

His eyes widened in surprise. "What are you doing?"

"You did the same for me before. Now it's my turn."

His lips curved in a tender smile, and his eyes slipped shut. He gathered her in his arms.

"...That was when I met Yukizasa. Back then, he was just one of the candidates to succeed the clan, but he was also the most powerful. We shared the same worries and frustrations, so it was easier to breathe when

I was with him. That's why I say our relationship is a little different than friends."

"I see. He seemed really concerned about who you married."

"There's a part of him that still can't let go of the past. That's why he's still fixated on me to some extent. But it's impossible for us to stay the same as we were back then." Saku snickered. "What a little punk he is."

Their gazes locked.

Saku's eyes showed his usual unwavering strength of will.

His hand came up around her head, and he drew slowly closer. She could have dodged if she had wanted to, but she stayed where she was.

Their lips touched. They felt each other's warmth through the kiss.

"...People say if pushing doesn't work, try pulling," Saku said.

Where had his fragility from earlier gone?

He smirked. The usual cocky despot was back.

Hana gaped.

"When Yukizasa pressed you to divorce me, unlike the time with Kikyou, you shot him down flat, or so I heard."

"Y-you heard wrong."

"I don't think so," Saku said. "You're always going on about getting divorced. I never imagined you actually loved me so much. I'm thrilled."

"No! I just said that because he was pissing me off!" Hana protested.

Her fluster and desperate excuses only made him happier.

Delighted by her reaction, he laughed. "Ha-ha-ha. Don't be embarrassed."

Hana shot him a glare. "Dumbass!"

She had been genuinely worried about him, and he had cruelly tricked her. She hammered him with her fists, but he only seemed more pleased than before.

"Stop that. You're a patient. You're going to hurt yourself," he said.

"It already hurts! Whose fault is that?"

Saku cradled her injured arm and continued the treatment. He finished off by binding the wound securely.

"Aren't you overdoing it a bit?" Hana said.

"Just in case. Go to the hospital if it gets worse."

"Sure, sure."

Saku had finished treating her injury, but he still wouldn't let her go. She looked at him, wondering what was up.

He leaned over and dropped a kiss on top of the bandages.

His touch was tender as if he were handling something broken.

Hana was suddenly at a loss for words. Her mouth opened and closed.

With his lips still pressed to her arm, Saku peered up at her.

She was paralyzed by his solemn gaze.

His lips slowly lifted away.

"I will warn Yukizasa off. If the same thing happens again, come to me for help right away," he said.

"...Okay."

"Good girl."

Saku stroked her hair gently one last time before leaving her room.

Alone, Hana blushed fiercely and hid her face with both hands.

"What the hell...?"

She thought back on the range of emotions Saku had shown her. She knew she had been played by him, but she couldn't fight the feelings blooming inside her.

Chapter 3

Several days passed after Hana's encounter with Yukizasa.

Thankfully, the pain in her arm had receded, and the bruise had faded to the point where it was largely unnoticeable.

She had intended to hit him if she ever ran into him again, but apparently, Saku had gone to talk to him in person and had punched him in her stead. Out of consideration for Saku, she figured she would let this one go.

However, she wouldn't forgive that guy a second time.

She had steeled herself to be ready to take him on at any time, but realistically, it wasn't every day one could lay eyes on the Sankourou successor, and the days passed by peacefully.

Then over lunch period one day, Hana was paged through the PA system.

"Ooooh, they want you in the principal's office. What did you do?" Suzu asked teasingly.

But Hana drew a blank. "Nothing. I don't think I did anything, at least."

She was on her best behavior in school, relatively speaking.

Her grades weren't stellar. That was a sore spot for her.

"They're not gonna chew me out for failing all my classes, right?" Hana said.

"Well, it's not a great look for the wife of the Ichinomiya lord."

Suzu didn't deny it, so the possibility wasn't zero.

"Saku already gave me an earful. I don't want to hear it from the teachers, too. Maybe I should pretend I didn't hear it."

"You can't. If you don't go, you're giving them more to scold you about."

It seemed that in Suzu's mind, Hana being chastised was an inevitability. Hana wanted to go less and less.

However, Suzu was right. She wanted to avoid a longer lecture, so she went to the principal's office obediently.

When she got there, she knocked on the door. She didn't have to wait long before she heard someone say, "Come in." She opened the door and nervously walked in, her mind racing to find excuses for her poor grades.

Her gaze was drawn to the two people sitting on the sofa, and her eyes widened.

Opposite the principal sat Hana's parents.

Seeing the two faces she never wanted to lay eyes on again, her brows furrowed automatically.

"Why are *you* here?" Hana demanded in a low voice, her anger simmering.

The principal stood and said, "Calm down. I don't know what misunderstandings you have had, but you shouldn't worry your parents. I'll excuse myself here, so please make up."

"Come again?" She scowled, not following what he was talking about.

He left the room with a smile.

Most likely, her parents had fed the principal a pack of lies. After he disappeared, laboring under whatever false impression he had been given, the smiles vanished off her parents' faces, replaced with glowers filled with loathing, as if she was their enemy.

Theirs weren't expressions one would give to their own daughter.

Granted, the same could be said of Hana. She glared at the two with an irritated face unbefitting a child seeing her parents.

Behind her stood Aoi and Miyabi, invisible but on guard. Unlike Saku, her parents showed no sign that they had noticed the shikigami.

Ah, but it was too pitiful to compare them to an Obsidian practitioner like Saku, so she revised her thinking.

The two people Hana had never wanted to see again.

It would be easy for her to ignore them and leave. She could just as easily have Saku wield his authority as the clan lord and order them not to come near her. However, they had purposefully come all the way to her school, and she wanted to know their intentions.

If she ran, next time, they might summon Hazuki instead, and that was just not okay. She decided to hear them out and sat down on the sofa across from them, throwing one leg over the other.

Her father instantly reacted to her arrogant gesture. "How dare you take that attitude with your parents?!"

His rage failed to move Hana. She projected an air of *What're you gonna do 'bout it?* and didn't change her demeanor one bit.

"I don't consider you my parents, so it makes no difference," she said dismissively. "So? What is so important that you got the principal involved?"

"Isn't it obvious?! Go talk to Lord Ichinomiya and win his favor for the family. We have given you ample time, and yet you have done nothing. If you call yourself an Ichise, you should work for the sake of your family!"

Hana's heart froze over in an instant.

She was disappointed.

She was surprised she could still be let down by her parents at all, but miniscule though it might have been, she had held a flicker of hope.

Hazuki, whom they had cherished so dearly, had fled the house. Might they be worried for her?

Hana thought nothing of herself. She had given up long ago in that regard.

But Hazuki wasn't the same as her, right? Or so she wanted to ask her parents.

Yet their concern wasn't for the child they had raised, but for the family name.

Had they said a single word of worry for Hazuki, Hana might have revised her opinion of them.

However, reality was cruel.

There was no sign they were going to mention Hazuki at all.

Hana had crossed beyond anger to utter apathy.

"I shouldn't have to explain something as basic as this!" her father yelled. "Now that you're the clan lord's wife, entice him and promote the Ichise name! You're so useless!"

He showed no trace of regard for Hana.

The complete lack of respect for her feelings was shocking.

Who did he think he was, blaming her like this?

What optimism to believe that she would act on behalf of the Ichise name though he had never treated her like part of the family.

The gaze Hana trained on her parents was horribly cold.

"Are you stupid?" she sneered.

"What did you say?" her father demanded.

"Why should I have to seduce Saku for your sake? There's no way I could do something so outrageous. Just because *you* are shameless doesn't mean that I am."

"Who are you calling shameless?!"

"Who else but the two of you?" Hana said sternly. "You treated me as an outsider all my life, and now you come slithering to me as if you've changed your tune. That's what I mean by shameless. Get it, birdbrain?"

She dumbed down her insults so that fools as thickheaded and cowardly as they would understand.

Her father gaped in shock. Then his face flushed red with indignation.

Hana hoped he would burst a blood vessel and pass out then and there. She no longer had the slightest hint of affection for her parents.

"You are an Ichise! It is only right that you sacrifice for the family!" he shouted.

"Hmm, but when I went back to pick up Hazuki, didn't you say I had no place in the house anymore?" Hana drawled. "In other words, I'm not an Ichise. Besides, I'm married to Saku now, so my family name is different."

Ichise, schmichise. Go to hell.

She wouldn't give a damn if the family were to fall to ruin.

"You plan to throw away the family?!" he demanded.

"What do you want me to say? Would you be satisfied if I said *yes?* If so, I'll say it as many times as you want. I don't need this sham of a family!"

"H-how dare you!"

Hana's father swung his hand back in a broad arc. Needless to say, he was aiming for her. He was going to slap her.

However, Hana didn't try to dodge, but merely glared back steadily at her father. Aoi and Miyabi leaped into action.

A split second before his hand struck Hana, the door burst open.

The intruder was someone unexpected. It was Yanagi, her older brother.

"Stop right there, Father," he said.

"Yanagi... Why are you here?!"

"I have told you time and time again, Hana is Lord Ichinomiya's wife. She is the lady of the main family whom we are obliged to serve. How dare you presume to raise a hand against her?"

"N-no! This is... It's discipline! I am merely disciplining a child who refuses to obey her parents."

"Lord Ichinomiya knows that you were scheming to contact Hana,"

Yanagi said. "If you don't want to anger him any further, leave immediately."

"Whose side are you on?!"

"Leave."

Their father was cowed by Yanagi's tone, which brooked no argument.

Their mother grabbed his arm worriedly. "Dear. Let's end it here for today."

"Shit!" he cursed.

He shot Hana one more sharp glare before exiting the room.

Once they were gone, Hana let out an exhausted sigh. Yanagi walked up to her. She watched him approach warily. The invisible Aoi and Miyabi had their guards up as well.

"Sorry, Hana. Are you okay?" Yanagi asked.

"Uh, y-yeah…," Hana said, shaken by the concern he was showing her.

It might have been the first time he had said a kind word to her.

Yanagi scanned her over to see if she was telling the truth.

It was rare for the two of them to be so close, for them to make eye contact at all, at least in Hana's memory.

"I didn't expect them to come all the way here. I'm sorry I didn't stop them," he apologized.

Hana was shocked by his show of remorse. "It, uh, it was nothing. I'm fine…" She could only muster trite words in response.

"I have been summoned by Lord Ichinomiya, so be careful on your way home. If possible, go together with Hazuki."

"S-sure…"

After hearing her reply, Yanagi spun on his heel and left.

Hana found herself speechless for a moment. Out of concern for her, Aoi and Miyabi manifested themselves.

"You okay, Master?" Aoi asked.

"Master?" Miyabi chimed in.

"I'm okay. Just a little surprised."

To think Yanagi, who she had hardly ever spoken to, would be worried about her.

Their conversation had been almost like that of regular siblings.

She had thought that Yanagi considered her a stranger—as she did him—but just then, he had seemed genuinely anxious.

There were truths Hana had yet to discover. About Hazuki. About Yanagi.

In various ways, she may have been blind until now.

She had lost sight of what was true and what was false.

◆

Hana did as Yanagi instructed and went home with Hazuki.

In the car on their way back, she told her sister that their parents had come to see her.

Hazuki was horribly shaken. "Don't tell me they came to take me home."

"If that had been the case, I would have given them a little bit of credit as parents," Hana said. "Actually, not a single syllable of your name came out of their mouths. The only thing they're concerned about is the Ichise name."

Hazuki's face clouded over. "Oh…"

Unlike Hana, who had thrown away any affection she had had for their parents long ago, for Hazuki, it had only been a few days since she had left the Ichise household, and her feelings toward their parents might not match Hana's.

"You still have expectations for them?" asked Hana.

"…"

Hazuki neither confirmed nor denied the statement. Perhaps it wasn't that she didn't, but that she *couldn't*.

"They might be planning to get a hold of you, too. Don't let yourself get swept up in their scheming," Hana warned.

Hazuki had always followed their parents' commands. It was impossible for her to combat them all of a sudden.

She had only been able to say her piece when she had run away because momentum had been on her side.

"They might try to butter you up, but it doesn't matter how kind their words are; they haven't changed one bit. Your feelings won't ever get through to them. I'm sure of it," Hana said.

She couldn't imagine their parents saying anything nice, but she threw in the warning just in case.

"...Yeah," Hazuki mumbled.

It wasn't clear whether she truly understood what Hana was saying or if her emotions had yet to catch up.

She hadn't thrown away their parents completely the way Hana had.

Well, that was hardly unusual.

It had taken Hana a long time to abandon all her feelings for their parents.

Demanding Hazuki cut off all ties immediately would be too harsh.

"Shitty bastards," Hana grumbled in a small, small voice.

They would harass her to the ends of the earth, until the end of time. Sometimes, the bonds of blood proved to be nothing but a burden.

The twins returned to the Ichinomiya residence without incident, and Towa came to greet them.

"Madam, Miss Hazuki, dear Junior has called for you. He says to come to the sitting room upon your return," she relayed.

"There you go again with the 'Junior,'" Hana said. "Saku's going to be angry."

"Ho-ho-ho-ho." Towa merely laughed, showing no inclination to change her ways.

Saku was surely doomed to be "Junior" forever. The thought made Hana want to giggle.

It was even more funny because of his usual pretentious attitude.

"Pfft..." Hana snickered.

"This is no time to laugh," Hazuki chided. "We have to go. We can't keep Lord Ichinomiya waiting."

"Let him wait," she said, still nursing a grudge from the teasing Saku had subjected her to a few days before.

"We mustn't."

Hazuki dragged Hana to the sitting room and found not only Saku but Yanagi waiting for them. Both the twins were equally surprised.

"What? Why...?" Hana said.

She had heard from Hazuki that Yanagi stopped by the Ichinomiya residence on occasion, but she hadn't known he would be here.

"You're back. Come on in," Saku said.

The two of them approached, their expressions bewildered.

"Never mind Yanagi for now. More importantly, I heard your parents visited you, Hana. Are you okay?"

"Yeah, no problems there. I was more worried about Aoi and Miyabi going ballistic."

Suddenly, it occurred to Hana that she might as well have had the two of them manifest and threaten her parents a little bit.

"Good. Just to make sure, what did they want?"

"Something along the lines of convincing you to favor the Ichise family," Hana said. "I refused, of course."

Who in their right mind would help such an awful family? Not her.

She wasn't so soft as to obey orders from people who had mistreated her horribly.

If she had been asked to help destroy the family, on the other hand, she would have happily cooperated.

"Water under the bridge and all that. So what's he doing here?" Hana asked. It was obvious to anyone she was talking about Yanagi even without her saying his name. "He didn't come to take Hazuki back, did he?"

Hazuki twitched in surprise.

"If that's the case, I won't hand her over without a fight. Even if it's you asking, Saku," she added.

Hana had no intention of giving Hazuki back to the Ichises. She could predict how their parents would treat Hazuki if she were to return.

"Relax. It's not about that," Saku said.

Hana was relieved, but that didn't explain why Yanagi had come.

"I've thought this from the start, but you all need to talk to each other more!" Saku yelled, raising his voice suddenly. "Especially *you*!" He stabbed a finger at Yanagi.

Yanagi's expression didn't change one bit.

"The two of you, come sit," Saku ordered.

"Huh? What do you want?" Hana asked.

"Don't sweat the details. Sit across from us."

His tone left no room for refusal.

Hana and Hazuki exchanged a look. Hana could feel her sister's confusion, but they took a seat facing Yanagi.

"Wh-what now, Saku?"

It wasn't as if anything would change if they talked.

"It's a problem that you three don't communicate, this affair with Hazuki being a prime example," he said. "In fact, Hazuki, if you had confided in Hana from the beginning, you could have avoided several years' worth of misunderstandings, right? You keep too much bottled up." He turned to Hana. "That applies to you, too, Hana. Giving up immediately is a bad habit of yours."

"Easy for you to say, but... You know. Right, Hazuki?" Hana said.

"...Yeah."

Sure, her relationship with Hazuki might not have soured had they spoken openly with each other, but their household environment had made such communication impossible.

"It's true that your parents did the most harm. However, the way I see it, you each created whatever excuse was convenient for you and didn't try to look any further," Saku said.

"Hmm..."

Hana couldn't refute what he was saying, but she was reluctant to accept it, too.

"It was wrong of you, Hazuki, to keep everything to yourself to the point where you self-destructed, but Hana, you're also at fault for being indifferent!"

"I don't get what you're trying to say," Hana said.

"Stop interrupting. Let me finish. The two of you were wrong, but the one who kept quiet all this time is also to blame. I mean you, Yanagi!"

Yanagi looked down at the floor.

Saku continued. "If you had paid more attention, your sisters wouldn't have drifted apart, don't you agree? Hazuki's problem could have been resolved earlier, right?"

"I apologize. I have no excuses," Yanagi said.

"*Sorry* isn't going to cut it! I know you treasure your sisters. Yet I haven't heard them utter a single syllable of your name since they came to live here! Are you fine with that?"

"As long as they are happy..."

"I told you to stop trying to solve everything on your own!" Saku shouted. "Your sisters have a right to know the truth. It's wrong of you to shoulder everything alone. You're siblings."

Hana and Hazuki listened to the conversation with bewilderment.

"Saku?" Hana said.

Saku turned toward the two of them and asked, his tone equal parts angry and exasperated, "Don't you find it strange at all? Despite Yanagi being the youngest practitioner to rise to the Lapis rank, he is ignored by your parents in favor of Hazuki. He may not have a human shikigami, but with a brilliant practitioner like him in the family, the Ichises' future should be secured, no? There should be no reason to hound Hazuki to study."

"That's...true," Hana said.

She hadn't realized until he had explained it. Yanagi was already an established Lapis practitioner working in the field. To have such an accomplished heir should have been the greatest blessing for the Ichise family.

However, their parents' expectations were placed not on Yanagi, but on Hazuki.

Why?

"If you don't know the answer, ask *him*. That's all I have to say," Saku concluded.

For a moment, no one spoke, and silence filled the room.

"*Ask*," Saku had said, but neither Hana nor Hazuki knew what to say. They looked at each other with troubled expressions, glancing at Saku and Yanagi in turn.

Then Yanagi abruptly bowed his head.

"I'm sorry," he said, to Hana and Hazuki's surprise. He straightened up again and looked at them with solemn eyes. "Let's talk. I'll tell you the story behind our family. It has to do with you, too."

They nodded, confusion still written on their faces.

Yanagi began his tale—a tale neither Hana nor Hazuki knew about the Ichise family and about their parents.

"It starts before you were born. At the time, the previous family head—our grandfather—was still alive. He was an upright man, but ambitious, too. After I was born, he was overjoyed to see my talents as a practitioner bloom at an early age. He favored me, and our father couldn't forgive that."

Their grandfather had passed away while Hana and Hazuki were still infants. They only knew him from photos.

Needless to say, they had no clue what his relationship with their father had been like.

"Why?" Hana asked.

"To our grandfather, our father was inferior. He had concerns about passing the head seat of the family down to our father, so he considered passing over Father and making me his heir instead.

"Inferior... Is that shitty old man of ours that weak? Did you know anything about that, Hazuki?"

"Come to think of it, I don't think I've ever seen him use his powers," Hazuki said. "What about you, Hana?"

Hana hadn't, either. She shook her head.

Their father had derided her constantly for being good-for-nothing. Looking back, she couldn't remember seeing him work as a practitioner.

The same could be said for Yanagi, but he was known to be a Lapis practitioner, so she didn't need to see it to believe it.

"Do you know what our father's shikigami is?" Yanagi asked.

"Huh. I don't think I've seen it," Hana said.

"Me neither," Hazuki agreed.

His expression bitter, Yanagi revealed, "It's a dragonfly. His shikigami is an insect."

"...Are you kidding me?!" Hana snapped without thinking.

Her voice was loud and angry, and no wonder. She had been constantly derided after she had summoned Azuha, a butterfly.

Hazuki was stunned into silence.

"That bastard. Who is he to call me worthless when his shikigami is a bug, too?!"

"Exactly," Yanagi said.

"I can't believe it...," she muttered.

She was so amazed that she was at a loss for words. Their father had pitted her against Hazuki and had oppressed her mercilessly, and yet he, too, was a washout.

"Normally, wouldn't you think he'd treat me with more kindness?"

They were comrades in arms, both having insect shikigami. He should have empathized with her.

"His shikigami is the root of his inferiority complex," Yanagi said. "He saw his own weakness reflected in Hana, and he couldn't bear it."

How impossibly selfish...

For such a petty reason, he had hurt Hana so deeply.

"That's why, when he saw the way our grandfather doted on me, he felt I was trying to snatch the Ichise inheritance away from him. He has treated me harshly since long ago, even more so than he does you, Hana."

"No way..."

She was surprised to hear it, having never witnessed their father behave cruelly toward Yanagi herself.

That said, she couldn't recall seeing the two of them having a pleasant chat, either.

Part of the reason was that Yanagi was usually away from the house for work, so it was rare to see him and their father together in the first place.

"Well, there's no point in comparing or asking which of us is more pitiful," Yanagi said.

"...Right."

Hana and Yanagi were in agreement on that front. She didn't know anything about how he had been treated, so she couldn't compare them anyway.

"Our grandfather wanted me to succeed the family line, but he passed away before it could happen. He wrote it in his will, but it was impossible for a minor to inherit, and our father became the head of the family instead. Nevertheless, that wasn't enough to erase his feeling of inferiority."

"Did something else happen?" Hazuki asked nervously.

To be honest, Hana had already heard enough, but she, too, was curious.

"The shikigami you two summoned were another trigger. One, an insect shikigami like his own and the other, a human shikigami even I hadn't managed to create. Your shikigami further fueled his inferiority complex. On the one hand, Hana's insect shikigami was like a blow to his bruised ego, and on the other, through Hazuki's human shikigami, he had his first taste of superiority. Keeping Hazuki, who has more talent than me, by his side was his way of restraining me."

"Ugh... How pathetic."

Hana felt disgusted that she and Hazuki had been used for such a worthless purpose, and she heaved a deep sigh.

"The reason why our father is obsessed with the family name is because he wants recognition from his peers that he is superior to me. His feelings toward our grandfather whose approval he never received have completely warped..."

Yanagi paused, his expression dark.

An unpleasant hush filled the room.

Hana's voice cut through the tension. "...Hazuki and I are nothing but convenient tools to him."

Their father had rejuvenated himself by abusing Hana. He had gratified his desires by treating Hazuki favorably.

She didn't know what Saku had wanted them to talk about, but what she had realized through their conversation was that their father was a piece of garbage through and through.

Of all the shitty parents she knew, he was the king.

"So? What's your point? What do you expect us to do after hearing this story?" Hana asked Yanagi, pinning him with a direct gaze.

"I want you to think about what happiness means to you," he answered.

"That's no business of yours. It's not like you care what happens to us. I can count on one hand the number of times we've talked. It's all the same to you if we live or die, right?"

"That's...right."

She had only stated the facts, but Yanagi looked upset. If she couldn't figure out the reason behind his gloomy expression, then...

Saku had been staying quiet, but he cut in and said, "I don't know about you two, but Yanagi cares a lot for you."

"What...?" Hana said.

Saku stood and dug through the inner pocket of Yanagi's suit jacket.

"W-wait, Lord Ichinomiya!" Yanagi protested, flustered.

He desperately tried to hold Saku off, but Saku called out, "Tsubaki," and bade her to pin Yanagi's arms behind him.

Saku ignored Yanagi's glare, snatched the other man's notebook from the jacket pocket, and flipped through its pages.

"You should know when to give up," he said to Yanagi. "If you don't express the important things in words, no one's going to get it!" He took out something sandwiched in between the pages and handed it to Hana. "Look."

It was a photo. Pictured were Hana and Hazuki when they were little. Yanagi was with them as well.

"What...?" Hana muttered.

"Yanagi always keeps this picture of you three on him. He wouldn't carry around a photo of people he cared nothing about or treasure it as he does. He cherishes you as his younger sisters in his own way."

The sudden revelation was hard to believe.

Hazuki looked at Yanagi doubtfully. Her eyes seemed to say, *We're talking about Yanagi, right?*

"Then why did you act so coldly all this time?" Hana asked. "You didn't try to help me or Hazuki. If you had at least tried to mediate, Hazuki wouldn't have nearly been forced into marrying against her will."

She wasn't angry so much as resentful.

Frankly, she couldn't care less about herself. She had already cut off all ties with their parents, and Saku had come to her rescue.

But Hazuki hadn't had such assistance.

Left behind in the Ichise house, maybe she wouldn't have had to suffer had Yanagi been her ally.

"I thought that my interference would make things worse…," Yanagi said.

"Why worse?"

"Like I said earlier, Father's inferiority complex causes him to see me as a rival. Hypothetically, let's say I tried to arbitrate. He's a man who doesn't listen to a word anyone says. My intercession would only anger him more. Who do you think would end up bearing the brunt of his anger? Undoubtedly, he would lash out at the two of you. The more I cherish something, the more he'll try to trample over it. All I could do was feign indifference and stay away from you."

Yanagi was hunched over as he spoke. Hana had never seen him like this. She looked over at Hazuki, who was making a complicated expression. She thought she must surely look the same way, and she didn't know how to respond.

That showed how remote of an existence Yanagi was to her.

Even knowing that there had been a reason for his apathy, Hana found it hard to accept it the way she had with Hazuki. Her confusion showed on her face. She looked like a child who had lost her way.

Hazuki grabbed Hana's hand. Judging from the steely look in her eyes, it appeared that she had made up her mind.

"Thank you for sharing that. I didn't know you felt that way about me and Hana. I'm genuinely happy. There is a part of me that has always looked up to you as a Lapis practitioner."

Yanagi looked at Hazuki as if he couldn't believe his ears. "Hazuki..."

"But that was a lot of information, and both Hana and I need time to process it. Please give us a while to organize our thoughts."

Seeing Hazuki's reaction, Hana thought that her sister was much more put together than herself, twins though they may be. She may be a mess inside, but Hazuki had given Yanagi a proper response.

"Lord Ichinomiya, do we have your consent as well?" Hazuki asked.

"Yes," Saku said. "You really are more levelheaded than Hana." He turned to Yanagi. "Don't you feel better now that you got that off your chest?"

"Against my will, but yes," Yanagi said. Then he faced Hana and Hazuki with a bitter expression. "Hazuki, did you hear that *those two* contacted Hana today?"

"Yes."

"I doubt they'll give up after one try. I have heard rumors that they are surreptitiously starting to act. Be careful just in case," he warned the two of them. "Don't be alone."

Hana clicked her tongue reflexively.

"I knew I should have had Miyabi knock them upside the head with her squeaky hammer."

If they want to come, then come, she thought and vowed to herself that when the time came, she would beat them up without a second thought.

"Saku, I'm counting on you for the cleanup," Hana said.

"Hey, what are you planning?!" he snapped back. "But anyway...if they'll do us the favor of firing the first shot, it'll be a golden opportunity."

A sinister smile rose to Saku's face. Hana felt a chill run down her spine.

"Yanagi," Saku said, "if those two slip up, we can use their blunder as an excuse to have them surrender their position. You'll succeed the Ichise family in their stead. That will tie up everything neatly."

"Will it go that smoothly?" Yanagi asked.

"Making sure things go according to plan is the fun part."

Saku's wicked expression made Hana feel a twinge of sympathy for her parents.

However, they were only getting what they had asked for.

◆

Hana was lazing about in her own room after their discussion. Her thoughts were occupied by Yanagi's confession.

She hadn't imagined their family had been embroiled in such a struggle before she had been born. She now knew that there was a reason for her father's animosity toward her.

That said, knowing was hardly enough to make her suddenly warm up to her parents.

If anything, she only felt more anger toward her father, and it was growing stronger as time passed. She didn't know where to release her pent-up rage.

"I won't feel better until I punch him," she said.

But alongside her anger was disbelief.

"Who would have thought he has an insect shikigami, too?" she muttered to herself.

In that case, had he also been ridiculed for being a good-for-nothing like she had been?

After the birth of his talented son, had he suffered from the comparisons?

Question after question popped into her head.

"What's with this feeling...?"

She felt an inexplicable unrest swirling in her heart.

That was when Saku came into her room.

Hana sat up from her prone position on the floor.

"You okay?" he asked.

"What do you mean?" she replied.

It wasn't as if anything had been done to her.

She had merely listened to Yanagi's story.

Granted, just remembering what he had talked about was enough to make her feel nauseated.

"Did you know?" Hana asked. "About the Ichises' situation?"

"I found out recently. I judged that it was too heavy a burden for Yanagi to bear alone, so I created an opportunity for him to talk to you and Hazuki. Did I stick my nose in where it didn't belong?"

"Yes, but maybe it was for the best." She paused. There was an air of sadness around her when she began to speak again. "I never knew... I never knew why my parents—my father in particular—hated me so much. True, I was a failure compared to Hazuki, but now that I think about it, there are plenty of people with insects as shikigami, right?"

"Yeah."

Practitioners summoned their shikigami for the first time when they turned ten.

However, since they were still children, yet to mature fully, many of the produced shikigami were insects.

Over time, their powers strengthened, and they created new shikigami.

Just like Hana. Once she had awoken to her powers, she had summoned Aoi and Miyabi. Human shikigami were the rarest of the rare, but on the other hand, an insect shikigami was hardly proof that a practitioner was talentless.

Of course, it was undeniable that practitioners with insect shikigami were looked down upon. However, it had been premature to jump to conclusions just because she had summoned a butterfly.

There were even practitioners who used the bare minimum power during the process in order to create an insect shikigami on purpose because they were easier to control.

In Hana's case, because Hazuki had been next to her and had summoned a human shikigami, and because she herself had shown no signs of growth, she had been called worthless and her sister's scraps. However, a weak insect shikigami did not equate to having no skill as a practitioner.

But her parents had treated Hana as the villain.

"I understand his feelings of inferiority, but to me, he is a failure as a father and as the head of the house," Hana said.

"I agree."

As the master of an insect shikigami—just like Hana—he should have understood her feelings and extended a helping hand instead of turning his back on her...

She might have been able to breathe easier in the Ichise house.

She might have gotten along with her brother.

Hana couldn't stop thinking about the what-ifs.

She hugged her knees to her chest and buried her face in them.

Saku came closer to her and stroked her hair gently.

She couldn't remember her parents petting her head even once, but Saku did it as if it were the most natural thing in the world.

"Are you feeling down?" he asked.

"It's not that, but I feel restless," she admitted. She felt antsy when she thought about Yanagi, too.

Hana was glad they had talked. She had never known the reason her parents hated her and had blamed herself for being a failure. She used to pour her heart into her studies, working herself to the bone in the hopes that her parents would look her way.

Not realizing it was wasted effort.

Saku was right. The Ichise siblings needed to use their words more.

"I have you to thank…," Hana said.

She finally knew the reason behind her mistreatment in the Ichise house.

If Saku hadn't stepped in, Yanagi would likely have kept the knowledge a secret.

Saku was still stroking her hair. He pulled her head toward his chest. She felt like she could already hear his heartbeat.

Normally, Hana would have resisted, but just this once, she couldn't muster the will. She let her head be guided to rest on his chest.

She soaked in his pleasant warmth.

Saku chuckled. "This isn't like you. You usually fight me tooth and nail."

"Don't talk about me like I'm some sort of vicious brute," she said sulkily.

He laughed. "There's your usual bite. If you have something to say, say it. Sticking together in tough times, that's what it means to be husband and wife."

He continued petting her head, which leaned against his chest. His hand was gentle and soothed the turmoil in Hana's heart.

When had Saku become a place of repose for her?

The one who was most surprised to notice the truth was Hana herself.

Hana abruptly tilted her head up and locked eyes with Saku.

"I…might like you."

The confession slipped out of her mouth without any prompting.

Once the words were out of her mouth, she found herself badly embarrassed and hid her face from Saku.

However, she immediately became anxious to see his reaction and peeked up at him.

He did not seem about to tease her and was watching her with gentle and fond eyes.

"You've finally caught on to my charms," he said.

Hana was amazed that, even in a situation like this, he was such an egomaniac. She grabbed his face.

"That hurts," he complained.

"Where do you get your bottomless confidence from?"

She was peeved that she was the only one who seemed to be nervous. She had expected a bigger reaction from him, but he was acting surprisingly normal.

But this was par for the course for the two of them.

"What can I say? I was born extraordinary," Saku bragged.

Hana stared at him coolly. "Aren't you embarrassed to say that about yourself?"

He was unaffected by the scorn in her gaze.

Saku's bluster and arrogance drove away the indescribable unrest she had been feeling.

"Whenever I talk to you, everything else starts to feel trivial," Hana said.

"That's good. Worrying alone won't solve anything. At times like this, you should come to a genius like me for help."

"Stop making fun of me! I'm way smarter than you."

"Says the one failing all her courses. Even in my rebel days, I never had a red mark."

Nestled against each other, Hana and Saku continued to argue.

Their equilibrium had been restored.

Even as they shrieked at each other, their expressions were soft.

◆

Around the same time, a visitor came to the Ichise house, one with no prior relation to the family.

The visitor was Yukizasa Sankourou.

Hana's father had been shocked when he received Yukizasa's request for an audience.

Since the Ichises were but a humble branch family of the Ichinomiya clan, he could not refuse the Sankourou successor, and even if he could, he would not have.

Hana's father, ambitious as he was, welcomed Yukizasa with open arms, thinking that this might prove the turning point he had been looking for.

When Yukizasa came calling, the Ichise parents greeted him at the door. "W-welcome to our humble abode!" they exclaimed, unable to hide their excitement.

The servants were visibly nervous as well.

After all, the visitor belonged to the Sankourou clan. A man nominated by the current clan lord as heir. A distinguished individual.

It was hardly every day that someone of such rank dropped by the Ichise house. There was no higher honor.

The Ichise parents bowed and scraped to Yukizasa as they invited him in. The holier-than-thou attitude they took with Hana was nowhere to be seen.

Yukizasa was smiling as he was led through the halls, but anyone looking would have felt a shiver of fear.

They ended up in the sitting room, and the Ichise patriarch ordered everyone else to leave. Yukizasa had demanded that their conversation stay between them.

Hana's father was so eager to do as he'd been bid that it made it easy to forget that the Ichises were part of the Ichinomiya clan, not the Sankourou.

The Ichise parents sat down across from Yukizasa.

Hana's father hesitantly asked, "I have cleared the room... May I inquire as to what business brings you to our home?"

"I despise talking in circles, so I'll get straight to the point," Yukizasa said. "Haven't you any desire to take back your daughter? To get revenge?"

"O-our daughter, you say?" Hana's father asked. He hadn't expected to hear such a suggestion and did not follow.

"Yes. The elder twin. The talented one. Hazuki, I believe her name is?"

"Yes, Hazuki is her name. How is it that you know of our daughter, Master Sankourou? In addition, what do you mean by 'revenge'?'"

"You know that the older twin was the top candidate to be the bride of the Ichinomiya clan lord, yes?" Yukizasa said.

"Excuse me?"

Hana's parents were shocked.

"You didn't know? She had the endorsement of Mio, Lord Ichinomiya's mother."

"We hadn't…"

"If all had gone accordingly, she would have married Lord Ichinomiya, and the Ichise family would have received great boons from the clan. What a shame," Yukizasa said. "If only the younger sister hadn't meddled and stolen the seat."

The corners of Yukizasa's lips drew upward in a sharp smile.

Hana's father didn't notice. He was trembling with rage. "That wench!" he cursed.

"Yes, her. If it weren't for her…," Yukizasa said wistfully.

"Yes. She ruined everything. If only that good-for-nothing hadn't been born. We should have thrown a pest like her into an orphanage a long time ago!" Hana's father slammed his fist down on the table.

"She's now living happily in the Ichinomiya residence, unconcerned about her parents' struggles."

"Damn it—…"

Imagining the picture of Hana's life Yukizasa had painted, Hana's father clenched his fist in frustration, so tightly it seemed like blood would come gushing out. The enormity of his rage was obvious to anyone watching.

"It's not too late," Yukizasa murmured, his words as sweet as honey. The Ichise parents looked at him. "If the older twin, Hazuki, returns to this family, all will be resolved, no?"

That was right. If only they had Hazuki...

Hana's mother grabbed hold of her husband, her eyes expectant. "Darling, Master Sankourou is correct. Lord Ichinomiya would surely prefer Hazuki to that disappointment."

"However, would we not incur Lord Ichinomiya's wrath by following through with this plan?"

A step before the precipice, and Hana's father was still hesitant.

Yukizasa gave him one last push. "What can you do for the sake of the Ichise name? Who is fit to lead this family? The answers are obvious, right?"

"Y-yes. It is as you say. I am the head of this family. I won't yield the position to anyone," Hana's father said.

"Exactly, darling!" Hana's mother cried.

"Let's fetch Hazuki back," he resolved. "I'm certain that two-bit wench, Hana, will interfere. What should we do...?"

"There's no need to worry. I will lend you my aid," Yukizasa said. From his words shined the light of hope.

"Thank you kindly, Master Sankourou!" Hana's father said.

"We will not forget this debt!" her mother added.

They bowed their heads low as if they were prostrating before him.

Yukizasa chuckled with delight.

The Ichise parents had leaped at the opportunity Yukizasa had presented them without wondering for a second why he was helping them.

They didn't know they were making a deal with the devil.

Chapter 4

Hana started going to and from school with Hazuki, since there was no guarantee that their parents wouldn't try to contact them again.

If they came for Hana, she would send them flying before they could say a word, but Hazuki wasn't one for violence. Therefore, staying together was the most reassuring option for them both.

Without fail, Nozomu would tag along as well. He had heard from his beloved brother that Hazuki might be hassled by their parents and was gung ho to help.

Considering Hana was the more powerful one, she had low expectations, but Nozomu did directly descend from the Ichinomiya bloodline when all was said and done. His birthright could provide a sturdy shield against their parents who folded easily in the face of social status.

"I'll protect you while I'm at it, since you're Saku's wife and all," Nozomu said to Hana bashfully.

He was definitely a softy beneath his bluff and bluster.

It was rare for him to act sweet toward her. She was amused, but since he was genuinely trying to help for once, she didn't try to tease him.

So far, they hadn't encountered any trouble. Perhaps they had Nozomu's overattentiveness to thank for that.

Yanagi had warned them that their parents were scheming something behind the scenes, so Hana had her guard up, but it might all have been a waste of effort.

That said, until they could be absolutely positive their parents had given up, they couldn't afford to relax.

Hana figured they should be safe on school grounds, but she still asked Kikyou and Kiriya for their cooperation.

"—Basically, our trash parents might be planning to trap Hazuki. I can't be by her side since I'm in Class C, and Nozomu can't cover for her all the time, right? That's why I'm asking you two to keep an eye on her when you have time. Will you help?"

Hana told the twins about their toxic parents and explained the general situation. Kikyou responded to her request with frightening enthusiasm. "Understood. Your sister is my sister! It's my job as your best friend to come running when you're in a pinch!"

"That's going a little too far…," Hana said.

"I'll rain punishment down on any pests that come buzzing! Think of me as a gigantic lifeboat. You can count on me, your BFF!"

Not only was Kikyou not listening to Hana, she was also hyperfixated on being Hana's "best friend."

Hana was suddenly worried about whether she could rely on the other girl at all.

Was this so-called lifeboat made of mud, or was she just imagining it?

"Please, Kiriya. Make sure Kikyou doesn't run wild, and look out for Hazuki for me," Hana said.

"Sure. Kikyou's always like this. I'll think of something. It'll be okay. Don't worry." Kiriya gave her a thumbs-up while staying perfectly expressionless.

He and Kikyou might have been twins, but his words sounded much more trustworthy.

With Nozomu and the twins watching over Hazuki at school, Hana could relax and spend her time in Class C. The regular reports the twins texted her gave her further peace of mind.

Incidentally, unlike Kikyou's impassioned reports, Kiriya's were logical, easy to read, and explained the current situation. They were a lifesaver.

From Kikyou, she received nothing but emotional texts along the lines of, *"Hazuki's followers were bad-mouthing you! How dare they insult my best friend,"* and *"Nozomu acts like a shy girl when he talks with Hazuki. It's creepy."*

There was too much extraneous information. Hana only wanted news about Hazuki.

Her replies to Kikyou's messages were perfunctory, but she read Kiriya's carefully.

Previously, Hazuki had played the part of the perfect honor student. Now that she had dropped the act, the sycophants were keeping their distance. On the other hand, she was starting to make friends she could actually talk with.

Hana had given some thought to the problem of Hazuki's followers, who did nothing but flatter her, so it was a blessing that they had distanced themselves of their own accord.

Nozomu was constantly attentive toward Hazuki and treated her kindly, so there were whispers that there was something going on between the two.

In any case, the two of them had been close from the start. There had always been rumors here and there that they were dating. They had merely increased.

It was a golden opportunity for Nozomu. Unfortunately for the poor boy, Hazuki had not even a flea-size inkling that he had feelings for her. Even Kiriya pitied him.

Nevertheless, Nozomu ardently protected Hazuki day after day. Such nobility could inspire one to shed a few tears, but for Hana's part, she didn't intend to help him one bit.

Hana kept up with Hazuki's situation via the twins' reports. Meanwhile, she was having a tough time of her own.

As a result of the assault on their school, their curriculum had changed, and Hana's class bore the brunt of the changes.

The number of lecture-based classes had been reduced to the point where she no longer had the time to nap, and the number of practicals had increased.

Practicals were classes for practitioners.

The ones who had been most freaked-out by the incident were none other than the teachers who were responsible for the students.

They were frenzied in their mission to teach the students to protect themselves, and their desperation influenced the classes. Every day, the students were subjected to such hot-blooded instruction.

Hana had already had more than enough, but to her consternation, her teachers, having found out about her powers, were determined to put her to use.

One time, the teacher had her erect a barrier, which her classmates all attacked at once.

Another time, they had a shikigami battle where it was Aoi versus everyone else.

So Hana was made to participate.

She felt taken advantage of to some extent, but when she saw the enthusiastic faces of her classmates, it was hard for her to say no.

At first, when the extent of her powers had been revealed to the public, there had been some who questioned why a master of two human shikigami was in Class C. However, that only lasted until she became infamous for failing her exams across the board. Afterward, the consensus became that, given her awful grades, her placement was understandable.

Magically powerful but intellectually weak. This was the scenario she had wanted to avoid the most.

The compassionate way Arashi—the softy—looked at her hurt. She would rather he have laughed at her outright.

She should have been happy to be accepted into the fold, but the day she had been told, *"Don't be too hard on yourself,"* she had felt her eyes grow hot.

The busy days continued, until one day, a rumor swept through the school that a short-term instructor was going to come.

"Did you hear, Hana? About the new teacher?" Suzu asked Hana with interest.

"Yeah."

"Apparently, they were hired for our sake."

"I guess our class is even weaker than our teachers gave us credit for," Hana joked.

They might have been vaguely aware of Class C's incompetence, but now the reality they had been avoiding was staring them right in the face, especially given how little hands-on experience the class had.

The students' performance was so atrocious that even their teachers were throwing in the towel.

That was where the short-term instructor came in.

"Apparently, they're an active-duty practitioner, and an accomplished one at that," Suzu said. "Do you think they could be an Obsidian-rank practitioner?"

"No way," Hana said. "Obsidian practitioners are like protected species. That's how rare they are, and therefore, they're busy. They wouldn't come just to teach washouts like us."

She could say that with confidence because she knew how busy Saku was.

Admittedly, Saku also had his duties as the clan lord to contend with.

"I guess you're right. I had my fingers crossed. That's too bad," Suzu said.

"You said 'active-duty,' but realistically, isn't a third rank on the cusp of retirement the best we can expect?"

"That's still amazing."

Their teachers all belonged to the Association, too, but they were all first or second rank.

Low-ranking practitioners were rarely ever deployed to the front lines.

A third rank might not be the elite of the elite, but they would still have real experience fighting on the front lines. Their teachings would no doubt greatly impact the students' growth.

After such a discussion, who should come but a practitioner newly promoted to the fifth rank, Yukizasa Sankourou.

"Hello. I'm Yukizasa Sankourou. I'll be your instructor temporarily. It's nice to meet you all. I'm an Obsidian practitioner, though I achieved the rank only recently. I plan to very *nicely* and *thoroughly* work you to the bone, so be prepared."

Yukizasa introduced himself, oozing with an overconfidence that rivaled Saku's.

Hana was shocked by the turn of events.

What surprised her wasn't that their teacher came from the cream of the crop, but that it was someone she knew.

Hana was stunned into silence, but around her, her classmates were shrieking and clamoring.

They were abuzz over the fact that a fifth-rank practitioner had come and that they were going to be taught by him.

Not to mention that he was the successor to the Sankourou clan.

The triple whammy had the students whooping in joy.

"I can't believe it. This is awesome!"

"We're going to be taught by an Obsidian practitioner? Talk about extravagant."

"Not to mention that he's hot!"

"Do you think he has a girlfriend?"

But unlike her overjoyed classmates, Hana was in turmoil.

"Master, are you okay?" Azuha asked, her voice only audible to Hana in the din filling the classroom.

"Yeah, I'm fine."

The bruise Yukizasa had left on her had faded long ago.

However, that didn't mean that her anger was gone as well. Hana glowered at Yukizasa.

When break time rolled around, Kikyou came running to Class C. "Hana, are you all right?!" She was very worked up.

Kiriya trailed behind her, laid-back as always.

"I came here as fast as I could after hearing Yukizasa is the special instructor for your class! He hasn't done anything to you, has he?!" Kikyou cried.

"I'm okay. He hasn't tried anything," Hana replied levelly in order to calm down her hysterical friend.

Kikyou knew that Yukizasa had hurt her last time and had wasted no time coming to check on Hana.

Kikyou's fervor finally cooled. Kiriya, having arrived a second later, took his place beside her.

"Neither of you knew anything?" Hana asked.

"Not at all," Kikyou replied. "The request probably went through the Association. Students like us who have no affiliation with the Association wouldn't be told anything. Especially since we're not from the same clan.

"Makes sense."

"Anyway, it's unprecedented for an Obsidian practitioner to be an instructor. Sure, he only passed his trial recently, but it's amazing that the Association agreed to this. The same could be said of him taking on the assignment."

"...Do you think he had another reason for coming?" Hana asked.

Considering the awful way they had met, she couldn't help but be suspicious.

She hoped she was just reading too much into it, but her intuition said that he had an ulterior motive.

"I can go investigate, Master. What do you think?" Azuha suggested, fluttering in front of Hana.

Hana looked at her shikigami. That was certainly an option, but Yukizasa's rough handling of Azuha was still fresh in her mind. She didn't want Azuha anywhere near him.

"No. I'll wait to see what he does. Thanks," Hana said.

"Mmkay." Azuha flew back to perch on Hana's hair.

Hana had been wary of Yukizasa ever since her run-in with him and had been taking precautions to avoid him.

Yukizasa looked the part of a regular ladies' man, and he looked pleased by the excited shrieks of the female students. The guys were watching him with an air of respect because of his rank, too.

To Hana, the smile that had been plastered on his face since the beginning seemed fishy for some reason. Was it because she remembered his icy gaze from their first meeting? The Yukizasa she knew was an entirely different person.

Yukizasa had been Saku's friend in the latter's days as a teenage rebel, but you wouldn't know from his appearance that he had a wild past. In addition, he treated Hana's classmates with kindness and courtesy.

However, because of the dark memory of their first encounter, Hana made sure that she never had to interact with him. Nonetheless, she couldn't run forever, and one day...

"Hana Ichise," Yukizasa called to her from behind.

Hana automatically grimaced. She adjusted her expression as she turned around.

He was wearing a shady smile.

Hana put everything she had into keeping her features still and placid. "Do you have business with me?"

"Your tone sounds barbed, or am I imagining it?"

"Who's to say?"

There was no way she could keep the venom completely out of her tone, but it was surprising that he had picked up on it.

She glared at him with eyes full of wariness.

"You don't have to be so cautious of me. I won't do anything," he said.

"You want me to believe you? After what you did when we first met? With no apology, either," she sneered viciously, making her distaste for him clear. She was still holding a grudge.

Yukizasa shrugged as if he couldn't be bothered. He squared himself to face Hana and bowed without any prelude. He apologized while Hana was in shock. "I was wrong. I'm sorry."

They were in the middle of the hallway. The students streaming past gawked at the spectacle.

The one bothered by the stares was Hana, who had demanded Yukizasa apologize in the first place.

"W-wait a second!" she stammered.

"I won't do it again. Please forgive me," he added without raising his head.

Hana was greatly agitated. "Stop it!"

"I will if you forgive me."

"I do. I forgive you!" she shouted, unable to bear the icy looks from onlookers.

Yukizasa straightened, a wide grin on his face. His expression was exactly the same as Saku's when he had fun at her expense.

Hana's eyes narrowed. "I think I understand why Saku used to get along with you."

"Hold up. It's not 'used to.' We still get along," Yukizasa retorted.

"If you say so. Hope it's not just your delusion," she said coldly. She turned to flee, but he grabbed her arm.

The way he had manhandled her last time was still fresh in her memories, and she shook off his hand violently. This time, he let go immediately, but that did not make her feel any better.

"Will you stop pawing me whenever you please? You already have a previous offense on your record."

Yukizasa raised his hands in surrender. "My bad," he apologized with a grimace.

He was acting sincere, but Hana was still watching him with suspicion.

He squirmed under her unflinching gaze.

"You're acting like a completely different person. Did you eat something weird?"

"Saku tore me a new one after the last time I saw you. He told me not to mess with you again."

"Oh, really? I'll have to praise him when I see him at home."

"You don't understand. He was terrifying. My stomach still hurts from his punch." He rubbed his abdomen gingerly.

Apparently, Saku had sucker punched him in the gut.

"You get what you deserve." She snorted disparagingly.

"You have an awful personality."

"Don't worry about me. I'm leagues better than some guy who would hurt a girl he just met. Be grateful I'm holding back from giving you another punch to the stomach while you're still hurting."

Hana made to leave again, but he blocked her way.

His repeated attempts to thwart her escape pissed her off, and she glared up at him in irritation. "What? What do you want?"

"I apologized, right? Make sure you report that to Saku."

Her fed up gaze stabbed into him.

"I thought you actually felt bad for what you did to me, but it turns out, you're just afraid of Saku. Pathetic."

"He's terrifying when he snaps, you know."

"Who? Saku?" Hana tilted her head in puzzlement.

What was he talking about? She had never once felt scared of Saku. Yukizasa's words were incomprehensible to her.

"Have you never seen him blow his top?"

"It's a little different, but I've seen him angry before," she said. "He's so expressive, it's a piece of cake to tell when he's happy, sad, angry, what have you."

"What?!" he burst out, shock painted across his features.

"What?" she asked.

"Full of expressions? Easy to read? Are you serious? Poker-faced robots like him are one in a million."

"I should be the one asking if you're serious. Poker-faced? That doesn't describe Saku in the slightest. Who are you mistaking him for?"

"You're—..." Yukizasa suddenly cut off and looked at Hana fixedly.

"What?" His eyes were boring holes into her, and she grew uncomfortable.

"Right, okay. I see. I get it." He nodded to himself like he had figured something out and tousled her hair roughly.

"Hey!" she protested, brushing her hair back into place.

Their eyes met. His eyes were solemn.

"I can't wait to see what you'll do," he said. His lips curved in a smile cold enough to give one chills.

Hana was startled by his sudden change in expression. "What do you mean?"

"You'll understand soon enough." He turned away. "Make sure you tell Saku I apologized," he said and left.

She watched him walk away. *Maybe he's not such a bad guy after all,* she thought, revising her opinion of him.

Perhaps she had been a little excessively cautious because they had gotten off to a bad start. He seemed to have reflected on his actions, too.

Hana decided there was no reason for her to purposefully avoid him anymore.

The thought that she would be betrayed didn't cross her mind.

◆

After school, Suzu was still in the classroom after everyone else had gone home because she had been asked to stay behind.

Across from her stood the person who had been animatedly chatting up Hana earlier: Yukizasa.

"Um, I don't understand. Why?" Suzu asked in consternation.

"You don't need to know," Yukizasa said. His frosty, cold gaze scared her. "Just do as I say and bring your best friend, Hana Ichise, to the abandoned factory north of the school."

"Why do I have to take her there? Plus, the Association forbids entry to that place...," she said timidly.

The words were hardly out of her mouth before a loud *crash* rang through the room. Yukizasa had kicked a desk and chair and sent them flying.

Suzu flinched at the noise.

Yukizasa's smile was reflected in her pupils.

"The only answers you are permitted are *yes* and *of course.*"

The words were neither angry nor loud, but his quiet, threatening tone was terrifying.

Suzu looked as if she were ready to burst into tears. She clenched her shaking hands and said, "N-no way..." She forced the words out of her mouth, her voice a high and tight whisper.

But they were erased by Yukizasa's menacing "What?!" He went on to say, "My bad. I didn't hear you. Say that again?"

They were inches apart. There was no other sound in the classroom. There was no way he hadn't heard, and yet he was asking her to repeat herself.

Pressured by his threat, Suzu bit her lip. Then, determined, she declared in a louder voice than before, "No way! I won't bring Hana to such a dangerous place!"

She looked down at her feet, afraid of Yukizasa's reaction. When she looked up again, she found his face, smooth and cold like ice, much closer than she had expected. She gulped.

"Who do you think you are, huh?" he growled.

"Uh...um..."

"Your family belongs under the Sankourou clan. You're not going to listen to a request made by the next clan lord? You're going to disobey me?"

Suzu was quaking. "I won't do it... I don't know what you're planning to do to Hana, but I won't put her at risk..."

"You're picking your friend over your loyalty to the head family? That's courageous, in a manner of speaking."

"P-please excuse me!"

She couldn't stay there.

Sensing the dangerous position she was in, she scrambled out of the classroom.

Suzu ran and ran and ran until she was finally away from the school grounds. She looked back to make sure Yukizasa hadn't followed her and sighed in relief.

That was when...

"Are you Suzu Mitsui?"

She flinched in surprise and turned toward the voice to see a middle-aged man and woman she didn't recognize. She looked at them suspiciously. "Who are you?"

"Oh, please don't be so wary. We're Hana and Hazuki's parents," the man said.

"Wh— Really?!" Turmoil warred with shock as she remembered her manners and bowed. "It's nice to meet you."

"No, no, there's no need for all the formalities. We heard you're friends with our daughters. You seem like a lovely girl."

"Aw, shucks. I can't believe Hana talks about me," she said bashfully, not knowing that Hana was on bad terms with her parents.

Hana had thought there was no need to expressly tell Suzu about the nature of their relationship, so Suzu talked amicably with the Ichises under the assumption that they had a normal parent-child relationship.

"Actually, we have a favor to ask of you," Hana's father said.

"What is it? I'm happy to do anything I can to help," Suzu said with a smile.

There was no way she was going to refuse a request by the parents of her cherished best friend. However, her smile soon turned into bewilderment.

"Can you contact Hazuki and ask her to come to the abandoned factory nearby?"

"Um, you said the factory...?"

Yukizasa's face popped immediately into her head, and her smile disappeared—soon replaced by a confused expression.

"Yes. Right away. Can you do that?"

"I'm sorry. I...don't know Hazuki's number," she lied. She had a feeling that she shouldn't tell them.

The moment Suzu refused, Hana's father clicked his tongue. Startled, she glanced at him. The warm smile he had been wearing a second ago was gone. Instead, he was glowering at her, his features twisted in irritation.

"In that case, I'll give you her number. Can you call her?"

"Um...ah..."

If they know her contact information, why can't they contact her themselves? she wondered.

They were her parents...

Suzu sensed danger, realized it would be best not to get involved, and slowly started to back away. "I'm sorry. I have somewhere to be, so please excuse me."

I'll have to contact Hana right away when I get home, Suzu thought and turned away. At that moment, her mouth was covered with a cloth.

She breathed in, and in the next second, she started feeling dizzy. The strength slowly drained from her limbs, and she collapsed to the ground.

"Hurry, dear," Hana's mother said.

"I know without you telling me!" Hana's father snapped.

He lifted the unconscious Suzu and loaded her into the car. The two of them climbed in and drove off.

A distance away, Yukizasa had witnessed the entirety of the brief incident. He picked up the phone Suzu had dropped.

"...Christ. If she'd just cooperated, we wouldn't have had to resort to violence," he muttered.

With a snap of his fingers, he dispelled the concealment barrier that Suzu hadn't noticed.

He tapped on Suzu's phone to bring up her newly added contacts.

She had exchanged numbers with Hazuki only recently, and Hazuki's name was on the list.

Having found what he had been after, Yukizasa's lips curved into a cruel smirk.

◆

Nightfall. Hazuki had come to the abandoned factory.

She scrutinized the Do Not Enter sign in front of the roped-off grounds with anxiety and fear, but she pushed herself to step past the rope.

The door of the factory was rusty and hard to open. Hazuki threw her entire body into the door, and it slowly screeched open. She peeked inside before entering.

The building should have been abandoned long ago, but the lights were on.

Naked bulbs lit the interior.

Hazuki checked her phone again. The location of the factory was included in the text she had received from Suzu along with the message, "*Come alone if you want to save her.*" It was clear as day Suzu had gotten herself wrapped up in something.

Hazuki scanned her surroundings nervously, but Suzu was nowhere to be seen. Just as she was about to head deeper into the building to search, she heard footsteps coming from within. She was instantly wary.

From the dark emerged…her parents and Yukizasa.

Hazuki's eyes widened, and she slowly backed away.

Seeing her, joy rose to her parents' faces.

"We've been waiting for you, Hazuki," her father said.

"We're so delighted to see you," her mother said.

"......me......," Hazuki mumbled. She wasn't looking at her parents but at Yukizasa. Warily, she eased farther away from the trio.

Her parents watched her in confusion.

"What's wrong? Hurry up and come here," her father said.

"You must have been lonely not being able to see us. Everything's okay now. We know everything. You're not the type of child that would turn her back on her parents and leave home," her mother said.

"Hana led you astray, didn't she? That worthless whelp. She's a bad influence. Talentless. Useless. She's a piece of trash! The position next to the head of the clan belonged to you, but she swiped it from you. How could we have raised such a despicable child?"

There was no one to stop the stream of complaints pouring out of the Ichise parents' mouths.

"But it's all right now," her father said with a bright smile. "You might have gone down the wrong road, but you need only to turn back onto the right one. Knock down that good-for-nothing and become the clan lord's wife. That way, our family will be able to stand on top of the Ichinomiya branches. Master Sankourou is lending us his hand for that purpose."

Hazuki goggled at Yukizasa. He ignored her gaze and plastered an eerie smile on his face.

Her father walked up to her and said, "Come, we're going home."

He grabbed her arm...

" We're not going anywhere, you stupid piece of shit!" Hazuki shouted. Profanities that were unexpected of her spewed from her mouth as she kicked her father in the gut.

"Ugackh!" he screamed, falling flat on his butt. "Ha-Hazuki...?"

Greater than the pain in his stomach was the shock from the fact that she had kicked him. He stared blankly up at her.

"Hazuki! How could you do that to your father?!" her mother berated her, rushing to her father's side.

Hazuki sniffed as if she found her mother's rebuke not worth her time.

Then a butterfly glowing in iridescent colors appeared out of nowhere and landed on Hazuki's head.

Hazuki's form flickered, and she turned into Hana in the blink of an eye. She looked down on her parents with scorn. "Sorry, I'm not Hazuki."

"Wh—!" Her father gasped in shock. Her mother was speechless with surprise; her mouth flapped open and closed without any words coming out. "You wench! Why are you here?! Where's Hazuki? Where is she?!"

Her father twisted his head to look around the space, but there were no signs of anyone besides Hana.

"She was never here in the first place. The one you've been talking to is me, cloaked by Azuha's illusion to look like Hazuki, you idiot."

Her parents had been fooled completely, not having the faintest suspicion that something had been off.

Hana wanted to bask in the moment and roar with contemptuous laughter, but...

Her eyes flicked over to Yukizasa.

Judging by his utter lack of surprise, he had noticed from the beginning that she wasn't the real Hazuki. She hadn't expected in the first place to trick an Obsidian practitioner like him, so that wasn't a problem.

Granted, his presence in and of itself was a *huge* problem.

She hadn't thought he would come, too, so she had been quite surprised.

"What happened to Hazuki?!" Hana's father demanded.

"She's in the Ichinomiya residence, house-sitting. After she received the upsetting text from Suzu's phone, she was going to come here alone, but her shikigami realized her plan and came to talk with me. Then it all became clear. There was no way I was going to let Hazuki go by herself to a place where some sketchy guy who sent that sketchy message could be waiting."

Hana had given Hiragi, Hazuki's shikigami, two big thumbs-up for his good work. Hiragi had returned the gesture. He had been scolded by Hazuki for spilling the beans, but he was on the same page as Hana with not wanting to expose his master to danger.

Hazuki, on the other hand, was scolded by Hana.

Even kids these days knew not to follow a stranger, not even for candy, so why was Hazuki going to obediently do what she was told?

It was an option to ignore the message, which reeked of bad news, but the catch was that it had been sent from Suzu's phone.

Hana had tried calling, but Suzu hadn't picked up, of course. If Suzu was really in danger, she couldn't ignore it. She had immediately tried asking Saku for help, too, but for some reason, his phone had been shut off, and the call hadn't been able to connect.

Without any other recourse, she had decided to check out the factory herself, but the problem there had been Hazuki, who had argued that the message had been sent to her so she should be the one to go. She wouldn't listen to Hana at all.

However, the sender's goal was to lure out Hazuki. Therefore, it was too risky to send Hazuki.

Before Hazuki had been able to fly out the door, Hana had trapped her in a barrier, borrowed Azuha's illusory powers to look more like her sister, and come to the factory herself.

Which led to the present moment.

Thank goodness Hana had found out beforehand. It would have been too dangerous for Hazuki to come alone.

She had known there was a possibility, but to think that their parents had actually been lying in wait.

When she got home, she would have to thank Hiragi again for his distinguished service in preventing Hazuki from running wild.

Plus, she would need to lecture Hazuki more about the importance of staying alert.

It was incredible that a naive lamb like her had gone so long without being deceived.

She was the polar opposite of Hana and her crooked personality.

Hana's rule was to doubt first. That way, everything would go exactly the way she expected.

Hana glared at her parents. "You're still planning to take advantage of Hazuki?"

The two had regained their will to fight and were back to making a fuss.

"Why did you come here?! We didn't call for you!" Hana's father yelled.

"Bring Hazuki here!" her mother added.

"'Yes, of course, my lady.' Did you think that's what I would say? There's no way I'd bring her. Are you stupid?" Hana sneered. "Oh wait. That's right, you are. Otherwise, you wouldn't dream of kidnapping Hazuki, who's officially a ward of the Ichinomiya clan lord." She snorted derisively, which had the effect of making her parents' faces turn an interesting shade of crimson.

"How long are you going to be a pain in our side, you failure?! Who do you think raised you?!" her father shouted.

"Not you. I know that much."

Hana had been raised by Sae and the kind servants in the Ichise house. If they hadn't been around, she would have never been free from her inferiority complex and would have lived a lackluster life. Repairing bridges with Hazuki would have been out of the question. Their relationship would have stayed broken and faded into nothing.

But the reason behind all of that was these parents of theirs.

"I'll do you a favor and leave if you promise never to come near Hazuki again," Hana said.

"Don't joke around. We're her parents!"

To tell the truth, Hana had not even a molecule of intent to withdraw. They had responded as she had predicted, but having to confront them in person, she couldn't help but be irritated.

"Master, is it time?" Hana heard a voice say.

Miyabi was by her side, invisible. She could sense that the shikigami had lifted the giant squeaky hammer and was just waiting for the go sign. She grinned unconsciously.

Hana's father, who hadn't realized Miyabi was there, thought she was making fun of him.

Well, he wasn't exactly wrong, so that wasn't an issue.

"What's with that disgusting smile?! Call Hazuki here already!" he demanded, spittle flying everywhere. "Hurry up and move out of the way so your sister can become the lady of the clan. Then everything will be as it should. Don't you know that you're not suitable to sit next to Lord Ichinomiya?!"

Did he really think that Hana would do as he said? If so, she would have to get him hospitalized.

"I regret to inform you that Saku has absolutely no desire to leave me," Hana said.

"There's no way that's true. Between you and Hazuki, it's clear as day who is more suitable to be his wife."

And as a result, Saku had chosen Hana. Where had her father gotten the misunderstanding that Saku would take that decision back?

They had even thrown a lavish wedding. Her parents had been present, so they should be well aware of Saku's feelings.

"Haaah…" Hana heaved a deep sigh. It was too tiresome to deal with them.

It didn't matter what she said. She couldn't have a proper conversation with them; from the start, they'd had no interest in listening to her. They would believe what they wanted to and ignore everything they didn't want to hear.

It was impossible for Hazuki to be chosen as Saku's wife at this stage.

"What a pain," Hana said.

She had made the right decision leaving Hazuki behind. Up until now, her sister had been wrapped up in their parents' affairs and tossed around for their benefit. Hana would have felt sorry to make Hazuki listen to their parents' bad joke.

"If you want glory for the Ichise family so badly, why don't you do something about it yourself without relying on others?" she sneered. "Oh, but I guess that's asking too much. Your shikigami is an insect, after all." She smirked meaningfully. Her father felt fear for the first time. "A dragonfly, was it? You belittled me to your heart's content for having a butterfly, but yours is just a bug, too. You're in no position to talk smack about others...and yet."

Azuha might have been an insect, but that didn't change how important she was to Hana. Hana couldn't care less what others thought. However, her father was different.

True to character, he was trembling with shame. Her attack had been an even more effective blow than she had expected.

"H-how do you know that...?" he demanded.

"My esteemed older brother told me."

"Th-that bastard..." Even his voice was shaking. He tamped down on his fury.

To Hana's father, the fact that he had an insect shikigami was a huge disgrace. Never mind that it wasn't anything to be ashamed of.

"You're pathetic," Hana spat.

"What do you know?! I was born as the successor, but my shikigami made me a target of ridicule. My father despaired of me, and my own son threatened my position. All because my shikigami is an insect! Can there be anything more idiotic? Shikigami are hardly a complete indicator of one's ability. Yet everyone and their mother treated me like I was nothing!"

"That's why you demeaned me for having an insect shikigami just like you and applauded Hazuki for her human shikigami? But you see, Hazuki isn't a tool for your convenience. She's a living, breathing person with a beating heart. Her life is hers alone. Not yours."

"Then what am I supposed to do?! I need Hazuki to show that I'm powerful. I'm the parent of a genius with a human shikigami. I couldn't possibly be powerless. Isn't that right?"

His selfishness knew no bounds.

He wasn't thinking of his children nor the Ichise family, but about himself.

He needed to be acknowledged. That was the only thing he was working for.

"You're not going to listen, no matter what I say... I see..."

This wasn't the time to be depressed. But Hana couldn't deny that a gloom had stolen over her.

She realized that this man would never change.

Anything anyone said to him would be meaningless.

Hana looked at her mother for the first time, the woman who never lifted a hand to stop her husband, who conformed to him. Even now, she was standing behind him, watching him with searching eyes. She might have had a will of her own, but Hana felt that she was merely drifting through life, swept along by the current. There was no doubt that nothing Hana said would change her mother, either.

A feeling similar to despair welled up inside Hana.

"You should trust yourself more," she said to her father. "There's nothing wrong with a dragonfly. I have never felt ashamed of Azuha. Stop comparing yourself to others and do the best you can with all your power. Your position was threatened? So what? A trifle like that? Just pass it on. Aren't there more important things than a little title?"

Something absolutely irreplaceable.

However, Hana's feelings didn't get through to her father.

"A child shouldn't put on airs! You know nothing! The head of the Ichise family is me. I won't give up this seat to anyone. It's mine!" he shouted with bloodshot eyes. He refused to listen to a word.

Hana took a deep breath. She turned away from her father to face Yukizasa. "Where's Suzu? I won't forgive you if you did anything to her."

"There seems to be a misunderstanding. The ones who kidnapped that girl were your parents," Yukizasa said.

Her gaze flicked over to her parents before returning to Yukizasa. "But you can't tell me you're uninvolved. They said it before: You're helping them."

She had just begun thinking he might actually be a good person. This was a horrible betrayal.

For him to lay a hand on Suzu of all people, she could only assume that he wanted to piss her off.

"What business do you have with Hazuki?" she demanded.

"…I don't have any interest in Hazuki Ichise. The one I wanted brought here wasn't your older sister, but you, Hana Ichise." He chuckled darkly under his breath, staring at Hana with amusement in his eyes.

Hana was already married to Saku, so she was already an Ichinomiya. Had "*Ichise*" been a slip of the tongue, or had he said it on purpose?

Her brows furrowed in puzzlement. "Me?"

"I wasn't confident I could lure you out with your best friend alone, but if I used your twin as bait, I was sure you would come running. I hadn't expected you to come pretending to be your sister, but you were my goal from the start, so I was delighted that you saved me the effort."

Hana didn't understand what he was thinking at all.

"What are you planning? You went as far as to take Suzu just to bring me to this factory. Is she safe?!"

"Could be. Who knows?" He smiled eerily.

She mustered her courage to confront him, but inside, she was panicking.

Since Hazuki had been the target of the summons, Hana had suspected their parents were the ones pulling the strings. She hadn't bargained that Yukizasa would be with them.

She had dropped her guard after his apology. That was her mistake.

It didn't pay to be trusting of others.

Hana had figured she would be able to take down her parents one way or another, so she had left Arashi behind as Hazuki's bodyguard.

However, with an Obsidian practitioner as her opponent, how long would she be able to hold her own? Without knowing the full extent of Yukizasa's abilities, she couldn't say.

On top of that, there was something about this place that had been bothering her the entire time.

She'd heard that the Association had declared it off-limits, but she didn't know why.

Nonetheless, she'd had an ominous feeling for a while now.

The alarm bells were going off in her head telling her to get out of there as soon as possible.

"Sorry, but I have no time to waste. I'm going to pound you into dust now," Hana declared. "Aoi. Miyabi."

The two shikigami manifested themselves at Hana's summons. They were both raring to go, their weapons drawn. Aoi had his great sword and Miyabi her giant squeaky hammer.

Yukizasa's expression didn't change one bit seeing the two human shikigami as if to say he was confident he could take them down.

Hana felt a twinge of irritation at being looked down upon.

"It's not too late to retreat. I'll permit it. How about it?" She laughed boldly.

Even though Yukizasa's Obsidian rank was newly minted, Hana was sweating inside at the prospect of facing an Obsidian practitioner. However, she didn't let an ounce of her fear show on the outside. Her pride wouldn't allow her to look weak in front of someone who was conspiring with her parents and their cowardly schemes.

"What...what is that? Human...shikigami? Are they Hana's? But her shikigami is a butterfly. And there's two of them. Impossible...," her father muttered in a daze.

How must he feel knowing that Hana, who he had denounced as worthless, had obtained human shikigami, which not even the talented Yanagi had. She wanted to interrogate him, but she had no time to waste on small fry at the moment.

"Where's Suzu? Spit it out," Hana demanded.

If her parents were behind the kidnapping, all she had to do was beat the answer out of them, but there was no guarantee Yukizasa would wait quietly in the meantime.

She had to deal with him somehow...

While Hana was thinking about what to do, Yukizasa abruptly took out his phone. He held out his screen, which showed an ongoing call, and smirked. "I'm connected with a buddy of mine who's with your friend. The moment you lay a hand on me, I'll give him the signal. What do you think would happen to your friend then? Want to find out?"

His flamboyant provocation had Hana grinding her teeth.

"Aoi, Miyabi, wait," she ordered.

She couldn't afford to make any bad moves. Her hands were tied.

Suddenly, loud clangs of something breaking rang through the building, and the structure trembled.

"Wh-what?" Hana said.

"Aha. Looks like it's time for our star to make its appearance," Yukizasa said. Unlike Hana, he was perfectly calm. He turned away from Hana and started walking toward the entrance.

"Wait!" she cried.

She scrambled after him, but before she could reach him, the door slammed shut. She tried to open it, but it was being held shut from the other side. Knowing it was useless, she banged on the door and shouted, "Open the door!"

In the next moment, a powerful barrier was thrown up around the entire factory. It was no exaggeration to say that it was the strongest one she had ever seen, and even when she threw her power against it, it didn't so much as shudder.

"What? What's going on?"

She didn't have a clue what was happening.

From the other side of the door came Yukizasa's voice. "Just now, multiple Sankourou practitioners erected this barrier."

She recalled Hazuki saying that the Sankourous were defense specialists. Of the five clans, they could produce the most durable barriers. Hana had no hope against a barrier constructed with the combined power of several Sankourou practitioners.

"You plan to trap me here? What are you trying to do?!" Hana yelled. She didn't understand what he was thinking.

"I left a present for you. Please accept it."

"Say what?! A present? Now I'm even more lost," she shouted, but she received no response.

Confined in the barrier, Hana was at a loss for what to do.

"Master," Miyabi said, her brows drawn worriedly.

Aoi was wearing the same expression. "Master."

But Hana was in the same predicament.

She tried kicking the door one more time, but because of the barrier, it stayed shut.

In the meantime, the ominous feeling she had was growing steadily stronger.

Then the sound of glass shattering reverberated through the space, and she was assaulted with a malignant force that brought goose bumps to her skin.

"Eek!" her mother shrieked.

"Wh-what was that?" her father asked nervously.

Among practitioners, her parents were weak and their senses dull. Even so, they could still sense the presence of the powerful shade.

Hana's gaze sharpened. "The bad feeling I've had all this time was from a shade?"

It was coming from deeper in the factory than where Hana and the others were.

The sound of something dragging along the floor grew closer and louder.

"Something's coming from inside," she declared.

Aoi and Miyabi raised their weapons.

It was strong, the deadliest out of all the shades she had ever encountered.

The pressure it was exerting made her skin prickle, and she found herself sweating bullets.

It appeared out of nowhere.

It lashed out from the depths of the building and attacked them with shocking speed.

Hana immediately yelled, "Expand!" and erected a barrier around herself, but the shade was sure to break through it easily.

The barrier had been created reflexively, so it wasn't the most durable, but it served the purpose of stopping the shade's attack.

Hana's parents, on the other hand, hadn't managed to create a barrier and were snatched up by the grasping presence and thrown toward the ceiling.

"Gwahhh!"

"Eeek!"

Hana clicked her tongue instinctively.

She had her hands full protecting herself and her shikigami. She hadn't had the time to throw a barrier around her parents, standing apart from her as they had been.

It would have been convenient if they could by themselves, but all they were managing to do was scream.

"H-help! Master Sankourou! Where did he go?!" Hana's father yelled.

"Hurry up and do something!" her mother cried.

Aoi glowered at Hana's so-called parents, who were failing to do anything but make a racket, and said, "Master, can't we just leave them for dead?"

"Aoi is right. Trash is meant to be thrown out," Miyabi said, denouncing the two of them as the garbage that they were.

The same thought had flashed through Hana's mind, but she caught herself just in time. "No, nuh-uh, that's out of the question."

As far as Hana was concerned, they were getting their just deserts, but they were still human beings, and she couldn't abandon them.

She wouldn't be able to sleep if she let them become shade kibble.

"Really? You're gonna help them?" Aoi whined.

"Don't complain. Sure, them kicking the bucket here would solve a lot of problems, but I have no choice."

Aoi looked displeased, but he agreed and said, "Fine."

"I suppose it can't be helped," Miyabi said. "However, if I mistakenly attack them instead of the shade, it'll be nothing more than an accident, right?" A dark but delighted smile rose to her face, and she raised the hammer.

Aoi smirked, approving of Miyabi's strategy. The expressions of the two shikigami became positively malicious.

"Oh-ho-ho-ho," Miyabi chuckled.

Aoi joined in. "Heh-heh-heh."

It seemed to Hana that their original goal had changed, but if they were still able to destroy the shade as a result, there was no issue.

"I'm pumped. Let's go, Miyabi," Aoi said.

"Let's," Miyabi agreed. "Make sure you take good aim at the target, Aoi. *Very* good aim."

"Obviously."

They charged. From their gleeful expressions, one wouldn't think they were heading into battle.

Hana watched over them with fond exasperation and turned to head deeper into the factory to seek out their enemy who had yet to show its true form.

"Oh, dear! I made a mistake," Miyabi said.

"Gwahh! That's my leg," Hana's mother screamed.

"Whoops. My hand slipped," Aoi said.

"Eeyahh," her father groaned.

From behind her came her parents' shrieks of pain and Aoi's and Miyabi's accidentally on-purpose exclamations, but she paid them no mind. She didn't have the time.

She casually dodged incoming blows from her attacker as she followed the reaching limb back to its source. She arrived in an inner room to find a fat, bulging shade.

"Ugh, gross."

Of all the shades she had encountered before, this one was particularly repulsive. Its distended body filled the entire room. It was so massive, it couldn't leave. It was trying to pry its way out using the limbs extending out from its body.

Hana cast her eyes down toward the floor. Lying on the ground was the same rope that had been strung on the outside of the factory grounds, only this one was in pieces.

She hadn't noticed when she had first come, but looking at the rope closely, she could sense the faint trace of a practitioner's power.

"I see. This rope was used as a medium to maintain the barrier," Hana mumbled to herself.

She now understood why the Association had forbidden entry to the factory. Most likely, this shade had been sealed here, and the ear-splitting noise from earlier was from the shade destroying the barrier.

"Why did they seal away a monster instead of killing it outright?"

The seal had been broken. Had Yukizasa known?

Why had he left without destroying it? Not just that, he escaped first and trapped Hana and the others.

"Hmmm. I still don't get the reason."

She didn't understand what his goal was.

"Wait, is Suzu safe?"

The factory wasn't very large. There were no signs of other people, so Suzu was definitely not inside the building.

Hana was relieved but also worried about Suzu's safety.

"There's too much I don't know. But first, I suppose I have to take care of this fatty…"

She had left Saku a voicemail saying she was coming to the factory. How long would it take him to notice and come help?

Before then, she would just have to do what she could.

"Expand."

The energy she felt from the sickening shade was so powerful it gave her goose bumps.

Knowing she couldn't afford to hold back, she constructed a heavy-duty barrier. It sealed shut with a quiet, high-pitched *ting*.

All that was left was to crush it.

"Eli—"

But before she could finish, the shade lashed out and smashed the barrier in an instant.

"You're kidding!!!" Hana cried, gaping at the shade.

She rapidly retreated, dodging its grasping tendrils by a hair's breadth. Occupied with trying to evade the shade's attacks, she had no chance to retaliate.

"Aoi! Miyabi!" she screamed.

After a moment, Aoi came running. "Master, are you okay?"

"Where's Miyabi?" Hana said.

"The situation over there is pretty dire. She has the dead weight to look after, and the limbs have multiplied, too. I managed to get away to help," he explained. "This SOB's limbs split every time you cut one down. We have to hurry. Miyabi won't be able to protect her cargo for much longer."

"Shit. Impudent bastard."

She concentrated her power in the palm of her hand and hurled it at the shade.

The ball of energy exploded with a bang as if it were a bomb and tore at the shade from its center.

"Score!" Hana was elated her attack had been effective, but not a second later, the shade's injuries started healing with unbelievable speed. "Damn. Its regenerative abilities are crazy."

However, possibly because it was exhausting its energy healing, it had shrunk slightly.

Hana saw a spark of hope. She threw another energy bomb at the shade, then started pelting it before it could recover.

"Aoi, I'm going to bombard this guy with all I have. In the meantime, keep those limbs away from me," she ordered.

"Got it. Brute force. Master's specialty," Aoi said.

"Don't make it seem like I'm a muscle head!"

He had hit a sore spot. At school, she was ridiculed for being magically strong but intellectually weak.

"Take this! And this! And some of this!" Hana screamed.

Somewhat desperately, she continued to assault the shade with her powers, and it continued to shrink smaller and smaller.

"Yes!"

She kept up her attacks, confident that things would work out at her current pace, when all of a sudden, a slew of limbs sprouted from the shade in a last-ditch effort at resistance.

"Eww! That's disgusting..."

The shade concentrated its attacks on Hana as if it knew that she was doing it harm.

The one who panicked at the situation was Aoi, who was protecting Hana. "W-wait a sec. This is too much even for me!"

"My hands are tied here so figure it out!" she yelled.

"No, no, no, no, no. This is literally insane! Big Sis! Can't you do something?" he cried, begging Azuha for help.

The butterfly was batting away lashing limbs and simply replied, "Nope."

"You gotta be kidding me."

Alarm colored his features. It was obvious that he was at his wit's end, too.

"Azuha has been using her powers to enthrall it this entire time, but it seems that it's a bad matchup for her," Hana explained. "Just a little longer. Don't give up, Aoi."

Hana had no time to rest. Attacking the shade took everything she had. But then, she was struck by a tendril that had evaded Aoi's guard.

"Shi—!"

Hana flew through the air and slammed into the wall, momentarily stealing the breath from her lungs. Excruciating pain shot through her back, but she had no time to waste on her injuries.

"One last push. Eat this!" she cried, throwing all the rest of her energy at the shade as hard as she could.

The shade had already sustained a lot of damage. Its limbs whipped through the air, but its body collapsed in on itself, shrinking until it disappeared entirely.

Silence reigned over the factory.

Hana let out a deep sigh, reassured that the shade had been destroyed. "Haaah… It's over."

Aoi ran over, worried about Hana after seeing her get hit. "Master, are you okay?!"

Azuha was similarly concerned and fluttered to Hana. "Master."

That was when Tsubaki appeared out of nowhere. "My darling," she cooed, embracing Aoi from behind.

"Gwahhhh! Where the hell did you come from?" Aoi cried.

"I'm hurt. Wherever my darling is, that's where I am!"

"Don't be!"

The tension was blown clean away with Tsubaki's appearance.

Hana watched Aoi and Tsubaki with an air of resignation. They were still making a ruckus when Miyabi came to join them from the room at the factory entrance. She looked worriedly at Hana, who was slumped against the wall, unable to move.

Miyabi went to Hana's side. "Are you all right, Master?!"

"I'm fine. I'm fine." She put on a tough face so as not to worry Miyabi further, but her back hurt so badly she was finding it hard to stand up. "If Tsubaki is here, the barrier must have been broken."

"It appears so," Miyabi said. "Lord Ichinomiya and your elder brother came inside together earlier."

"Then I guess I should go. Sorry, Miyabi, but can you lend me your shoulder?"

"Didn't you say a second ago you're fine? Are your injuries so severe that you can't walk without support?"

"Ah-ha-ha…" Hana laughed to avoid the question.

Miyabi exploded. "This is no laughing matter! Please rest here."

"I'm sorry, really," she said, "but I have to go. There are my parents to deal with, too."

Miyabi, who always prioritized Hana, seemed displeased, but Hana knew that the shikigami would do as she said.

Miyabi glared at Aoi, who was being grossly lovey-dovey with Tsubaki, and smacked the other shikigami with her squeaky hammer. With her masterful control, she hit him on the head, and Aoi finally turned his attention their way.

"Aoi, save the flirting for later and come carry our Master."

"I'm not flirting! …Hold on, are you okay, Master?!"

"She's not. That's why I'm asking you for help," Miyabi snapped. "I don't want her pushing herself, so hurry up and get over here."

"R-right."

"Aww, boo. I'm so jelly! I want my darling to sweep me up in his arms." Tsubaki watched Hana with envy in her eyes, biting on her thumbnail in frustration. Of course, she couldn't go as far as to tell him to put down an injured person, lest she wanted to be treated to a death glare from Miyabi.

Hana was carried by Aoi back to the room where her parents were. The two were sitting on the ground, their faces pale. Looming above them were Saku and Yanagi, who were glowering at them frostily.

Intimidated by the two men, her parents were finally silent, lucky to be alive.

"Saku," Hana called.

The group turned her way.

Saku's eyes widened seeing her in Aoi's arms. "What happened?"

"Just got bruised a little in a scrap with a shade," she said flippantly. "More importantly, why didn't you pick up? You're late."

"Ah, sorry about that." He averted his gaze guiltily. "Did you take down the shade that was here?"

"Yeah. Why was something so disgusting left sitting under a seal? Wait!" She turned to her father. "Suzu! Where is she, shitty old man?!"

She struggled in Aoi's arms. He did his best not to drop her.

"Calm down," Saku said in an attempt to soothe Hana, who looked like she was about to leap at her father's throat. "Your friend is safe. She's under our protection."

"Good." Her face finally went slack with relief.

Saku took up a stance in front of her parents again and glared down at them.

Her parents couldn't muster the energy to stand, pinned as they were by his stern gaze. Those were the eyes of the Ichinomiya clan lord, not Saku. He had never subjected Hana to this side of him.

"You have caused a lot of trouble this time."

"Lord Ichinomiya... W-we just...," Hana's father stuttered.

"I don't need your excuses. You kidnapped the daughter of a San-kourou branch family. Do you understand what a grave matter this is? One misstep, and you could have ignited a dispute between our clans."

"It was all for Hazuki's sake."

"Shut up."

Her father went white at the sharp rebuke and closed his mouth.

It was refreshing to see him scolded by Saku, who was young enough to be his son.

Her parents had always had an endless supply of abuse for her, but they were as well-behaved as a trained pup with Saku. If only they had been obedient from the beginning.

"I lowered my head to the Sankourou family myself to ask for forgiveness. I, your lord, had to prostrate myself because of *you*. I won't let you plead ignorance as to how big of a disgrace that is for the clan."

"We…ah…" Her father had broken out in a cold sweat.

Her mother couldn't say anything, either. She was staring hard at the ground.

"I cannot face the Sankourou clan without dealing you a punishment appropriate for your role as perpetrators of an incident that could have led to an interclan dispute. You will yield the head of the family position to Yanagi and retire, effective immediately."

"No!" Her father gasped, his face twisted in misery. He looked as if he had just been handed a death sentence.

Hana watched him with cold eyes.

To be blunt, he had made his bed.

"What? Are you unhappy? Do you think you have the right to complain after what you did? Have you no shame?" Saku yelled.

Raked over the coals by Saku, Hana's parents shrunk in on themselves, trembling.

"I am not giving you a choice. It is useless to protest. As the lord of the Ichinomiya clan, I hereby declare that Yanagi Ichise is now the head of the Ichise family!" Saku said. "Yanagi, I trust you are okay with that?"

Yanagi kneeled in front of Saku and bowed deeply. "I understand, my lord. I am terribly sorry for the trouble that my blood relations have caused."

"Send your parents to the countryside at once."

"As you say. I thank you for your benevolence."

In other words, he was only making them retire from the public eye. They wouldn't be punished conspicuously.

They sure were getting off easy considering they had kidnapped someone.

Hana would rather the police step in and lock them in jail, but the Ichinomiyas would end up targeted by the other clans for inadequate management. Saku kowtowing to the Sankourou clan for their pardon would end up all for naught.

In addition, to ensure that Yanagi could smoothly succeed the position of family head, his blood relations couldn't be marked as criminals. Hana was an Ichise by blood as well, so Saku likely didn't want to blow up the incident.

At least what had needed to be done was done.

Yanagi led their depressed parents out of the building.

Hana finally let herself relax, believing that it was all over, when all of a sudden, the sound of clapping rang out through the space.

"Wow, all's well that ends well. Congratulations are in order."

The interloper was her parents' coconspirator, Yukizasa. He approached the group, his lips curled in a shady smile.

Hana didn't hesitate before focusing her energy and chucking it at him. She didn't hold anything back.

Yukizasa's cheek spasmed. "Wait a sec."

"Why should I, you creep?!" She whaled on him, forgetting about the pain in her back.

Flustered, Yukizasa looked at Saku for help. "Yo, Saku! Do something about your woman."

Saku shrugged tiredly and stayed Hana's hand. "Calm down, Hana."

"How do you suggest I do that?! Why are you stopping me? Isn't he the root of all the evils?!" She hadn't forgotten that he had been in on her parents' scheme.

"That was all a cover."

Hana stopped in her tracks, failing to understand what he was saying. "...Excuse me?"

"I asked for his help to force your parents from their position."

"What are you talking about?!"

"I'll explain. You remember when Yanagi warned you that your parents could be cooking up something unpleasant?"

"Yeah..."

"Once in a while, minor irritations grow out of proportion, so I wanted to have control over the chain of events. That was why I had Yukizasa make contact with your parents, pretend to by their ally, and report to me about their plans."

Hana's jaw dropped. She slowly turned to face Yukizasa.

He gave her a glowing smile and two thumbs-up. "That's the gist!"

"What about Suzu?" Hana demanded.

"Your little friend? The one who suggested using her as bait to bring the two of you twins here was me. Saku said he needed a reason to kick out your parents, so I gave him one. Messing with a kid whose family belonged to another clan is plenty of reason, don't you think?"

"Saku said he prostrated himself to the Sankourou clan..."

"I mean, technically, he did to me. His head dipped a whole inch."

Hana's eyes glazed over as he talked.

"I sent one of my people to collect her right away. By this time, she should be home already."

"What about the shade?"

"Oh, that was a job the Association asked me to do, but I had my hands full with your parents and didn't have the time to deal with it. The Association asked Saku for a substitute, and he volunteered you."

Hana gave Saku the stink eye. He avoided her gaze.

"For my part, I wanted to know how strong Saku's woman is, so it was a win-win situation," Yukizasa went on to say. "It's amazing you took down that shade in such a short time. Ah-ha-ha." He laughed without any trace of ill will.

However, having been wrapped up in another annoying scheme against her will, Hana wasn't laughing.

"…Aoi, let me down," she said in a low voice that shook with rage.

Aoi hesitantly did as she bid.

Hana moved in front of Yukizasa, who was still laughing away without a care, and thrust her hand into the air. "Eat this, you damn rich kid!"

Her vicious blow slammed into him. "Gak!" He squatted down in pain.

Hana gazed down her nose at him and snorted.

◆

It was the day after Hana's first encounter with Yukizasa.

That day, Yukizasa had agreed to the short-term instructor job. When he returned to his temporary residence, the servants ushered him inside in a panic.

"Master Sankourou, Lord Ichinomiya is here to see you!"

"Is that so?"

As I expected, he thought, grimacing like he had just bitten into a lemon. He figured the other man had come to complain about the fact that Yukizasa had reached out to his wife.

But Yukizasa didn't see what the problem was.

The Saku he knew kept a cool head and never got serious no matter who his partner was.

Yukizasa was confident that the only reason Saku had chosen Hana Ichise was to complete the barrier around the pillar.

He had heard that the older sister, Hazuki, was the stronger one of the two, but he had realized the truth immediately after meeting Hana: the younger twin was leagues more powerful.

He had always assumed insect shikigami were weak, but Hana's butterfly shikigami was strong enough to completely bust up what he had thought was common sense.

The girl appeared to be hiding her powers, but she was clearly a force to be reckoned with. Yukizasa was impressed Saku had managed to dig up such a strong candidate to be his bride, a true gem whom Yukizasa would have considered marrying had he found her first.

At the time, he had thought Saku, like him, would pick a lady of the clan solely based on power, with no consideration for love or such rot.

The barrier masters who protected the pillars had to give up on various things for the sake of the country.

Even if that weren't the case, there was a part of Yukizasa that was frigid toward women. He and Saku shared that in common.

He felt sorry for Hana being forced into her position, but she was a necessary sacrifice for the country.

Such were Yukizasa's thoughts as he went to meet Saku in the reception room.

When he entered, Saku was waiting for him with displeasure written across his face.

Saku grabbed Yukizasa by the collar and sucker punched him in the gut without so much as a "How do you do?"

"Ugh!"

With zero concern for Yukizasa, whose thoughts had been short-circuited by the pain, Saku twisted his fist and drove it deeper into Yukizasa's stomach.

Unable to bear the pain, Yukizasa sunk to his knees, clutching his abdomen. Saku looked down at him with frosty eyes.

"That hurts like a bitch. You bastard," Yukizasa groused, breathing heavily. "What did you do that for, Saku?"

Saku's leg moved.

Yukizasa immediately leaped out of the way and managed to avoid the blow, but had he not, he would've been kicked mercilessly as if he were a ball. There was a hole gaping open in the paper sliding door, which had taken the hit in Yukizasa's stead. The merciless attack proved that Saku was dead serious.

Yukizasa broke out in a cold sweat. "Hold on, man. That's not funny."

"Of course. I'm not joking around."

"What's with you?"

"...I'm just repaying you for what you did to Hana." He was expressionless, but the anger in his eyes was plain for all to see.

"Hana's your bride, right? I just went to give her my regards."

"Her arm is bruised. You're the one who put it there, right?"

"My grip was a tad too tight. So what?" Yukizasa said flippantly. "Besides that, when are you going to divorce her? Sure, it's for the good of the country and all, but you don't want a woman hanging around, right? I think it's a pain, too, but I won't have a choice since I'm next in line to be clan lord." Yukizasa laughed freely.

Saku's eyebrow twitched, and fury filled his expression. "...A tad?"

He grabbed Yukizasa by the collar again and raised his fist.

Yukizasa desperately held him back. "Hold on, calm down." He didn't understand why Saku was so angry.

Without loosening his grip on Yukizasa, Saku slammed him into the wall. "You listen to me. There will be no second time. Don't you dare lay a hand on my Hana again."

Yukizasa was taken aback by Saku's humorless gaze. He nodded. "I—I got it. It won't ever happen again."

Satisfied by Yukizasa's shocked expression and acquiescence, Saku harrumphed and let him go. "I'm leaving," he said and made to exit the room. As his parting words, he declared, "FYI, I'm never going to divorce Hana!"

Yukizasa looked at him in disbelief. "What? That's really all you came for?"

"What else could there be?"

"Hold on. Nothing comes to mind? I'm an Obsidian practitioner now," Yukizasa said.

"So what?" Saku's expression didn't change one bit; he seemed like he couldn't care less.

Yukizasa was disappointed by his utter lack of interest. "Isn't this where you're supposed to congratulate me? Aren't we friends?"

"I don't remember being friends with you," Saku said, shooting him down point-blank.

That was the Saku that Yukizasa knew. Poker-faced, cold as ice, iron defenses he didn't let anyone through in order to protect himself, a frigid personality that made it clear that he rejected the world with every particle of his being.

"Don't say such heartless things. To make it up to you, I'll do whatever you say. Any one thing," Yukizasa said jokingly to lighten the mood.

Saku stroked his chin with one hand, pondering Yukizasa's offer. Then a sinister smile rose to his face.

Suddenly, Yukizasa wanted to take back his words.

"In that case," Saku said, "I'll put you to work. I've been wanting a lackey to help me take out the trash." He looked so evil even a demon would have run from him on bare feet.

Yukizasa's face spasmed. "I shouldn't have said anything..."

That was when he learned about the Ichise family's circumstances and the compromise.

His mission was to get rid of the family trash and install Yanagi as the new head so the young man could revitalize the Ichise name.

Even he had heard of Yanagi, who had been the youngest practitioner to claim the Lapis rank, so he wasn't against Yanagi becoming the head of the family per se. However, he didn't see why he had to get his hands dirty to solve some other family's problem.

Yukizasa let displeasure show only to have Saku pin him with a sharp gaze. He wasn't even allowed to complain.

"There's something different about you, Saku."

"What?"

"How do I explain it? It just feels like the atmosphere around you is different from how it used to be."

"That's—"

It seemed like he wanted to say something, but Tsubaki appeared out of the blue and finished his sentence. "That's the power of love," she cooed. "Master's eyes have been opened by his love for Hana. Just like mine were by my love for my darling!"

"Don't say anything unnecessary, Tsubaki," Saku scolded, karate-chopping her on the head. She giggled and disappeared.

"Hana...," Yukizasa muttered. "Do you get along?"

"We're a married couple. Of course we do." Saku tried to play it cool, but his voice went mellow and soft when he said *couple*.

"I see," Yukizasa responded simply.

At the time, he had been mildly impressed that Saku was making an effort, but now that everything was over and he was seeing the two of them together with his own eyes, he realized he had been wrong.

"Saku! Don't abuse other people whenever you feel like it!" Hana yelled. "Let me punch you once. This is grounds for a divorce! Divorce, I say!"

"What would you have had me do? This was all for the sake of a peaceful resolution."

"Is this what you call peaceful, idiot? It was pure mayhem!"

Yukizasa watched the two argue with exasperation.

"It's all good and well that Hazuki and Suzu are both okay, but what were you going to do if Hazuki came here alone?" Hana demanded.

"Don't fret. We had a plan B," Saku replied proudly.

"That's nothing to brag about!" Suddenly, Hana's face twisted in pain, and she crouched down. "Ow, ow, ow..."

Saku's impish expression turned on a dime, and he rushed to Hana's side. "Are you okay?"

"The shade slammed me into a wall. It hurts so badly."

"Sorry..." His eyes were full of genuine concern with no hint of a lie. They made it clear that he was worried about Hana with all his heart.

Saku lifted Hana up gently.

"Oh my god! Put me down," she shrieked.

"If you're in pain, hold still. It's best we treat you right away."

The Saku who was smiling tenderly at Hana was a completely different person from the Saku Yukizasa knew.

Saku helped Hana into the car that was waiting in front of the factory, then turned back toward Yukizasa and said, "I'll leave the rest to you."

"You got it."

Yukizasa waved. Saku climbed into the car and drove away.

Left alone, Yukizasa smiled wryly and said, "He's changed a lot."

He hadn't believed it when Hana had said Saku was expressive, but it was true; when Saku was with her, his expressions changed all the time.

But not in a bad way.

It felt like he had been freed from his burdens.

Yukizasa muttered, "You found a good woman to be your bride." His expression was one of relief.

◆

With the incident resolved, the next day, Hana's parents were forced to move to a house in the countryside.

The servants who had been close with her parents had been replaced, so it was a lot easier to breathe in the Ichise house.

Between the move and the preparations, Hana was made to realize how thoroughly everything had been planned in advance.

Hana, having been totally oblivious, felt conflicted. The same could be said of Hazuki.

Because she had been thrown into a wall during her battle with the shade, a large bruise bloomed on Hana's back. Just when the bruise on her arm courtesy of Yukizasa had finally faded. Talk about bad luck.

Hazuki blamed herself, but in Hana's book, Saku and Yukizasa were at fault for everything.

Hana had to take a few days off from school, but the day after the whole incident, Suzu called her. Suzu's voice was full of pep, which put Hana's mind at ease.

Although Suzu had been kidnapped without knowing a thing, she had been rescued immediately and was informed of the broad strokes of the situation. She had cooperated in order to help Hana, but at first, she hadn't understood what was going on at all and had been terrified. Or so she explained cheerfully.

Hana felt horribly guilty that she had gotten Suzu involved. She made a big fuss with Saku—this time, she would have her divorce, for sure—but he had offered a lavish full-course French dinner as compensation, and she had taken back her threat right away.

In addition, apparently, Saku had been chewed out by Mio. She had blown up, demanding to know what he'd been thinking, sticking Hana, who was still a *student*, on a shade that required the expertise of an Obsidian practitioner without any prior information.

Truer words had never been spoken.

Hana had been made to help with Saku's work several times in the past, but previously, she had always consented, so Mio had stayed quiet. However, Saku had sprung the latest job on Hana.

Mio had been feeling anxious about Hana's involvement in Obsidian-rank work for some time, and she finally snapped, reaching the limit of her patience.

Plus, Aoi and Miyabi had been complaining as well, pointing out Hana's unending parade of injuries, which had started since she had gotten married to Saku. Getting divorced as soon as possible would really be for the best.

Saku had been powerless against his mother and had listened to his lecture like a good boy.

Between this and that, the days passed, and right around the time the pain in Hana's back had gone away at long last, Yanagi came to the Ichinomiya residence to pay a visit to Hana and Hazuki.

The three siblings were alone in the room.

Yanagi spoke up first. "Our parents have been moved away from society and are living under supervision. From now on, you'll have no more contact with them unless you so choose."

To Hana, there could be no happier news. However, Hazuki had yet to throw away all her attachments to their parents and was making a complicated expression. Nonetheless, she didn't protest Yanagi's decision and merely nodded without a word.

Yanagi added, "We've overhauled the staff and cut everyone who had no love for the family in the first place."

"What about Sae?" Hana blurted out, unable to help herself. Sae was the person she was most concerned about.

"She'll continue working in the household."

Relief washed over Hana.

Sae was the reason Hana and Hazuki could be together like this. Had she been turned out into the streets, Hana would never have been able to forgive herself.

Hazuki, too, whispered a quiet "Thank goodness…" It was apparent that Sae was an invaluable presence to her, too.

"Now, to the crux of the matter," Yanagi said. "Hazuki." He paused before continuing with some trepidation. "Won't you come back to the Ichise house?"

"What?" Hazuki said, surprised at Yanagi's suggestion.

"The parents who tormented you are no longer there. You can live however you like, doing whatever you want. It's true that here, you can be with Hana, but won't you live with me?"

Hazuki was silent for a moment. Then she nodded. "Okay. I'll go back with you."

"What?!" Hana gasped unintentionally. "You're going to leave?" Just when she was finally able to be with Hazuki.

A wistful expression crossed over Hazuki's face, plain for all to see. "I love spending time with you, too, Hana," she said, "but I'm not a part of the Ichinomiya family. I don't think I should be here. Think about how it looks to the other branch families."

Hana was disgruntled. The other branch families could go to hell for all she cared.

Hazuki pressed on. "Besides, I don't want to leave our brother alone in that house."

Hazuki's words blew all of Hana's protests away. Yanagi's eyes widened.

"You won't be lonely with me around, right?" Hazuki said to Yanagi, smiling softly.

Yanagi smiled back, looking as if he might cry. "Yeah. You would give me strength."

Hana looked at the two of them grinning at each other. She shoved herself forward. "Then I'm going with you, too!"

She was dead serious, but her proclamation made the atmosphere in the room sour.

"You can't, Hana," Hazuki said.

"Why not?!"

"Don't you have any pride as Lord Ichinomiya's wife?"

The only answer that came to her mind was *none at all*. Her confession to Saku of her budding feelings was long forgotten.

"Got it. Let me go get divorced real quick," Hana said glibly, as if she were talking about going to the convenience store to buy ice cream.

She flew out of the room without hesitation—no time like the present, right?—barged into Saku's room, and demanded a divorce.

However, when it looked like she was about to be jumped, she ran away and returned to the room where her siblings were.

"It didn't work...," she said, her shoulders slumping.

Hazuki and Yanagi both looked like they had nothing to say.

"Hana...," Hazuki said.

"Lord Ichinomiya would never give you up," Yanagi said.

And thus, it wasn't long before the day came when Hazuki would return to the Ichise house with Yanagi.

Hana saw her off with a melancholic expression.

Saku put an arm around her shoulder. "You can see each other whenever you want."

Her face instantly lit up. "Yeah, you're right. Not to mention, if we get divorced, I can go back to the Ichise house," she said brightly as if she had put her worries behind her.

The corner of Saku's mouth convulsed. "Are you still going on about that?" A vein throbbed on his temple.

Without giving Hana any time to respond, he laid a hand on her chin and brought their lips together.

"Mmngh!!"

When they broke apart after the intense kiss, Saku smirked shamelessly. "You'll be my wife until death do us part. Give up and accept it."

"Dummy!!! Kiss fiend!" Hana yelled.

"Was that a compliment?"

"Not at all!"

Azuha fluttered leisurely above their heads. Constantly bickering though the two might have been, they were nevertheless thick as thieves.

Printed in Great Britain
by Amazon

List of Acronyms

ASEAN	Association of South-East Asian Nations
COMESA	Common Market of Eastern and Southern Africa
CSO	civil society organization
CSSDCA	Conference on Security, Stability, Development and Cooperation in Africa
EAC	East African Cooperation
ECOMOG	ECOWAS Military Observer Group
ECOWAS	Economic Community of West African States
EO	Executive Outcomes
EU	European Union
ICRC	International Committee of the Red Cross
IGAD	InterGovernmental Authority on Development
IHL	international humanitarian law
IPMC	international private military company
MPRI	Military Professional Resources International
NAFTA	North American Free Trade Area
NGO	non-governmental organization
OAU	Organization of African Unity
OSCE	Organization for Security and Cooperation in Europe
RPA	Rwandese Patriotic Army
RUF	Revolutionary United Front
SADC	Southern African Development Community
SPLA	Sudan People's Liberation Army
TNC	trans-national corporation

The Ultimate

Cooking Experience

Delicious Finnish Recipes for Everyone

By: Valeria Ray

DELICIOUS HOMEMADE FOOD

Recipes

License Notes

Table of Contents

Introduction

Finland - one of the most beautiful countries in the world is home to some of the best landscapes, villages, towns and welcoming local people.

This brings us to what we really want you to discover today! Finnish Cuisine! Finns are extremely passionate about their food and their recipes. They celebrate a wide variety of foods, flavors and textures and they have a huge respect for their culinary roots.

Finns love their local ingredients, their original and traditional dishes and maybe that's why Finnish food tastes so great!

Mushrooms Omelet Roll

Known locally as sieni munakas, this breakfast recipe looks absolutely delicious and tastes even better!

Preparation time: 10 minutes

Cooking time: 20 minutes

Servings: 6

Ingredients:

- 6 eggs, whisked
- 1 cup milk
- 2 tablespoons flour
- A pinch of salt and black pepper
- 3 tablespoons olive oil
- 1 pound mushrooms, chopped
- 2 onions, chopped
- 1 tablespoon basil, chopped

Method:

1. In a bowl, mix the eggs with the milk, flour, salt and pepper and whisk well.

2. Heat up a pan with 1 tablespoon olive oil over medium high heat, add the eggs mixture, spread into the pan, cook for 3 minutes, flip, cook for another 3 minutes and transfer to a plate.

3. Heat up the same pan with the rest of the oil over medium high heat, add the onions, stir and sauté for 3 minutes.

4. Add the mushrooms, stir and cook for 5 minutes more.

5. Spread this mixture over the omelet, sprinkle basil, roll the omelet, place it in a greased baking dish, introduce in the oven at 390 degrees F for 5 minutes, slice and serve for breakfast.

Enjoy!

Breakfast Pasties

These traditional pasties are a tasty and very rich breakfast idea!

Preparation time: 10 minutes

Cooking time: 45 minutes

Servings: 8

Ingredients:

- 4 and ½ cups white flour
- 1 cup olive oil
- A pinch of salt and black pepper
- 1 and ¼ cups cold water
- 5 and ½ cups potatoes, peeled and diced
- 2 carrots, shredded
- 1 yellow onion, chopped
- ½ cup rutabaga, chopped
- 1 and ½ pounds beef, ground
- ½ pound pork, ground
- 1 beef bouillon cube, dissolved in hot water

Method:

1. In a bowl, mix the flour with the oil, salt, pepper and water and stir until you obtain a dough.

2. In a separate bowl, mix the potatoes with the carrots, onion, rutabaga, beef, pork and bouillon cube and stir well.

3. Roll the dough on a working surface, divide it into squares, divide the stuffing in the center of each, fold and seal edges and arrange them all on a lined baking sheet.

4. Introduce in the oven, bake at 425 degrees F for 45 minutes, divide between plates and serve for breakfast.

Enjoy!

Salmon Soup

Salmon fish soup – or Lohikeitto - is a sinfully easy and delicious soup that will surprise you for sure!

Preparation time: 10 minutes

Cooking time: 35 minutes

Servings: 4

Ingredients:

- 1 pound salmon fillets, skinless, boneless and cubed
- 4 tablespoons butter
- 1 leek, sliced
- 5 cups fish stock
- 1 pound potatoes, peeled and cubed
- 1 carrot, chopped
- 1 cup dill, chopped
- 1 cup heavy cream
- ¼ teaspoon allspice
- A pinch of salt and black pepper

Method:

1. Heat up a pot with the butter over medium heat, add the leeks, stir and cook for 10 minutes.

2. Add the stock, stir and cook for 10 minutes more.

3. Add potatoes, carrots, allspice, salt, pepper and half of the dill, stir and cook for 10 minutes.

4. Add the salmon and the cream, stir and cook for 5 minutes more.

5. Add the rest of the dill, toss, divide the soup into bowls and serve.

Enjoy!

Leipäjuusto – Squeaky Finnish Cheese

This delicious cheese recipe can be served warm or cold and is great with a fresh cup of coffee!

Preparation time: 10 minutes

Cooking time: 25 minutes

Servings: 6

Ingredients:

- 2 and ½ gallons milk
- A pinch of salt
- 1 tablespoon cornstarch
- 1 tablespoon sugar
- ½ tablet Hanson's rennet

Method:

1. Put the milk in a double boiler and heat it up over 88 degrees F.

2. In a cup, mix the salt with cornstarch and sugar and stir.

3. Add some of the milk, and the crushed tablet, whisk well and pour over the milk.

4. Stir and set aside for 45 minutes.

5. Pour the jelled mixture into a cake pan in which you arranged a wet cloth.

6. Gather the corners of the cloth, take it out of the pan and squeeze the liquid as much as possible.

7. Remove the cloth, press the cheese in the pan, introduce in the oven and bake at 400 degrees F for 15 minutes.

8. Cool the cheese down and serve it for breakfast.

Enjoy!

Vispipuuro - Lingonberry Porridge

A smooth and delicious semolina based porridge cooked with delicious lingonberries and eaten throughout Finland!

Preparation time: 10 minutes

Cooking time: 25 minutes

Servings: 4

Ingredients:

- 3 cups water
- 1 cup lingonberries, mashed
- 3 tablespoons sugar
- 1 cup semolina

Method:

1. Put the water in a pot, bring to a boil over medium heat, add mashed lingonberries and sugar, stir, cook for 10 minutes and strain the cooking liquid into a clean pot.

2. Add the semolina, bring to a boil again over low heat and cook for 15 minutes more.

3. Cool the porridge down completely, whisk it well, divide into bowls and serve cold for breakfast.

Enjoy!

Meat Pasties

Another traditional recipe, pasties are quite common around Finland and rightfully so! They are both fulfilling and delicious!

Preparation time: 10 minutes

Cooking time: 20 minutes

Servings: 4

Ingredients:

- 1 and ½ cups flour
- 1 cup milk
- ½ tablespoons yeast
- ½ tablespoon sugar
- 1 pound beef, ground
- 1 yellow onion, chopped
- 4 tablespoons white rice
- A pinch of salt and white pepper
- ¼ cup sour cream
- 1 egg, whisked
- Oil for frying, a drizzle

Method:

1. In a bowl, combine flour, milk, sugar and yeast, stir well, shape a dough out of this mix and leave aside to rise.

2. Heat up a pan with a drizzle of oil over medium high heat, add the onion, stir and cook for 2-3 minutes.

3. Add the rice, the beef, salt, pepper and sour cream, stir, brown for 5 minutes more and take off the heat.

4. Divide the dough into medium balls, flatten each, divide the meat mixture equally into the center of each flattened dough ball dough's Fold the dough over the meat and seal the edges, making sure to brush all the pasties with egg wash.

5. Heat up a pan with a drizzle of oil over medium high heat, add the pasties, cook them until they are golden on both sides, drain excess grease on paper towels, divide between plates and serve for breakfast.

Enjoy!

Scandinavian Crab Cakes

It's easy to make these crab cakes and they taste so good!

Preparation time: 10 minutes

Cooking time: 10 minutes

Servings: 6

Ingredients:

- 1 egg, whisked
- ¼ teaspoon curry powder
- 1 tablespoon homemade mayonnaise
- 3 drops hot pepper sauce
- 1 teaspoon Worcestershire sauce
- 1 tablespoon lemon juice
- A pinch of cayenne pepper
- ½ teaspoon paprika
- 1 pound crabmeat
- ¼ teaspoon mustard seeds, ground
- 1 tablespoon lemon pepper
- 5 tablespoons bread crumbs
- 5 tablespoon olive oil

Method:

1. In a bowl, gently combine the crab meat with the egg, curry powder, mayonnaise, pepper sauce, Worcestershire sauce, lemon juice, cayenne, paprika, mustard seeds, lemon pepper and bread crumbs, stir well and shape medium cakes out of this mix.

2. Heat olive oil on med heat. Add the crab cakes, cook them for 5-6 minutes on each side, divide between plates and serve for breakfast.

Enjoy!

Finnish potato flatbreads –
Perunarieska

This recipe makes for an easy and quick traditional Finnish bread that requires absolutely no kneading!

Preparation time: 10 minutes

Cooking time: 15 minutes

Servings: 4

Ingredients:

- 1 and ½ cups potato, boiled, peeled and mashed
- ¾ cup barley flour
- 1 egg, whisked
- A pinch of salt
- Butter for serving

Method:

1. In a bowl, combine mashed potato with the flour, egg and salt and stir well until you obtain a dough.

2. Transfer dough to a floured working surface, flatten it and divide into 4 servings.

3. Shape your disks, arrange them all on a lined baking sheet, prick them with a fork, place into the oven and bake at 428 degrees F for 15 minutes.

4. Divide the breads between plates, spread the butter over them and serve for breakfast.

Enjoy!

Kanttarellikeitto - Chanterelle Soup

Made from the king of mushrooms, this creamy soup is an absolute crowd pleaser!

Preparation time: 10 minutes

Cooking time: 50 minutes

Servings: 5

Ingredients:

- 6 cups chicken stock
- 6 tablespoons butter
- 2 tablespoons flour
- 1 pound chanterelle mushrooms, sliced
- 2 shallots, chopped
- 3 egg yolks
- ½ cup heavy cream
- ¼ teaspoon saffron powder
- A pinch of salt and black pepper

Method:

1. Heat up a pot with 2 tablespoons butter over medium high heat, add the flour and stir well.

2. Add the stock, whisk well and cook for 20 minutes.

3. Heat up another pot with the rest of the butter over medium high heat, add the shallots, stir and cook for 5 minutes.

4. Add the mushrooms, stir and cook for 5 minutes more.

5. Add the stock, stir, bring to a boil, cook for 10 minutes and blend using an immersion blender.

6. In a bowl, mix the cream with egg yolks, saffron, salt and pepper and whisk well.

7. Add some of the cooking liquid and whisk well again.

8. Pour this into the pot, stir, cook for 10 minutes more, ladle into bowls and serve.

Enjoy!

Karjalan Rice Pies

A delicious rye based pastry with a rich rice filling in the centre!

Preparation time: 10 minutes

Cooking time: 55 minutes

Servings: 4

Ingredients:

- 1 cup white rice
- 1 cup rye flour
- ¼ cup white flour
- A pinch of salt
- 2 cups milk
- 3 tablespoons butter, melted
- 2 and ½ cup water

Method:

1. Put 2 cups water in a pan, add the rice, bring to a boil over medium heat, cover and cook for 20 minutes.

2. Add the milk and salt, stir well and cook for 20 minutes more.

3. In a bowl, mix the rye flour with the white one and ½ cup water and stir until you have a sticky dough consistency.

4. Transfer dough to a floured working surface. Divide into 16 servings and roll each piece into a circle.

5. Divide the rice mixture in the center of the circles, spread almost until the edges, fold the edges and crimp them shaping small boats.

6. Arrange all the pies on a lined baking sheet, introduce in the oven and bake at 450 degrees F for 15 minutes.

7. Serve them for breakfast.

Enjoy!

Pyttipanna - Fast Potatoes and Eggs

Meat, eggs, and potatoes - an absolutely amazing breakfast combination!

Preparation time: 10 minutes

Cooking time: 10 minutes

Servings: 6

Ingredients:

- 6 bacon slices, cooked and crumbled
- 8 potatoes, boiled, peeled and diced
- 1 yellow onion, chopped
- 2 tablespoons butter
- 2 cups lamb, cooked and shredded
- 6 eggs, fried

Method:

1. Heat butter in a pan. Add the onion, stir and sauté on med for 5 minutes.

2. Add the potatoes and the lamb meat, stir and cook for 5 minutes more.

3. Divide the potato hash between plates, top each serving with a fried egg, sprinkle the crumbled bacon on top and serve for breakfast.

Enjoy!

Pannu Kakku – Baked Finnish Pancake

This recipe makes for an eggy, buttery, baked pancake!

Preparation time: 10 minutes

Cooking time: 15 minutes

Servings: 4

Ingredients:

- 6 eggs
- 1 and ½ cups milk
- ¼ cup sugar
- 1 tablespoon vanilla sugar
- ½ teaspoon of lemon zest, grated
- 1 and ½ cups flour
- 1/3 cup butter, melted
- 1 teaspoon of baking powder

Method:

1. In a bowl, mix the eggs with the milk, sugar, vanilla sugar, lemon zest, flour, baking powder and butter and stir well.

2. Pour the batter in a round baking dish, introduce in the oven and bake at 450 degrees F for 15 minutes.

3. Slice the pancakes, divide it between plates and serve for breakfast.

Enjoy!

Sienisalaatti - Great Mushrooms Salad

The Finnish mushroom salad is made with salted milk caps. Before salting, don't forget to soak the cleaned mushrooms in water for a few hours.

Preparation time: 10 minutes

Cooking time: 0 minutes

Servings: 4

Ingredients:

- 1 pound salted milk cap mushrooms, soaked for several hours, drained well and sliced
- 1 yellow onion, diced
- 1 cup sour cream
- 2 teaspoons lemon juice
- ½ teaspoon sugar
- A pinch of white pepper

Method:

1. In a salad bowl, mix the mushrooms with the onion, sour cream, lemon juice, sugar and pepper, toss well, divide into smaller bowls and serve cold.

Enjoy!

Smoked Mackerel Mix

Smoking is a traditional Finnish method of cooking delicate proteins such as seafood - so healthy and delicious!

Preparation time: 10 minutes

Cooking time: 0 minutes

Servings: 8

Ingredients:

- 7 ounces smoked mackerel fillets skinless and flaked
- Juice of ½ lemon
- Zest of ½ lemon, grated
- 4 tablespoons crème fraiche
- A pinch of black pepper
- A small bunch of chives, chopped
- A small handful dill, chopped
- 1 chicory head, shredded

Method:

1. In a bowl, mix the mackerel with lemon juice, lemon zest, crème fraiche, chives, black pepper, dill and chicory, toss, divide between plates and serve.

Enjoy!

Balsamic Potato Salad

This potato salad is so yummy! Use Finnish potatoes for a truly authentic feel!

Preparation time: 10 minutes

Cooking time: 20 minutes

Servings: 4

Ingredients:

- 2 pounds potatoes
- A pinch of salt and black pepper
- 2 tablespoons mustard
- 3 tablespoons olive oil
- 2 tablespoons balsamic vinegar
- 1 tablespoon chives, chopped

Method:

1. In a pot, add water to cover potatoes. Bring to a boil over medium heat, cook for 20 minutes, drain, peel and cut them into cubes.

2. In a salad bowl, mix the potatoes with salt, pepper, mustard, oil, vinegar and chives, toss and serve.

Enjoy!

Finnish Cucumber Salad

It's a perfect summer salad! It pairs perfectly well with a salmon dish!

Preparation time: 10 minutes

Cooking time: 0 minutes

Servings: 4

Ingredients:

- 3 cucumbers, thinly sliced
- 1/3 cup cider vinegar
- ¼ cup water
- 2 tablespoons olive oil
- 4 tablespoons sugar
- A pinch of salt and black pepper
- 1 tablespoon dill, chopped

Method:

1. In a salad bowl, mix the cucumbers with the vinegar, water, oil, sugar, salt, pepper and dill, toss and serve cold.

Enjoy!

Great Beef Stew

A mouthwatering, hearty soup made with a tasty combination of traditional ingredients!!

Preparation time: 10 minutes

Cooking time: 2 hours and 10 minutes

Servings: 6

Ingredients:

- 1 pound beef sirloin, cubed
- 1 tablespoon olive oil
- 1 tablespoon butter
- A pinch of salt and black pepper
- 2 yellow onions, chopped
- 1 teaspoon sugar
- 2 pounds potatoes, peeled and sliced
- 2 cups beer
- 2 cups beef stock
- 1 tablespoon thyme, chopped

Method:

1. Grease a baking dish with the butter and layer the potato slices on the bottom.

2. Heat up a pan with the oil over medium high heat, add the beef, toss, brown for 5 minutes and transfer over the potatoes.

3. Heat up the pan again over medium high heat, add the onions, stir and cook for 2 minutes.

4. Add the sugar, stir, cook for 3 minutes more and transfer over the meat in the baking dish.

5. Add beer, stock, salt and pepper, introduce the dish in the oven and cook the stew at 360 degrees F for 2 hours.

6. Divide the stew into bowls, sprinkle the thyme on top and serve.

Enjoy!

Stuffed Cabbage

Finnish cabbage rolls are stuffed with cabbage, rice and ground beef, and makes for a delicious meal!

Preparation time: 10 minutes

Cooking time: 1 hour and 10 minutes

Servings: 5

Ingredients:

- 1 cabbage head, leaves steamed and separated
- 1 pound pork, minced
- 1 yellow onion, chopped
- 4 cups veggie stock
- 2 cups cabbage, chopped
- 1 cup rice, cooked
- A pinch of salt and black pepper
- 1 teaspoon marjoram, dried
- 2 tablespoons butter
- 1 tablespoon flour
- 1 tablespoon cream

Method:

1. Heat up a pan with 2 teaspoons butter over medium high heat, add the onion and cook for 2 minutes.

2. Add the pork, rice, salt, pepper and marjoram, stir, cook for 4-5 minutes and take off the heat.

3. Arrange the cabbage leaves on a working surface, divide the pork mixture, roll and seal edges.

4. Arrange all the rolls in a baking dish and add the stock on top.

5. Heat up a pan with the rest of the butter over medium heat, add the flour and the cream, stir, cook for 2 minutes and pour over the cabbage rolls.

6. Introduce the dish in the oven and bake at 400 degrees F for 1 hour.

7. Divide between plates and serve.

Enjoy!

Herbed Salmon

This is a very elegant and special dish, perfect for any dinner party!

Preparation time: 10 minutes

Cooking time: 25 minutes

Servings: 4

Ingredients:

- 4 salmon fillets, boneless, pockets cut in the center
- A pinch of lemon pepper
- A pinch of salt and black pepper
- Cooking spray
- 3 tablespoons lemon juice
- 4 tablespoons mozzarella, shredded
- 2 tablespoons dill, chopped
- 2 tablespoons chives, chopped
- 2 tablespoons thyme, chopped

Method:

1. Season fish with salt, pepper and lemon pepper. Drizzle with lemon juice.

2. Arrange the fillets in a baking dish greased with cooking spray, stuff them with shredded cheese, dill, chives and thyme, introduce in the oven and bake at 400 degrees F for 25 minutes.

3. Divide between plates and serve.

Enjoy!

Finnish Beef Mix

Another great traditional Finnish stew – packed full of flavour and oomph!

Preparation time: 10 minutes

Cooking time: 7 hours

Servings: 5

Ingredients:

- 1 and ½ pounds beef, cubed
- 2 beef stock cubes
- 1 yellow onion, chopped
- 2 carrots, sliced
- 2 tablespoons flour
- 4 tablespoons butter
- 2 cups cream

Method:

1. Heat up a pan over medium high heat, add the beef mixed with the flour, stir, brown for 5 minutes and transfer to your slow cooker.

2. Add beef cubes, onion, carrots, butter and the cream, stir, cover and cook on Low for 7 hours.

3. Divide the mixture into bowls and serve.

Enjoy!

Creamy Rutabaga Bake

It's such a rich dish! You can serve it for lunch anytime!

Preparation time: 10 minutes

Cooking time: 1 hour

Servings: 4

Ingredients:

- 6 cups rutabagas, diced
- 3 tablespoons butter
- ¾ cup half and half
- ¾ cup bread crumbs
- A pinch of salt
- A pinch of nutmeg powder
- 2 eggs, whisked

Method:

1. Put the rutabagas in a pan, add water to cover, bring to a simmer over medium heat, cook for 20 minutes, drain, mash and put in a bowl.

2. Add the eggs, bread crumbs, half of the butter, salt, nutmeg and half and half and stir well.

3. Grease a baking dish with the rest of the butter, pour and spread the rutabaga mix, introduce in the oven, bake at 350 degrees F for 45 minutes, slice and serve.

Enjoy!

Fish Dinner Mix

The Finns absolutely love their sea food. And with how delicious this recipe is, we aren't surprised!

Preparation time: 10 minutes

Cooking time: 25 minutes

Servings: 4

Ingredients:

- 1 pound salmon fillets, boneless and cubed
- ½ teaspoon dill, dried
- 1 yellow onion, chopped
- A pinch of salt and black pepper
- 4 cups water
- 4 potatoes, cubed
- 2 cups milk
- 2 tablespoons butter
- 1 tablespoon chives, chopped

Method:

1. Put the water in a pot, add potatoes, salt, pepper, dill and the onion, stir, bring to a simmer over medium heat and cook for 20 minutes.

2. Add the milk combined with the butter and whisk.

3. Also add the salmon, toss, cook for 5 minutes more, divide into bowls and serve with the chives sprinkled on top.

Enjoy!

Finnish Meatballs - Lihapyorykoita

Serve them right away! They are so good!

Preparation time: 10 minutes

Cooking time: 10 minutes

Servings: 6

Ingredients:

- 4 whole wheat bread slices, crumbled
- ½ cup whole milk
- 12 ounces ground pork meat
- 12 ounces ground beef meat
- 1 egg, whisked
- ½ cup yellow onion, chopped
- ¼ teaspoon ground allspice
- Salt and black pepper to the taste
- ¼ teaspoon nutmeg powder
- 2 tablespoons butter
- 1 tablespoon white flour
- 2 tablespoons olive oil
- 1 cup chicken stock
- 1 cup fresh cranberries
- ¼ cup heavy cream
- 1 teaspoon lemon zest, grated
- 1 tablespoon lemon juice
- 2 teaspoons sugar
- 1 teaspoon ginger, grated
- 2 tablespoons dill, chopped
- 2 tablespoons parsley, chopped

Method:

1. Put bread in a bowl, add whole milk, soak for 5 minutes, drain well and put in another bowl.

2. Add pork, beef, egg, onion, nutmeg, allspice, salt and pepper, stir well and shape medium meatballs out of this mixture.

3. Heat up a pan with half of the oil and half of the butter over medium heat, add the meatballs, cook them for 4 minutes on each side and transfer them to a plate.

4. Heat up another pan with the rest of the oil and the rest of the butter over medium heat, add the flour and whisk it well.

5. Add stock, salt, pepper and cream, stir, bring to a simmer over medium low heat, add the meatballs and cook them for 10 minutes.

6. In your food processor, mix cranberries with lemon zest, lemon juice, sugar, ginger, salt, pepper, dill and parsley and pulse well.

7. Divide the meatballs mix between plates, add the cranberry sauce on the side and serve.

Enjoy!

Flavored Chicken Mix

This chicken recipe is simple but absolutely delicious!

Preparation time: 10 minutes

Cooking time: 1 hour

Servings: 2

Ingredients:

- 3 ounces morels, sliced
- 2 tablespoons white flour
- 2 tablespoons butter
- Salt and black pepper to the taste
- 2 chicken breasts, skinless and boneless
- 1 teaspoon tarragon, minced
- 1 and ¼ cups chicken stock
- 4 shallots, diced
- 4 tablespoons heavy cream
- 1 tablespoon dry sherry
- 1 tablespoon lemon juice

Method:

1. In a bowl, mix flour with salt and pepper, stir and dredge the chicken in this mix.

2. Heat up a pan with 1 tablespoon butter over medium high heat, add chicken and brown for 4 minutes on each side.

3. Transfer chicken pieces in a baking dish, add half of the chicken stock, introduce in the oven at 300 degrees F and bake for 40 minutes.

4. Heat up another pan with 1 tablespoon butter over medium high heat, add shallots and morels, stir and cook for 4 minutes.

5. Add the rest of the chicken stock, stir, bring to a simmer and cook for 10-15 minutes.

6. Add lemon juice, cream and the sherry stir and cook for 10 more minutes.

7. Slice chicken breasts, divide between plates, add the morels mixture on the side and serve with tarragon sprinkled on top.

Enjoy!

Trout and Spinach

It's so fantastic and easy to make! You'll see!

Preparation time: 10 minutes

Cooking time: 30 minutes

Servings: 4

Ingredients:

- 1 and ¼ pounds trout fillets, boneless
- Salt and black pepper to the taste
- 1 small yellow onion, chopped
- 6 ounces mushrooms sliced
- 2 tablespoons vegetable oil
- 9 ounces spinach, torn
- 2 garlic cloves, minced
- 3 tablespoons pine nuts

For the sauce:

- ¾ cup fish stock
- ¾ cup whipping cream
- ¾ cup Parmesan, grated
- 4 tablespoons white wine

Method:

1. Put the stock in a pot, heat up over medium heat, add the cream and the wine, stir and simmer for 15 minutes.

2. Take this off the heat, add the Parmesan, whisk well and cool down a few minutes.

3. Heat up another pan with the vegetable oil over medium high heat, add mushrooms and onions, stir and cook for 3-4 minutes.

4. Add garlic, spinach, salt and pepper, cook for 2 minutes and spread into a baking dish.

5. Add the fish fillets, season them with salt and pepper, spread the creamy sauce you've prepared, introduce in the oven and bake at 425 degrees F for 15 minutes.

6. Divide the fish, the spinach and the sauce between plates and serve.

1. Enjoy!

Smoked Salmon Bowls

This is one traditional Finnish recipe you simply have to try!

Preparation time: 5 minutes

Cooking time: 0 minutes

Servings: 8

Ingredients:

- 3 tablespoons white horseradish cream
- 1 cup heavy cream
- 2 teaspoons mustard
- 1 pound smoked salmon, boneless, skinless and flaked
- ¼ teaspoon black pepper

Method:

1. In a bowl, combine the horseradish cream with the heavy cream, mustard, salmon and black pepper, toss, divide into small bowls and serve.

Enjoy!

Finnish Cookies

These cookies are so delicious! We love them!

Preparation time: 10 minutes

Cooking time: 10 minutes

Servings: 4

Ingredients:

- 1 cup soft butter
- ½ cup sugar
- 1 teaspoon almond extract
- 3 cups flour
- 3 eggs, whisked
- 1 and ½ cups almonds, chopped

Method:

1. In a bowl, combine the butter with the sugar, eggs, almond extract, flour and almonds, stir well and shape medium sticks out of this mix.

2. Arrange the cookies on a lined baking sheet, introduce in the oven and bake at 350 degrees F for 10 minutes.

3. Serve the cookies cold.

Enjoy!

Blueberry Pie

This looks incredible and it tastes so amazing!

Preparation time: 10 minutes

Cooking time: 30 minutes

Servings: 5

Ingredients:

- 1 cup almond milk
- 2 teaspoons dry yeast
- 2/3 cup sugar
- 1 egg
- 3 cups flour
- 1/3 cup butter, melted
- 4 cups blueberries
- 3 tablespoons almond flour

Method:

1. In a bowl, combine the milk with the yeast, sugar, egg, white flour and butter and stir well.

2. In another bowl, mix the blueberries with the almond flour and toss.

3. Pour the batter into a pie pan, spread the blueberries all over and bake in the oven at 350 degrees F for 30 minutes.

4. Slice the pie and serve it cold.

Enjoy!

Rhubarb Puddings

This is one dessert both adults and kids will adore!

Preparation time: 10 minutes

Cooking time: 40 minutes

Servings: 4

Ingredients:

- 5 tablespoons sugar
- 12 ounces rhubarb, chopped
- Zest of 1 orange, grated
- Juice of 1 orange
- 2 tablespoons water
- 1 and ¼ cups heavy cream
- ½ cup milk
- ¼ cup sugar
- 1 teaspoon vanilla extract
- 2 gelatin sheets

Method:

1. In a bowl, mix the rhubarb with orange zest, orange juice, 5 tablespoons sugar and 2 tablespoons water, toss, spread into a baking dish, bake at 350 degrees F for 30 minutes and cool down.

2. Heat up the milk in a pot over medium heat, add the heavy cream, ¼ cup sugar and vanilla extract, stir, bring to a simmer and take off the heat.

3. Put gelatin in a bowl, add cold water to cover, soak for 5 minutes, drain, add over the cream mixture and whisk well.

4. Strain this into 4 ramekins and keep in the fridge for 3 hours.

5. Heat up the rhubarb in the microwave for a few seconds.

6. Take ramekins out of the fridge, put the bases in hot water for 30 seconds, then tip them out between plates, top each with the rhubarb mix and serve.

Enjoy!

Rich Rice Pudding

The Finns love their rice – they use it in everything - savories to desserts!

Preparation time: 10 minutes

Cooking time: 1 hour

Servings: 8

Ingredients:

- 3 cups milk
- 1 cup rice cooked
- 3 eggs, whisked
- ¼ cup butter, melted
- ½ cup sugar
- 1 teaspoon cinnamon powder
- ½ cup almonds, sliced

Method:

1. In a bowl, mix cooked rice with eggs, sugar, milk and melted butter, stir well, pour into a baking dish, sprinkle cinnamon and almonds on top, introduce in the oven at 350 degrees F and bake everything for 1 hour.

2. Transfer to dessert bowls and serve.

Enjoy!

Conclusion

And there you have it! Delicious Finnish cuisine prepared in the comfort of your own home. We hope you have a great time reading through the different recipes and learning about the wonderful Finnish Cuisine!

About the Author

A native of Indianapolis, Indiana, Valeria Ray found her passion for cooking while she was studying English Literature at Oakland City University. She decided to try a cooking course with her friends and the experience changed her forever. She enrolled at the Art Institute of Indiana which offered extensive courses in the culinary Arts. Once Ray dipped her toe in the cooking world, she never looked back.

When Valeria graduated, she worked in French restaurants in the Indianapolis area until she became the head chef at one of the 5-star establishments in the area. Valeria's attention to taste and visual detail caught the eye of a local business person who expressed an interest in publishing her recipes. Valeria began her secondary career authoring cookbooks and e-books which she tackled with as much talent and gusto as her first career. Her passion for food leaps off the page of her books which have colourful anecdotes and stunning pictures of dishes she has prepared herself.

Valeria Ray lives in Indianapolis with her husband of 15 years, Tom, her daughter, Isobel and their loveable Golden Retriever, Goldy. Valeria enjoys cooking special dishes in her large, comfortable kitchen where the family gets involved in preparing meals. This successful, dynamic chef is an inspiration to culinary students and novice cooks everywhere.

•••••••••●●●●●●●●••••••

Author's Afterthoughts

Thank you for Purchasing my book and taking the time to read it from front to back. I am always grateful when a reader chooses my work and I hope you enjoyed it!

With the vast selection available online, I am touched that you chose to be purchasing my work and take valuable time out of your life to read it. My hope is that you feel you made the right decision.

I very much would like to know what you thought of the book. Please take the time to write an honest and informative review on Amazon.com. Your experience and opinions will be of great benefit to me and those readers looking to make an informed choice.

With much thanks,

Valeria Ray

1

SEEKING COHERENCE IN PEACE-MAKING

This book is an attempt to develop some new insights into the challenges of peace and security in Africa. It takes a fresh look at some enduring problems, introducing some new frameworks for analysis, and some new conceptual language. It is 'work in progress' rather than a polished thesis. It aims to stimulate debate, rather than argue towards a clear conclusion.

Our starting point is that conflict in Africa is both complicated and indeterminate. There is no single theory that explains everything and no single approach that can address all aspects of the problem. The causes and nature of conflict are multiple, and the mechanisms needed for building peace, resolving conflict, and ensuring that peace lasts, are also very complex. A simplified model, outlined below, identifies five levels of engagement (from local to international), three stages of the conflict cycle, and three principal areas for action (military, political and economic). The interactions between these different levels and areas are exceptionally complicated.

Conflict is also indeterminate, in that all actors—including both mediators and belligerent parties—have imperfect information, and their actions have unanticipated outcomes. The weakness and opacity of institutions in Africa, especially those engaged in fighting wars, also means that it can be very hard to predict how wars will start and escalate. The weakness of institutions combines with the centralization of power to create a situation in which a handful of senior members of a government—usually security officers—can make the major decisions concerning war, peace and governance. They are overworked and may have little time for reflection and consultation, and their sources of information and analysis may be narrow. A major conflagration can be ignited by an apparently trivial spark. Often, the management of a war effort appears chaotic, and the success of a peace initiative can appear to rely on chance. Even such an apparently trivial factor as the personal disposition of a leading player on a particular day, can completely undo months of patient diplomatic preparation.

Amidst this bewildering confusion, we can identify some important main themes. This book seeks to highlight the much neglected theme of militarism. We do not attempt a comprehensive definition of militarism, but rather a diagnosis of how it is present in the political parties, liberation movements, commercial enterprises, governments and inter-governmental structures that predominate in much of Africa. Militarism is akin to a political culture, a predisposition to use violence. One of its most important components is the tendency to use force in pursuit of political objectives.

The militarization of governance is prevalent across Africa, but has received insufficient scholarly attention. This is despite the fact that militarism is antithetical to all the precepts of good governance demanded by African citizens, espoused by the international community and echoed by African leaders. Conflicts of various kinds are a normal facet of political life. It is when these conflicts are combined with a readiness to turn to violence, that there is danger of war. And once war has broken out, the military logic of war supersedes the political logic of peacetime. As Clausewitz noted, war tends to the absolute. Thus a war that has broken out for a particular reason tends to escalate, bringing in other issues and factors as well.

In this context it is striking to note how little of the recent military history of Africa has actually been written. There are huge and very important gaps in basic understanding of military events in Ethiopia and Eritrea, Sudan and the Democratic Republic of Congo for example. Most of those who have been engaged in the wars are reluctant to write. They are too busy, or they do not have the training or tradition of writing, or they are fearful of exposing secrets. As a result, the insider perspective on many important issues of peace, security and governance must be filtered through others. But most academics and consultants have very limited access to the key decision-makers. For obvious reasons, writers tend to concentrate on what they know about, and can measure and can describe. As a result, the published literature is a very incomplete guide to conflict in Africa, and the actual processes of decision-making in government—especially in the security services—remain a black hole.

This book cannot fill the gap. But the analysis presented tries to draw as much as possible on insights provided by those who have themselves been engaged in recent wars, as participants or mediators. This allows us to begin to develop frameworks for analysis that will, in time, provide the scaffolding for building a much more complete account of conflict and militarism in Africa.

An Organizing Framework

This introductory chapter develops a simple organizing framework that can reflect some of the complexity and indeterminacy surrounding conflict and peacemaking in Africa. It seeks to provide the basis for examining the range of contributory factors in creating war and escalating or continuing war. Its added value is its attempt to identify linkages between different levels at which conflict occurs, different stages in the conflict cycle, and different components of conflict. These linkages operate both in conflict causation and in effective response.

The causes of conflict are complex and occur at many different levels, ranging from the individual factor in leaders to wider issues of political ethnicity, control over resources, etc. None of these factors can be discounted. The particular challenge for those seeking to prevent or resolve conflicts is to attend to all these different factors. This calls for a multiple approach, involving different institutions and stakeholders, to acknowledge these different components. However, this is not an argument that a comprehensive settlement is necessary for every conflict, on the spurious grounds that anything less than a settlement that takes account of every grievance will not be a settlement at all. In some cases, achieving an 'unjust' or incomplete peace may be better than failing to achieve a peace at all. As Alia Izetbegovic, President of Bosnia, said of the Dayton Accords, 'this is not a just peace. But it is more just than a continuation of the war.' Under some conditions, seeking a 'just' or comprehensive peace that addresses all the 'root causes' of a war may be a recipe for indefinite prolongation of that war. And in fact those who want to continue a war often use this argument, adding that it would be a betrayal of those who have died in the struggle if their ideals were abandoned at this stage. Many issues are best postponed for resolution in a post-conflict phase. A peace settlement can be the beginning of a political process, rather than the solution to all a country's ills. Peacemaking requires *awareness* of the complexity of conflict, it does not necessarily involve *solving* every conflict-related issue.

We can identify three main stages of the conflict cycle, with corresponding elements for conflict management:

1. The underlying factors that create conflict—conflict prevention and peace-building;
2. War itself—conflict resolution and containment;
3. The post-conflict period—management of post-conflict transitions.

The main components of conflict creation and escalation can be schematically organized under three main headings: military, political and economic.

Military factors include, among others: the security calculations, both rational and irrational, of leaders on all sides; the nature of the army; the militarization of society, and the response to any outbreak of violence. When war has actually broken out, military factors become more high-profile and salient, as leaders seek to mobilize human and material resources for war, and calculate whether they can gain a decisive military advantage over their adversary. Purely tactical military calculations may become the driving force in the development of a conflict, superseding any political reasons for the outbreak of conflict, and revising war aims upwards. Post-conflict, factors such as the effectiveness of disarmament and demobilization measures and the demilitarization of politics are key to the success of peace agreements. There are strong indications that the most important factor determining the likelihood of a conflict breaking out is the military history of the country: where there has been a war before, and former war-leaders are in power, war is more likely. The second most important factor is the presence of conflict in a neighboring country.

Political factors include: the nature of political control over state power, the extent to which the government includes effective representation of all groups in society, government responses to the expressed grievances of constituencies, the manipulation of political ethnicity or politicized religion, the felt need for those in power to appear strong and decisive, struggles for control of party or military apparatus, etc. A particular concern is militarized governance: militaristic parties of any political complexion have a tendency towards using violence for political ends. When conflict has broken out, the political dynamic changes, and the conduct of the conflict itself can become the most salient political issue. Questions such as the degree of resolve in pursuing popular war aims, the level of conscription and the level of loss of human life, perceived competence in conducting the war, the deployment of ethnic, nationalist or religious ideology, human rights abuses and humanitarian questions, all become new ology, human rights abuses and humanitarian questions, all become new factors in the political equation. As human losses and financial expenditures mount, the political demands of the adversaries tend to harden and heighten. Regional factors may become salient as neighboring states are drawn in, as belligerent parties, as hosts for refugees or rebel groups, as diplomatic allies, or as mediators.

Economic factors include: control over natural resources, perceived benefits of control over state power, especially in winner-takes-all political systems (and penalties of not gaining such control), the commercial benefits of using violence to acquire physical assets, and the weakness of constituencies that have vested interests in peace and security. During conflict, certain groups and individuals prosper: although peace will bring a net economic gain for a country, it does not necessarily follow that those in charge of the war effort on either side will gain. In post-conflict periods, the economic factor can become the most important. Peace agreements need to be underwritten by economic rehabilitation programmes, targeted at various levels: the state, local government, essential service provision, rehabilitation of former combatants, etc. There are some indications that the single most important factor in a peace agreement actually holding is the personal financial interests of the former war leaders.

All the above factors operate at different levels. These range from the individual and community to the international level. Each level has its own dynamics, distinguished by the nature of the actors involved, the institutions available for organizing violence or for mediating conflict, and the salience of the issues at stake.

Turning to the tools we have to respond, we can distinguish a number of levels. These include the community/grassroots level, the civil society/private sector level, the national political level, the regional level, and the international level. These levels can of course be sub-divided, but this simplified categorization appears useful. The following three tables indicate some of the measures that are possible at different levels, addressing different components, and at different stages in the conflict cycle. The listing of measures is not exhaustive in any way, but merely indicative.

5

Conflict prevention and peace-building

	Military	Political	Economic
Community	* Teaching of non-military values in schools. * Promoting inter-communal dialogue. * Small arms control.	* Maintenance of effective dispute resolution mechanisms. * Empowerment of women and youth.	* Management of common resources in a way so as to minimise conflict potential * Provision of work, education opportunities for youth
Civil society/ private sector	* Engagement of civil society stakeholders in public debate on security issues.	* Promotion of civil and political rights, transparency and good governance. * Inclusion of all constituencies, promotion of gender equity.	* NGO/CBO promotion of service provision, sustainable development. * Good corporate citizenship
National political	* Limited use of emergency measures. * No proliferation of special forces or militias. * Transparency about military spending * Civilian control of the military and security services.	* Equitable representation of different ethnic/ religious/social groups in government. * Devolution of powers. * Freedom of movement and regional citizenship. * Respect for constitutionalism.	* Adequate remuneration for soldiers, including health care and pensions. * Limitations on military spending. * Controls on military and security involvement in commerce.
Regional	* Creation of credible regional intervention forces. * Development of national and regional security doctrines to promote predictability and transparency in inter-state relations.	* Promotion of norms of good governance, utilising peer pressure. * Establishment and development of regional fora for dialogue and dispute management. * Regional civil society organisations also have roles in this regard.	* Functioning of regional mechanisms and institutions for e.g. management of shared riperine resources, cross-border pastures. * Promotion of intra-regional trade
International	* Development of credible international intervention forces. * Training for military, police, security services.	* Enhancement of conflict early-warning and timely intervention systems. * Support to civil society initiatives.	* Increased predictability, mutual accountability in aid relations. * Increased support to key social sectors.

6

Conflict resolution and containment

	Military	Political	Economic
Community	* For local conflicts, traditional moral restraints on conflict can be invoked. * For national conflicts, less is possible.	* For local conflicts communities can invoke adapted traditional dispute resolution mechanisms. * For national conflicts, little can be done.	* Promotion of fair and equitable access to and control over local resources.
Civil society/ private sector	* For local conflicts, civil society initiatives are possible. * For national conflicts, very little is possible.	* Human rights monitoring. * Advocacy for peace (where possible). * Promotion of dialogue across conflict lines, e.g. contact with counterpart groups on the 'other side.' * Promotion of dialogue on post-conflict issues.	* Provision of assistance to people affected by war. * Observance of business codes of conduct, especially regarding human rights.
National political	* Measures to ensure respect for the Geneva Conventions and provide humanitarian access to war-affected populations. * Ceasefire, augmented by mechanisms for monitoring. * Mechanisms for separation of forces, creation of security zones, encampment, etc.	* Proximity talks; preparatory talks, high-level talks, adoption of common values and principles; all the modalities for mediation available, either bilateral, facilitated or mediated. * Political liberalisation, opening up space for civil society. * Increased respect for human rights and humanitarian principles/ promotion of culture of peace.	* Avoidance or minimisation of military and security involvement in commerce.
Regional	* Restrictions on arms flows, prohibition on use of military bases in neighbouring countries	* Measures to contain the conflict and prevent its spreading to neighbour-ing countries. * In regional conflicts, the range of peace initiatives outlined above. * Facilitation or mediation of peace talks of various kinds. * Regional CSOs can support or augment national CSO efforts.	* Monitoring and controlling illegal export of commodities from the affected country. * Assistance to refugees, combined with protection, demilitar-isation of refugee camps etc.
International	* Monitoring adherence to IHL. * Arms embargoes.	* Carrots and sticks to encourage the parties towards negotiation. * Support to community-based and civil society initiatives * Facilitation or mediation of peace talks.	* Humanitarian assistance. * Monitoring and controlling illegal export of commodities from the affected country. * Advance planning for post-conflict economic rehabilitation and recovery

Management of post-conflict transition

	Military	Political	Economic
Community	* Rehabilitation and reintegration of former combatants. * Local control of small arms supplies. * Humanitarian mine action.	* Reconciliation between formerly hostile communities. * Rebuilding of judicial institutions.	* Rehabilitation of essential services.
Civil society/ private sector	* Assistance to veterans' associations to become articulate and responsible members of civil society.	* Promotion of democracy, human rights etc., including active participation in rebuilding institutions. * Promotion of reconciliation	* Support to social service provision, income-generating projects, micro-credit etc. * Engagement in policy debate and monitoring of post-conflict rehabilit-ation programmes.
National political	* Creation of a national army and security forces committed to democratic sovereignty. * Establishment of a comprehensive nationwide programme for disarmament, demobilisation and reintegration of former combatants and security officers.	* Establishment of democratic procedures and institutions. * Civilianisation of national political life. * Rebuilding national institutions.	* Development of plans for rehabilitation of war-stricken areas, return and resettlement of refugees and IDPs; economic reintegration of demobilised former combatants; and relaunching the economy. * Development of new financing schemes for rehabilitation.
Regional	* Provision of peace-keeping forces as appropriate. * Monitoring adherence to military protocols in peace agreements.	* Supporting and monitoring implementation of peace agreements. * Promotion of regional civil society initiatives and networks.	* Assistance for refugees to return. * Promotion of regional integration, cross-border trade and other measures.
International	* Provision of peace-keeping forces as appropriate. * Monitoring adherence to military protocols in peace agreements. * Support financial and technical to military reform and demobilisation.	* Institutional support to key ministries, departments for reconstruction. * Engagement in policy dialogue to promote democratisation and reconciliation plans over a realistic time frame. * Support to civil society initiatives.	* Sequenced economic assistance to support transition from conflict through rehabilitation to growth/development. * Providing conditionality-free assistance to rehabilitation and recovery plans through trust funds and similar initiatives. * Accelerated debt relief.

8

The Centrality of Militarism

The problems posed by militarized governance form a theme that knits together the different levels, stages and areas of peace-making, and the different chapters of this book. At a regional or international level, our analysis uses the concept of 'security communities.' A security community shares a political culture in which it is unacceptable to use force to settle disputes. It is therefore the antithesis of militarized governance. Chapter 2 is concerned with a framework for regional peace and security that can respond to this challenge.

The regionalization of conflict is prevalent across Africa, where wars display a disturbing tendency to spill over borders, and engulf neighboring states. For a number of key conflicts in Africa, notably the Great Lakes and Sierra Leone, peacemaking needs to be pursued at a regional level. Among African institutions, there are comparative advantages that can be utilized in approaching the complexities of peacemaking. The OAU has a degree of political legitimacy that can be crucial in bringing the parties together. However its capacities remain limited. The implicit analysis in the table above implies that the OAU, in partnership with other regional organizations, can play a key role as a facilitator in synthesizing actions at different levels and establishing linkages between different organizations. As the OAU transforms itself into the African Union, one of its challenges will be to create the institutions, norms and procedures necessary for the forging of a security community across the continent.

Subregional organizations have emerged as the premier peace enforcers in the continent. This is a highly significant development which has so far been a series of ad hoc responses to particular conflicts. The UN continues to play a pivotal role in certain conflicts. As yet there is no institution in Africa devoted to strategic planning concerning the social and economic components of conflict and post-conflict transitions. This is a potential role for the Economic Commission for Africa in coordination with subregional organizations and the Bretton Woods institutions.

Among international partners, different institutions also have comparative advantages in their specialist areas. For example, there is general specialization of defence ministries in military affairs, foreign relations in political affairs and development cooperation in economic affairs. However, the division of labor is not that simple. A foreign ministry is better able to deal with national, regional and international issues than it is with civil society and community-based issues. Thus there is a strong rationale for a specialization that provides development cooperation departments with a lead role when it comes to supporting peace-related civil society initiatives. In addition, many issues have cross-cutting implications. Notably, disarmament, demobilization and the reintegration of former combatants is an issue that has military, political and economic aspects, and is salient at the national, civil society/private sector and community levels. (It may also have regional implications.) At an international level there is a need for more coordination to avoid the problem of multiplication of overlapping initiatives.

The core chapters of this book examine different components of militarism, conflict and society. At a national level, the issue of constitutionalism is key: it is the antithesis of militarism in governance. Chapter 3 is concerned with a set of issues relating to this. It focuses upon the prevalent doctrine of 'exceptionalism'—the assumption of emergency powers by a government in response to real or perceived threat—which is the constitutional manifestation of militarized government. This is best tackled through a process of constitution-making and constitutional implementation. The involvement of the widest possible groups of stakeholders should be a means for ensuring that a national constitution has the highest degree of legitimacy, and is least likely to be abrogated or undermined.

Chapter 4 is concerned with the main vehicle for militarism: political parties, movements and the elites that control governments. This chapter develops a schematic typology of forms of militarism, and their implications for political culture and the possibilities for wider mobilization of social forces for peace. A particular focus of this chapter is 'left-wing militarism,' particularly as it is manifest by former liberation movements in power. This implies an ambitious agenda for governance, for transforming many of Africa's political movements into closed vanguardist parties into more open organizations, permeable by civil society, in which the militaristic values of discipline, authority and secrecy are replaced by more democratic and consensual methods of organization. Unfortunately, the record of former liberation movements in power suggests that most of them have failed to respond to these challenges. Many of them have been embroiled in both internal and international conflicts, and have suppressed all internal challenges to their grip on power.

Centralized, vanguardist parties are in part a product of a 'winner takes all' political system. The contest for power in such systems will always be hard-fought, with the contenders trying to exert maximum control over their party apparatuses, and thus tending towards militaristic modes of party governance—with implications for state governance should they win. In this regard, it is possible that means for debating and contesting *policies* may be an important intermediate mechanism for democratizing political systems. Forums for engaging with civil society, the political opposition, and the general public, to discuss specific policies may be a means of introducing democratic policy debate and influencing policy, without the confrontational politics that are associated with elections for state power.

Chapter 5 turns to civil society and social mobilization, dealing with the options for and constraints upon citizens' involvement in peace-making. This also develops new schemata for understanding the possibilities for social action under different political systems. The analysis highlights the difficulties faced by major groups of stakeholders—specifically women, young people and the poor and marginalized—in mobilizing to pursue their collective interest in peace. Specifically, it shows how the mobilization of social movements and the emergence of a wide range of civil organizations are dependent upon the development of a mature democratic governance, with a strong state apparatus. Once again, we see how militarized governance is the enemy of any organized civil society, and any social mobilization for peace.

Chapter 6 is concerned with commercial militarism—mercenaries and the wider engagement of business interests, both national and international, in warfare in Africa. This chapter seeks to place the phenomenon of international private military companies in the wider context of the 'mercenarization' of warfare in Africa. It develops the concept of the 'military-commercial complex,' whereby armies and their commanders develop commercial interests, while some businesses find it profitable to deal with the military, especially in zones of conflict. This analysis leads to an agenda of Demilitarizing commerce and separating the military from business activities.

The final chapter deals with the demands of a post-conflict transition. Perhaps the most common cause of conflict is a failed transition from the previous conflict. For this reason alone, post-conflict demilitarization demands special attention. It is evident that planning for post-conflict transitions should begin even while conflicts are still underway. This will make it possible to exploit effectively the opportunities that arise during the first months of a post-conflict transition, putting in place effective policies and programmes. There is a danger that if these critical moments are missed—because policymakers are simply too busy with pressing concerns—important issues will remain unresolved. Early planning and constituency-building on post-conflict issues will facilitate smooth transitions. In addition, it is possible that serious and concrete planning for peace may help to focus the billigerents' minds on the benefits of peace, and help to mobilize pro-peace constituencies in the countries concerned, thereby hastening peace itself. This requirement for planning ahead reflects a more fundamental reality: conflict has become a fact of life in many parts of Africa and cannot be regarded as an aberration. Planning for peace must be a long-term strategic affair.

The major onus for peace-building falls upon African leaders and citizens themselves. The category 'leaders' should include not just political leaders but social leaders at all levels. In this respect, this book seeks to bring into particular focus the pervasive problem of militarism and the propensity of militaristic parties to resort to violence. The fundamental challenge is to demilitarize politics and business, and ultimately 'demilitarize the mind.'

2

TOWARDS A FRAMEWORK FOR REGIONAL PEACE AND SECURITY

This chapter asks, can we identify (and hopefully construct) a workable framework for regional peace and security in Africa? What would such an order look like? The structure of the chapter is based upon asking the questions about whether the necessary preconditions exist for constructing any such framework. In doing so, it attempts to identify what strategies are open to governments, civil society and international organizations seeking to promote an international peace and security order.

Approaches: 'Security Communities'

A basic concept utilized in this chapter is Karl Deutsch's 'security community' (Deutsch, 1957; Adler and Barnett, 1998). Breaking away from the traditional realist conception of international relations, which held that states pursue their interests in an anarchic international order in which armed conflict is inevitable, Deutsch argued that community is possible at an international level. He believed that it is possible for different countries to engage in social, economic and political interaction in a way that made war between them unthinkable. This can be seen as a form of regional non-militarism: the dismantling of the capacity to engage in militaristic governance at a regional level.

Deutsch was specifically concerned with western Europe, and believed that liberal democracy was an essential component of this common trans-national community creation process. Subsequently, others have applied the concept elsewhere in the world, for example to U.S.-Canada and U.S.-Mexico relations, to the southern cone of South America, to the Gulf Cooperation Council, and to the Association of South East Asian Nations (ASEAN). These other cases raise questions about how the model of security communities can be adapted to different circumstances (Fawcett and Hurrell, 1995).

The OSCE Model

The Organization for Security and Cooperation in Europe (OSCE) is seen by many as a model case of an institution that has provided the framework for deepening an existing security community (democratic western Europe) and expanding it. The extension of the European security community eastwards began in the 1970s and '80s, by promoting the preconditions for peaceful change in the Communist bloc. To the surprise of most—both the Communist leaders of the Eastern Bloc and the elected leaders in Europe and North America—it was peaceable citizens' action, inspired by civil values and human rights, that ultimately brought down European Communism. The 'Final Basket' of the 1975 Helsinki Accords can be seen as akin to a secret weapon against totalitarianism. But it was not a secret weapon in the hands of 'the West'—it was a tool of basic human values, and it was the citizenry of Eastern Europe who used it and won the victory.

Subsequently, the OSCE has played a central role in extending the values of dependable peaceful change into the former Eastern Bloc. It has done this by setting values and standards which the former Communist countries can aspire to, bringing them one by one, little by little, into the European security community. Turkey is in the same category. Rather than a conventional regional alliance, which defines member states as an in-group, set against an external enemy, the OSCE—along with other European and North Atlantic institutions—has been a coalition *in process*. It does not reject European applicants to join, instead it responds, 'yes, but'. The carrots—and they are considerable, given the extraordinary wealth of the western states—are more important than the sticks. It is like a peaceful imperium, slowly spreading, regarding its borders as only temporary. The OSCE is a nexus of institutions and fora. Its processes are complex. It has many rules. The institutional framework is expensive. Implementing the obligations required by the OSCE and other European institutions (notably the European Union itself) requires considerable institutional capacity within governments.

There have of course been major problems. One has been the wars in former Yugoslavia, which have dramatically illustrated the limits of the OSCE's approach. (However, the fact that change in Belgrade ultimately came through civil means is a remarkable demonstration of how deeply internalized the security community's values were among large sections of the Serbian citizenry.) Another problem has been the refusal to entertain the case of Morocco. Other difficulties will arise if Turkey becomes a member of the EU, because this brings the European security community face to face with the problems of the Kurds, and the Caucasus, Syria, Iraq and Palestine/Israel. And lastly, the supplicant Eastern European states have lost much independence in the arena of social and economic policymaking, as they have submitted to the unregulated capitalism of the west.

The ASEAN Model

The creation of the Association of South East Asian Nations (ASEAN) in 1967 has achieved, over the succeeding three decades, in eliminating armed conflict between its member states. This is a considerable achievement, especially given the inauspicious preconditions surrounding its formation. At the time ASEAN was set up, many of the member states had been recently in dispute with one another and several had ongoing border disputes (e.g. Malaysia, which has border disputes with each of its neighbors). In addition, there is much cultural and political dissimilarity between the south-east Asian nations. They did not share a common identity. Perhaps most seriously, several of the countries have had ongoing internal conflicts (e.g. Indonesia's war in East Timor and conflicts with various separatist movements, the guerrilla war in southern Philippines). However, the geography of the region (notably the fact that the armed conflicts in ASEAN countries have been on islands) means than these conflicts have limited potential for destabilizing neighboring countries. And finally, none of the states have been liberal democracies throughout this period. ASEAN has also been ready to embrace highly authoritarian states including Myanmar (Burma) and Vietnam, provided they adhere to the ASEAN principles (which do not include human rights or democracy). During the formative period of ASEAN, the nascent 'security community' was however facilitated by a number of important factors. These included, first, the perceived common threat of Communism, in Vietnam and China. A second factor common alignment with the United States, which provided an overarching strategic security framework during the Cold War period. Thirdly, rapidly growing economies delivering unprecedented prosperity. Although intra-regional trade is less important than trade with Japan, the U.S. and Europe, the network of commercial and financial ties has been dense and growing. Lastly, none of the inter-state disputes in the region involved very large territories or military-political hegemony.

The ASEAN model is more modest than the OSCE framework. It is based on state-to-state relations. It focuses on security and stability, emphasizing non-interference and sovereignty, excluding reference to human rights, democracy and civil society. The institutional apparatus of ASEAN is far more limited than the ambitious mechanisms established in Europe, with much resting on the personal interaction of heads of states and senior government officials from the member states.

As with the OSCE, ASEAN began with like-minded states, but included a mandate that allowed it to incorporate others.

The toughest test for ASEAN was the recent economic crisis in Asia, with ensuing political crises, especially marked in Indonesia. The region emerged from this turbulent period without an inter-state conflict. Newly-independent East Timor has no reason to thank ASEAN or its member states: but the new nation will be too small and weak to play a significant role in the subregion. However, the incorporation of Burma with its highly repressive regime and insurgencies will prove a greater test. Should a democratic regime acquire power in Burma, what will be its attitude to ASEAN members that turned a blind eye to the abuses of the current government? An important shortcoming of ASEAN is that it provides no mechanisms for promoting internal conflict resolution or democratization within its member states. This may yet prove to be a critical shortcoming.

ASEAN has succeeded, however, in creating a subregional identity. This may be limited to the governments and may not have percolated down to wider society, but that is at least a beginning. The longer the subregional inter-state peace prevails, the more difficult it will be for ASEAN states to envisage fighting one another.

Security Communities in Africa?

Can the existing regional and subregional organizations in Africa can provide a foundation for an African security community or communities? Let us examine some significant historical experiences and models in Africa, which can allow us to pose some broader questions about what may be possible in the future.

The Organization of African Unity

The OAU is Africa's premier continental organization. Since shortly after its inception it has been the butt of sustained criticism from numerous quarters. From the leftist perspective, the OAU represented a betrayal of the Pan-Africanist principles that enthused Africa's independence movements. The preamble to the OAU Charter begins, 'We, the Heads of State and Government,'—from the very outset reflecting the statist orientation of the organization, which was to become, in the words of the late Mwalimu Julius Nyerere, 'a trade union of heads of state.' Repeatedly, the OAU insulted basic principles of democracy and human rights by agreeing to have some of the continent's most disreputable dictators as its chairmen, including Idi Amin Dada and more recently Gnassingbe Eyadema. All international summits have an element of theatre, but some OAU Summits have been more akin to comedy or farce. Other critiques of the OAU have focussed more on its lack of institutional capacity. It may have adopted many enlightened and far-reaching resolutions, but have these actually been respected? For example, the OAU's convention on mercenaries has been routinely flouted by numerous member states.

The OAU has, however, to be seen in the historical context in which it was created and first developed. Although a number of writers have described the background to the creation of the Organization, to date there have been no detailed accounts of the considerations and processes whereby it evolved in its first decade or so. Such an account would begin to identify some of the unacknowledged strengths that the OAU possessed, and might seek to regain. Some of the elements that might form the basis for such an account include the following:

1. The unity of the OAU itself. Until the very first OAU Summit, it was unclear whether Africa would have a single continental organization, or whether there would be two, one aligned with each of the Cold War blocs. The Unionists, led by President Kwame Nkrumah, wanted a single sovereign African entity; the functionalists, led by (among others) Emperor Haile Selassie, wanted to use the existing entities as the building blocks. This debate was never fully resolved, and the OAU itself was a piece of ad hoccery that simply postponed the question: what is the fundamental rationale and conceptual framework for African cooperation? Instead, the OAU developed in response to events, which in the early 1960s were fast-paced, dramatic and threatening. The Cold War was erupting into Africa at the time and the gains of African independence seemed in very real jeopardy. The very existence of the OAU as a non-aligned continental organization was a remarkable achievement, but possible only by focussing on prautilized concerns rather than basic principles.

17

2.   Non-alignment of the OAU. From the outset, the OAU had extremely limited room for manoevre because of the Cold War context. However, in a few instances, it did succeed in insulating some African problems from Cold War interference. Examples include the 1964 mutiny in Tanzania, the 1964 Ethiopia-Somalia war, and the Algeria-Morocco border war.

3.   The regular meetings of the OAU. Unlike a number of regional and subregional organizations, for example the Arab League, the OAU actually *meets*. It has held an annual summit every year and has regular meetings at the ministerial level. This provides for a level of continuity and the evolution of diplomatic practice that provides some legitimacy to the Organization and its decisions. The meetings of the OAU also provide an opportunity for all kinds of other bilateral meetings between Heads of State and foreign ministers. In common with most regional organizations, the bulk of the real business of handling security, building alliances, and responding to common challenges is conducted outside the conference chamber. It is notable that the OAU has not generated a regular parallel forum for NGOs or citizens.

4.   Principle of non-interference in the internal affairs of sovereign states. For many African rulers, this has been interpreted as a charter for doing what they like with impunity within their own jurisdictions. However, the stimulus for this principle was very different: it was the solidarity of newly-independent states in the face of interference by former colonial powers. The experience of Congo in the early 1960s was the leading case of the systematic subversion of a newly sovereign state by imperial interests. The OAU's member states were determined to delegitimize such activities. African leaders at the time were aware of the possibility of potential problems inside African states. The fundamental concern was that, to have allowed interference in the internal affairs of African states would have led to chaos.

5.   Principle of upholding boundaries inherited from colonial rule. This principle was reluctantly swallowed by leftist Pan Africanists in the early 1960s, who dreamed of dismantling colonial boundaries to create a single African nation. It was always contested by the Somali Republic, which harbored claims on the Somali-inhabited areas of Kenya, Ethiopia and the then French-ruled territory of Djibouti. (Which was in turn one reason why Emperor Haile Selassie of Ethiopia was enthusiastic about the principle.) But the key experience influencing Africa's leaders at the time was Congo, and the attempts by western mining interests to sponsor secession in Katanga.

18

6. The OAU Liberation Committee. Based in Dar es Salaam, the OAU Liberation Committee was entrusted with providing African diplomatic and political support to Southern African nationalist movements. This was probably the OAU's most successful activity during its history. It created a unity of purpose among African states that in many other respects had divergent interests. It is notable that even the most conservative states on the continent, such as Imperial Ethiopia, actively supported the continental agenda of liberating southern African countries from colonialism and Apartheid. Even while closely aligned with the U.S., Emperor Haile Selassie provided military training to Nelson Mandela. It is notable that this continental success was in a collaborative military-political project.

7. OAU Convention on Refugees in Africa. The 1951 UN Convention on Refugees was the outcome of the European experience immediately before and following World War II. Its shortcomings with regard to Africa were evident by the 1960s, and the OAU took the lead in adopting its own broader legislation concerning refugees. Among other things, the OAU Convention shifts the focus away from exclusively the individual fleeing persecution, to include groups affected by conflict. It is unfortunate that the OAU, having taken the lead in this area, has since taken no active role in monitoring the Convention or developing refugee law and practice in Africa.

8. OAU Convention for the Elimination of Mercenaries in Africa. This is the only international legislation of its kind in the world. Although it has some shortcomings (see Chapter 6), it is still the foundation for any envisaged international action on the phenomenon of mercenaries. Again, it is unfortunate that the OAU has not taken the necessary steps to monitor and enforce this legislation.

9. The OAU has been active in encouraging its member states to sign and ratify a number of international conventions, such as the UN Convention on the Rights of the Child and the Ottawa protocol on land mines. In both these cases, the African signatories were more than half of those required for the treaties to come into force. These treaties have often been honored in the breach. But the eagerness of African states to accede to them reflects a deep desire to be part of a stable, rule-based international order.

Clearly, there were ferocious external structural constraints on the development of a security community in Africa during the 1960s and thereafter. These doomed the OAU to be at worst, a hollow shell, and at best, a mechanism for salvaging some individual remedies for individual problems in a very adverse environment. There was no hegemonic power to underpin the OAU, and no dynamic economic processes to draw African countries together. In this context, we should perhaps be more generous to the OAU for its achievements, however modest they were, in the 1960s and '70s. In particular we should notice the elements of innovation and authenticity. Although the OAU itself was a pragmatic compromise, some of its activities were innovative and not in any sense copied from non-African models. (E.g. the refugee and mercenary conventions.) The OAU was in an important sense an authentic *African* process. However, by the 1970s its limits had been brutally tested.

The OAU has now lasted forty years. This cannot be considered an achievement in itself. Is it a learning organization? Has it adapted to the challenges of the post-Cold War realities in Africa? This question will be considered in the context of the CSSDCA initiative.

The CSSDCA utilized conflict Management at the OAU

The Conference on Security, Stability, Development and Cooperation in Africa (CSSDCA), is explicitly modeled on the OSCE, which was an inspiration for the initiative of (now President) Olusegun Obasanjo that resulted May 1991 Kampala Conference. At the time this was ambitiously dubbed 'the African Helsinki'.

The impulse behind the CSSDCA was the recognition that Africa's peace and security needed a new approach. The OAU risked simply becoming an irrelevance. Its structure and procedures were becoming an impediment to any effective response to conflicts in Africa. The complex nature of African crises, especially the way in which political, economic and security crises interact, demanded a much broader approach. The Kampala agreement focussed on the 'calabashes' of security, stability, development and cooperation.

For various reasons, progress has been modest in the intervening decade. But many of the ideas were subsequently adopted by the OAU, and the CSSDCA process still continues, now folded into the OAU itself. OAU decisions such as the 1997 resolution not to recognize any forcible change of government, and the creation of the Central Organ (akin to an OAU 'Security Council') and the Conflict Management Centre reflect the spirit of the CSSDCA.

Although the CSSDCA closely follows the format of the OSCE, in important respects it is closer to the ASEAN model. Notably, it follows ASEAN in stressing inter-state stability and respect for sovereignty, with human rights conspicuously downplayed. On the other hand, it follows the OSCE—and indeed the OAU—in its elaboration of formal agreements and instruments.

These characteristics have led to criticisms that it the CSSDCA a mere copy of non-African models rather than an authentic African response. This criticism seems to be somewhat misplaced. First, security problems have common elements across the world, and there is value to learning from the experiences of elsewhere. Africa is not unique. Second, many of the basic building blocks of African politics and international relations, such as the sovereign state itself, have their origins elsewhere (Davidson, 1992). Insofar as Africa's political elites are going to be part of an international world order that includes states, the United Nations, international financial institutions, and all the other institutions and arrangements of the globe, their regional security arrangements will also have to be consonant with existing international models in a similar way. Third, any organization or conference is a vehicle that can be used by its members to mobilize participants. Even though its basic architecture may be derived from elsewhere, it can still be moved in the direction of developing a specifically African praxis. The OAU demonstrated that this could be done in the 1960s. It can be repeated. An African ethic will develop from practice, and not philosophy alone.

The real questions is, where is the OAU's conflict management system including the CSSDCA going? Is it going to be able to deliver tangible results, which could be the foundation for the evolution of an African security community? Or are we going to remain at the level of ad hoc responses and initiatives that promise much and deliver little?

The danger remains that instruments and treaties for regional peace and security run far ahead of realities. There is a continuing tradition of progressive continental legislation in Africa. African countries have taken the lead in adopting international legal measures against land mines and child soldiers. Many have ratified the convention for the International Criminal Court. However, enforcement of these commitments has been very weak and in some cases it is evident that there has been very little genuine intention to adhere to the agreements. For example, Angola has signed the Ottawa Convention on anti-personnel land mines but there has been no indication at all that its use of the weapons has been reduced. Sudan has signed up to the International Criminal Court but is very unlikely to meet and mobilize commitments. (By contrast, Sudan showed greater honesty when it refused to sign the Convention on the Elimination of All Forms of Discrimination Against Women, because it is incompatible with its Islamic penal code.) In fact, it could be argued that signing and ratifying international agreements without serious intent to honor them only serves to undermine and discredit those agreements. There is a parallel here with many national constitutions: the legal frameworks are there for democracy, due process of law and the protection of human rights, but the provisions are routinely ignored or abused or undermined by governments. The challenge is not to draft and negotiate more agreements: it is to enforce the ones already in place.

East African Cooperation

Perhaps the most ambitious attempt at subregional cooperation in Africa today is the resurrection of the East African Community (EAC) of Kenya, Tanzania and Uganda in a new form (Magaga Alot, 2000). The EAC started as an inherited colonial apparatus binding together the three newly-independent East African countries formerly under British rule. Following disagreements between the member states, the EAC broke down in 1977. Tanzania and Uganda were jealous of the disproportionate benefits that accrued to Kenya, the most industrialized of the countries and therefore the one best placed to take advantage of free trade. Kenya was dominating, but not so powerful that it could impose its will on its neighbors, nor so economically dynamic that it could hold out the promise of an economic bandwagon that others could join. Just two years after the breakup, two of the member states were at war with one another. The subsequent mismanagement of the state corporations that had previously been jointly and profitably managed by the EAC contributed to the deepening economic crisis in the subregion. Cross-border trade declined and for some time the Kenya-Tanzania border was closed, with dire economic consequences.

However, a vestigial apparatus remained that allowed for continuing negotiation, used initially to secure an agreed division of the assets in the 1984 Mediation Agreement. This agreement also bound the countries to explore opportunities for greater cooperation. Public opinion and business interests helped push the East African heads of state to resume negotiations to restart cooperation. In 1993 they agreed to establish a permanent Commission for East African Cooperation and in 1996 a Tripartite Commission was established in Arusha, former headquarters of the EAC. In 1999 the Treaty for the Establishment of the East African Community was signed. This envisages economic and political union as the ultimate outcome of the process, with the establishment of joint governmental institutions including an East African Parliament as intermediary measures. Further cooperation was cemented by the January 2001 Summit of the three Heads of State.

The model has been cautious, led by governmental and business interests. Increased subregional trade and improved economic growth have been the fundamental aims of the cooperation agreements. Ultimately, the new EAC will stand or fall on the success of economic cooperation in delivering tangible benefits.

An essential precondition for the moves towards cooperation was peace and security between the partner states, specifically outlined in the East African Cooperation Development Strategy (1997-2000). The states committed themselves to maintaining peace and security, principles of good neighborliness and peaceful resolution of conflict, addressing the root causes of conflict and observing good governance, including promoting food security and poverty eradication, and preparedness of peacekeeping and conflict and disaster management. A Memorandum of Understanding on Defence Matters was signed in 1998 and the 1999 Treaty contains Articles safeguarding peace and security in the region. The possibility of any of the partner states going to war against each other have been massively reduced, while the opportunities for joint diplomatic and political action to help resolve conflicts in neighboring states (e.g. Burundi) have been enhanced.

These principles are fine on paper and encouraging. However, they have yet to be tested by a serious security crisis in one of the partner states. The security agreements remain ambiguous about the status of internal conflicts in partner states, with the implication that the existing principle of domestic jurisdiction will prevail. It is far from certain whether the states have yet achieved sufficient stability to be able to guarantee collective security.

The convergence has been greatly facilitated by the previous colonial and post-colonial histories which laid a foundation of common legal and administrative systems, and the use of the English language. It has also been aided by the changing economic orthodoxy, in which the language of exploitation and domination has been replaced with one of the common benefits of growth, even if it is not equitably distributed. Thus, 25 years ago, Uganda and Tanzania were distrustful of disproportionate economic benefits accruing to Kenya, while today they are more ready to accept unequal distribution of benefit, provided that all are gaining some advantages. Lastly, a highly significant component of the EAC is the East African Parliament, an elected body that will provide the EAC with a crucial element of democratic legitimacy.

Advocates of the EAC regularly compare it with the European Community, which, they argue, evolved over more than four decades to approach economic and political union. The EC was also founded on a much higher level of intra-regional trade and much more robust economies.

Hence, we should not expect rapid results from the EAC.

Basic Issues

Many other experiences from across Africa can be adduced, including ECOWAS, SADC, IGAD and various attempts at economic integration. There is certainly no paucity of inter-governmental initiatives. But all have a disappointing record. Is this due to the formidable external constraints they face? Are African states simply not strong or capable enough to be the building blocks for such systems? Or are there intrinsic weaknesses in the initiatives themselves—do they lack a coherent philosophy or are they not dealing with the right institutions and stakeholders? Or perhaps we are witnessing the slow and painful evolution of a new and uniquely African model of peace and security?

The remainder of this chapter asks four basic questions about the development of a security community or communities in Africa:

1. What are the preconditions in terms of internal peace within states that are part of a security community? Specifically, is prevailing internal peace an essential precondition for an inter-state security order? Or can internal conflicts be bypassed, or perhaps internal peace and inter-state security should be developed simultaneously? And, secondly, should internal conflicts within states be regarded as solely a domestic issue or as a question of international concern and engagement?

2. What are the preconditions in terms of an inter-state power order? Specifically, does a security community require an established inter-state power hierarchy (which can take various forms), and what can be done in the absence of this? (Another important issue, economic inter-dependence, will only be discussed briefly here.)

3. What are the preconditions in terms of democracy, civil society and demilitarization? Can a security community be established between authoritarian governments, or does it require the engagement of an active, democratic civil society?

4. What is the sequencing of establishing a security community? Specifically, if the above preconditions are not fully met, is it possible for international organizations to take the lead in establishing a security community?

Internal Peace

The concept and approach of 'security communities' is based on the sup-position that inter-state power relations are primary, and internal conflicts within states are secondary. This is questionable with regard to Africa, where most conflicts are internal, and many inter-state conflicts arise over-whelmingly from the internal problems of one or more states. In all the existing cases of actual or nascent security communities (Europe, ASEAN, North America), internal conflicts within states have been absent or rela-tively minor. The same cannot be said for Africa. This section asks, first, can we build inter-state security communities in the absence of internal peace within member states? Second, assuming that we can at least begin to do so, how should inter-state security communities handle internal con-flicts?

Can Inter-State Security Communities Precede Internal Peace?

The theorization of security communities implicitly assumes that each member state is internally at peace. In Deutsch's typology, security com-munities fall into two categories: 'amalgamated' and 'pluralistic'. 'Amal-gamated' security communities occur when multiple entities merge together into a single sovereign entity. The USA after the Civil War is an example of this; the United Arab Emirates may be another case. 'Pluralistic' secu-rity communities consist of associations between separate sovereign en-tities, that are willing to pool (and hence dilute) some of their sovereign powers in pursuit of collective security. They can be either 'loosely' or 'tightly coupled', depending on the degree of juridical and institutional interdependence.

Implicit in this typology is the question of whether African states, as they exist should not be considered as candidates for *internal* amalgam-ation to become security communities. In important respects, many Afri-can states resemble the USA before the civil war, with different territorial or ethnic components of the state extending their primary loyalty to these more localized components rather than to the state itself. Some African constitutions have been crafted with the primary aim of balancing regional and ethnic allegiances against national/state allegiance in the aftermath of civil war. (Nigeria and Ethiopia are cases in point, and Sudan will need to go through a similar process if its civil war is to be settled.) It is argu-able that before Africa can begin to develop interstate 'pluralistic' secu-rity communities, its states need to consolidate themselves as internal 'amal-gamated' security communities themselves.

Achieving the resolution of internal conflict is a question primarily for states' domestic policies. Some aspects of this are discussed in chapters 3, 5 and 7, which deal respectively with constitutionalism, engaging stakeholders in peace and post-conflict demilitarization. These will not be detailed here.

We can compare two general approaches to this challenge. First is the 'European' approach. This is to treat the internal conflicts of a member state as a subject for international concern. No European country engaged in a major internal conflict could become a member of the EU, until that conflict is settled and human rights are respected. The second alternative is the ASEAN approach. This is a non-interventionist approach that leaves each state to deal with its internal problems in whatever way it feels fit, with the implicit understanding that it will not cause regional destabilization in doing so.

Is there an African Version?

Is either of the two approaches appropriate for Africa? Note that both approaches are based on the similar foundation of building on a core of stable, like-minded states that comprise a subset of the region. Both Europe and South-East Asia are helped in this by the indeterminacy of their external boundaries: there is no easy definition of where the regions start and end. This makes it easier for a core of states to set up an association without being seen to exclude others on arbitrary grounds.

Adopting either approach in Africa give rises to the problem: where to start? No region—and hardly any major states—have the necessary preconditions. There is simply no stable, prosperous and powerful 'core' that could form the foundation of such a strategy. In addition, because Africa's continental boundaries are so clear, and there are already continental organizations that include all states, there is less geographical indeterminacy to be exploited. Once a formal continental security initiative has been set up, it will be difficult to exclude any existing African state. The African Union explicitly includes all member states of the OAU: it starts with the maximum.

This problem is particularly acute in the case of the 'European' approach, which relies on a high level of internal peace and civil society development for its 'core' states. Even South Africa, which is by far the most economically and militarily powerful state, with the most developed civil society, can only fit this description with difficulty. In particular, there is some distance to go before South Africa can be said to be consonant with its northern neighbors in terms of its basic values.

Adopting the ASEAN approach can bypass the problem of internal peace in the core state or states. However, this runs the risk that it might lead to a common security policy that added up to the indiscriminate repression of internal problems by all states. This would be a regression to the discredited days of OAU indifference to human rights and democracy. It would face the additional problem that few 'internal' African conflicts are purely internal. Most will, sooner or later, involve a neighboring country, through flows of refugees, the fact that major ethnic groups straddle international borders, or other reasons. In this respect, Africa is more like Eastern Europe than South-East Asia.

Africa has already taken steps indicating that it is charting a middle course that combines elements of the two options. Consonant with the European model, African intergovernmental organizations have taken the following decisions:

1. The 1997 Harare Summit decision by the OAU not to recognize the unconstitutional transfer of power, followed by the refusal to recognize the coup d'etat in Sierra Leone and support to military action to reverse it.

2. The adoption of the four 'calabashes' of the CSSDCA, which include references to governance and human rights.

3. The IGAD 1994 Declaration of Principles with respect to its mediation in the Sudanese civil war. These principles go beyond merely mediating in the conflict and lay down a set of basic principles concerning democracy, human rights, the separation of religion from the state, and self-determination.

4. The ECOWAS intervention in Liberia in 1990. This was the pioneering case of subregional responsibility for peacekeeping and conflict resolution. Although the ECOMOG force cannot be said to have achieved any of its aims, and in significant ways has complicated the situation not just in Liberia but in West Africa as a whole, the precedent has enormous international significance.

5. The 1999 Sirte commitment to an African Union, reaffirmed in Lome in 2000 and finalized in Lusaka in 2001, that would entail the pooling of much sovereignty in a set of common institutions.

On the other hand, there is also a strong element in African institutions that reflect the more statist approach of ASEAN. Notoriously, the OAU Charter begins with 'We, the Heads of State and Government,' rather than 'We, the Peoples of Africa' or a similar reference. Moreover, while the CSSDCA includes provisions concerning human rights, these are subordinate to considerations of stability, development and cooperation. And most significantly, the OAU continues to make decisions that are contrary to the spirit of its commitment to constitutionalism, such as the decision to appoint Togo as the chair for 2000/01.

We can ask, do the decisions taken at the OAU, CSSDCA and subregional organizations add up to an emerging doctrine of African security, that could form the basis of a security community? Or are these still merely a set of ad hoc initiatives, modest attempts to grapple with issues that are too huge and intractable for African leaders to see means of really solving them? But let us leave this question aside, and conclude instead that Africa certainly needs a combination of the 'European' and ASEAN approaches. Exactly how that variant can be made into a reality is the next challenge.

Strategies: A Linked Approach

The basic principle for an African approach should be that internal and interstate conflicts in Africa are inextricably linked. This is due to various characteristics of African political geography, the historical legacy of colonialism and the Cold War, and the nature of African conflicts. In general, we cannot solve interstate conflicts without also addressing internal conflicts, and neither can be resolve civil wars without dealing with their regional dimensions. In particular, it has become clear that an internal conflict in any one African country quickly becomes a subregional problem. The civil war in Liberia in the 1990s destabilized the entire West African subregion; the Sudanese and Somali conflicts have affected their neighbors, and the war in the Democratic Republic of Congo is affecting many countries. No threat can any longer be regarded as purely internal: all have trans-national significance.

Several options for tackling this problem include the following:

1. Regionalizing/internationalizing internal conflict resolution. African subregional and regional organizations should take the lead in internal conflict resolution within member states. This has of course occurred in many cases already. However, too often this means no more than the subregional organization or the OAU becoming the mediator and the forum for negotiation. Basic principles are rarely set out, and still more rarely elaborated into a detailed agenda for building a sustainable peace.

The IGAD Declaration of Principles (DoP) for settling the war in Sudan is a good model for how such basic principles might be formulated. Unfortunately in the case of IGAD, the adoption of the DoP was not followed up by sustained diplomatic effort to ensure that the parties really accepted them as a framework for ending the conflict.

2. Broadening representation in international organizations to include levels other than the state. This is partly a matter of making civil society fora function effectively. But other options can be considered too, especially for countries with federal constitutions. Sub regional organizations could, for example, include representations at sub-state level including states or regions of member countries. This could help to anchor sub-national identities within a wider framework of peace and security.

   Part of this approach could focus on conflict prevention mechanisms. It is unfortunate that an imminent armed conflict in a country is still an 'internal' matter, and international concern begins only when armed conflict actually breaks out. Regional or subregional fora that allowed for the expression of sub-national concerns could be a means of providing early warning for such conflicts, and also mechanisms for preventive action.

3. Institutionalizing concern for minorities. The OSCE has a permanent office of a high commissioner for ethnic minorities, and 'missions of long duration' in chronically unstable countries (usually on account of ethnic tensions). African institutions could create similar positions, endowing them with sufficient autonomy to relate to a wide range of international, regional, and subregional organizations, governments, and non-governmental actors.

4. Formalizing the legitimacy of regional concern with the powers and operations of security services. This is one of the most politically sensitive areas in Africa (and elsewhere). All agree that security services and armies should be under constitutional control, but there is no quick process whereby common standards of practice will change. A first step might be to agreeing on common standards for states of emergency and exceptional powers.

This list of challenges is a sobering one: it strikes to the heart of sovereign power in many states. It is a reminder of just how great the sacrifices in terms of arbitrary use of state power will be if we are to create security communities in Africa.

Inter-State Power Order

The foundation of all existing security communities is a core of states that can underpin regional stability. There must be a stable power order between these states, such that none feels its position threatened by another. Security is concerned with power, and the more obvious the power relations are, the simpler it will be to construct a security community. This is an historic reality. Whether or not the existence of hegemonic power is desirable, and whether there is an alternative route to regional peace and security that does not involve dominant powers, are separate questions that will be considered below.

The question of how to deal with regional rivalries and dominant states has been the subject of much analysis in international relations. There are a number of strategies adopted in response to different situations. Where there is a dominant power, the foundation of a security community is recognising the hegemonic status of that power—and then either accepting that position or containing it (Hurrell, 1995). Strategic options might include:

1. Smaller states may seek to contain the hegemon within a wider system, thus diluting its power and obliging it to act according to a set of wider rules. The dominant power thus becomes the core of the security community.

2. Smaller states may align with a dominant power in order to obtain some of the benefits of its hegemonic status, including protection.

3. The dominant power may itself see a wider coalition as a means of sharing the burden of its role, distributing the economic, military and diplomatic costs among other members of the community.

4. Smaller states may mobilize an alliance to provide a counter-force to the hegemonic threat. In this case the dominant power is outside the security community. Such a strategy also requires a long-term strategy for defusing that threat.

Where no dominant power exists, the creation of security communities is more problematic. In the case of both Europe and ASEAN, the Cold War was a crucial context: U.S. strategic interest in the two regions meant that the security communities could be nurtured against the backdrop of the U.S. as an outside protector. But where no such strategic superpower interest exists, it is necessary to fall back upon the old European idea of the 'balance of power.' This operated effectively in Europe for much of the 19th century, when the European monarchies decided it would be more effective to use their military capacities mostly for internal repression rather than inter-state warfare.

Creating stability or parity pacts between historic rivals is a strategy that can be envisioned for parts of the world where there is no dominant state. This may create a 'dominant axis' that can exercise the role of a subregional hegemon. Alternatively, it can entail a 'spheres of influence' approach, in which major powers decide to focus on their own backyards.

In all cases there is both the challenge of the objective existence of a potentially stable inter-state order, and the second challenge of enabling leaders to recognize this as an acceptable reality. This second, subjective challenge, is as important as the existence of the objective conditions.

Is there a Stable Inter-State Power Order in Africa?

Until the late 1990s, inter-state conflict in independent Africa was a rarity. Cases such as the Tanzania-Uganda war, the Somali invasion of Ethiopia, and the Chad-Libya conflict were sufficiently rare as to be considered as exceptions. It is rare for African states to have major territorial ambitions on their neighbors. In cases such as Liberia and D.R. Congo, it is notable that neighboring states have been actively engaged in the commercial exploitation of the resources of the collapsed country, but have not taken the opportunity to annex territory. (The Kenyan annexation of the Ilemi Triangle in Southern Sudan, facilitated by the absence of any Sudanese administration on account of the civil war, is exceptional in this regard.) In the 1970s, the situation certainly contrasted with the Middle East, India-Pakistan, and Vietnam, leading to the impression that at an inter-state level, independent Africa was moving towards achieving a security community. However, subsequent to the war in D.R. Congo and the Ethio-Eritrean war, we cannot be so sanguine. The different subregions in Africa can be briefly considered, one by one.

1. The dominant status of Nigeria in West Africa is clear but the dimensions of that dominance are open to dispute. There is as yet no consensus on what Nigeria's role in the region should be, or how other countries in the region should engage with it. Subregional confidence in the stability and predictability of Nigeria is limited. Nigeria is unable to provide either a model for good governance or an economic powerhouse that could uplift its neighbors. Hence while in theory Nigeria can underpin a subregional order, in practice it is some distance from being able to do so.

2. The hegemonic status of South Africa in the SADC sub-region is clear, but exactly what this amounts to is not yet the subject of consensus. Some of its smaller neighbors have accepted South African dominance (Lesotho and Swaziland have no option) but others are jealous of their independence and have sought to counteract its political influence in the sub-region (e.g. Zimbabwe). South Africa is the one country on the continent that has the economic potential to achieve rapid economic growth, and also provide the dynamism that could develop its neighbors at the same time. Collective economic advancement would certainly help create an environment in which mutual trust could be reinforced and a security community could be established. But currently, due in part to the economic impact of the HIV/AIDS pandemic, it is unable to do that.

3. In East Africa, the EAC is probably the closest there is to a security community in Africa. The three countries of Kenya, Uganda and Tanzania have developed close ties and multiple transactions at many levels, especially the economy, free movement of people, and common institutions. But the region is still subject to disorder, destabilization and tension on several of its borders, and the abilities of Kenya and Uganda to handle a smooth handover of power remain to be tested. In principle, were the three countries to act together with a common security policy, they could become a hub of stability for the region.

4. In Central Africa, the internal and inter-state power order is hotly contested. The potential core state of the region, D.R. Congo, is a force for instability not stability. Its mineral resources have attracted pirates from inside and outside the continent, who prosper from the ongoing insecurity. Meanwhile Rwanda, which has a major regional influence despite its small size, has a security policy highly colored by the experience of the 1994 genocide. There are groups in the Great Lakes subregion that do not accept the rights of others to exist, or to have any political power. Under these circumstances, the elementary preconditions for mutual trust do not exist. Creating a consensus on common security issues in this subregion will be extremely challenging.

5. North-east Africa is almost as difficult as the Great Lakes area. The internal and inter-state power order is hotly contested. Egypt envisages itself as the hegemonic power in the region, seeking to control the Nile waters. However, its historic role and the style of its diplomatic and political initiatives often prove counterproductive to its aims. It seeks to control rather than cooperate, seeing inter-state politics as a zero-sum game. Briefly during the mid-1990s, the Ethio-Eritrean alli-

ance provided not only a common front against Sudan but also a check on Egyptian ambitions. Currently, inter-state power relations in the subregion are in a situation of extreme flux, which has allowed Egyptian influence to be reasserted in Sudan. There is also rapid internal change within several of the countries. The subregional organization, IGAD, is very weak relative to the political and military power exercised by the states of the region.

6. In north Africa, the existence of strong cultural, historical and commercial linkages have not inspired a security community. The big states of the region, Egypt, Algeria and Morocco have to contend with the huge resources of a relatively smaller country (by population), Libya and its militant claims to continental and trans-regional leadership. Morocco and Algeria have a traditional rivalry for dominance in the subregion, which has flared into proxy war over the Western Sahara. This dispute has paralysed the Arab Maghreb Union and has led to Morocco's withdrawal from the OAU.

These are not auspicious conditions for the emergence of security communities within Africa's subregions. However, it is clear that the challenges of some regions—the EAC, Southern and West Africa—are much more manageable than those of the Great Lakes and the Horn.

The possibility of dominant powers in several of Africa's subregions is evident. This may be reinforced by selective representation of the biggest African countries at the UN Security Council. But is this acceptable to Africa? There is much resistance across the continent to the idea of domination by potentially hegemonic powers such as South Africa, Nigeria and Egypt. Medium-sized countries with assertive security policies such as Uganda, Ivory Coast and Zimbabwe are particularly suspicious of any system founded on hegemonic states. They would much prefer a security system built without any dominant states. For them, and other smaller countries, sovereignty is too precious for compromise. There is much criticism of the leadership failures of Nigeria under military governments, which is unfavorably compared with the more effective and enlightened leadership of some smaller countries.

The previous section has outlined possibilities of responding to regional hegemonies that do not entail uncritical acceptance of the leading role of that hegemon: for example smaller states can combine together to act as counterweights to a large state. However, any strategy must be premised on recognising reality. We may reject the idea that big states are entitled to exceptional status, but we must expect more of them, and respond to them differently. Thus Nigeria should not be entitled to act with impunity in the West African subregion simply because it is the biggest country, but at the same time it should be expected to play a more significant role in maintaining peace and security than, say, Gambia or Guinea. And clearly, any security system that gives leading roles to the biggest countries must also enable others to exercise leadership as well.

Strategies and Opportunities

Creating the objective conditions in which a security order may emerge entails resolving all the major armed conflicts in Africa. Without peace in Sudan and the D.R. Congo there is no prospect of a viable security community. This section will not detail the peace processes in these conflicts, and the associated conflicts in neighboring countries. Instead, we will simply point out that any settlements should be pursued with the wider aim of constructing a regional order for peace and security in mind as well.

Creating a stable inter-state order is more complex than establishing the ascendancy of a particular power or axis of powers. The nature of the ascendancy, and its relation to other states in the region, will need to be established. In some cases, we can hope that inter-state disputes will be resolved completely, or rendered irrelevant by other developments such as economic integration. In other cases, disputes or hegemonic ambitions may be contained. Whether this will result in a sustainable long-term order for peace and security is another matter: containing a conflict of this kind requires a continual investment of political, diplomatic and economic resources. It is also possible that conflicts will simply be frozen, perhaps for an extended period of time. This is not intrinsically a problem: it is often better to freeze a conflict than to fight it out. In the meantime, means can be sought for resolving the conflict or rendering it irrelevant. Without such measures, the dangers of the frozen conflict re-erupting cannot be ruled out.

Creating the *subjective* conditions for a security community is an area that has been less studied. It is important discuss the process whereby security interests can be identified, defined and pursued. If a government can define its national security interest in a clear way then it can react in a clear way to internal and external threats. That government's actions can be predictable, which is an important step towards achieving security. For some African countries, national security is little more than elite or personal interests of those in power. This makes for unpredictability and insecurity. Other, more institutionalized states, can define their interests in a wider sense and can therefore develop national security doctrines. They can develop analyses based upon their interests and core values, the threats they face, their vulnerabilities and capabilities. This provides the building blocks for subregional and regional security orders, as these interests and doctrines can be negotiated and accommodated.

In the long term, it is in the interests of all to recognize common interests in a workable security order. However, one difficulty is that militarized or securitized states do not tend to think long term, at least when it comes to security issues. Security thinking concerns survival, and responding to immediate threats. In most cases, African security apparatuses are structured so that they only consider short term threats and strategies. In foreign ministries and among heads of state, there is a recognition that a longer term approach is needed. But there is much confusion about what it might entail. (African governments have adopted medium- and long-term planning for major economic issues. Surely this can be replicated and developed in the security arena?)

One challenge is to stimulate long-term security thinking in a manner that is realistic, practical, and rooted in African realities. This means clear thinking about power, clarifying where power lies and how that power may be used. If it is to work, collective security must be in the interests of the larger states.

The crucial subjective step is to define national security for each state. Or, to be precise, open up discussions that can identify security dilemmas, security needs and what thinking needs to be done in order to address these issues. The rationale is, if leaderships can begin to define what their national security means then they will be obliged to think in long-term ways and to incorporate a wider definition of national security than simply regime survival.

An essential element of this agenda is to take the security debate out of the military and security apparatuses alone. National security needs to be defined as broadly as possible, and the concept and process needs to be owned by all citizens. National security is security for all, not just for the regime and its highest echelons. What is to be protected? Whom is security for? These questions must be asked, and civil society should participate in providing the answers. There is a clear agenda for developing discussions on these issues. This might take the form of 'seminar diplomacy', as practised by the OSCE, or a variant.

Discussion and analysis of the security needs of states may come up with some surprises. The very exercise of openly debating this issue will have an impact on what is defined as national security. Without public debate it is possible for extremists, irredentists and others to impose an agenda. With public debate the outcome is likely to be more moderate. But such discussions need to be carefully managed and scheduled: in some circumstances, public platforms give an opportunity for chauvinists and militarists to impose an agenda.

Economic Integration

A crucial dimension of any African country's security dilemma is, how to pay for national security? Countries that are internally at peace have neighbors at war and face external threats, real and imagined. The dilemma is how can a country in an unstable region afford to pay for the military means whereby threats can be met? Meanwhile, economic weakness itself is a big contributor to instability. Common security cannot be addressed without attention to the economic dimension.

In the European case, economic integration has been a key factor in the development of common security. The extraordinary economic success of western Europe has created a very powerful incentive for states on the fringes of western Europe to join the club. Meanwhile, prosperous economies in the West meant that there was something very substantial to protect: security became a more comprehensive issue. In the ASEAN case, the economic integration has followed a somewhat different pattern. It is 'open regionalism' driven by the strategies of multi-national companies, many of them headquartered in Japan, to develop globalized production and marketing. In north America, the U.S. has promoted regionalism as a means of achieving globalization, or at the minimum as a response to the perceived threat of 'fortress Europe' and a supposedly impenetrable Japanese domestic market. Meanwhile, Canada and Mexico have moved from trying to counterbalance their dependence on their superpower neighbor, to 'economic bandwagoning' on the U.S.'s phenomenal economic growth (Hurrell, 1995). NAFTA and the emergent hemispheric bloc are however weakened because of the capacity—and not infrequently the willingness—of the U.S. to override multilateral commitments in pursuit of perceived national interests, sometimes based on narrow domestic lobby groups.

In each of the three most successful cases of regionalism—Europe, East Asia and the Americas—the core has been dynamic industrialized economies that have been sufficiently powerful to dictate the terms of integration on their neighbors. The poorer neighbors have tended to accede because they see the possibility of joining in the process of economic upliftment. In East Asia this has been called the 'flying geese' theory of regionalism (Gilpin, 2000): the 'lead goose' is Japan, at the cutting edge of technological development. As it develops, the less advanced sectors are passed to the following geese (countries such as Thailand and Malaysia), where labor costs are lower, which in turn pass on their less developed sectors to the geese following them (e.g. Indonesia). From the point of view of the less developed countries, it is more akin to a nascent globalized economic system than a regional trading bloc.

An overview of regional economic integration elsewhere in the world makes depressing reading: the same preconditions do not exist in the African continent. African economies are poorly integrated, at least at a formal level. Informal economies (some illegal) contribute to a much higher level of integration, but do not necessarily contribute to security (Bach, 1999: 12-13). (To the contrary, the multi-national looting of the D.R. Congo's minerals is a contributor to conflict.) The African economy has a low level of industrialization, and is largely dependent on the export of agricultural products, minerals and labor. Within the continent, only South Africa has the possibility of providing the economic dynamism that could help lift its neighbors out of poverty—and the prospect of South African regional or subregional hegemony raises significant political difficulties. The prospect of tying African economic growth and security to countries outside the region—such as former colonial powers—is politically unacceptable.

The establishment of security communities in Africa cannot wait for economic integration and development. However, greater levels of economic cooperation and integration, and a reduction in poverty, will not only be desirable in themselves but are also likely to advance peace and security.

Democracy and Civil Society

Deutsch's initial work on security communities was aligned with the 'democratic peace' theory of international relations, namely that democratic countries do not go to war with one another. This thesis has been extensively explored in the intervening years, and several variants of the hypothesis have been examined. A number of questions are relevant for Africa.

First, is this phenomenon true of all democracies? Or are transitional, young democracies prone to conflict, perhaps as nationalist politicians use ethnic platforms to build constituencies? (The recent history of the Balkans and the former Soviet Union suggests that democratization may be destabilizing, at least in the short term.)

Assuming that the 'democratic peace' is a reality, is it due to the internal structures of liberal democracies, which place severe constraints on leaders wishing to wage war, especially against another democratic state? A variant on this, is it that democratic states are likely to pursue foreign policies based on trade and peaceful coexistence, that means that the preconditions for war are less likely to arise? A second variant is that democratic states might have domestic political processes that prevent the emergence of civil conflict, which might be the sparks for bringing in neighboring states and creating inter-state war? Alternatively, is it that liberal democracies develop strong social, cultural and political ties between one another, which prevent war between them?

Or, is a third factor responsible for this phenomenon? For example, could it be the economic success of liberal democracies that has been the main engine of eliminating war? If democratic countries face very severe recession, might they become bellicose? Or might they relapse into authoritarianism which in turn entails a likelihood of war?

A variant explanation, consistent with the general hypothesis of this book, is that the central issue in Africa is militaristic governance. Militarism is generally aligned with authoritarianism, but there are non-militaristic forms of authoritarianism, and some broadly democratic systems of government can also have militaristic tendencies. The hypothesis would be that militaristic parties in government have a proclivity to use violence, both internally and against neighbors, and this is a fundamental obstacle to the emergence of a security community.

Africa has too few stable democracies for the 'democratic peace' hypothesis to be testable in the African context. However, some of the experiences and approaches from other parts of the world are relevant to Africa. Our basic question is, which comes first, peace or democracy? The European and ASEAN experiences point to different lessons. The European model promotes civil society and democracy as an intrinsic part of the security community. The European experience of the ending of the Cold War was that civil society played the key role in bringing this conflict to an end. More recently, the bellicose regime in Belgrade was brought down by civil protest. In Europe, lack of democracy and violations of human rights are seen as a legitimate concern for all.

The ASEAN model values stability over democracy. As with internal conflict, it treats human rights and civil society as matters that fall exclusively within the domestic jurisdiction of sovereign states. The historical experience of South-East Asia is that democratization has occurred in the context of regional stability (though economic frustrations and internal instability have also contributed to the downfall of authoritarian regimes). To date, the African response is a mixture of the two approaches. Some aspects of this will be examined below.

Stability, Democracy or Both?

A strong argument can be made that stability is the essential prerequisite for the emergence of a democratic order. Democracy has historically emerged within the matrix of the sovereign state at peace. This is a context that has enabled social and economic processes to mature that have helped to create civil society, and enabled democratic activists to focus on democratic change during periods of internal crisis. In short, inter-state stability allows for internal flexibility and democratization. States need confidence that their neighbors are stable and predictable. In this context, they are less likely to develop over-strong military establishments and aggressive military postures, which are antithetical to inter-state stability and internal democracy.

In the African context, these arguments may be particularly strong. African countries have a high degree of mutual interdependence when it comes to security: conflict in one country is very likely to impact on its neighbors. Any attempts at democratization where no regional security exists are therefore hazardous, and are liable to be destabilized by insecurity next door.

The previous section has argued that the foundation for regional peace and security is a stable interstate power order, in which power rivalries are resolved, contained or frozen. Given the weak institutional infrastructure of Africa, it is more likely that these conflicts will merely be contained or frozen, rather than fully settled. But this provides at least a breathing space in which democratic systems can develop.

On the other hand, there are strong arguments for prioritizing democracy, for arguing that democracy itself is the main force for stability. Many conflicts have arisen through lack of democracy, and many people are fighting because they aspire for democracy. To deny them this right would be tantamount to challenging them to return to armed struggle.

A frozen conflict is a cause for alarm, because it will need to be addressed sooner or later. It may explode, perhaps with even more ferocity than before. So a security community that has frozen a conflict should also entail a means of addressing this frozen conflict so that it no longer becomes a problem. The most effective way of doing this, as illustrated by Eastern Europe, is the promotion of human rights and democracy. Civil society in Eastern Europe was the additional factor that resolved the frozen East-West conflict of the Cold War eras.

A similar argument holds for regime stability. The demand for domestic stability in Africa does not mean that countries should be left in the grip of rigid, unchanging regimes. Examples such as Ivory Coast illustrate the danger of governments that are so stable over decades that they do not respond to accommodate the changing demands of their people. Instead of stability for its own sake, what is needed is a constitutional order that can accommodate the need for incremental change in response to circumstance, and which can allow for the regular peaceful transfer of power.

Liberalism and democracy are all conducive to the development of transnational security communities. Liberalism implies tolerance, openness. Democracy implies the peaceful transfer of power and respect for human rights. Both imply the development of a political culture that can handle change, which is flexible enough to respond to changing circumstances without falling apart. By contrast, authoritarianism—particularly of the militaristic variety common in Africa—is a standing danger to security communities. Security communities are predicated on the demilitarization of regional governance.

Lastly, it can be argued that the real transnational community that is developing in Africa is at the level of civil society. It is members of religious organizations, NGOs, professional associations, academics and their civil society colleagues who are taking the lead in creating the networks that can be the basis for a future African security community. Governments are arguably lagging behind. Hence to prioritize states' concern for stability over citizens' demands for democracy is to hold back the processes that are already underway.

Both these sets of arguments have some force. In some situations, the argument for stability is stronger, in others the argument for civil society and democracy. But the African experience and the wider arguments suggest that the overwhelming need is for the right mixture of the two.

Perhaps the key issue is constitutionalism: this brings together the citizens' demands for rights and representation, and the state's need for stability and predictability. This is explored in some detail in chapter 3. It entails, first, restraints on the use of emergency or exceptional powers—demilitarization of internal governance. Second, the inclusion of all ethnicities in a shared national identity is essential. Third, it needs a popular, participatory process that involves all, so that all citizens can identify with the nation and its constitution.

A commitment to constitutionalism also has another major implication: it makes possible the formal construction of international institutions with real power. Any security community requires its member states to share some powers. Although transnational security arrangements (the OSCE is the classic case) do not formally involve surrendering any sovereignty (in contrast, say, to the European Union), they do involve adopting common elements of political culture by a number of countries, including most especially a commitment not to use force against one another. The commitments that are thereby undertaken are more like the unstated socio-cultural understandings that maintain a peaceful order within a state (akin to Britain's famous 'unwritten constitution'). But conforming to them involves abdicating much of the power so cherished by many heads of state—especially the power to use force. This is possible only in the context of constitutionalism. The only means whereby a state can surrender some of its power and maintain its legitimacy is when it has a stable constitutional order, and a constitutional procedure is followed to abdicate that power.

How to achieve the co-terminous development of stability and democracy in Africa? One possible scenario is that a powerful democratic state, or association of democratic states, form the core of the security community, and then admit other members when these achieve the required criteria. This roughly follows the model of the OSCE. Meanwhile, the international structures set up by the core state or states would help to promote democracy in the applicant countries. Such a proposal has the obvious difficulty that it is diplomatically unacceptable in Africa for states to evaluate one another's internal political situations. Moreover, it is unclear if the potential core states have sufficient democratic stability themselves to undertake this exercise.

The second strategy is intrinsically more difficult, but is the more likely trajectory for Africa. This is to embark on the exercise in a collective multilateral manner, using institutions such as the OAU and CSSDCA, and the subregional organizations. Such a process would have only very limited enforcement mechanisms, and few economic incentives to offer. Instead it would be founded very strongly on common moral thinking, and especially a shared understanding that common security is the basis for long-term common prosperity. This is an uncertain and very long term enterprise. However, it is the course that Africa is adopting by setting up the African Union, which aims to incorporate all the OAU member states from the outset.

International Organizations

Following on from the tentative conclusion that multilateral agreement and institution building—as envisaged in the African Union is likely to be the main mechanism for an African security community, this section asks, how? In what ways existing regional and subregional organizations can incrementally contribute to building mutual trust, strengthening transactions and exchanges, deepening common understanding, promoting constitutional values, and thereby bring security communities closer?

This final section begins an overview of the existing institutions and mechanisms in Africa. It sketches an approach. One of the most important tasks of the immediate future is for African scholars and policymakers to subject these organizations to critical scrutiny, and open debates on their roles and possible functions, based on the African experience.

International Organizations as Fora

An international organization can be just a forum for governments to pursue their own interests and initiatives. This is a minimum purpose, which is worthwhile as far as it goes. The OAU was precisely such a forum for a long time and this is still one of its major functions. Institutions that are no more than meeting points can be useful. Such institutions create the impression that the real business of international politics: security cooperation, building alliances, making economic deals, is transacted elsewhere, on a realpolitik basis, bilaterally between ministers and heads of state.

Most inter-African diplomacy is conducted in this bilateral, secretive and command manner. It is characteristic of militarized or securitized states, and is marked in other regions of the world that have high concentrations of militaristic authoritarian governments, such as the Middle East. This will continue, in some form, for the foreseeable future.

The drawbacks of such fora include:

1. Their moral authority is undermined by the addiction of member states to realpolitik. Commitments to peace and democracy are not given credibility when their sponsors are engaged in secretive back-door deals, and when formal commitments and conventions are not honored.

2. Such fora do not develop collective trust, and so they are not well-placed to develop multilateral cooperation among member states.

3. The institutions are unable to develop some autonomy with regard to initiatives; they are unlikely to have the legitimacy, resources or mechanisms to develop their own agendas and provide leadership. And, by their very existence, they may stand in the way of the development of other more practical institutions, that could for example actually implement enforcement measures.

4. These institutions can be 'set up to fail': they are a means of giving the illusion of cooperation without its substance. For a government determined to pursue a realpolitik foreign policy using bilateral mechanisms, it is useful to have a formal but hollow international forum within which it can act out its pretence of international solidarity.

Bilateral diplomacy and the use of the OAU and other fora as meeting places for these processes will continue. The challenge is to augment and complement them with other forms of inter-governmental and international association.

Stability Pacts and Security Cooperation

A minimum agenda for peace and security focussing on the most unstable regions is the development of stability pacts, with the aim of containing armed conflict. This is a minimalist agenda, which does not require a theorization of why wars occur, and what a sustainable security community would look like. It just needs a commitment to stopping the wars. For Africa, this would be an achievement.

To date, most security cooperation in Africa has been based on bilateral relations between countries, often conducted in a secretive, informal way at the highest level. It has been ad hoc, organized in response to specific threats and opportunities. As the conflicts between Ethiopia and Eritrea, and between Rwanda and Uganda, have shown, these kinds of leadership level understanding are fragile. They are prone to break down, in part through lack of institutional mechanisms that would allow the parties to manage their difference. Coalition instability is a feature of intra-African foreign policies.

Undoubtedly, bilateral deals, ad hoc alliances, and informal 'clubs' of like-minded leaders will continue. But their limitations are evident. What is needed is a more open, formal mechanism for establishing stability pacts, that will allow them to be institutionalized, and subject to some scrutiny and monitoring.

A basic stability pact in Africa would consist of two complementary commitments. The first is non-interference in the internal affairs of the other state, and especially no support for rebel movements. The second is a counterpart commitment to respect democratic principles, ethnic diversity and human rights, to remedy the legitimate causes of discontent within countries.

It is more likely that the first element will be taken seriously than the second, which may be neglected by all parties. Stability pacts may become little different to security cooperation that is intended to preserve the status quo and in fact put a brake on democratization. One can imagine cooperation on internal security matters (on the model of, for example, the Gulf Cooperation Council) becoming popular across Africa. It is also possible that such cooperation may extend to mutual defence if countries are threatened by a common enemy, though it is less probable that they would actually coordinate their military training, coordination, equipment, and doctrines. This is in fact militarized regional governance, which works solely in the face of a common external threat. However, even in the absence of a genuine commitment to democratization, any such security and military cooperation can prove to be a positive development. It can create conditions for stability, which is not only valuable in itself, but in turn can make it possible for civil society and democracy to develop. The pressures for, and processes of democratization have their own momentum that cannot easily be reversed by intergovernmental security agreements.

Economic Associations

Economic cooperation and integration has value in itself, and can also be an indirect way of promoting regional peace and security. Given their economic desperation, most African governments have sought ways to promote regional economic cooperation in the hope that this may become a means of promoting economic growth. The results so far have been modest, which also means that the sacrifices that governments have had to make in terms of giving up control over their economic command have also been modest.

If economic integration is to proceed further, governments must be ready to surrender some power in terms of economic control, and political/juridical sovereignty. Most African governments are not in a position to do this readily. Their revenue bases are too heavily reliant on extracting rent from their sovereign status, and they are understandably reluctant to surrender the control they have in this area, and introduce the measures of transparency that would follow. African governments have so little leeway in economic policy making, being so deeply in debt and reliant on the goodwill of international donors and financiers, that it is difficult for them to give up what little power they do have.

For some African governments, if they were to abandon most of their frontier controls, their patronage over awarding contracts, raising revenues, and nominating individuals to posts in which they too can extract rents, they would lose much of their raison d'etre. Some African countries would similarly have little reason for remaining sovereign: it would be titular status only. It will take remarkably farsighted and selfless leadership in Africa to recognize some of these realities, accommodate them, and provide the foundation for development opportunities accordingly.

There are important moves in the direction of economic integration. The EAC has been mentioned. COMESA is developing. Recently, the Anglophone countries of West Africa have signed a common currency agreement with the hope that after two years this new common currency will be merged with the CFA of the Francophone countries.

Globalization is challenging Africa's complacency. The challenges posed by globalization, the World Trade Organization, and the regional integration of the EU and NAFTA, is also pushing Africa to seek its salvation in numbers. Current arrangements for economic association may be weak and ineffectual, but as they develop they may gather momentum. Economic integration may in turn entail other complementary elements that can help lead Africa towards collective security. It is not possible to cooperate economically without also having some cooperation on regional peace and security. Economic integration also entails more than a common market in goods and services: it entails free movement of people, which has implications in terms of residence and citizenship.

Challenges of an African Union

The challenges of creating an African Union, as agreed in Sirte, Libya, in 1999 and agreed at the OAU Summit in Lusaka, in 2001, are huge. It seems improbable that the challenges have been comprehensively studied in advance of the proposal being put to the OAU member states. This discussion will outline two major problems with the idea, along with potential responses to these problems, and one major advantage it brings.

The first problem is that any intergovernmental organization that takes on real constitutional authority—judicial, legislative, and executive powers perhaps including military capacity—places huge demands of trust and due process on its member states. In Africa, for the time being, the prospect of governments yielding real decision-making, judicial, legislative and executive, to a regional body appears remote. In addition, any such body would undoubtedly be held to higher standards than many national governments would be comfortable with. It would demand a degree of transparency and accountability that would embarrass some member states.

A strategy for responding to this challenge must incorporate both the ideals of the African Union and the practicalities of making it work. The ideal is a continent-wide Union, and hence all African states should participate in establishing the overall framework and direction of the Union. The practicality is that some states are more ready for membership of a Union than others. Even in existing subregional organizations, we are seeing tendencies towards first track and second track cooperation. E.g. the signing of a common customs union by eight members of COMESA: the number that are ready have gone ahead regardless of the others. Also in ECOWAS, the security component has become stronger than the economic cooperation aspect. ECOWAS has also committed itself to the creation of a West African parliament, similar to the East African parliament that is planned by the EAC.

The idea of a 'two-speed' (or 'three-speed') African Union, or 'variable geometry', may be anathema to some states, which are jealous guardians of their sovereign equality, but it should be taken seriously if the project is to be feasible. It is also possible to envisage several semi-independent groups of core states, in different parts of Africa, first moving towards sub-regional unions, as a basis for a subsequent continental union. Africa already has many subregional organizations that could form the basis for this incremental approach.

The second problem is that economic and political union presupposes lack of armed conflict. In Europe the EU was possible because of NATO and the military umbrella it provided. The idea of promoting a union in a region marked by instability has rarely been tried before. One of the few cases in recent history includes the United Arab Republic of Egypt and Syria, which had a short history. The considerations outlined in earlier suggestions indicate that we must be cautious in expecting more rapid and positive outcomes in Africa.

How to meet this challenge? Establishing robust mechanisms for regional peace and security must be the foundation of any African Union. The scaffolding for any economic and political union must be the establishment of a security community.

Social and economic decisions will have important security consequences. For example, a guarantee of freedom of movement across Africa may help to lessen tensions arising from issues of disputed citizenship. The African Union process may lead to the creation of an African citizen, which will help nullify some of the issues of national and regional conflict. But many African states will be fearful of uncontrolled movement. Egypt, for example, is likely to resist any such suggestion because it fears the security implications of allowing Islamist groups to move freely.

On the other hand, the African Union proposal has one immense virtue. After many half-hearted commitments towards incremental progress, the idea of an African Union returns to the simplicity, idealism and energy of the early years of Africa's independence. By focussing minds on a clear goal, that is both Utopian and achievable (the European Union was an Utopian ideal fifty years ago), it may be able to mobilize governments, regional organizations and civil society across the continent in a way that has not been possible before. The African Union may confound its detractors and cynics, but only if there is a major investment in developing the institutions and processes at all levels that could make this dream into a reality. This in turn requires a frank and thorough analysis of the existing institutions and processes, and a commitment to creating new modalities whereby these organizations can work together.

The proposal to create an African Union provides an opportunity for civil society to engage and help shape the future of African organizations. Civil society was absent in 1963 but has an opportunity to make its presence felt in the current review of the OAU Secretariat and the OAU Charter itself. A number of issues are emerging. These include, first, how to make the African Union more a people-driven process than a government-led one, with inputs from a much wider range of institutions than only states. A second challenge is moving away from traditional economic integration approaches to a Union, towards wider issues of general human security and peace.

An Architecture of Regional Organizations in Africa

At present, while achieving the African Union remains a distant ambition, the main question to ask is, can Africa's existing intergovernmental institutions play a leading role in promoting a security community (or communities) in the continent? The obstacles they face are formidable.

1. The problems are severe and complex, and the institutions are weak. While ASEAN benefited from strong, stable states, and Europe had both capable states and strong inter-governmental institutions, Africa has neither.

2. There are strong vested interests in international organizations failing, or at the minimum not developing sufficient autonomy to exercise real influence. Many governments, both African and non-African, prefer to bypass regional and subregional organizations, and even sometimes undermine their efforts. Many African governments are also possessive of their sovereign privileges, and are thus averse both to surrendering any powers and to the implications of 'variable geometry' approaches to inter-state activities.

3. The relationships between the OAU and subregional organizations is unclear. To date, there has been no disciplined approach to managing these relationships. For example there is no forum solely for the senior executive officers of the OAU and subregional organizations to meet and coordinate their strategies: this has been left to ad hoc initiatives.

4. The formal mandates and resolutions of Africa's organizations are not matched by genuine collective commitments and capacities for monitoring or implementing these resolutions. There is an imbalance between form and substance. This is not a problem if the realities are regularly catching up with the aspirations after a time lag, but in the case of Africa, this is often not the case.

5. Most of the organizations are not situated at a nexus of power. That is, they are neither backed by a dominant power, nor are they a critical intermediary in the mediation of power relations.

6. Real enforcement capacities remain elsewhere. For mediating the most difficult problems and implementing peace agreements, Africa looks to Europe and the U.S. (sometimes bilaterally, sometimes under a UN umbrella). To date, this has been done solely on an ad hoc basis, without a coordinated analysis of how the relations between African intergovernmental organizations and the UN are interfacing.

This is a daunting list. What we see is not planned architecture but an amalgam of ad hoc initiatives, and stand alone institutions. Some work, others do not. Institutional coherence, coordination and learning is poor. However, the very multiplicity of institutions and initiatives indicates the high degree of concern about the issue of peace and security in Africa. The resolutions of these organizations, the direction in which they are evolving, and even their very existence, marks an emergent consensus about the importance of containing and resolving armed conflict across Africa. One of the priorities for the objective preconditions for security in Africa is creating a synergy between the existing institutions, enabling them to complement and support one another.

Given the lack of real power in regional and subregional organizations, much of the focus must be on developing the subjective conditions for security cooperation, namely developing common understandings of security and enriching the moral consensus against armed conflict and unconstitutional means of acquiring power. Meanwhile, there are also some specific measures that can assist making this institutional architecture into an operational reality. Some include the following:

1. Building the capacities for understanding, analyzing and warning of conflicts among African institutions (governmental, intergovernmental and civil society). Part of this agenda is 'seminar diplomacy', focussing on building and disseminating a body of knowledge about conflict, conflict resolution, democratization, etc., among key players.

2. Monitoring and following up commitments made, and at the minimum, documenting those who have failed to live up to their promises. The establishment and reassertion of moral norms can (slowly) contribute to changes in state behavior.

3. Working out relationships between the UN, OAU, regional and sub-regional organizations and initiatives, so that they work in complementary ways. Much can be done in terms of mutual learning, and formal and informal networking and information sharing.

4. Finding means of engaging with civil society initiatives, so that they complement and augment inter-state processes.

Given the absence of real mechanisms for enforcement in the hands of African institutions, much of the work for the foreseeable future must consist in developing consensus, thereby promoting the subjective conditions for a possible peace and security order.

Conclusion

Conditions are not auspicious for the development of a robust framework for regional peace and security in Africa. Many of the basic preconditions for establishing security communities have not been met. The opportunities for following either the OSCE or ASEAN models are not encouraging.

However, Africa should not feel constrained to follow the same path as Europe or Asia. An African path towards common security can be developed that reflects the unique problems, challenges and opportunities in Africa. Above all this entails linking regional peace and security to internal conflict resolution and governance in African states, utilizing the existing architecture of regional and subregional organizations as a key component.

The challenges Africa is confronting the call for 'thinking the unthinkable' and being creative in responding to these challenges. Other regions can provide lessons and parallels but Africa has to develop its own collective institutions through its own political will. The much-maligned slogan 'African solutions to African problems' does not mean that Africa is an island untouched by global forces, but is a call for African ownership and originality in these matters.

3

CONSTITUTIONALISM AND CONFLICT PREVENTION

This chapter asks the question: in what ways can constitutional rule avert or contain conflict? And, on the assumption that constitutions, well-drafted and well-implemented, can play a role in conflict prevention, how can we promote constitutionalism in some of the most conflict-prone countries of Africa? But constitutions also have their limits. They are not a solution to every problem. They can have a totemic status. One of the symbols of an independent state is a constitution, and a government can use the label 'unconstitutional' to make any activity seem tantamount to treason. While accepting the importance of democratic constitutionalism, this chapter also seeks to examine its weaknesses in Africa today.

Our basic argument in this chapter is that constitutionalism can work in three main ways to prevent or contain conflict. Underpinning each of these is the basic argument that constitutionalism is opposed to militaristic forms of governance.

First, constitutionalism provides means of non-violent, civil and democratic representation whereby individuals and groups can express their aspirations and grievances, thereby preventing recourse to violence. However, constitutional rule has in some cases led to weak or paralysed government, and democracy has led to government that is captured by special interests, preventing governments from planning strategically for the future. Constitutions can be used to perpetuate tyranny or entrench privilege and inequality. Can some constitutions give citizens inflated expectations, fuelling their grievances? The mere existence of a good constitution may not be enough to guarantee the resolution of conflicts peacefully. The process of bringing the constitution about and the integrity of the constitution are also very important. Otherwise constitutions could be used to justify or legitimize unequal power relations or an unfair political order.

Second, constitutionalism ensures legality (especially separation of powers) and should promote transparent decision-making in the executive, which in turn means that arbitrary measures likely to provoke violence are less likely. Against this, it can be argued that every government, including the most constitutionally-constrained such as the U.S. or Germany, has a secretive executive. It may be the political culture and activism of opposition parties, newspapers, etc., that is the key to promoting legality and transparency. There are those who will argue that matters of national security are often too sensitive and often have to be decided quickly, so that they may not be open to democratic discussion or control. The powers of declaring war may be constitutionally vested in the president, subject to parliamentary approval, but it is not unusual for such powers to be exercised without reference to parliament, which may just be presented with a fait accompli. In some cases war could be a creeping process or disguised as a routine law and order matter. Constitutionalism can be a cover for militarism, both in internal and inter-state governance.

Third, constitutional rule provides mechanisms for managing change, including new aspirations and grievances among citizens, and the peaceful transfer of power. African countries have suffered from inadequate mechanisms for transfer of power, so that there tends to be either extreme regime stability to the point of paralysis (followed by violent changes that come too late), or acute disorder without effective government at all. Constitutions should be able to prevent both of these extremes. But on occasions constitutions may also imprison countries, making it more difficult to make the rapid and flexible changes that may be required.

The chapter will focus on the following central issues in constitutionalism and its relation to conflict, both internal and inter-state. Each major theme can be seen as an enemy of constitutionalism.

The first theme is emergency powers, including the doctrine of 'exceptionalism', and the removal or suspension of constitutional constraints on the use of force by the executive. Exceptionalism the main underpinning for avowedly constitutional militaristic governance. However, there are also legitimate uses for emergency powers. How are governments to be given the necessary means to deal with violent threats, without entitling them to assume unlimited arbitrary powers?

The second issue is failure to respect the rights of minorities, or the failure to manage diversity. Democracy implies majority rule, which can entail the marginalization of minorities, and the imposition of other measures that have majority support but which may entail violations of rights (such as Islamic law). Marginalization of certain ethnic, religious or regional groups is often a recipe for violent conflict. Failure to manage political competition between diverse communities can create conflict. But there are also strong arguments against giving special rights to ethnic entities. How are we to balance the demands of minorities with the demands of stability, statehood and globalization?

Thirdly, we will consider lack of legitimacy and 'ownership' of a constitution. If the citizens of a country are aware of their constitution and the rights it awards them, they are more likely to resist unconstitutional rule than if not. The processes of constitution-making and constitutional implementation are vital: how to ensure that the people of a country—and *all* the people—feel that the constitution represents them?

Finally we must ask, is a constitution implemented or enforced? Some constitutions contain the most wonderful wording about democracy and human rights, but these are wholly ignored by those in power. For example the independence constitution of Malawi was a model in this respect, but President Hastings Banda made a mockery of the constitution through his style of rule.

Emergency Powers

A study of the recent history of Africa suggests that emergency or exceptional powers are over-used by governments and this is a major contributory cause of conflict, both internal and international. It follows that a close analysis of emergency powers and how they can be constrained is an important facet of peace and security. The doctrine of exceptionalism has widespread acceptance in Africa's political cultures and has generated its own jurisprudence. The idea that exceptional events, including threats to national security and natural disasters, warrant exceptional responses, is widely accepted. This even includes the idea that the executive can violate human rights with impunity in these circumstances.

How are emergency powers assumed? There are four main ways. The first and commonest is by coup d'etat. Two kinds of regime appear to be most vulnerable to a coup: elected governments in a country which has a history of alternation between parliamentary and military rule, and military governments that came to power by coup themselves. Elected governments with a long history of continuous civilian rule, and countries ruled by a unified political-military executive arising from a victorious liberation war, display much greater regime stability. This points to one important contributory factor to coups: a history of coups, with the implication that the military has a tradition of political ambition at the highest level, and there is some legitimacy for organized violence in the political arena. It also points to the importance of well-managed transitions to democratic rule, to ensure stability.

This is not the whole story. Apparently very stable regimes, such as Cote d'Ivoire, are vulnerable to coups as well. This is a salutary warning that stability does not always entail legitimacy.

Historically, the coup d'etat has enjoyed some legitimacy in leftist circles. This dates back to the Nasserite coup in Egypt and the belief that a group of left-leaning nationalists such as the Free Officers could achieve radical progressive change by seizing state power. There was also a phase in African political history when coups by junior officers were invested with popular and revolutionary ambitions, described as a revolt of the masses against the generals and illegitimate political classes. The coups of 4 June 1979 and 31 December 1982 in Ghana and Thomas Sankara's coup in 1983 in Burkina Faso were typical of this. On the right, equally, some argue that a nationalist senior officer can prevent chaos and disorder by taking charge. For many, the question is not, 'is it right to have a coup?' but, 'is it a good coup or a bad coup?'

In theory, coups can be overcome by internal resistance. A courageous supreme court judge could rule a coup illegal, and/or the people could take to the streets to protest. In practice this rarely if ever occurs. This is indicative of the weakness of the traditions of the rule of law under an independent judiciary, and of mass popular democratic protest in Africa. If both these traditions are encouraged, then coups will be less likely, and less likely to succeed.

However, encouraging internal resistance has its dangers. What if the judges and civil society leaders who stand up are simply rounded up and detained, or worse? The Ghanaian constitution goes further than simply ruling military coups illegal: it also has provisions that protect those who challenge coups. How these provisions can be enforced is of course open to question, but their inclusion sends a strong message and begins to establish a body of best practice. The establishment of the International Criminal Court and the adoption of its statute by many African countries also opens the possibility of criminal prosecution of putschists.

The decision by the OAU at its 1997 Harare Summit to refuse to recognize the forcible transfer of power was a landmark decision. Implementing the resolution will take time, as the Organization and its member states do not have the capacity or will to respond decisively to every situation. The Christmas 1999 Coup in Cote d'Ivoire provided a test of the OAU resolve and it refused to recognize the regime. It is an important step: a strong gesture of intent that, in time, could make it impossible for any putchists to succeed. The fact that other international bodies such as the Commonwealth are adopting similar principles is also helpful. The logical implication of this is that constitutionalism will be regionalized, i.e. that there will be mechanisms for protecting constitutional rule that cross borders, and that each country will become guardian of its neighbors' constitutions as well as its own.

This discussion raises several questions. First, are there indicators that can be monitored that give warning of the likelihood of a coup? Clearly, deterrence will be much more effective than any measures to reverse a coup that is already in progress. What should be the responses, domestically and internationally, if the lights start flashing red? And, given that coups do not come out of the blue, and that the incumbent civilian regime may be sorely in need of reform itself, how are such governments to be supported and yet encouraged to make the necessary reforms?

Second, where a coup is in progress or has taken place, what are the appropriate measures for the international community—including African regional and subregional organizations—to reverse coups? In particular, what recommendations do civil society and democracy activists in the concerned have?

Third, more widely, what is the role for scholars and other intellectuals in examining the phenomenon of the coup in Africa? Do they have a responsibility to challenge the historical and ideological legitimacy of the coup d'etat? Can there be such a thing as a 'good coup?'

After the coup d'etat, the second most important mechanism for exceptionalism utilized is the imposition of state of emergency. Across Africa, all governments—whether elected or non-elected—have tendencies towards authoritarian or militaristic rule. The imposition of a state of emergency is one of the preferred mechanisms for manifesting this. There are many pretexts, some of them more credible than others, for imposing states of emergency. Natural disasters such as droughts and floods are one of the less convincing pretexts. Insurgency or the threat of a coup are more credible reasons. However there is a standing temptation for a government to inflate the supposed threats it faces, even to the extent of inventing threats, in order to take on exceptional powers. In many cases, 'democratic' government is little more than a façade for emergency powers that enable the executive to act in an arbitrary way. In Sudan, all elected governments have used emergency powers extensively. In Kenya, civilian governments have imposed near-continuous states of emergency in whole regions of the country, continuing the colonial practice.

Learning from the experience of Apartheid rule—in which superficial rule of law was combined with extensive use of draconian emergency powers—the democratic South African constitution contains much detail on how and when emergency powers may be used. South Africa also has the post of an inspector general for the armed forces and security services.

As well as allowing for arbitrary measures, one of the disturbing consequences of exceptional rule is that it creates an environment in which the security services can build themselves up as institutions beyond the reach of the law. Security forces can become autonomous institutions, extra-budgetary and accountable to no-one but themselves, the self-appointed guardians of state sovereignty. Their powers are easily abused and they can be a major threat to democracy and stability.

There are legitimate reasons for exercising emergency powers. Governments do face real threats such as terrorist attack, destabilization or invasion, and in these circumstances they will need to impose a state of emergency.

There are international standards governing states of emergency: when they can be imposed, what powers can be assumed, how the security forces should behave, and how they should be monitored, reviewed and lifted. Several questions arise with regard to making such standards effective and operational throughout Africa. The first set of questions is, how widely known are international standards governing emergency powers? Should there be a specifically African convention on this subject or is there only a need for greater education on the standards that are already developed? A related set of questions is, what sorts of threat should be considered as legitimate reasons for emergency powers? Do we need a typology of threats, each with its appropriate powers to react? Concerning human rights protection, there is a need to ask what powers should be included under states of emergency? What individual rights should never be abrogated? Lastly, it is necessary to ask, who has the right to impose emergency powers? What process of judicial and/or legislative review is required? How long should the powers be exercised before they are reviewed? Should they automatically lapse after a certain period?

A third mechanism for emergency rule is a unified political-military executive refusing to relinquish its exceptional powers after a military victory. Africa is remarkable in having a substantial number of governments that spring directly from liberation movements that achieved military victory, either over a colonial power or over an incumbent post-colonial regime. These have proved some of the most stable regimes on the continent, in terms of their ability to hang on to power. They are marked by unification of the political and military command in a single leadership of a close-knit group of former comrades in arms.

A number of factors all contribute to a resistance to political liberalization. These include: a left-leaning political ideology, strong personal commitment to social and political ideals, and established structures for mass mobilization. Moreover, the first steps of a liberation front on taking power are to consolidate control. Typically, after a civil war, government institutions and key economic sectors are controlled by groups whose loyalties lie with the former regime and what it stands for. Hence, initial steps are likely to be towards greater centralization and control, including intervention in ownership of the economy and the appointments to the civil service, including the judiciary. Once power is centralized in this way it can be very difficult to liberalize.

Also, liberation movements have rivals and take power in the context of militarily-contested state power. Hence, opposition parties are likely to be rival armed groups, initially at least. In this context, political pluralism may imply civil war. It is logical to create a de facto one-party state at first, with the idea of a subsequent transition to multi-party democracy. But the first step is rather easier than the second. Experience shows that most liberation movements in power continue to consolidate power in the years after their victory, and that dissent becomes less tolerated as the regime consolidates itself.

It is possible that the phenomenon of former guerrillas in government is the outcome of a particular historical period in Africa, which will not recur. But a range of important issues still need to be addressed. How can executive, legislative and judicial powers be separated in a post-victory liberation movement that has become a government? How can government, army and party be separated in these circumstances? What are the appropriate periods to allow for transition to constitutional rule, separation of powers and institutions, etc.? If regime stability is to be valued, should this transition be a slow process? If democratic rights are to be valued, should it be a quick one, perhaps at the cost of political stability? And, lastly, are there means of liberalizing *within* the single-party hegemony that can be pursued without jeopardizing regime stability?

A fourth route to exceptionalism occurs when a government simply refuses to relinquish power. Whatever means governments utilized to come to power, they are likely to seek ways to retain it. African heads of state are well-known for seeking to rewrite constitutions to enable them to seek additional terms of office, or to prevent potential adversaries from standing against them. One tactic is to rewrite citizenship laws so that opposition candidates are no longer eligible to stand for election. Although a sitting head of state may initially believe that only a minor legal change is required, in fact the decision to subvert the possibility of a peaceful and legal transfer of power has very far-reaching consequences. Very often, the incumbent has to then assume wide-ranging special powers to enforce his decision and to suppress the popular discontent it may have provoked.

Liberation movements that have fought long wars to gain power are likely to be very unwilling to relinquish office to others who have not fought or sacrificed so much. They will tend to justify their continued hold on power on the basis of their own protracted struggle and heavy sacrifice—implicitly legitimizing armed struggle as the only means of taking power. They may intimidate opposition parties with the threat of a coup, should the front lose an election. More likely, they will simply use their control of the executive, the media and the electoral process to frustrate free and fair elections, thereby winning a very unequal contest.

A variant of this is to formally hand over power to an elected leader, but to continue to exercise real power behind the scenes. This can be done if the transition is skillfully manipulated so that any elected leader is beholden to military patrons. In this case, there is only an illusory transition, that runs the additional risk of discrediting civilian or democratic politics.

National and international monitoring of elections is becoming increasingly common and more and more sophisticated. It is no longer sufficient simply to have no irregularities on polling day and during the count: it is recognized as important to have a free and open pre-election campaign, complete voter registration, party and press laws that enable democratic debate, etc. These measures make it more difficult for incumbents to fix elections in their favor. (But might these difficulties encourage some rulers to dispense with elections altogether?)

A variant of this may be called 'constitutional unconstitutionalism'. This is when a government uses measures that are allowed within the constitution in order to put itself beyond the reach of civil politics. A government can become a constitutional Frankenstein, enlarging its powers by apparently lawful means in such a way that it is out of control. Such cases raise the question, who has ultimate authority over the constitution?

Achieving peaceful and lawful transfer of power is something that very few African countries have achieved. There is considerable debate among African democrats and constitutional lawyers about how this may be promoted. However it is rare for the question to be posed to a head of state, 'How will you lose power? And what will you do afterwards?' Some questions can be posed in a more general manner. For example, should there be a continent-wide term limit for heads of state and heads of government? If this is not legally possible, are there informal ways to lessen the international standing of heads of state who have overstayed their welcome?

Another approach is to ask, can heads of state and government be given incentives to assist them retire peacefully? What special privileges and guarantees should be extended to a former head of state? For example, what pension should he be awarded? Could there be a 'house of statesmen' attached to the OAU where such figures could have due recognition as elders? How do such measures square with the growing demand for accountability, which means that some former heads of state may be brought to court for actions undertaken during their years in power? And should such privileges and guarantees be extended to other senior political figures?

This discussion also raises the uncomfortable question, in situations in which a 'constitutional' ruler has abused his power to stay in office indefinitely, can there be a 'good coup' to remove him? Or is forcible transfer of power to be opposed under all circumstances?

The final road to emergency rule that we will consider is a transitional vacuum in which the security forces acquire exceptional power. Transitions, after peace agreements or the dismantling of dictatorships, are periods of change and danger. In some circumstances a power vacuum can develop, which is filled by the security apparatus flexing its muscles. In such a case, the weakness of the executive can therefore translate into de facto emergency rule, as the security institutions arrogate powers to themselves. In some cases, security forces can foment unrest with the aim of justifying a military takeover in the name of 'national salvation'.

Can the management of transitions be planned and supervised in such a way as to minimize this risk? What checks and guarantees can be built into a transitional process? Should restructuring of security forces be one of the first components of a transition? This is primarily a task for political leadership and civil society in the country concerned (see chapter 7).

Internationally, there are possible sources of leverage. Where there are international peacekeeping forces or there is some international oversight over a transition, what levers should these external forces utilize for managing the transition?

Lastly, the phenomenon of permanent, unending or illusory transition needs attention. Any benchmarks or schedules can be manipulated and undermined by those cynical and determined enough. Governments can postpone constitutional rule by a range of stratagems. The ultimate guarantee on the success of a transition is not the degree to which it meets certain formal criteria for elections, legal reform etc., but the extent of genuine democratic participation by citizens. This is something that only citizens and civil society can achieve and guarantee.

Minority Rights and Management of Diversity

Repression of minority rights is arguably the single most common contributor to insurrection and instability in Africa. It can also contribute to inter-state tension, as many ethnic groups live in more than one country, and any measures against communities that stimulate refugee flows or involve expulsions will generate an international dimension. Although the debate is usually framed in terms of 'minorities', it may be more accurate to describe it as the challenge of managing diversity. There are oppressed and marginalized majorities as well as minorities in some countries, while in many others the problem is less one of deprivation of minority rights and more one of managing ethnically-based competition for political and economic rewards.

The issue of community rights can become particularly important under democratic governments, especially newly-elected ones. Democracy entails majority rule, which has risks for minorities. Ethnic minorities that enjoyed some protection under authoritarian states may find their position vulnerable during a transition to a multi-party system. Religious minorities—especially non-Moslems in a Moslem majority state—may become subject to discrimination through a majority decision to favor religious laws. Parliamentary systems can also promote competition between regional, ethnic and religious communities, compounding the problems of managing diversity.

Most constitutions recognize the individual as a legal being, and some (e.g. federal constitutions) award rights to intermediate institutions such as states, which may have an implicit or explicit ethnic color. Once the question of awarding rights to ethnic, regional or religious groups becomes a constitutional issue, complex issues arise. This section looks at three axes for analyzing this question. In each case, arguments for and against recognising special group rights are presented. The argument against group rights is presented first each time.

First, we have the *'liberal rights' argument*. This argument is based on the case that each individual has inalienable human rights, including freedom of conscience, assembly and expression. These individual rights should be sufficient to protect the rights of believers in particular religions and members of ethnic groups who wish to organize themselves, use their language, practice their customs etc., provided they do not infringe the rights of others.

Once we start to award rights to *communities*, however, we are likely to begin to impinge upon the rights of individuals, and may even create instability and conflict. Several possibilities need to be examined, from both points of view:

1. Communities' customs may deny certain rights to members of that community, especially women and members of small castes. A Moslem minority may for example choose to adopt an extreme version of Islamic Law that involves denying some basic rights to women. To some extent this problem can be overcome by national legislation that makes international standards of human rights enforceable. But if the issue is politically contentious, then it may be that the national or federal government thinks it is more prudent not to seek a confrontation with local or state authorities, thereby allowing human rights abuses to proceed.

   A counter-argument runs like this: In a mature multi-ethnic liberal democracy such an argument is valid. In such a case, ethnic or religious groups will have the freedom to organize, and individuals will have the option to join or refuse to join such ethnically or religiously based communities of their own free will. However, the reality of Africa is that these conditions do not exist. To the contrary, ethnic and religious politics is a reality and cannot be wished away. One instrument of ethnic and religious politics is denying cultural, linguistic and religious rights to minorities. For example the Nuba people in Sudan have suffered for years because many valued customs such as dancing, wrestling, etc., were suppressed by the authorities. This was one reason why many Nuba took up armed struggle against the government. For such marginalized people, constitutional recognition of their cultural rights is a sine qua non of their fair participation in national politics.

2. Individuals may not want to identify themselves with *any* ethnicity (or faith); they may want to simply be *citizens*. In Apartheid South Africa, it was an act of resistance to write 'human being' in the space reserved for 'race' in official registration forms. In former Yugoslavia, some citizens took the option of being simply 'Yugoslavs'. In Ethiopia after 1991, some objected to being required to identify their 'nationality' (i.e. Amhara, Oromo, Tigray, Gurage, etc.), preferring instead simply to be 'Ethiopian.'

   A counter-argument is this: For most citizens of ethnically complex countries, uniform national identity is only a dream. In these countries, ruling elites like to pretend that their (dominant) ethnic status is identical to 'national' identity. Real national identity can only be created by a realistic consensus, that begins by recognising that other (chiefly ethnic) identities are more significant.

3.   Ethnic groups are usually defined geographically, and members of other groups living in those areas may find themselves deprived of some rights. As almost ethnic boundary is blurred, creating an ethnic entity is likely to involve tensions along the border. Some individuals or communities may feel pressured to move, and will argue they have been subjected to ethnic cleansing. Alternatively they may find themselves in permanent opposition to the ethnic entity within whose borders they live. Hence, any form of ethnic federalism will create conflicts.

A counter-argument runs like this: In some places, different ethnic groups live together in harmony. In such cases, no-one would advocate creating political boundaries between them in a way that creates conflict. But the reality is that for many other ethnic groups, there is conflict already, and it is illusory to talk about 'creating' tensions. Often, the indigenous group is marginalized because of its lack of political and economic clout, so that, for example, it finds outsiders coming in and buying up land and mineral rights. In such circumstances, special legal protection is needed to prevent undue exploitation which will lead to violent resistance. The challenge is to find a way of containing these conflicts that delivers the best (or least bad) deal to all involved. There is no solution to an ethnic or territorial conflict that will satisfy all. Ethnic federalism is one solution, appropriate in some cases. There are special cases like Burundi, Rwanda or Somalia where the social geography does not conform to ethnic territorialism. What are the implications of constructing democracy on an ethnic basis that means communities are either permanently privileged or disadvantaged?

4.   Awarding rights on the basis of ethnicity (or religion) forces individuals to identify with communities. Thus it undermines the foundation of citizenship, and promote sub-national (ethnic, regional, religious) identification. The intention of creating a federal or devolved system of government may have been to lessen political competition at the centre. But in some circumstances it can have the opposite effect: it may create new locations for competition for political power, in the regional or state capitals. If the regions or states are ethnically homogenous, or largely so, then there will be greater temptation among leaders to play the ethno-nationalist card. Hence, a federal system aimed at creating stability may in fact end up by promoting fragmentation, conflict and even war.

The counter argument runs something like this: If we are dealing with a country without ethnic or religious tension, then this is correct. But what of those countries that are *already* at war? And, especially, what of countries with a history of genocide? In such cases, ethnic identity is so deeply engraved into the social consciousness and political culture, that there is simply no option but to provide special constitutional protection to endangered groups.

In conclusion, it seems that the particular histories of specific countries are an essential component in determining the balance between liberal individual rights and the rights of ethnic and religious communities. The received wisdom of modern western liberal democracy and the consensual assumptions behind it may not be grafted on to the African situation without modifications and creative adaptation. The preliminary audit on current democratization that is sweeping across Africa raises more questions than answers. States like Tanzania that have enjoyed relative political stability for a long time and built a nation state amidst multiplicity of cultures and ethnic diversities have seen new tensions and potential conflicts consequent to multi-party competition. Democracy and democratization have produced new conflicts that are testing liberal gains. A country like Nigeria may not be said to be democratic but rather to be 'civilianizing'. It appears to be far from being able to build institutions that can peacefully manage diversity and difference.

The second argument can be called the *'globalization' or 'modernization' argument*. This argument is essentially that, in order for a country to be competitive in the international environment or global economy, it needs to have a social, economic and political culture founded on individualism. If customary practices are protected by law, and local languages are encouraged, then the country will suffer in terms of international competitiveness.

This argument, and its counter-arguments, are complicated and subtle. Some considerations include the following:

1. Is there an incompatibility between speaking local languages, following aspects of traditional culture, and also speaking an international language and having access to the internet etc.? The European experience suggests not. The Finnish language is spoken only within Finland (and is unrelated to almost all other European languages), but Finland is the world leader in mobile phone technology. On the other hand, can African countries support the educational infrastructure to allow multilingual teaching? Do they have an alternative?

2. There are different considerations applicable to different countries. For example, Sudanese who favor Arabism and Islam will argue that Arabic is an international language, and those who are proficient in Arabic will have access to an immense international cultural archive,

to the international Arabic media, etc. Some Ethiopians who would like all their fellow citizens to use the Amharic language cannot make such a strong argument, because although Amharic has the richest literature and media in Ethiopia, it is not an international language comparable to Arabic. In most African countries, English or French is the language that allows citizens to become members of the global information system and global economy.

3. The 'modernization' version of this argument was common in the 1960s and '70s, when it was expected that the route to development lay through industrialization, which entails urbanization and the development of a working class. In turn these imply some cultural homogenization. However, in the global information age, the qualities that promote competitiveness may be different. Cultural richness and diversity may be a great asset. Tourism, entertainment, and music are rapidly growing sectors of the world economy. Those with the greatest cultural diversity to draw upon may be those best placed to exploit these niches. The ideal is therefore to combine global access, high levels of education, with cultural richness and authenticity.

The globalization argument has no answer. Rather it poses questions and challenges, which are especially relevant to economic and social policymakers. One consideration is key, however: it is only countries that are free of violent conflict that stand any chance of achieving rapid development such that they can compete in the global economy.

The third argument is the *leftist or Marxist argument*. This argument opposes granting special rights to ethnic groups on the grounds that the problems are economic disparities and uneven development, and that ethnic consciousness and conflict is merely a symptom of this deeper problem. Under this approach, nationalism and ethnic consciousness is a transitional stage. For example, many Marxists in Sudan have argued that regional ethnic consciousness is merely a reflection of the exploitation of these areas by the central regions in which economic development has been concentrated. They argue that although resistance in the South, West and East of Sudan has taken on an ethnic color, in fact the fundamental problems are land alienation, unequal provision of education and other services, and other mechanisms of under-development that force many from the regions to become labor migrants to the agricultural schemes and cities of the centre. Resolve these economic inequalities, and the ethnic problem would disappear.

The counter-argument to this is that history does not support it. Nationalism and ethnic feeling have not died away. The historical fact is that ethnicity matters, a lot. Note that when Communists were presented with

64

the reality of nationalism and ethnicity, as in the former USSR, they evolved their own theories and set up a federation based on nationalities in order to cope with this.

In addition, it is perhaps optimistic to expect that the problem of uneven development will be solved. At least, it will not be solved quickly. In the meantime, are the minorities not entitled to some rights?

However, the Marxist critique makes an important point: economic inequalities should not be overlooked in any analysis of ethnic or religious discord. While it may be futile to try to ignore ethnicity and simply to address the economic challenges of unequal development, equally it would be wrong simply to treat ethnic conflict as a matter that can be resolved through administrative or constitutional mechanisms. No matter how robust the legal protection of a minority, it will be worth little if that minority remains without any economic clout. If there is a federal system in which one state, or the federal government, retains overwhelming economic power, then the system will be a sham.

The three arguments outlined here, and their variants, will not be resolved quickly, if at all. One challenge for constitutions is to recognize what can be resolved through constitutional means, and what cannot and must instead be left to other mechanisms of politics and social and economic planning.

Clearly, the issue of minority or community rights is not one for which there is a right answer. All circumstances are different, and all are subject to change. All are the outcomes of particular histories. Constitutional measures for protecting minority rights are more akin to a gyroscope than a cast iron guarantee: they are a mechanism that must be subject to adjustment over time.

Constitutional Process

The third main area of discussion for this chapter is the question of the legitimacy or 'ownership' of a constitution. Clearly, if the citizens of a country know little and care less about their constitution, it will be easy for a government to override it. If, however, they feel that the constitution affects their lives in a positive way, and they are mobilized to defend their constitutional rights, then the legislature and executive will be much more cautious. In the U.S., the gun lobby is so powerfully mobilized around the constitutional right to bear arms that successive governments have been unable to challenge them, despite the overwhelming evidence that easy access to firearms causes thousands of unnecessary deaths in America every year.

At a very general level, there are two models of constitution. One is a short and simple constitution (or in the British case, an unwritten one). In countries with a long tradition of rule of law and peaceful and regular transfer of power, such constitutions may be appropriate. The second model is an elaborate constitution in which a wide range of rights and duties are spelled out in detail. Most African countries have such constitutions (or would, if they were able to adopt a constitution). The rationale for this is that they tend not to have long continuous histories of lawful government, and therefore much more needs to be spelled out in the basic law.

Most African constitutions have been revised or radically changed since independence. The revised constitutions usually reflect an attempt to remedy the problems existing immediately before the new constitution was adopted. They are attempts to try to learn the lessons of the immediate past. Many also try to look further back into history and learn lessons from decades ago. But as times change, all will need to adapt to accommodate new realities. No constitution can be a panacea; it cannot anticipate and prevent all future problems.

Three questions dominate. One is how a constitution is arrived at, the second is, how it is implemented (i.e. how institutions are made to function in accordance with the constitution, and how citizens come to understand, accept, support and defend it), and the third is, how is a constitution reviewed?

First, how is the current constitution arrived at? Here we may identify a number of processes used historically to adopt and change constitutions in Africa.

1. Inherited constitution from a colonial hand-over of power. These constitutions were generally formulated more or less along the model of that of the former colonial power. They may be criticized as foreign implants. Few have lasted. But many basic principles have been retained, such as separation of powers. Although these principles have mostly been honored in the breach, there is at least an acceptance that such principles are basic to a democratic constitution. By the very fact of these principles being retained for decades, they have acquired some stature and legitimacy.

2. Constitutions adopted during the handover from military to civilian rule. Currently, the most significant case in Africa is Nigeria, though there are other important instances that are variants. Such constitutions are typically adopted in order to placate domestic and international pressure for democratization, while preserving important elements of the power and privilege of the military. Because of this it is

unusual for the constitution-making process to include widespread popular participation or democratic decision-making. Such constitutions are typically highly elitist, and would not stand up well to democratic scrutiny or popular participation in their revision.

3. Constitution negotiated between parties as part of a peace (perhaps under the auspices of a third party negotiator such as the UN, the Commonwealth or the OAU). (Variants include South Africa, Namibia, Zimbabwe, and Mozambique.) Such constitutions are less formulaic than independence handover constitutions, because they have gone through lengthy processes of negotiation between different parties, and in some cases reflect a history of previous failed constitutional experiments. Because they are the outcome of these sometimes fierce processes of negotiation, these constitutions may be very robust, accurately reflecting the true balance of power in the country. On the other hand, pragmatic compromises made simply to achieve an agreement may become elevated to become permanent constitutional principles.

4. 'Revolutionary' constitutions adopted by fiat by victorious belligerent parties. No such constitutions now exist. Perhaps the closest are the Ethiopian and Ugandan constitutions, adopted after wide consultation but with the domination of a single party. These constitutions may be the most innovative; for example Ethiopia's introduction of nationality-based federalism and Uganda's 'no-party' system. They may thereby find creative solutions to major structural problems that have bedeviled the state. On the other hand, such constitutions may not command universal assent from citizens, some of whom may see them as imposed by a victorious party.

5. Theocratic constitutions adopted by religiously-oriented states. The Sudanese constitution is an example. In the Arabic text it is evident that authority is vested in Islamic Law as interpreted by select scholars (the English version appears considerably more liberal). While theocratic principles may command legitimacy among believers (or some of them at least), such constitutions are likely to exclude substantial groups from full enjoyment of their rights, and will become a source of conflict.

6. Constitution drafted by specialists brought in for the purpose by a government. A case of this is the unrecognized Republic of Somaliland, which hired legal experts to draw up a constitution. Some processes of constitutional review (e.g. Nigeria) have also been opaque, elitist and remote from any participation by ordinary people. This process has the virtue of being potentially rapid.

7. Constitutions adopted by a process of popular consultation and participation. While several constitutional drafting processes have involved wide consultation, the Eritrean constitutional exercise was exceptionally wide ranging in how it involved a wide section of the populace, actively soliciting their views.

In this context, the issue of group participation can be as important as widespread participation by individual citizens. In a multi-ethnic state, historically-constituted ethnic constituencies may seek to safeguard their interests and identities within the state, at the expense of the legitimacy of the common national constitution. A Bill of Rights that awards rights to citizens may not be sufficient (as indicated in the section on ethnic minorities, above). Finding answers to the questions of safeguarding ethnic identities within the constitution is an issue for the *process* of constitution-drafting, as well as the substance resulting in the constitution itself.

Most constitutions involve a mixture of the above. In addition, we may note that many are, at least in part, evolved constitutions, amended over a period by parliamentary procedures, decisions by an activist judiciary, peace agreements with insurrectionary parties, popular referenda or other methods.

In Europe, constitutions have evolved because national governments have signed up to the Single European Act and have agreed that the European Court of Human Rights has jurisdiction. African constitutions have yet to move far down this road, but with the rise of the influence of subregional and regional organizations, and the commitment to a future African Union and its continental juridical institutions, this will be an important issue for the future.

Can we say that any one procedure is better than another? Or is each appropriate to a particular set of political and historical circumstances? Arguments can be adduced in favor of each constitutional process. Perhaps just as important as the type of constitution is the process whereby it is implemented, changed from being a piece of paper into a living reality.

A second question is, how is the constitution implemented? We must distinguish between the formal, paper constitution, and the real, living constitution that informs the power relations between executive (including military and security forces), legislature, judiciary, and people. By focussing on 'real' constitutions we can see, for example, that exceptionalism is in fact the rule and not the exception at all. Most African executives seek to bypass constitutional procedures whenever possible, especially as regards security affairs. Too often, legislatures and judiciaries readily comply without examining the constitutional implications of emergency actions. This highlights the importance of constitutional implementation: this is how citizens can restrain the arbitrary exercise of power.

The implementation of a constitution includes the following general principles (the actual implementation will of course depend on what is included in the constitution in question):

1.   Actions by the relevant arms of government to ensure that the legal and institutional aspects of the constitution are in place. If the constitution demands a federal system, then the executive is obliged to set up the relevant structures. If it demands a multi-party system, then the requisite laws should be drafted and passed into law as quickly as possible.

     In terms of the prevention and containment of conflict, it is particularly relevant to ask what are the relevant constitutional procedures for (a) enacting emergency powers, (b) declaring a state of war, and (c) authorizing the use of force outside these procedures. How are these constitutional provisions to be followed, enforced and monitored?

2.   Permissive action by the government if citizens run ahead of the government in implementing constitutional rights. For example, if a constitution specifies freedom of the press, then it should be possible for citizens to start newspapers even before the government has promulgated a press law.

     In such a case, the government itself may not react favorably to the initiatives of its citizens. What procedures at the regional or international level could be called upon to encourage respect for constitutionalism? For instance a recent judicial decision in Harare, Zimbabwe, affirmed the right of any Zimbabwean to establish a radio station. The opposition saw it as an opportunity to break the government monopoly of the airwaves and set up a radio station. The government ordered it closed as illegal because appropriate licensing laws have not been passed by the government. The government says it is a law and order issue while the opposition claims it is a constitutional issue.

3.   All institutions, governmental and independent, should be able to explore the limits of their rights and obligations under the constitution. It is by engaging in activities that test the constitution, that the constitution will be implemented, strengthened and legitimized. Again, there may be a role for regional and international solidarity. International associations of universities may encourage their academic colleagues to take commitments to academic freedom seriously.

4. Public education. Citizens have both a right and a duty to know the contents of their constitution, and to be informed about what this means in practice as well as in theory. Public education should not be passive: citizens learn through doing, through exercising their rights. Constitutional documents should be translated into local languages and broadcast, with commentary, on radio.

5. Use of public and democratic mechanisms when the government incorporates international treaties and conventions into law. It is easy for a government to collect UN conventions and protocols, earning applause in international fora. It is unlikely that many citizens are aware of these commitments and their implications. The government may not take them seriously at all. It would be much more effective if there were mechanisms such as referenda to decide whether these treaties should be adopted. In most cases, there would be little difficulty in securing a 'yes' vote, but the process of conducting the vote and educating the electorate would be an extremely important one.

6. International engagement. All African countries are signatory to a range of regional and international treaties, declarations and conventions that should be binding. All African governments have signed and ratified the Convention on the Rights of the Child for example (Somalia and the U.S. are the only states worldwide that have not done so). All have signed and ratified the African Charter on Human and People's Rights and are bound by the statutes of the African Commission on Human and People's Rights. These commitments are valid whether or not they are reproduced in national constitutions. The international organizations that are custodians of these treaties have an obligation to use whatever mechanisms are available to promote their implementation, and by extension, national and international civil society organizations have the right to pursue this too.

Constitutions are too important to be left to lawyers and politicians. They are the property of citizens. A constitution becomes real through the active engagement of its citizens in exercising their constitutional rights and obligations. This is the fundamental guarantee on a constitution, and the fundamental deterrent to those who may seek to overthrow it or ignore it.

For a constitution to be implemented, it must be relevant to the country in its particular stage of social, economic and political development. Unconstitutional acts such as coups d'etat may be a symptom of a deeper malaise, in which the system of government has become irrelevant to the needs of the population. For example, parliamentary politics may become dominated by an elite with its particular narrow concerns. These may be cast in terms of rights, but this discourse can become remote from the social and economic realities of the majority of the population. A constitutional discourse that is remote in this way can easily become discredited, helping to create the conditions for military rule.

An effective constitution should therefore be a product of a wider project of nation-building, including the establishment of institutions and mechanisms for democratic government, social and economic development etc. A constitution is reliant on the establishment of common core values among citizens including a democratic political culture.

Mechanisms for constitutional implementation can also be sought at a regional level. Countries should be aware of their neighbors' constitutions, and involved in deepening the constitutional process of their neighbors. This is particularly the case where countries are partners in cooperative arrangements at a subregional level (such as SADC, EAC etc.). In addition, the OAU principle of non-acceptance of forcible seizure of power puts a responsibility on all member states to protect all others' constitutions. This goes beyond contemplating diplomatic and perhaps military measures to reverse unconstitutional takeovers, but should also include encouraging democratic constitution-building and implementation internationally across the African continent.

Finally, we must ask, how is the constitution reviewed? Constitutions must be open to processes of review and revision. One the one hand, it is important that the constitution should not be changed too easily: it needs to retain its status as fundamental law that cannot normally be abrogated or changed during political or legislative process. A constitution that is too easily changed will create problems. On the other hand, a constitution is a living document and needs to be amenable to review. A constitution needs to have an aura of permanence, while also being sufficiently flexible. Having the appropriate mechanisms for review and revision are as vital as the wording of the constitution itself.

In 2000/01, approximately twenty African countries are undergoing some form of constitutional review. Most of these processes have been initiated by civil society, sometimes in the teeth of opposition from governments.

The situation in Kenya is an interesting example in which two parallel processes of constitutional review were initiated. There was a formal parliamentary review process. This is clearly the legally preferable option, as it is the elected legislature that should have the legal authority to make any constitutional amendments. However, in common with many other African countries, parliament is dominated by the party of the executive, which therefore has a wide scope for amending the constitution in favor of its short term or sectarian interests. Parallel to this there has been a constitutional review process set in motion by the churches and civil society, involving a much wider range of stakeholders. This is a much more open and democratic process, in which the concerns of the people are being voiced much more clearly. However, the constitutional status of this review process is uncertain as it has no formal status under the law. To accept it as a legitimate process would raise fundamental issues about the supremacy of the legislature. However, if parliament is politically incapable of conducting the necessary review process, are the people not entitled to initiate their own? The situation is comparable to the popular pressures that led to sovereign national conferences in many west and central African countries in the period 1990-92. Recently, the two processes have merged.

Conclusion

This chapter has focussed on asking questions rather than answering them. But some basic themes stand out. The most important is that a constitution must be seen as a living thing, not merely as a piece of paper. Constitutions can be abused or subverted; the spirit of constitutional rule needs to be protected by an array of institutions and organizations, ranging from the formal institutions of state (especially the judiciary and legislature) to civil society organizations and the citizens themselves.

The discussion also shows how vulnerable constitutions are in the African context, especially how they may be subverted by militarism or 'exceptionalism.' Many struggle to deal with the realities of organized ethnic communities that continue to command the loyalty of citizens. Many constitutions fail to command the loyalty of much of the populace because there has not been a participatory and inclusive process of adopting and implementing the constitution. Lastly, the discussion indicates that constitutionalism is central to the possibility of establishing a national and international order in Africa that can create peace and security. Robust and well-implemented constitutions, that command legitimacy and respect from citizens, can protect countries and indeed the entire continent from armed conflict. However constitutions are not an end in themselves but a means (though very important) to the end of good governance and human security.

4

THE POLITICAL CULTURES OF MILITARISM

It is a sad reality that Africa is a militarized continent. This can be demonstrated by documenting the numbers of ongoing conflicts, the level of military spending, the availability of armaments, and the number of heads of state and government who are or have been military officers or liberation fighters. This chapter is concerned with an equally significant but less well-analyzed phenomenon: the political cultures of militarism. This is an issue that has received little scholarly attention.

War is the pursuit of political aims by armed methods. War implies having an enemy to whom one is opposed. But war also entails certain kinds of internal power relations within the belligerent party and state. This kind of political culture can then also be manifest during peacetime. Militaristic governance is a characteristic of many governments that have either emerged from war, or which feel themselves to be threatened by insurgency or destabilization. It is manifest in the absence of inter-state security communities, as discussed in chapter 2, and constitutional exceptionalism, as discussed in chapter 3.

Mobilizing for war and fighting war commonly entails a culture of militarism in one form or another. This chapter focuses on militarized political parties, movements and fronts, both in power and struggling for power. It distinguishes several variants: right-wing, left-wing, liberal, reactive, and commercial/opportunistic. This is an ad hoc typology, utilized to undertake a preparatory exploration of the phenomenon of militarism and to spark a debate. The concept of left-wing militarism, in particular, is likely to prove a controversial one.

The analysis of militarism developed in this chapter is intended to provide a framework for understanding how different social groups can mobilize to promote peace, which is the subject of the following chapter. The three social categories focussed upon are women, youth and the poor: these categories are therefore given special reference in this chapter. Militarism, in each of its variant forms, imposes tremendous constraints on the ability of social groups to mobilize and pursue their interests. Worse, it can stand in the way of them even *identifying* their interests with a degree of clarity.

Right-wing Militarism

Right-wing militaristic cultures have been well-studied, particularly in the European and Asian context. But they have also occurred in Africa, both on the side of colonial and Apartheid regimes, and in some post-colonial states. Although specific African examples are not mentioned in detail below, the reader can supply his or her own examples to fit every case. We can identify a number of common elements in these militaristic cultures.

The first element is *authoritarianism*. Militarism entails a certain form of power, based on absolute authority, hierarchy and obedience. Some form of authoritarianism is intrinsic to military organization of any kind. Junior officers are required to obey the orders of their seniors without thinking, and private soldiers in turn are required to have unquestioning loyalty to their immediate commanders. Some armies try to instill this obedience through developing a sense of camaraderie and loyalty, others through fear, most use drill and behavioral conditioning: the rationale is that the soldier should be just as frightened of his commanding officer as of the enemy, so that he will not flinch in combat. It is very difficult to teach people to kill: most ordinary individuals need to be bullied and coerced into doing it. This type of authoritarianism becomes so deeply entrenched within the militarized individual, that it is reproduced in his relations with his friends, family, and colleagues at work after he leaves the army. In right-wing militarism, authoritarianism is raised from being an instrument of organization to the level of an ideology. Hierarchy itself becomes worshipped.

Because of the importance of these values and forms of organization for any form of effective military structure, armies have a built-in rightward tendency. Militarism tends towards the right: it needs exceptionally strong efforts to steer left if it is not to internalize these right-wing values.

A second characteristic is *elitism*. Many militaristic societies are characterized by an officer class or caste. This is a group, perhaps aristocratic, that sees itself as superior to all others. Its members believe that they embody certain values and morals—such as discipline, courage, loyalty, the qualities of command—that are lacking in wider society. They may see themselves as custodians of these values, which they fear would be lost if society were to become more democratic and open. Perhaps these ideals may also be bound up in notions of ethnic superiority or racial purity. The codes of honor among these elites recognize and respect one another: officers from one militarized society, fighting another, will greet their captured adversaries as fellow members of the officer caste, and treat them honorably. (This concept of 'the warrior's honor' underpins the acceptability of the Geneva Conventions among many militarists (Ignatieff, 1998).)

A third component commonly found is *racism, ethnic chauvinism or religious extremism*. Many right wing militarisms become closely bound up with ethnic mobilization. In most societies, armed conflict generates closer identification with ethnicity, so that all forms of militarism have a tendency to develop ethnic components. However, among right-wing militarists, we often see an ideology of ethnicity developing, resulting in outright racism. A variant of this is religious extremism, and the declaration of Holy War (often with an ethnic or racial dimension as well as a religious one).

Another variant is 'militarist ethnicity.' Europe and Asia have historically had 'warrior castes' and even 'warrior nations' such as the Cossacks. These are groups whose identity is bound up with the very idea of fighting. Africa has its variants on this too. Some ethnic groups—such as the Nubi of Uganda and neighboring countries—are comprised of the descendants of 19th century soldiers, some of whose descendants still retain a militarist ethos. Other ethnic groups have strong warrior traditions, and even today some of them supply disproportionate numbers of recruits to national armies. It is notable that these groups tend to be either livestock herders or aristocrats. In many cases, the domination of the military by one particular ethnic or regional grouping is disguised by a non-ethnic nationalist ethos that minimizes the level of racism in the military system.

An important element associated with any form of military organization is *secrecy*, and tight control of information. The truth is hidden by trenches and embankments of lies. Along with authoritarianism and elitism comes a cult of secrecy. While there may be some collegiality and openness among the highest military elites, this trait is not shared with other ranks or more widely with society.

Secrecy is essential to effective military organization. A general must keep his plans secret from his adversary, and this entails keeping them within the tightest possible circle of his own staff, for fear of spies or leaks. In addition, a general cannot be too open with his troops or civilians: if he were to reveal the risk of military failure, or the likelihood of a long and costly campaign, then morale would suffer and public support for the war effort would trickle away, along with public confidence in the command. A general must therefore exude self-confidence and certainty, and must have a public relations or propaganda office to work to convince the public, and the rank and file, that the war is winnable and the sacrifices are worthwhile. Even in peacetime, secretiveness is central to rightist militarism. Among other things, it enables generals to become closely involved in commercial activities, away from any requirements of transparency.

Lastly, we must identify the *cult of violence*. For many soldiers, violence is a regrettable necessity; it is an instrument. But for a militarized society, violence has virtues. It is a means whereby a man can prove his real manhood, demonstrate his courage and loyalty. It can be seen as a means of achieving a higher, purer self. It is an expression of 'decisiveness', a demonstration of virility. For some right-wing militarists, violence also exemplifies superiority: the military commander is like a cattle herder: by his display of violence he demonstrates that other, lesser human beings are like dumb animals who can easily be commanded.

It is well-documented that the majority of individuals have a profound aversion to killing others, even during combat (Grossman, 1995). After the Second World War, research in the U.S. Army found that even in the thick of battle, as few as 20 per cent of soldiers actually fired their personal weapons. Comparable findings have been validated for all major western armies. (Crew operated long-distance weapons such as artillery are different, and partly as a result are responsible for the great majority of casualties in most wars.) Subsequently, in the Korean and Vietnam wars, the U.S. Army has sought to overcome this aversion to killing by psychological conditioning during training. However, considerable long-term psychological damage is inflicted on individuals who have been trained in this way. Research also finds that a small minority of individuals—perhaps 2 per cent—do not have this handicap, and are ready to kill. These are not psychopaths or criminally insane people, and nor are they indiscriminate killers. In fact many of them can be highly effective leaders in civilian life. They are simply lacking in the mental block that inhibits killing. This small group of individuals can be responsible for the majority of kills by light weapons during combat. Although research on militarist ethnicities is lacking, it is possible that, the processes of socialization of boys and young men in these societies helps to overcome the inhibition on killing. It is also possible that these societies enable 'natural' killers to rise to leadership positions more readily.

No research has been published on killing rates by African armies. However, compiling overall statistics for numbers killed in these wars with information about the size of armies and the types of weapons used suggests that African wars are probably no different to European, Asian and American conflicts in terms of the readiness of the individual soldier to kill. The numbers of soldiers killed are usually much smaller than the length of wars and the level of destruction and displacement would indicate. Most deaths are inflicted by mechanized weaponry (e.g. Ethiopia-Eritrea) or in massacre frenzies (e.g. Rwanda). Most combat casualties occur when one army has broken and is retreating in disorder. This implies that most soldiers serve without actually killing any enemy combatants. It also implies that an army or armed organization that has overcome the psychological obstacles to killing will thereby become a more effective killing machine, and can be far more effective at waging war than its small size might indicate. (There are also some indications that one reason for commanders' use of child soldiers is that children have yet to develop fully their inhibitions on killing.)

All the characteristics outlined above have implications for power relations within the militarized society. The implications reach to the most intimate aspects of social relations.

The militarized society is *not gender neutral*: it has profound implications for the position and role of women. It elevates a particular kind of masculinity, praising certain 'manly' virtues, and despising other qualities as 'feminine'. In most right-wing militaristic societies, women are valued as carers only: as mothers, wives and nurses. (They may also be valued, less openly, as sex workers.) There is no gender equality. Women who rise in such societies do so by exemplifying 'feminine' values, or sometimes by replicating the 'masculine' values of militarism—in which case they are seen as exceptions. Within right-wing militaristic organizations, we may see women participating in atrocities such as massacres; they may assist by 'dutifully' revealing the location of people due to be killed, by providing food and succor to the soldiers, or by participating in the atrocity themselves.

Militarized societies value *youth*, but only in certain forms. The army is seen as an ideal organization for channeling the virtues of youth in a useful and moral direction. These values include physical energy, readiness to take risks, idealism, and courage. For those too young to serve in the army, there may be specialized youth organizations (boy scouts etc.) in which the young can serve their militaristic apprenticeships. These youth organizations replicate the values of the military: they instill discipline, respect for hierarchy, commitment to physical fitness, and conformity. They may train boys to kill, trying to block the full emergence of the inhibition on killing. Organizations for boys and girls are strictly separated. Official stress on discipline should not obscure the reality that one of the attractions of joining a proto-military youth wing is the chance for licensed thuggery that it brings. These youth may be the shock troops for war on unarmed opponents of the regime; they may delight in smashing up shops or beating up opposition party members and other real or imagined enemies.

The *'poor'*, or the economically marginalized or impoverished, as a category has little place in the schema of the militarized society. In rightwing ideology we may distinguish the 'conjunctural poor' from the 'structural poor'. The 'conjunctural poor' are the disabled, the old and infirm, and those who have suffered an unfortunate disaster (e.g. orphans, victims of natural calamities). Such people are 'deserving poor', worthy of charity. But they have no political claims. The 'structural poor'—those impoverished by social and economic processes—by contrast, are merely expected to conform and better their condition by working harder. Hence, again we see the authoritarian, hierarchical model of socio-political organization at work.

In summary, a right-wing militarist system will mean that individuals who are authoritarian, elitist, secretive and exult in violence will rise to the top. Moreover, it is evident that right-wing militarism leaves little room for social mobilization to promote peace. The power relations inherent in this manifestation of militarism are antithetical to any form of civil action of this kind. And while fully-fledged right-wing militaristic systems are relatively rare in Africa, elements of this ideological pattern can be seen clearly in a number of armies, regimes and political parties.

Left-wing Militarism

The very concept of left-wing militarism is a controversial one. Many thinkers and political leaders on the left reject the very idea of left-wing militarism: they argue instead that there is left-wing *militancy*, but *militarism* is exclusively a right-wing phenomenon. Marxists will develop arguments to prove that left-wing militarism is a contradiction in terms. Perhaps this may be philosophically defensible. However, if we examine revolutionary parties and regimes in Africa (and Asia and Latin America), we see a characteristic syndrome of military-type organization and ideology coupled to ideals of social transformation. Revolutionary regimes in power tend to continue or even intensify military-style mobilization in order to achieve their social and economic goals. Even (and perhaps especially) when the ideals of comprehensive revolutionary social justice have been abandoned, the military-style of socio-political organization remains. Therefore, *prima facie*, there is a strong case to be made that left-wing militarism is an actually-existing phenomenon. This discussion will attempt an empirical analysis of revolutionary regimes in power, using the label 'left-wing militarism' for convenience.

Historically, left-wing militarism has two variants: resistance and state-revolutionary. Leftist popular resistance to oppression has been a common theme throughout history. Much popular resistance to imperial conquest in Africa, although led by traditional rulers, falls broadly into this category. In Europe and Asia there is a long history of peasant revolts, some of whose leaders developed proto-socialist philosophies: the Levellers and Diggers in 17th century England are some of the more celebrated martyrs of this tradition. Unfortunately for its practitioners, the radical tendency to democracy and tolerance often tends to undermine effective military organization, so such movements have a tendency to fragment and collapse. State-revolutionary left-wing militarism began (in modern times at least) with the French Revolution and the concept of 'the nation in arms'. Citizenship was bound up with the idea of the right and duty to bear arms to defend the Republic. A significant variant of this was the militarism of the first Republic of Haiti led by Toussaint L'Ouverture following his successful slave rebellion.

In post-colonial Africa, left-wing militarism has two broadly comparable variants. The first variant has been bound up with ideas 'people's war', as developed by Mao Zedong and Che Guevara, and widely practised on the African continent, initially in anti-colonial wars in Algeria, Southern Africa and Guinea Bissau. A second wave of people's warriors refined the methods in Eritrea, Ethiopia and Uganda. The state-revolutionary variant is generally bound up with the idea of the 'free officers', nationalistic army officers committed to promoting emancipatory social change by taking power, on the model of Gamal Abdel Nasser. A whole generation of leaders in Africa, including Muammar Gaddafi, Jaafar Nimeiri, Siad Barre, Jerry Rawlings and Thomas Sankara were inspired to some degree by this model. The state-revolutionary militarism of Mengistu's Ethiopia was a particularly violent variant of this.

Left-wing militarism is a more complicated phenomenon than its right-wing counterpart. The chief structural reason for this is that it is rooted in a reactive militancy: it is motivated by the desire to right a perceived wrong, and driven by an agenda of progressive social transformation. One of its targets and enemies is militarism (the right-wing variant). Left-wing military leaders are therefore motivated in part by a coherent ideological critique of right-wing militarism, and they consciously strive to avoid its errors. Left-wing militarism has its own variant of the 'just war' theory: its advocates argue that in certain circumstances, the people have no option but to resort to armed struggle to achieve their rights. In certain historical circumstances, they may be right. What option did the nationalists in Algeria, the Portuguese colonies, and Eritrea have except to take up armed struggle? Would the imperialists in Congo in the early 1960s have responded to non-violent civil protest? Would Apartheid have surrendered if it had not been faced with the prospect of war to the finish? And in certain key cases, armed struggle has proved an effective way of resolving the problems it set out to address. Algeria, Eritrea and the Southern African states all achieved their independence, and Apartheid was removed. Some may argue that the cost was too high, and that some of these gains might have been achieved anyway: but it is a historical fact that in some cases, armed struggle has worked.

Once in power, leftist revolutionary leaders have often enacted progressive measures that have substantially improved the lot of ordinary people. And the removal of the old oppressor is, on its own, a positive development. However, in the tradition of George Orwell's *Animal Farm*, leftist military rulers often end up resembling the autocrats whom they overthrew. But even when they do not, and the new regime is markedly different and more socio-politically radical than the old, left-wing military leaders tend to create their own unique brand of militarism. We may notice some of its characteristics.

The first element is *centralism and vanguardism*. There can be no purely democratic form of military organization. Some leftist military organizations have developed structures for popular consultation and participation. However, these tend to be hierarchically-organized councils, in the form of a pyramid leading to a central committee or high command which takes ultimate control. There is no place for the liberal ideals of separation of powers and public expression of dissent. (Within the upper echelons of the party, open debate may be permitted and frank evaluation encouraged. But this rarely permeates far.) In fact, with a few exceptions, leftist militarists adopt, in one form or another, the Leninist idea of a vanguard party. This has many far-reaching implications.

To begin with, vanguardism elevates the role of the party above other commitments and loyalties. The party becomes both means and end to its members. Absolute loyalty to the ideals and procedures of the party is required. To its members, the party can become as important as the state and even the country: preserving the position of the party, its unity and coherence, can become an objective that swallows up all other aims, including the goal of taking power or running the country. The abandonment of principles of justice, equality and freedom can be justified through the dictat of the party.

When a vanguard party is in government, it tends to create command structures that run parallel to the state structures, and are present in every workplace. These become the real circuits of power. While the existing executive structures may already be slow and cumbersome, the imposition of a parallel authority with arbitrary powers tends to paralyse such structures. The party will increasingly resort to its own independent and militarized means of action in order to achieve the goals of the leadership. Thus, broad social agendas such as literacy, school construction or drought relief will be undertaken through mass campaigns in which party cadres, military style, mobilize task forces to implement programmes. These may be effective in the short term but are rarely sustainable. The party may also impose its priorities on schools and workplaces, in extremis even taking over wide swathes of 'private' enterprise. While such exceptional measures may initially be justified in the name of the rapid and effective implementation of social transformation, it is in the nature of institutions that they become self-serving and self-preserving. As a vanguard party expands its social and business activities, its bureaucracy ends up serving its own sectoral objectives. Given the party's disciplined command structure and lack of transparency, this can also be a recipe for party leaders' abuse of power for personal gain. A vanguard party can become a monster that devours the ideals for which it once stood.

Next, the vanguard is assumed to have privileged understanding of the objective situation, and the right and duty to act on behalf of the broad masses, if necessary in a dictatorial manner. This is elitism under another name. Under some circumstances, the vanguard may be ready to consult widely and accept the views and proposals of the masses. This is particularly the case when the movement is dependent upon the wholehearted support of the masses, for example in times of extreme stress and threat. This usually occurs in opposition, when a liberation front needs the active support of the people in a liberated area in order to survive. But when that threat is removed, and the leadership of the movement finds itself able to act with more autonomy from the dictates of its followers, vanguardism tends to reassert itself. The leaders assume the right to *think for* the wider populace, and they acquire a condescension and arrogance towards the masses, and also towards other intellectuals who are not members of the vanguard.

In addition, the ideological orientation of leftist vanguard parties, towards Marxism-Leninism, creates an insoluble contradiction. Marxism-Leninism claims to offer a scientific, objective understanding of and response to any situation. This is the theoretical underpinning of the privileged power exercised by the vanguard. But the world is more complicated than scientific socialist analysis allows, and consensus cannot always be obtained on a 'correct' analysis and course of action. Because the inner sanctum of a Marxist-Leninist party must act on total consensus on the basis of 'objective' analysis, the leadership cannot make policy on the basis of compromise and uncertainty, as is the norm in more open systems of government. Dissent is 'error' and can only be dealt with by purging the dissenters, who may then admit the 'errors' of their ways and return to the 'correct' analysis. As complex problems multiply and the 'correct' line is harder to identify, cohesion can only be maintained within the vanguard by relegating power to a smaller and smaller circle, which then imposes its views on the rest. This is a recipe for schism and dictatorship.

Not all leftist militaristic regimes have succumbed to the extremes of vanguardist politics. Some have worn their Marxism-Leninism more lightly, using nationalism to construct a broader front, which can also be a means of accommodating greater diversity of views. However, a centralizing, vanguardist tendency can be identified in many leftist regimes, particularly former liberation fronts. It is a phenomenon that demands a study of its own.

The second broad characteristic of leftist militarism is that it demands *discipline* in service of its ideals. Unquestioning loyalty has been discussed above. Some of the discipline required is self-denying. For example, people's warriors are required to serve the people they live amongst; they should not take food without paying, they should refrain from sexual relations, they should always be respectful of their civilian hosts. Other aspects of discipline are more common to all effective armies, namely a readiness to obey all orders, to be loyal to one's unit, etc. Similarly, nationalistic 'free officers' are expected to live austere and simple lifestyles, eschewing pomp and lavish ceremonies. Colonel Gaddafi likes to live humbly in a Bedouin tent. Such leaders should be accessible to the people, and avoid awarding themselves senior ranks. In the early days of his rule, Colonel Nimeiri would drive his own car. Similarly, Siad Barre would leave his palace and walk openly in the streets of Mogadishu to mix with the people. Thomas Sankara received his visitors informally and entertained them by playing the guitar. These examples of personal modesty can be inspiring but they are only symbolic. A leader who is honest and humble in his personal life can also abuse power, and may indeed spuriously feel that he has the moral authority to act in an arbitrary way because he is making no personal material gain. Discipline and unquestioning loyalty becomes a problem if a leadership insists on marching an army in the wrong direction.

Associated with this, leftist militarism requires total, wholehearted *commitment* to the party and its cause. There may be opportunities for open discussion within certain restricted confines, but there can be no dissent from the overall goal and strategy, which commands total loyalty. Any disagreement, however small, is tantamount to treason. Leftist militarist organizations are normally very intolerant and unforgiving of their internal critics. Splits and fractions occur on account of the most obscure ideological differences, that to the outsider may seem irrelevant to the strategic goals of the struggle. Internal purges and denouncing 'traitors' and 'sell-outs' are characteristic. This in turn generates a high degree of self-censorship and secrecy. The ideology of the struggle generates its own self-reinforcing mythology. Leftist vanguard parties are closed political systems, that speak largely to themselves.

A related characteristic is the tendency of left-wing militarists to eliminate their leftist rivals, whether inside the same organization or in another leftist camp. A classic example is the Ethiopian revolution, which in the 1970s generated a very large number of armed leftist organizations. In addition to the extremely bloody government massacre of the opposition, especially in Eritrea and on the streets of Addis Ababa during the Red Terror, the opposition groups fought and eliminated each other with total ruthlessness. The groups that survived into the 1980s were those that had a geographical location and regional agenda solely to themselves. Other leftist armed groups that have differed have also been quick to settle their differences through violence. The civil war in Angola in the 1970s is another example, as is the bloody repression of the Sudanese Communists by President Nimeiri in 1971. Although right-wing militarists also fall out among themselves, their internal struggles seem to be less protracted and bloody.

Left-wing militarism tends to promote *nationalism*. All conflict generates attachment to ethnic or national sentiment. Left-wing militarists have only rarely managed to mobilize armies on ideological grounds alone. Usually they also appeal to nationalist sentiment. Unlike right-wing militarism which is commonly associated with racism—which propagandizes the adversaries as demons—left-wing nationalism tend to praise the virtues of the nation or ethnicity, while also espousing respect for individual members of the opposing group. It is the enemy leadership and its ideology that is demonized, described as 'chauvinist' or 'imperialist'. However, among many ordinary soldiers and citizens, this distinction may be unclear: the line between nationalism and racism sometimes becomes blurred. And once in power, it is more difficult to label one's adversaries as 'chauvinist', when they are not well able to exercise that chauvinism. It becomes even more difficult when former state officials, merchants, professionals and other bourgeois elements successfully align themselves with the new leftist regime, and the regime finds it necessary to accommodate these elements as tactical allies.

Lastly, left-wing militarism can, despite its ideology and best intent, encourage a *cult of violence*. Many leftists engaged in people's war are very reluctant warriors. They see violence as a last resort, and as an instrument to be used sparingly and reluctantly. Their version of 'the warrior's honor' includes treating prisoners of war—especially the lower ranks—with kindness and respect, providing them with political education, and giving them the opportunity to join the struggle, should they wish, or return home, if that is possible. However, leftist militarism has also embraced its own cult of violence. The most notable exponent of this is Frantz Fanon, who celebrated violence as a means for the oppressed to achieve psychological and social emancipation, freedom from the burden of inferiority complex imposed on them. In other cases, violence is seen as the weapon of the masses, as a cleansing, pure and democratic expression of the people's will. The willingness of people to suffer and die for a higher cause is seen as the highest sanctification of that cause. The self-sacrifice of 'martyrs' becomes the strongest reason for fighters not to abandon the cause for which their comrades have given their lives. In addition, when armed struggle fails to achieve success rapidly, its leaders tend to elevate the concept of 'the struggle' to an ideological level, which means participation in the armed struggle itself becomes a virtue. As time passes, the warrior ethos becomes internalized in the people's army.

Left-wing militarism has one component that markedly diverges from its right-wing counterpart. Revolutionary regimes in power pursue ambitious programmes for socio-economic transformation. These normally require the decisive and unconstrained use of state power. The campaign model of enacting social change is particularly attractive to such leaders. They may use it for literacy or immunization campaigns, for mobilizing labor for infrastructural projects such as building railways or schools, for land reform, for agricultural transformation, for purging counter-revolutionary elements (merchants, landowners, sell-outs), or for mobilizing a citizens' army to face a military threat. The cadre system can mobilize society on a wider scale than many right-wing militarist systems. Moreover, the claim that the goals of the revolution are not yet achieved provides a standing justification for maintaining the militarist system intact.

The similarities between right-wing and left-wing forms of militarism are as striking as the differences. In fact, the two militarisms have as much in common with one another as they have with right- and left-wing civil politics. It is probably easier for a left-wing militarist system to become a right-wing militarist system, than for it to become a civilian system.

These power relations have implications for how social groups can mobilize to press for peace. The possibilities are rather more complex than in the case of right-wing militarism. Let us begin with analyzing *the position of women*. Leftist militarists commonly have an agenda for the emancipation of women. Leftist coups d'etat in the Nasserite model have often been followed by legislation that gives women unprecedented legal rights. People's war has often included the mobilization of women as combatants and even commanders, and programmes for women's literacy, health, and empowerment (e.g. reforming customary law to give women more rights in marriage, rights to own land, etc.) Leftist movement also set up women's associations that give a formal voice to women in policymaking.

But there are many reasons to suspect that these reforms, while laudable, do not go far enough. In many cases, once victory has been won, women find that the gains they made during the struggle are being eroded. Once their brothers-in-arms have achieved power, solidarity with sisters-in-the-struggle seems to slacken. More generally, the emancipation of women in Leninist-style organizations consists of the promotion of women within organizational and power structures that are inherently 'masculine'. As outlined above, left-wing militarism replicates the 'masculine' values of hierarchy, elitism, secrecy and violence, albeit in subtly changed forms. There is no 'feminization' or liberalization of these values; there is little room for free association, free expression, harmony and consensus.

Leftist militarism replicates many of the militaristic forms of organization for *youth*, but with a different ideological gloss, and (sometimes) with different gender characteristics. Socialist countries had powerful youth organizations (pioneers etc.) which mobilized boys and girls in the service of socialism. During leftist struggles, the youth have often been at the forefront. Young people form the backbone of most guerrilla armies. They can be drilled and disciplined to be the most effective, undemanding and self-sacrificing volunteer soldiers. Young leftist guerrillas, fearless and fearsome in combat, can be extraordinarily courteous and respectful when dealing with their civilian elders, who are hosting them in a village. Another case is the struggle against the Apartheid regime in South Africa, youth were in the front line for much of the 1970s and '80s. The struggle was able to capture their energy, frustration, idealism, readiness to use violence and readiness to deal with danger, in its confrontations with the Apartheid authorities. In this case, the lack of discipline among youth could also be an asset to the movement: many youths could be turned out by the prospect of a riot (with the thrill that entailed) and looting. Many youths became 'social bandits', Robin Hood-type figures who stole from

85

the capitalist and oppressor classes, redistributing goods to the masses (first of all, themselves).

The *impoverished and marginalized* are the prime group on whose behalf leftist militarists act. (Leftists tend to dispute the validity of the term 'poor' and prefer to speak of the 'broad masses,' impoverished and marginalized people, and workers and peasants.) Leftist ideology stresses the centrality of the broad masses, and leftist organization provides for mass organizations that can mobilize the masses, in the workplace and the village. This form of party-led organization is also a form of control. The interests of the poor are identified solely and exclusively with those of the party. In many cases, leftist parties have indeed enacted reforms that have improved the lot of the poor, such as land reform, improved rural services, democratized local administration, fairer employment legislation, etc. However, the ability of the poor to mobilize outside the party apparatus is severely constrained. Thus, on key issues such as the decision to go to war, the party organization will ensure that the mass organizations faithfully follow the party line, with no room for dissent. The more the military ethos is entrenched within the party's mode of operation, the less opportunity there will be for independent organization or expression of different viewpoints.

Left-wing militarism is therefore a more complicated and contradictory phenomenon than its right-wing counterpart. It has space within it for an anti-militaristic ideology and practice, and for practical progress towards the emancipation of the marginalized and oppressed. But it replicates many phenomena such as a tendency towards authoritarianism, and the exclusion of dissident viewpoints from real influence or power. And, left-wing militarism or vanguardism tends to promote certain sorts of individuals. Those who gain power are those who best manifest the traits of vanguardism, discipline, commitment and skill in using violence. For many leftist military practitioners, violence is merely an instrument and not an ideal in itself. But, having achieved power, left-wing military practitioners have a poor record in moving towards civil politics in which violence is wholly abandoned as a legitimate instrument.

In many countries ruled by former liberation movements, there is a strong sense of betrayal of the ideals of the revolution by those on whose behalf the victory was allegedly won. Social categories such as women, youth and the impoverished feel that the promises of the leadership have not been kept; they accuse their leaders of being fraudulent, of reverting to self-interested power politics once they are in government, and neglecting the constituencies they relief upon during the struggle.

Many national liberation movements in Africa fall into the category of left-wing militarism, both because of their populist orientation and the historical context of the Cold War, especially the leftist implications of national liberation. On the other hand, right-wing groups such as UNITA and Renamo tend to have pro-West, anti-Communist orientations, adopting hybrid forms of militarism. (UNITA started out as a Maoist front.) In some cases such as Ethiopia, both the guerrilla groups and the regime they were fighting could adopt leftist postures.

Concluding the analysis of leftist militarism, we must ask whether this is a historical phenomenon whose time is passing. During the struggles against colonialism and Apartheid, and as recently as the 1996-7 war to defeat the Rwandese genocidaires in Zaire and topple the discredited autocracy of General Mobutu, it was not difficult to identify a 'just cause'. Left-wing militarists could easily identify the oppressed masses on whose behalf they were taking up arms. They could argue, easily and with justification, that there was no alternative to violence, and that the ends justified the means. But the moral certainties of even this recent past seem to be disappearing into a fog of war. Former allies find themselves fighting one another; former ideological allies seem to consider realpolitik and narrow interests more important than the ideals they earlier espoused. Africa's left-wing military leaders have done a good job of forcing their former advocates and apologists into embarrassed silence.

Variant Militarisms

Although the dominant modes of militarism are the left-wing and right-wing versions, there are also a number of other variants. One of these is 'liberal militarism': the phenomenon of military establishments within liberal or civilian states. This may also be called 'professional militarism': the ethos of a non-political army subordinate to civilian command. There is also 'reactive militarism', which is communities or nations mobilized to defend themselves from external onslaught; 'commercial militarism', the phenomenon of armies mobilized for the pursuit of greed; and 'opportunistic militarism', which is the military mobilization of political entrepreneurs who see armed force as a way of gaining power. The phenomenon of 'warlordism', much discussed in recent Africanist literature, is a combination of 'commercial' and 'opportunistic' militarism, with perhaps ingredients of others thrown in too.

This discussion will be much briefer because under these conditions there is much less of an ideology of militarism as such within the state apparatus or the army itself. However, any military establishment tends to nurture certain values. As mentioned in the discussion of right-wing militarism, these tend towards the right.

87

Our first category is *liberal or professional militarism*. Most military establishments within liberal states originate from right-wing military traditions. In Africa, many national defence forces were founded on the colonial model, which was a version of rightist militarism. Both for this reason, and because the demands of discipline and effectiveness within any army dictate certain forms of organization, the basic militaristic model of authoritarianism, elitism, secrecy and cult of violence are reproduced. It is even possible that some of these characteristics may be accentuated when the military feels itself remote from power. Officers may feel that civilian politicians do not display the required qualities of discipline or determination, and may come to exaggerate and promote those qualities within their own ranks. These officers will lose no opportunity to impress on the president the need to take national security more seriously, and to keep the forces of anarchy and destabilization at bay.

Militarism in a civilian state can also come from another direction. A head of state or head of government may feel the need to bolster the militaristic element in his (ruling) political party. This may be motivated by a desire to enact dramatic political reform, to intimidate the opposition, to mobilize the party's own ranks (introducing control and discipline where it may have been lacking), or even a desire to develop an alternative military force to keep the army at bay. The ruler of an impoverished African country is not in fact a very powerful individual. His budget is constrained by debt and the demands of international donors and creditors; his national bureaucracy is frustratingly inefficient and under-resourced, and the promises he made on gaining power may become more and more unattainable. One of the few areas in which he can increase his freedom of action is by organizing new security services and party militias or 'youth wings'. A more centralized, militaristic form of command and control, over at least some elements of executive or party power, will provide greater latitude for action.

Liberal, civilian governments differ from right- and left-wing militaristic ones in that they have structures that allow non-militarized individuals to rise to the top. But, liberal civilian government alone is not enough: there must be an environment that prevents the emergence of any form of militarism within the civilian system.

Our second category might be termed *reactive militarism*. Many communities and nations are mobilized in reaction to a threat to their identity or existence. This is the classic mobilizing rationale for militarists of all kinds. In some cases, it is the overwhelming reason for mobilization. Historically in Africa, resistance to colonial rule from the 19th century to the 1950s was in this form, and there have been a number of revolts and insurrections by peasants and pastoralists against the post-colonial state as well.

This form of militarism is driven largely by circumstance. The violence of the state or dominant groups drives marginalized peoples to the point of armed resistance. Ethnic modes of mobilization and discourse, and the militarization of administration and politics which have implications for ethnic identification, mean that most reactive military mobilization takes an ethnic form.

The ethnic component means that the mechanisms for mobilizing stakeholders including women, the youth and the poor, are specific to the society and culture in question. There may be traditional or (more likely) adapted-traditional means whereby specific stakeholders can make their voices heard. It may be possible to improvise on cultural traditions to enable women or youth to have an influence. Alternatively, these customary forms of social organization may marginalize or exclude women or youth altogether.

As long as reactive militarism remains confined to merely defensive measures, protecting land and cultures, then it is relatively easy to demobilize. However, if it becomes protracted, or bound up with other types of militarism, then it can be much more problematic.

Thirdly, we have *commercial or opportunistic militarism*. Commercial militarism ranges from the phenomenon of private military companies (mercenaries), through the involvement of armies and militias in commercial activities, to the initiation of war for economic reasons. (Elements of this are detailed in Chapter 7.) 'Pure' forms of commercial militarism are relatively rare. Outside mercenary companies, it is mostly a case of mixed motives: profit becomes one reason among others for engaging in war. However, as war becomes protracted, the 'fringe benefit' of getting rich through looting or trading may become the primary reason for continuing to fight, and military activities may become more and more structured around the necessity for provisioning troops and the opportunity for commanders enriching themselves.

In the absence of war, commercial militarism can entail the close engagement of senior army officers—who are usually also government officials—in commercial activities. The secretiveness and discipline of the military apparatus, combined with its exemption from normal democratic constraint, may enable military men to build business empires and acquire personal fortunes, away from any scrutiny. This in turn influences the attitude of the military towards any constitutionalism or handover to civilian authorities—they fear that their commercial activities may be exposed or halted. The protection of the commercial interests of army commanders may become a dominant factor in the political strategies of the military.

Opportunistic militarism is used to refer to the mobilization of an armed force simply with the aim of taking power. It is close to commercial militarism, because the motive is likely to be greed and little else.

There has been a lot of recent academic attention to the issue of 'warlords' and the economic incentives involved in African wars. Some of this literature implies that armed conflict is a rational economic choice for commanders and soldiers, and that war is little more than a business venture. For some commanders and businessmen, conflict is an environment in which certain business ventures can thrive, and they will do their best to profit from the opportunities it presents. These interests can become so powerful that they can sustain a war when other (political) interests dictate that it should come to an end. But these 'economic rationality' approaches to warfare suffer from some shortcomings.

First, the motives of the military commanders is usually to acquire power. Few if any aspire to be 'warlords'. No matter how much their decision-making is bound up with economic factors, they still have political ambitions and programmes. Most importantly, no commander will attempt to publicly justify a war solely as a commercial enterprise. Warlords such as Jonas Savimbi and Charles Taylor aspire to state power. Partly this is because they see state power as a means of generating still more riches for themselves. Commercial motives are thus interwoven with political ambitions.

Secondly, the demands of maintaining an army and fighting are different from those of running a business enterprise, especially an informal sector enterprise. Armies that do not maintain discipline and command structures are not likely to win battles. They may prevail for a while, if their opponents are very weak and disorganized, but they will be liable to defeat or fragmentation unless they adopt some militaristic ideology that can help maintain them as institutions. In theory, the gap can be filled by mercenaries, but this also has its hazards and shortcomings.

Lastly, for the majority of soldiers, serving in an army does not make much economic sense. The risks and hardships are not compensated for by the benefits. There may be a chance of getting rich, but it is a gamble. Keeping soldiers mobilized, and keeping a measure of popular support for the war, will require other justifications. Soldiers mobilized on the promises of riches, and then disappointed, are not likely to prove loyal or reliable. Hence, commercial or opportunistic militarization will tend to acquire other ethnic or political characteristics too.

One of the major challenges for commercial or opportunistic militarists is acquiring political and cultural legitimacy, both domestically and internationally. This type of war mobilization and warfighting is not approved of by cultures and ideologies. This means that there may be opportunities for stakeholders in peace, and their international coalition partners, to bring pressure to bear.

This discussion focuses on non-ideological militarism in its variant strands: militarism adopted simply as a means of trying to control the uncontrollable, or as a simple means to power or profit. Many forms of militarism are hybrid: they include elements of several of the above. But in turn, military modes of organization have their own logic: they exult authoritarianism, elitism, secrecy and the cult of violence. They have built-in right-ward tendencies. This implies that social groups will all face great obstacles in trying to make their voices and influence heard in peacemaking processes. The constraints and opportunities will depend crucially on the particular circumstances of the conflict: a framework for analyzing this is outlined in the following chapter.

Conclusion

Some preliminary conclusions can be drawn from the discussion above. Above all, the militarization of governance in Africa is an important and poorly-understood phenomenon that has far-reaching consequences. Militarism is prevalent in governments of all political shades, and deeply influences the ways in which power is exercised and decisions are made. It fundamentally influences the readiness of governments to go to war: militaristic leaders have a propensity to use violence as a first rather than a last resort. Any peace settlement that retains militaristic parties in power therefore suffers from a fundamental weakness: its principal beneficiaries may start another war.

Militarism represents a particular subset of authoritarianism. Militarist leaders exploit doctrines of constitutional exceptionalism; they seek an emergency mentality. Militaristic modes of governance are predicated on opacity and command, rather than transparency and dialogue. Therefore they utilize information and human resources in an efficient and slow manner. In a fast-changing and globalizing world, militaristic governance is an anachronism, and will undoubtedly prove to be a huge obstacle to African countries obtaining the kinds of democratic, participatory and accountable government that they need in order to achieve economic development. Militarism in government is a source of political paralysis, so that when change does come, it comes too late and in a sudden and often violent manner.

Left-wing intellectuals and leaders must seriously analyze the implications of their embrace of military modes of organization, and ask whether these have not proved self-defeating to the agenda of social justice and

91

economic emancipation that they espouse. The dominant generation of leftist leaders grew up during an era in which the moral polarities were clear: armed struggle against colonialism and Apartheid was justified, and in some cases people's war against post-colonial regimes was equally a 'just war.' But, leftist thinkers also need to examine whether these moral certainties are still as clear in the 21st century. The clear morality of fighting the Rwandese genocidaires in Zaire in 1996, and overthrowing the Mobutu regime, has transformed itself into the moral morass of the D.R. Congo war, in which no side can claim a monopoly on justification. What counts as a 'just war' now seems to depend on where you stand. In these conditions, the negative implications of leftist militarism come into sharper focus: there are no clear ends to justify these ambiguous means.

5

SOCIAL MOBILIZATION FOR PEACE

The previous chapter has highlighted some of the dangers of militaristic modes of governance, and in particular has pointed to their tendency to use violence to resolve political problems. Of necessity, any peace settlement must be negotiated among belligerent parties, and therefore give prominence to militaristic leaders. However, the sustainability of any such agreement will depend crucially on the demilitarization of governance. This in turn is closely related to the extent to which a wide range of social groups can be involved in a peace settlement.

This chapter is concerned with how three of the most important categories in any society—women, youth and the poor the impoverished and marginalized—who are also those with the greatest stake in peace, can make their voices heard and their presence felt during war, and help to promote peace. This is a laudable aim: who would be opposed to women, young people and the poor facilitating peace? There is no doubt that these are the people who suffer great burdens and risks during any armed conflict, and especially the protracted internal civil wars that are too common in much of Africa.

There are huge challenges facing those who wish to organize peace groups or peace movements in Africa. There are few successful 'issue-based' social movements in Africa, that are capable of effecting social or political change, such as ending armed conflict. The opportunities for civil society and social mobilization are few. In addition, the power relations inherent in armed conflict tend to further subjugate such people, and make their participation in the political life of the country more difficult. The prevalence of militarism, as analyzed in the previous chapter, is perhaps the single major constraint on effective social mobilization.

We must also note that these categories are not simple. 'Women', 'youth' and 'the poor' are not organic social groups that automatically adhere together. They all have multiple loyalties, and especially during times of war, some of these other loyalties—to ethnic group or political party—will be much stronger than their identification with other women, youths or poor people. Many youth and poor people and some women are themselves combatants. (It is often overlooked how ordinary rank-and-file soldiers are victims of war. They suffer the highest casualty rates, and although some of them inflict abuse, they are also victims of abuse. And because they are embedded at the bottom a military hierarchy, they cannot express their views without risking court martial for insubordination or worse.) For those who advocate for these marginalized groups, what strategies can be followed?

This chapter asks the question, how the representation of women, youth and the poor, who are among the key stakeholders in peace, can be promoted. It approaches this issue from several angles, including not only the mechanisms whereby these groups can be mobilized, but also how the means, material, political and ideological, whereby these groups are marginalized, can be tackled.

Civil Politics and Social Mobilization

The term 'civil society' is widely used, but with little analytical precision. As a prelude for approaching the challenge of involving key stakeholders in peace, we need to develop a more incisive framework for understanding how different categories and groups can become actively involved in pursuing their interests. The first requirement is to identify several kinds of civil society activities related to peace, governance, human rights and other mobilization for social progress and change.

1. *Primary mobilization.* This consists of the mobilization of multiple grass-roots organizations and constituencies; the mass mobilization of individuals in pursuit of what they see to be their own interests, or a wider moral cause. This 'primary mobilization' is the core constituency for any truly effective peace-building. Their intimate and ongoing involvement is the key to the maintaining the relevance, moral determination, sensitivity and sense of accountability of such mobilization.

2. Professional advocacy. Advocacy organizations represent the 'second generation' of human rights activism. Advocacy in this sense has policy-oriented and adversarial components. Policy-oriented advocacy is the activism of professionals in the area who can bring the issue to the public eye, provide legal and policy expertise, and advise governments and international organizations. Adversarial advocacy is the investigation and documentation of cases of abuse, and the extent of abuse, in different countries; and the exposure ('naming and shaming') of governments that have turned a blind eye or worse to the practice. This includes bringing cases to court and providing legal aid to victims. Journalism and law are key professions in this kind of work.

3. Material assistance. Assistance agencies, ranging from local NGOs and community-based advice centres, to international NGOs, to UN organizations, to governmental donors, all have a role in building peace. Aid provision can be a vital part of peacebuilding and especially of the success of post-conflict transitions. However, a focus on resources also has its dangers, because it may lead to a neglect of the essential social and political activities that must underpin effective peace-related activities.

4. Coalitions with concerned policymakers. Sympathetic individuals in governments (legislature, executive and judiciary), and also in business, the UN, foundations, etc., must be key parts of any coalition concerned with peace. These 'policymakers with a conscience' are strategic allies in terms of enacting policy changes and taking key leadership decisions.

Historically, the most successful social movements have consisted of a coalition between the 'primary mobilization' of constituencies—the mass mobilization of people in pursuit of their own rights and interests—and the 'secondary activism' of professionals, who can use the tools of publicity, the law, and international alliance-building to lead such movements. The principled activism of some lawmakers and judges has also been instrumental. Africa has had few of these successful primary-secondary coalitions. The non-violent independence movement in the 1950s and 1960s was one case. The anti-Apartheid movement was a variant on the theme. The short-lived civil coalition that overthrew the Nimeiri dictatorship in Sudan in April 1985 was another. The pro-democracy movements of the late 1980s and the sovereign national conferences of Francophone countries in the early 1990s were another encouraging case. But it is very rare in Africa (as indeed elsewhere in the world) for there to be a mass peace movement in a country that is at war, especially when the war is close to home. For many reasons, peace movements are easily divided or manipulated, and it takes remarkably courageous individuals to resist the taunts of 'traitor' that will be leveled by one side or the other.

In seeking to explain the paucity of effective social mobilization in Africa, we must turn our attention to the political environment. There are many dimensions to this, including the extent to which society is organized on the basis of citizenship or kinship, the extent of economic development and especially industrialization, and the nature of political culture, in particular the extent of militaristic governance. The following discussion seeks only to isolate one dimension among these, and suggests a simple four-fold categorization of kinds of political authority in Africa. The categorizations apply in variant forms both to governments and to rebel movements, and to left- and right-wing systems of rule (c.f. Moore and Putzel, 1999).

War—whether civil conflict or inter-state war—tends to destroy or distort systems for political representation. A tolerant liberal government will become much more authoritarian when it is in war mode. Suddenly, dissent may be regarded as treason, or just a step away. Rebel groups and militias usually depend upon total loyalty for their political survival. However, war does not mean that there are no channels of communication, no opportunities for organization and expression. Other socio-political structures remain intact, and some may even become strengthened. Hence, any state in one of the following categories is likely to shift towards a more repressive and authoritarian category, when it is afflicted by war.

The following categorization runs from collapsed states to liberal democracies. For each case, we ask what kind of civil society is possible, and what it can do. Note that in this context, civil society includes civilian political parties, trade unions and other organized interest groups, as well as NGOs and community-based organizations.

Category one is *collapsed states*, with the absence of any effective governing authorities, including organized administration by militia groups or former rebel fronts. The opportunity for any form of civil mobilization is very limited, and will probably be confined to local NGOs seeking to protect and assist displaced people, perhaps with help from international donors. No organized political representation is possible.

This draws attention to the fact that in most situations of armed conflict, the primary need for any individual is security and survival. These needs are best met by seeking the protection of a party to the conflict, which in turn means not mobilizing in any manner that may challenge that party. Where the conflict has a regional or ethnic dimension, these loyalties may become by far the most important organizing principle, so that individuals are uninterested in promoting their interests as women, youth etc., and instead identify with the political and military struggle. Those who resist this identification may be branded as 'traitors' and crushed.

However, we must not place all conflict-affected countries in this bracket, with the implication that nothing can be done. This is for several reasons. First, countries at war may still have civil politics in one form or another, especially in the capital city. For example, Sudan had a functioning parliamentary system during 1986-9, despite being at war. Despite the current war and collapsed state in the D.R. Congo, the city of Kinshasa continues to have civil space and political activities by parties and individuals. Second, the warring parties themselves differ greatly in terms of their internal organization. While some are highly authoritarian and may even be the personal fiefdoms of their leaders, others have the capacity for civil administration and the implementation of social programmes, that may actually promote the emancipation of marginalized groups such as women. In addition, in some countries with collapsed states, some areas may be peaceful, and civil organization around NGOs or grassroots organizations may be possible. Many parts of Somalia are like this. However, in other cases, there is such a widespread breakdown of the socio-political order that any form of organized representation of interest groups is impossible.

Category two is *personal rule or arbitrary rule*. This characterizes some governments, and many armed groups. Policies are unstable; political activity is focused on taking or retaining power and enriching those in power. Groups such as women and the poor have few or no political options, and effective public policies are improbable and if they do occur, they are unlikely to last long. Again, those who challenge the authority of the government or anti-government group may find themselves crushed. Even raising alternative agendas and viewpoints may be politically and personally dangerous.

In Africa, most such systems of government are dominated by a 'big man' who seeks to evoke traditional images as the 'father of the nation' or chief of the tribe. His citizens are infantilized as 'subjects,' who should be grateful for their leader's generosity and consideration, and should not be so insolent as to demand 'rights'. The 'big man' does not consult, he preaches. This kind of rule tends to be much more effective in rural areas, where adapted traditional forms of authority prevail, than in urban areas. Any civil society mobilization is antithetical to this neo-traditional rule. Commonly, civil society will therefore be largely an urban phenomenon, arising from the same social groups that mobilize opposition political parties and demand greater political freedoms. The government will tend to dismiss both civil society leaders and opposition politicians as elitists who represent only narrow urban interests. This charge may contain an element of truth: any form of social mobilization presupposes that people envisage themselves as citizens and bearers of rights, not as subjects, and if this kind of socio-political culture is confined to urban areas, this is where civil society and social mobilization will occur.

Some slender options for mobilization to represent civil interests offer themselves in such cases. First, there may be a small opening for organizing groups in a solidarity mode, avowing their loyalty to the ruling party, and those groups may then move on to undertake other forms of advocacy in a discrete way. But, when challenged or fearing challenges, such groups must always put their solidarity with the dominant political force above any other consideration.

Second, using external linkages may be an option, if used carefully. That is, a group will seek the protection of an international organization, or will build a coalition with an exile or expatriate organization, in order to press their case. Alternatively, the initiative may come from diaspora groups, who enjoy the silent support of people inside the country. The interests of women, or youth, or certain ethnic groups, will then be represented by leaders who are outside the country or who have positions or influence in international NGOs. These leaders may of course develop their own agendas, or may not effectively serve their constituencies— but in the absence of opportunities for the mobilization of the group in question internally, there may be no other mechanism for making their voices heard. The influence of such groups is likely to be marginal.

This type of mobilization will be effective in proportion to the weakness of the ruling authority. When that authority is weak—it has few resources and needs international respectability—then it may concede space for independent groups to operate, if doing so is its only means to gaining access to international resources. However, should the authority obtain its own sources of income, it is likely to squeeze that small space for civil action.

Lastly, if the government or opposition represents a coalition, then there will be political space provided by the differences between the coalition partners. A coalition entails a forum for discussion between the different party leaders. Any such forum is also an opening for civil groups to make their voices heard. Once again, managing this without falling foul of the parties will demand skill, sensitivity and patience.

Category three is *institutionalized government with limited political freedoms* and minimal pluralism (either left-wing, right-wing or simply authoritarian). Governments or (more rarely) opposition fronts may be able to run effective administrations and deliver social services.

In such situations there are much greater possibilities for the mobilization of interest groups. Where the authorities have a broadly leftist political programme, it may be easy for them to respond to some demands from women, youth, the poor etc. Mass organizations may have some autonomy which can be used to push the interests of their constituents. Under right-wing authorities, it is possible that religiously-based groups may be able to mobilize and represent interests. It is possible that there will be international NGO involvement in service provision, which increases opportunities for stakeholders to make alliances with external groups. However the authorities' response is likely to be top-down, and the institutional mechanisms whereby these groups are given some political representation are likely to be dominated by the political apparatus.

In such circumstances, internal constituencies may take the lead in mobilizing stakeholders, but only for limited agendas. Once again, we will find that civil groups are likely to define their primary loyalty to the political cause, and use this as a platform for pressing for their specific interest. Meanwhile external groups—either international organizations or expatriate or exile groups—may still play a crucial role, because they can provide an arena for more open debate and discussion of alternatives, that may be impossible within the limited political space available internally.

In such circumstances, civil groups can mobilize for peace, but only indirectly. Some may adopt a formal agenda for 'peace', but on examination their loyalty to one or other belligerent party means that they really mean 'peace through victory.' Others may seek peace indirectly by promoting local reconciliation within limited localities, or by developing independent civil society organizations in the small niches available. But civil groups will be able to openly call for peace only when the party that protects them endorses that call.

The fourth and final category is *institutionalized government with political pluralism*. These are stable and mature democratic states with legitimate organizations and civil and political rights. They normally provide a wide range of welfare services, and there is much debate and scrutiny of service provision. Interest groups have the scope to organize, though other axes of political mobilization (such as ethnicity) may dominate. Groups that are otherwise invisible politically (e.g. the handicapped, very small ethnic minorities) may find a voice. There are myriad opportunities for promoting the interests and mobilization of women, youth and other groups. International networking by these groups is possible and can be done in an open manner.

It is rare for such a government to be involved in a protracted armed conflict, internally or with a neighbor. However, there are transitional cases in which either or both government and opposition are engaged in open public debate about peace, creating a space in which pro-peace constituencies can organize. Where the government or opposition consists of a broad coalition with different political agendas, this political space is more likely. Under these sorts of government, there is the possibility for a genuine 'peace movement' that is independent of government or military opposition, and brings real political pressure for peace to bear on the parties.

Options and Strategies for Civil Society

The above categorization underlines how it is inherently difficult for civil society groups to mobilize when their need to do so is greatest. It emphasizes how the interests of stakeholder groups may be primarily linked to ethnic, regional or political affiliations, on which survival and security depend in the short term. It draws attention to the strategies that such groups are likely to follow.

During conflict, the primary identification of any civil society organization or social group is likely to be with the major agenda of one of the parties to the conflict, because of ethnic, religious, political and regional allegiance and because of the need for physical security. Only when the political tension relaxes, for example in the context of hopeful peace negotiations, will it be possible for cross-cutting allegiances to be mobilized. (This implies that civil society can mobilize for peace only when peace is already on the agenda of the principal billigerents.) A variant of this occurs when a group may work within the institutions set up by one of the parties, trying to test the autonomy of that institution (e.g. a women's organization or a humanitarian agency). Another variant occurs when an independent group may be in solidarity with one of the parties, with also an ulterior agenda of promoting the rights of specific interest groups. Thus, a women's organization may seek to promote the rights of women within a particular party or the territory it controls.

All groups will be extremely cautious in undertaking any visible mobilization in a way that challenges the warring party under whose authority they reside. A group with an existing constituency in the area— for example a church organization—will be very cautious in protecting the interests of its constituents, by seeking not to offend the controlling party. But, under certain circumstances, it may be ready to advocate boldly and publicly, confident that its combination of local constituency and international linkages will provide some protection.

Groups may utilize external links with international NGOs and exile groups in order to promote their particular interest and point of view, or to create a space in which wider issues such as peace can be discussed openly.

Certain categories of people—including our three target categories—

have particular interests in peace. But they are also categories of people whom it is difficult to mobilize as such. They have more interests that divide them and few natural structures for organization and authority, implying that any mobilization will probably be transient. The following sections of this chapter deal with these three groups, and the challenges of mobilizing them or representing their interests.

Women and Mobilization for Peace

The idea of 'engendering the peace', bringing women's outlook and voices to bear on peace processes, is gathering momentum. In most societies, women are seen, in one way or another, as a force for peace and harmony, as nurturers and carers. This may be a myth, a cultural construct, that actually originates in sexist values. However, if these cultural stereotypes can be used in the course of promoting peace, they may bring some benefits to women and men alike. This section looks at some of the challenges of mobilizing women and representing their interests in war-afflicted countries.

Women and War

Women suffer terribly during war. Women in Africa suffer from poverty, inequality, discrimination, and abuse during normal times. During conflict, all these elements are worsened.

Women suffer from changes in economic roles. Women already do the majority of the work in the home and in agriculture throughout Africa. War usually entails even greater workloads and responsibilities. Whether they are at home, with their menfolk gone (fled, conscripted or dead), or displaced (also commonly without their menfolk), women have to take on greater responsibilities. Women in female-headed households have to take on the exclusive responsibility for caring for the family members who remain, perhaps augmented by orphaned members of the extended family. They may find themselves with the sole responsibility of growing food and earning an income, perhaps from petty trade. They may have to venture into new economic areas, which may involve running risks when travelling to buy food or trade. While for some women it may be a liberating experience to be freed from the confines of domestic work and farming, for many it is simply an additional burden and an extra set of risks. Elder daughters may find themselves withdrawn from school in order to help look after younger siblings; their future is sacrificed for the immediate

101

needs of the family.

Women who are poor and desperately in need of food or money for themselves and their children are vulnerable to exploitation. They can be economically exploited by traders who buy their assets cheaply, or farmers who employ their labor at below-market rates. Young women may have no option but to become commercial sex workers or to attach themselves to a series of male partners for survival.

Women are vulnerable to sexual abuse. Particularly when they are outside the framework of their village, clan or extended family, women may be extremely vulnerable to rape. This has the attendant risks of HIV infection (and soldiers are one of the highest-risk occupational categories for transmission of HIV), other sexually-transmitted diseases, unwanted pregnancies, stigmatization, trauma, and perhaps being forced into commercial sex work.

For poor women during wartime, life can consist of trying to manage multiple risks. Nothing is certain. There are no reliable guides for how to act. No information can be relied upon. Many women find themselves with unacceptable choices every day: they have to choose between husbanding seed (not knowing if they will be able to plant at all) and feeding their children; between using scarce time walking a safe path to a well or risking land-mines on a shorter path; between risking HIV by offering sexual favors and the 'safety' of begging for charity that may not come.

Women are under pressure to support warring parties. Women in war-affected areas or refugee camps tend to have few possessions. But this does not deter soldiers or rebels who consider even the smallest contribution to the war effort, or their own personal welfare, a worthwhile sacrifice. Women may be forced to surrender crops, food rations, basic possessions to soldiers. They may be required to cook for soldiers, or even to abandon their homes and travel with army units as camp followers, cooking, doing the laundry, acting as porters, and providing unpaid sexual services as well.

Men, of course, suffer too during war. Especially poor men and youth, because, in most wars, it is men who predominantly suffer death or disability during combat. Widows and orphans may suffer, but they are still alive. In many wars, however, civilian casualties are greater than military, and women may suffer disproportionately from the combined effects of social vulnerability, sexual abuse, displacement and hardship.

Commonly, men also suffer most during food crises. For every single famine and refugee crisis for which statistical information is available, death rates for men have been higher than for women. This is true, with very few exceptions, across all age ranges from very young children to old people. This appears to be related to two factors. One is the greater physiological resilience of women, who survive prolonged undernutrition and related stresses better than men. The second is the fact that in the lower-status occupations, on which survival depends during times of extreme stress, women have advantages compared to men. (E.g. selling cooked food, collecting wild foods, domestic labor.)

The idea of men somehow 'escaping' from famine or conflict zones, abandoning women to suffer, is not generally borne out by the facts. We need to be cautious in assuming that men somehow 'benefit' from conflict: most of them do not.

Women in Peacemaking: The Case Against

There is a case to be made that women do not have a useful role to play in peacemaking. This is a 'realist' view. It should be taken seriously: responding to these arguments provides the foundation for organizing women in support of peace. The argument runs something like this.

Peace is made between those who control armed forces. In fact peacemaking is a futile exercise if it is merely conducted among those who desire peace but have no power to deliver it. Given the structure of power in Africa, especially military power, it follows that women's role in peacemaking will always be marginal.

Women's advocacy for peace is open to some common misconceptions. Some women argue that their sex is necessarily more pacific: they are the bearers of children, the nurturers, the bringers of harmony, and that therefore they should be peacemakers. It is almost certainly correct that women are less warlike than men. Also, it does not follow that women will make *better* peacemakers.

Women's primary loyalty is not necessarily to peace, nor to other women. Women often mobilize strongly in support of their ethnic group or community, taking militant positions. Women in formal political positions will hold to their party's line, even when it comes to taking a stand on women's issues that contradicts women's rights. Women can agitate for war, help promote war ideologies, and carry out other actions in pursuit of war. They can also participate in fighting, and commit atrocities.

Women have some traditional sanctions against war in Africa. For example, there are cases in which the women of some communities have refused sexual relations with their menfolk until those men have seen sense and abandoned their wars. However, this tool just shows how weak women's capacity for pressing for peace really is. How common is this strategy? How difficult is it to organize? And how long does it last?

It is important not to forget that men have as much interest as women in peace, if not more so. After all, it is mostly men who die. Why should women's voices be given a special privilege?

Most advocacy for peace by women's organizations has been by external organizations that do not directly represent the voices and interests of women inside the countries concerned. Foreign organizations have commonly organized or sponsored these initiatives. These may have good intentions at heart, but it is questionable whether they have the organic links and accountability to war-affected women for them to be true representatives of them or their interests. Without this foreign sponsorship, these 'women for peace' organizations and conferences would simply not occur. In extreme cases, critics argue that foreign women's organizations are meddling in affairs about which they understand little, and are pursuing their own interests at the expense of women in war-stricken countries.

Women in Peacemaking: The Case in Favor

Strong following arguments may be made in favor of women having a special role in peacemaking. First, women are not seeking a privileged role, or the sole role, in making peace. They are not seeking to exclude or marginalize men, merely to make warmakers aware of the impact of war on women, which is something that they may not know or may have chosen to ignore. Women are aware that it is up to the warmakers to make peace, but they believe that if their voices are heard, then warmakers are more likely to consider seriously the harm of war and the benefits of peace, which may bring peace closer.

Secondly, some women may be stakeholders in war; some may commit atrocities or benefit from conflict. But on the whole, women are purely victims of violence, while men are both perpetrators and victims. Women are also the prime carers of children, especially during wartime, and children are also solely victims of war and not its beneficiaries. Giving a voice to women therefore stresses the negative aspects of war. It makes it more difficult for warmakers to justify continuing war, if there is an option of peace. Also, the fact that some women participate in war and atrocity shows that women have a choice: when women advocate for peace, it is not because they are naturally programmed to do so, but because they have made a moral choice to do so. This should make their contribution all the more valuable.

Third, although women's role in *peacemaking* is limited, their role in *peacebuilding* may be much more substantial. Adult women are the prime carers of young boys and can play a crucial role in socializing them into becoming more peaceable men. Young women, if empowered, are the group who can help forge key values among their male contemporaries. If every young woman wants to marry an army officer, it will be difficult to overcome a culture of militarism.

Fourth, women cannot enforce peace. It is hard for women to organize to represent their common interests as women. It is particularly hard for them to do so in patriarchal societies such as are common in Africa, and even harder in war-affected authoritarian and militaristic societies. Women have very few sanctions. There is little direct pressure they can bring to bear. But their weapon is the weapon of the weak: an appeal to conscience and long-term good sense and self-interest. Precisely because women are so vulnerable, their voice carries a moral authority. Women should be listened to, not because they can enforce their demands, but because they speak on behalf of the powerless, and raise questions that cannot be ignored.

Finally, the international component of women's mobilization should be welcomed, not dismissed. Those women who are fortunate enough to be internationally networked and protected should speak out on behalf of their sisters who live in conflict-ridden areas, who are downtrodden and vulnerable and unable to organize or speak on their own behalf. Those who decry the international orientation of women's mobilization should provide the resources, opportunity and freedom for women at home to organize, and then listen to what they have to say. And if international mediators choose to listen to women's voices, while the warring parties are still not ready to do so, whose problem is this? Certainly there is a problem of foreign agencies having divergent agendas—but at least there is some overlap of aims between them and women affected by war, whereas the agendas of national war leaders and their female citizens seem often to have no convergence at all. Should women refuse to talk to the international community just because their national warmakers would rather that they remained silent?

Options for Women's Mobilization

The above discussion has some important implications for the strategies for women's mobilization in pursuit of peace. The main lesson is that we should not expect a mass women's movement in a war-affected country. It is simply too much to expect that hundreds of thousands of women will mobilize themselves to demonstrate for peace, pressuring and shaming their government or belligerent party into abandoning war in favor of negotiation. Women's activists may keep this as a vision in their minds, as an ultimate goal, but it is some way away.

The experience of women in Burundi, and their engagement in the long peace process in that country, is an important experience, from which many lessons can be learned. The voice of Burundi's women was heard at the Arusha talks, which was positive. But the women also brought with them their social and political agendas, associated with their alignments with social and political groups. The women were not an external, 'innocent' force: they were an integral part of the conflicted society.

The experience of the 'Engendering the Peace' initiative for Sudan, led by the Netherlands Government, also had strengths and weaknesses. It was an unprecedented opportunity for Sudanese women to make their voices heard internationally, and to meet with one another and with prominent women activists from across the world. But they too brought their politics with them. Most notably, the final conference in Maastricht did not include a delegation of women aligned with the SPLA, because the SPLA leadership took a political stand against the initiative. Meanwhile, the Sudan Government delegation to the conference was led by men!

For the time being, women's mobilization for peace is likely to be opportunistic, in a positive sense. It will take and utilize what opportunities exist for mobilizing women and representing their concerns. This strategy may include:

1. Contacting, informing and mobilizing whatever women's groups exist or can be brought into being, whether they are 'primary' constituencies of women in the affected country, or 'secondary' activist groups either inside or in the diaspora.

2. Researching the condition of women in war-affected countries. Documenting their plight, the difficulties they face and the risks they run. Recording their voices, so that their experiences and views can be known to the world.

3. Providing practical assistance to women affected by war. Encouraging humanitarian agencies to prioritize women's concerns and set up programmes that deal specifically with women's needs (this agenda is already well advanced). Helping women with access to information and legal protection where possible.

4. International networking, bringing together different women's groups interested in peace. Bringing women's viewpoints to international fora including peace negotiations. Using every moral pressure to make sure that the national parties and international mediators consider women's views.

Note that these strategies, or variants of them, can and should also be adopted as a preventive strategy. In countries that are not at war, but there is a clear risk of conflict, it is likely that the capacity for women's mobilization and advocacy will be greater than in a country already in the grip of conflict. Women's advocacy for preventing war may be both more possible and more effective.

Youth

Where would warmakers be without youth? The great majority of soldiers in any army consists of young men and boys in their late teens and early twenties. Many are conscripted, either forcibly or because they have no other options for a livelihood. Others join voluntarily because of grievance or frustration (closure of schools being a classic reason), or for excitement.

'Youth' is a problematic category. It is tempting to define 'youth' in terms of age (e.g. the group between ages sixteen and thirty). But this is an arbitrary measurement that misses the key point: youth is a category that is exploited by warmakers. The challenge for peacemakers is, can youth also be a category that can be mobilized for peace?

Youth Organization for War

As outlined above, both right-wing and left-wing militarists have sought to organize or at least mobilize youth. We may recap on this, add an additional category, and summarize the types of youth organization and ideology that are useful for military mobilization.

1. Right-wing proto-military youth organizations. The 'youth wings' of certain political parties are a variant on this, with discipline played down and wanton thuggery played up. These are hierarchical organizations, controlled from the top.

2. Left-wing youth organizations. These may have a (partly) pacific ideology, perhaps oriented towards 'development' or 'international solidarity'. But they can still form the basis for instilling discipline and loyalty, and be the foundation for military organization. These are also hierarchical organizations, and some 'youth' leaders may stay in the posts for many years, reaching ages that stretch

any age-based definition of 'youth' somewhat.

3. Traditional warrior organizations. Among some ethnic groups, particularly pastoralists, there were warrior age-sets or similar means of mobilizing fighters. Some of these mechanisms remain in adapted form and can still be called upon for mobilizing young men.

4. Youth mobs and 'social bandits'. The excitement of armed confrontation and the possibility of looting, may be sufficient to mobilize unruly mobs of youth for transient rioting.

5. There are hybrid cases. For example the Interahamwe militia of Rwanda include elements of right-wing proto-military organization, adapted traditional warrior mechanisms, and youth mobs. Given the dispersal of the Interahamwe throughout Central Africa, this model now has regional ramifications.

The fourth type of military youth mobilization raises questions. The youth mob, in this form, is a recent historical phenomenon, certainly in Africa. Why might this be so?

A basic point is that Africa is now a continent of young people. Rapid population growth means that there are far more children and young people than mature adults. In the past, and in European countries, stable populations meant that youths were a scarce commodity. States needed to nurture and develop them, as all would be needed for future mobilization. However, African countries have (relatively speaking) a surfeit of youth. Military planners and others seeking to mobilize youth can afford to be more wasteful and less efficient.

In addition, in contemporary Africa, the previously existing life trajectories for young people are no longer valid (Seekings, 1993). In traditional societies there were rites of passage for young people to become adults, at which point they were entitled and obliged to fight, and thereafter they would marry, own land and cattle, and become senior members of the community. In more recent times, there was an expectation that modernity entailed a new trajectory: living at home as a child; attending school; leaving school and finding work. For many this was just a hope, but it was at least, a norm. In the last decades, with the decline in the formal economy, we have a new trajectory: school-'youth'-uncertainty. Youths live with unemployment, some chances in the informal sector, with risk-taking, and with few expectations that they will achieve the same standard of living as their parents or grandparents.

Youth—or, to be precise, male youth—are seen as militant, rebellious, impatient, malleable, and risk-taking. If these energies cannot be chan-

neled into a courageous commitment to a national cause (national liberation, or *jihad*, or something similar), then there is the possibility of mobilizing youth in a violent and anarchic way. Some writers, observing the
apparently uncontrolled and irrational violence of the wars in Sierra Leone
and Liberia, have hypothesized that Africa's youth are now out of control;
a combination of frustration, lack of education, access to drugs, and the
readiness of cynical warlords to provide them with weapons, has created
a dangerous new class of armed thugs with no agenda other than enjoying
themselves at the expense of civilized values.

This is of course an exaggeration. The majority of young combatants across
Africa have rather conventional aspirations for their future lives. They would like
an education and a useful job. Like young people across the world, they rebel
against their elders, ignore advice, and enjoy taking risks. The advent of the AIDS
pandemic has shortened time horizons, narrowed expectations, and heightened
risks. But, given the option, is very likely that most young people would prefer a
future of security and domesticity.

It is striking how little research there is on this area. There are very few
surveys of the background and aspirations of young soldiers in Africa. There is
very little sociological or economic analysis of youth and their needs and strategies for survival. Any wide-ranging plans for bringing stability to Africa must
include intensive study of these questions.

Other Options for the Mobilization of Youth

Non-military means for mobilization also exist. We can identify several
types of formal youth organization, including especially:

1. Leftist youth organizations. Although, as mentioned, these organi-
    zations may be co-opted by militarists or neutralized by vanguardist
    organizations, they also tend to have a pacific and internationalist
    ideology, which can be the basis for autonomous action and interna-
    tional networking that can promote peace.

2. Student unions. Student unions are probably the most representative and
    influential civil organization for youth. Student politics has a dispro-
    portionate influence in many African countries. In 1964 it was the
    Khartoum Student Union that sparked the 'October Revolution' that
    brought down the military dictatorship of General Ibrahim Abboud.
    Many African governments closely watch student politics. Often they
    find it difficult to intervene and control student unions, perhaps be-
    cause student organization is so fluid and fast-changing that it is dif-

ficult to set up patronage and supervisory structures that can work effectively. By the same token, student unions can only mount short-lived challenges to political authority.

3. Church youth groups. Africa's main religions organize young people for self-advancement and as the core of their future congregations. Their politics tends to follow that of the parent religious organization. Although they may seem over-formal with a top-down hierarchical organization, such youth groups often succeed in capturing the energies and commitment of their members. They can be key intermediaries in spreading public health messages such as AIDS prevention. With the rapid growth of youth-oriented Pentecostal churches, this form of mobilization of young people is becoming more significant.

4. Sports groups. Football clubs and supporters clubs are some of the most vigorous and authentic youth organizations in Africa. They have loyal and dedicated followers.

Turning to less formal organizations, we can identify a wide range of other youth organizations. These include: student clubs (both male and female students have clubs that vary greatly in their degree of formal organization), music associations and clubs, secret societies (in west Africa, especially Nigeria, these are common), gangs of various kinds, vigilante groups, and community associations.

Generally speaking, more is known about male organizations than female ones. Their variety, informality and transience makes them difficult to study. Also, some are based on a culture of resistance: i.e. they will deliberately not cooperate with any authorities and may in fact react in an adverse way to any attempt to mobilize or co-opt them.

All these factors make it intrinsically difficult to mobilize 'youth' as a force for peace. However, the very fact that a large proportion of Africa's youth, especially in urban areas, is organized into clubs and societies of one form or another presents opportunities for mobilization. Such mobilization can be addressed incrementally. The best foundation for youth mobilization are the more durable and structured youth organizations, such as international leftist youth organizations, federations of students' unions, and church youth groups. But the effectiveness, authenticity and vitality of youth mobilization will be best served by a wider coalition that embraces other less formal organizations, such as football supporters' clubs, music clubs, etc. The latter have the particular advantage that they can potentially mobilize important celebrities and stars as role models and advocates.

The Poor

The political mobilization of 'the poor'—or the 'broad masses', the impoverished, and workers and peasants—in Africa has been a Holy Grail for the left on the continent for many decades. The limited success of sustained attempts by civilian leftist parties to mobilize workers and peasants as an effective political force should warn against any easy assumptions that poor people can be mobilized as a force for peace. Some guerrilla movements have proved effective at mobilizing the peasantry, with programmes of land reform and the removal of harsh taxes. However, extending this mode of mobilization to other groups has usually proven difficult. The poor are particularly vulnerable during wartime: any attempts to make their voices heard are likely to meet with violent repression. However, there are some limited options in terms of organizing the less poor through trade unions, and indirectly representing the interests of the poor through development organizations.

Trade Unions

The most successful mobilization of economic groups in Africa has been trade union activity in South Africa and a few other major cities. Miners, industrial workers and tenants on irrigated agricultural schemes have all scored some successes through trade union organization. Though poor by international standards, these groups are relatively well off in comparison to many of their compatriots, for example people who work in the informal sector selling cooked food or farmers on marginal land in remote areas.

Trade unions can play an important role in mobilization. For example, trade unions were at the forefront of the struggle against Apartheid, and they were the backbone of the 1985 popular uprising in Sudan. Their local base can be strong. Individual members of trade unions also tend to have a high level of political consciousness, especially when they are operating within the framework of union activities. Their leaders often have strong organizational capacities. Trade unions also have the important asset of international connectedness: they can call upon foreign partners and friends to press their case at the ILO and other international fora.

As a force for peace, trade unions suffer the same difficulties as general civil society organizations as outlined above. Their capacity to orga-

111

nize and present the case for peaceful settlement of conflicts is likely to be greatest when the belligerent parties have already begun to move towards peace. If they make claims before this point, they will be running the risk of major political confrontation with their governments.

Trade unions face special challenges arising from the current economic context of globalization, austerity measures that have cut back public sector employment, and the informalization of African economies. These developments have had a negative impact on trade unions, undermining their constituencies and reducing their influence. Outside a few industrial and mining centres, trade unions are generally a weakening force.

Development Agencies

Development agencies, whether they are local NGOs, international NGOs, inter-governmental organizations or other variants, do not seek to mobilize the poor. But they do claim, to some degree, to represent their interests. Depending on their position, their options vary considerably.

Domestic NGOs in war-affected countries are a component of civil society, and as such the constraints they operate under and opportunities they have are similar to trade unions and other civil society actors. There are options for indirectly promoting peace however, for example by initiating discussions on what policies and programmes should be implemented when peace has come. Merely talking about a peaceful future can help billigerents consider the rewards of peace more actively.

International development NGOs tend to work with local partner organizations and have to be careful about the implications of any advocacy activities for their partners. They also tend to prioritize their access and operationality over any advocacy on matters of principle. (This is a structural conflict of interest that regularly hampers international NGOs effectively addressing the underlying causes of poverty, war and famine.) Thus, a relief or development NGO operating in Southern Sudan may advocate peace in general, it is unlikely to call for a particular peace deal or a practical strategy to promote peace, because this may risk offending the party under whose auspices they must operate. However, if international agencies were to collaborate more closely with one another on such advocacy strategies, they might be able to achieve more: belligerent parties would be less likely to expel a whole group of them. There are also opportunities for documenting the effects of war on poor people, and presenting these in national and international fora, allowing the audience to draw its own conclusions. Much work has been done in this direction, but there is room for ensuring that these agendas and strategies are articulated more closely with regional organizations that may be more closely engaged in negotiating peace.

International organizations, including African and UN organizations, international financial institutions and western donor governments, well understand the devastating economic impact of war, and generally speaking their assistance and lending policies are run accordingly. There is, however, a clear lack of common principles and coordination, both between the assistance agencies themselves, and between them and any regional or international mediators involved in promoting peace. Achieving such coordination is difficult, because of the intrinsic problems of coordinating different bureaucracies across different countries and continents, and because the demands of peace mediation (flexibility, rapidity of action) are very different to the slow pace and formal procedures of decision-making in development assistance bureaucracies.

The route of using development institutions to advocate on behalf of the poor is fraught with complications. The most serious of these is that development agencies are not always run with the aim of relieving poverty. Economic development, environmental protection, tackling disease and a host of other mandates overlap with poverty alleviation but are not identical. In addition, those that have a specific concern with poverty alleviation do not always combine this with an approach that focuses on representing the poor. (The paternalistic outlook of some missionary organizations is an obvious case in point.) It would be very unwise to assume that any aid institution can advocate authentically and effectively on behalf of the poor. However, it may be that aid agencies, pursuing their own interests, can help promote peace by making it clear that peace is a precondition for generous or effective development assistance.

Implications

Africa's 'unarmed battalions' are intrinsically difficult to mobilize, but their involvement is important for sustainable peace and security. Creative means of ensuring that these groups can find a voice, and become part of broader coalitions, is an important task if we are to promote sustainable peace. Political settlements may be negotiated among the leaders of belligerent parties, but at the risk of entrenching militarized parties in power, with the attendant danger of militarizing governance over the long term. This is not only undesirable in its own right, but also undermines the long-term prospects for peace and the establishment of security communities.

The agendas of peace and democratization—including civilianization—are inexorably linked. As the analysis of constraints on stakeholders' mobilization has shown, it is only possible for the key groups to organize themselves when they are freed from the ideological and organizational shackles of militaristic-type mobilization. While conflict and militarism prevail, the forces of peace remain fragmented, disorganized and unable to articulate their agendas clearly. But, as civil society grows in confidence, and different stakeholder groups are able to mobilize themselves and ensure their voices are heard, it will be more and more difficult for militarists and warmakers to have their way.

6

MERCENARIES AND THE MILITARY-COMMERCIAL COMPLEX

This chapter seeks to pose some key questions about commercial militarism and African conflicts—a phenomenon most marked by the presence of foreign mercenaries.[1] The discussion does not start with a definition of what is a mercenary, but instead seeks to situate the phenomenon of soldiers who fight primarily for financial reward in the context of African conflicts today. The archetypal mercenary—a non-African professional soldier employed by a private company to protect foreign commercial interests—stands at one end of a spectrum of 'mercenarized' conflict. International private military companies (IPMCs) are part of a broader phenomenon, which has also seen the close engagement of African militaries in commercial activities, and military operations conducted primarily for commercial reasons. There is also the rapid growth of private security companies in many African countries, reflecting the deterioration of police forces. A focus on mercenary companies alone, and especially on the most high-profile ones such as Executive Outcomes and Sandline International, runs the risk of overlooking this wider structural issue. This does not negate the importance of finding the appropriate political and legislative measures to address the specific problem of these IPMCs. But it should caution us against believing that a successful prohibition on this kind of mercenary companies will resolve the wider problem of commercial engagement in warfare.

The debate on mercenaries is complicated by a number of other subsidiary issues. One of these is the proposal, forwarded by some, that IPMCs can play a role in peacekeeping and peace-enforcement, perhaps replacing UN or other multilateral forces. This is a very problematic proposal, as discussed in this chapter.

In addition, mercenary activity is very often closely associated with a host of other important political, economic and ethical issues. One of these is the rapacious extraction of Africa's natural resources by international oil companies, diamond traders and other commercial interests in alliance with some African elites. Another is the ideological agendas that further discolour many mercenary activities—notably associations with racism, colonialism or fundamentalism.

Overview of International Mercenarism in Africa

The history of international mercenarism in Africa goes back to the early imperial penetration of the continent. Schematically, we can identify alternate phases of mercenarism: a phase of foreign combat mercenaries engaged in high-profile, high-risk adventures, followed by a longer period in which foreign powers secured their interests in a more systematic and institutional manner. These 'non-mercenary' periods also witnessed close international engagement with military activities in Africa, usually through sponsoring African clients, thereby lessening the need to employ foreign mercenaries. When these African intermediaries have been afflicted by crises, then outside powers and international business interests have again turned to foreign combat mercenaries.

In the middle and later decades of the 19th century, individual European mercenaries and mercenary companies and their clients were prominent in the penetration and exploitation of much of Africa. Private military companies spearheaded the imperial penetration of the Nile Valley, Congo and Rhodesia, among other territories. The metropolitan powers subsequently changed their modus operandi. Some mercenary-type conquests were incorporated as official colonies (e.g. the Belgian Congo, Rhodesia), while other military-commercial entrepreneurs were labelled as bandits and slavers, and militarily defeated after their usefulness had expired (e.g. Tibbu Tib, Zubeir Rahma, Rabih Fadlallah). What followed was the formal apparatus of colonial rule, which made equal or even greater use of metropolitan armies and African intermediaries and foot-soldiers, but under a façade of legality—the Kings African Rifles and the French Foreign Legion were not formally 'mercenary' forces.

The post-colonial era, co-incident with the Cold War, saw a

comparable succession of phases. First, during the transition to independence, European combat mercenaries were active across the continent in defending the interests of former colonial powers. Although French and Belgian mercenaries garnered most publicity, British ones were also extremely active. The dismantling of colonial armies created an unemployed former officer corps with marketable military skills, often combined with a taste for adventure and right-wing or racist leanings.

European mercenaries came to prominence in the Congolese civil wars of the 1960s (Chapleau, 1998). The Katangan secessionist leader Moise Tshombe employed the services of about 650 Belgian mercenaries to fight against the government of Patrice Lumumba. The Belgian company Union Miniere du Haut Katanga was the paymaster, also employing soldiers of fortune from Britain, France, Germany and South Africa. In those early days the terms of employment were openly advertized: individual recruits were attracted by advertisements in South African newspapers, and recruitment centres were opened in cities in South Africa and Rhodesia. The Belgians offered contracts with daily pay of 13,411 francs and 10 million francs compenzation for the mercenary's family should he be killed. Those recruited included not only professional soldiers but also taxi drivers, waiters and former plantation owners from the Congo (Chapleau, 1998: 33-4). 'Mad Mike' Hoare commanded a contingent of 64 British mercenaries. Hoare later went on to serve Tshombe in fighting against Laurent Kabila's forces in eastern Congo, supporting Ian Smith's Rhodesia against the nationalist struggle, and attempting a coup d'etat in the Seychelles.

The next phase began in the 1970s, and for almost two decades there was relatively little overt mercenary activity on the African mainland. This did not reflect a decline in external interest in military activities in Africa, but rather a change in strategies. The relatively unsophisticated approach of recruiting individual soldiers of fortune as combat mercenaries became less preferred. It had proved too risky and too prone to adverse publicity. Instead, western countries adopted a range of alternative strategies to guarantee their interests. The first was by supplying arms to 'legitimate' governments. From the 1949 Mutual Defence Assistance Act, the U.S. packaged military assistance, economic aid and technical assistance. The first major beneficiary of this in Africa was Haile Selassie's Ethiopia, but from the 1960s onwards U.S. largesse was spread more widely. Independent African governments could be pliable clients. General Mobutu became Africa's foremost mercenary, his status camouflaged by the fact that he was ostensibly a head of state. The CIA's role in his coup and his subsequent reliance on U.S., French and Belgian military assistance was no secret.

Where possible, arms sales were preferred. From 1961, the Military Assistance Program was separated from the Foreign Military Sales Program, and successive administrations sought to earn cash for their military supplies. President Johnson stated, 'we will shift our military aid programs from grants to sales wherever possible' (McKinley, 1984: 35). In 1973 the Senate Foreign Relations Committee called for the State Department 'to get... arms sales business back to free enterprise where they belong' (McKinley, 1984: 59). Reflecting this, while arms assistance to Africa stagnated between the mid-1960s and the mid-1970s, arms sales rose from about $100 million in 1966 to about $3.5 billion in 1978 (at 1970 dollar values). But by the 1980s, few recipient countries could be relied upon to pay, so most arms transfers were on credit or outright gift. From a low point of approximately $40 million in 1974, U.S. military assistance rapidly expanded in the 'second Cold War', with each of the years 1982-5 seeing more than $300 million in military aid (Clough, 1992: 13). Most of this went to a few selected client states, notably Siad Barre's Somalia, Jaafar Nimeiri's Sudan, Mobutu Sese Seko's Zaire and Samuel Doe's Liberia. By 1988, as these regimes either fell or faced serious internal crises, the assistance levels had fallen to under $150 million.

United States arms transfers greatly understate the extent of western assistance to favoured U.S. clients, because U.S. policy was to encourage other western suppliers to provide arms on favourable terms. Thus Somalia also received significant arms supplies from Italy, France, Egypt and Pakistan. French arms exports to Africa rose tenfold between 1969 and 1978, and British arms sales doubled over the same period (McKinley, 1984: 59).

Among western countries, France was exceptional in its readiness to maintain large-scale military bases in Africa and when desirable even commit its troops to action. Britain and the U.S. preferred to use third parties, either countries such as Israel and South Africa, or private military advisors, keeping the role of its own military and security advisers to a minimum. Israel became engaged in the first Sudanese civil war as an arms supplier and adviser to the Anyanya separatist movement (Hutton and Block, 2001). South Africa was closely engaged in ongoing wars in Mozambique and Angola (where it committed its own army) and was active in destabilizing each of its independent neighbors. Although Israel and South Africa both had their own strategies and aims, during the Cold War each could be relied upon not to contradict the strategic goals of the United States.

The Eastern Bloc had a different pattern of military engagement. In line with Kruschev's doctrine of 'sacred' wars of national liberation, the Soviet Union provided military support, including training and equipment, to liberation fronts that were ready to align themselves with the USSR. The amounts supplied were modest, but welcome to impoverished and ill-equipped people's warriors. Lacking a doctrine of revolutionary guerrilla war, Soviet advice was often inappropriate, and many nationalist fighters looked to China and Cuba for inspiration and training. When socialist governments were in power, in many cases the Eastern Bloc sold or gave its cheap, mass produced weaponry and vehicles, often left-over inventory from World War II. In a few cases—notably Angola from 1975 and Ethiopia after 1977—the Soviet Union provided extremely large scale military assistance including military advisers. The Soviet Union also called upon its allies for specialist tasks. The East Germans provided security expertise and the Cubans sent combat troops.

There were however a few high-profile exceptions, in which old style mercenarism persisted. One example was the British mercenaries who went to Angola in 1976, some of whom were captured and executed, while others ended up fighting one another. Another was Idi Amin's employment of British military advisers. A third case was the repeated coup attempts in the Comoros. Bob Denard was a leading example of a mercenary commander who was able to act on his own as an autonomous agent, staging coup attempts.

The end of the Cold War and the surrender of Apartheid saw another period of instability and turmoil. The 1990s witnessed the return of white combat mercenaries in wars associated with state collapse, declining military capacity of governments, and high potential profits from mineral resources. This also coincided with heightened availability of a range of private military services. Between 1987 and 1994, worldwide military forces are estimated to have fallen from 28.3 million to 23.5 million (Chapleau, 1998: 86), so that literally millions of trained military professionals found themselves seeking work. For a while, it seemed as though mercenarism was to become the dominant mode of international military engagement in Africa. International mercenaries, who had been considered as pariahs for several decades, suddenly received a remarkably good press. In the mid- and late 1990s, a number of analysts suggested that it was time to question the unacceptability of IPMCs, and even to propose them as part of proposed solutions to African internal conflicts.

The role played by Executive Outcomes (EO) in assisting the government of Sierra Leone against the Revolutionary United Front insurrection, is usually cited as the exemplary case of the 'legitimate' use of IPMCs in certain circumstances. According to some journalists and analysts, EO contributed professional skills and discipline to a legitimate elected government, enabling it to hold off a serious military challenge from a rebel front with a regressive political programme that was also responsible for very serious human rights abuses. They argue that EO may have been paid handsomely, but its combat operations respected the Geneva Conventions, and it helped preserve a fragile democracy. Its departure was followed by a collapse of that democracy within one hundred days—as predicted by EO operatives. In its place, there is a complex and expensive multinational intervention to restore the elected government, and maintain it in power, which has not yet succeeded in bringing peace to the country.

This case raises a range of questions about the demand for mercenary services in Africa. These will be discussed in more detail below. In the meantime, it is important to sketch the transformation in the supply that occurred in the immediate aftermath of the Cold War and the end of Apartheid.

The demobilization of former Eastern Bloc militaries, military suppliers and military logistical specialists, had a profound impact on conflicts across the globe. The arms supplies unleashed onto the world market as a result of the running-down of Eastern Bloc militaries is well known. The same phenomenon exists for the military labor supply. Many well-trained soldiers, flight crews, arms suppliers, and engineers begun to seek work in the profession they know best.

Another major source of mercenaries is the international Islamist forces that were mobilized for the Afghan Jihad after 1979. Thousands of volunteers from across the Arab and Islamic world flocked to Afghanistan over a ten year period, where they were massively armed, funded and trained by the CIA and Pakistani military. Among them was the Saudi businessman and Mujahid, Osama bin Laden. Since the withdrawal of Soviet forces from Afghanistan, many former members of the international brigades of the Afghan Mujahidiin have sought to use their skills and weapons elsewhere, in conflicts ranging from Kashmir and Chechnya to Sudan and Algeria. The ideological orientation of these fighters sometimes means that they are seeking their rewards in the next life rather than this one. However, others are ready to be mobilized in a more conventional private sector manner.

At the opposite end of the political spectrum, former special service officers from Apartheid South Africa are also on the job market, both as individuals and in the form of companies. The case of Executive Outcomes fits this model well. EO started out as a state-sponsored clandestine destabilization unit, set up by the Apartheid government, and aimed at the Frontline States as part of the 'total strategy' of undermining black-ruled Southern African governments. By the early 1990s, South African policy had changed and EO's services were no longer required by the state. Instead, EO was encouraged to go private, to seek alternative markets for its services. Although the exact identities of EO's founders remain unclear, its rapid growth in the mid-1990s undoubtedly owed much to its aggressive promotion by Eeben Barlow. One of its first and biggest contracts was in Angola, serving the Angolan government—on the opposite side to that which South Africa had been supporting until very recently.

In its buccaneering image, notably its readiness to engage in combat operations, EO resembled the mercenary units put together for the Congolese civil war in the 1960s. These echoes proved too problematic for the company to maintain its respectability in the 1990s, and in due course EO was closed. However, this did not reflect the end of the careers of Barlow and his companions in EO. Instead, they resurfaced in new form, with greater ostensible respectability. The most important successor company is Sandline International.

Sandline is anxious to project its image as a 'legitimate' and responsible private military company. Its website states that 'the business was established to fill a vacuum in the post-Cold War era at a time when Western governments' desire to provide friendly governments support in conflict resolution has materially decreased' (www.sandline.com). In this context, 'conflict resolution' is a euphemism for 'military assistance.' Emphasising its credentials as an agent of western policies, Sandline quotes from a letter written by lawyers acting on its behalf to British Foreign Secretary Robin Cook: 'Sandline International is in the business of providing military assistance to lawful governments.' It has expended much effort in stressing that it can be a quicker, cheaper and more effective alternative to UN or British peacekeeping forces. This is more than an attempt at corporate re-branding, it reflects a definite shift towards a lower profile form of mercenarism, comparable to the way in which the likes of 'Mad Mike' Hoare were replaced by discrete military advisers attached to diplomatic missions.

Military Professional Resources International (MPRI) is another variant of the western private military company. MPRI is based in Virginia and boasts more than two thousand retired U.S. military officers on its books. It stresses the provision of technical expertise and training over direct intervention in combat. Although a commercial operator, it has very close links with the State Department.

The supply of western military professionals has an additional significance, because of the way in which these individuals were able to embed themselves in the structures of international corporate capitalism. International PMCs were able to build complex and intimate links with mining companies, oil companies, arms manufacturers and others. In earlier decades, mercenaries had sometimes acted as powerful autonomous players. In the 1990s, however, their autonomy was raised to a new level of sophistication. IPMCs could play hide-and-seek in the international corporate world. EO could dissolve itself, with many of its leading figures re-appearing in Sandline International. Their assets and interests could be hidden behind front companies; their modalities of payment tied up in complex financial dealings.

The market for professional military services is secretive and cynical. It can lead to bizarre alliances between former enemies (such as EO and the Angolan government) and even between those who remain adversaries in a different context (such as the coalition of Serbian mercenaries and French intelligence that came together to defend Mobutu).

Therefore, just as the wider strategic context changed, allowing governments of whatever political colour to hire IPMCs, the services of professionals from many different quarters were becoming available. Supply and demand coincided in this new market.

This piece of history holds an important lesson for policymakers who seek to pursue foreign policy aims by means of military mobilization. What happens when the government changes its policy, or when circumstances change? All those who were trained and mobilized for war remain, and they will continue to seek employment in the profession they know best. They may also retain their ideological orientation, and seek to continue the struggle in a freelance way, making opportunistic alliances as necessary.

However, beginning in the late 1990s we can witness a new era in which high profile international mercenary activity appears to be declining, and perhaps more discrete, targeted and long term security interventions will become the norm. The principal role for IPMCs is likely to be training African security forces, which will then actually conduct whatever military operations are required. Given the long-standing pattern whereby foreign powers prefer to protect their commercial and strategic interests through cheaper, more institutionalized, and more discrete means of military engagement, this is not surprising. Two events mark the probable passing of EO-style operations.

One is the last-ditch attempt by Mobutu Sese Seko to shore up his collapsing regime by hiring a range of French, Serb and other mercenaries to defend the city of Kisangani from the Rwandese-led coalition of forces in early 1997. The hastily-recruited mercenary force was decisively routed by the Rwandese Patriotic Army and its allies, whose discipline, skill and knowledge of the fighting conditions outclassed the fearsome reputations of Christian Tavernier and 'Dominic Yugo.' In their rush to escape from the city before its surrender, the mercenaries fired upon the defeated Zairean troops that sought to block their road to the airport. European mercenaries were re-learning the lesson of an earlier generation: success is not a foregone conclusion, and defeat if it occurs will be personally and politically catastrophic.

The second is the 'Arms to Africa' affair in Britain: the scandal in which the British Government appeared complicit in breaking the arms embargo on Sierra Leone, through facilitating EO's activities in support of the Tijan Kabbah government. In strictly military terms, EO ran a successful operation in Sierra Leone. Against a much less formidable adversary than the RPA, it rolled back the RUF insurgents with minimal combat losses. EO makes a strong case that its activities in Sierra Leone were cheaper and more effective than the subsequent UN military operation in that country. However, the controversy itself demonstrates the risks to a commercial company of being branded as 'mercenary'. It was a public relations disaster. Moreover, EO itself faced major difficulties in getting paid, and has probably incurred a financial loss over this contract.

Traditional style mercenarism is therefore risky: militarily, politically and financially. The niche of combat mercenarism may simply be too small and insecure to sustain a large international company. Hence, the transformation of EO to Sandline International and the continuing growth of companies such as MPRI that specialise in discreet military advice and training. Just as western governments devised strategies in the 1970s and '80s to protect their strategic interests without sending white mercenaries into battle, commercial interests are relearning the same lesson in a new context in the 2000s.

The Military-Commercial Complex in Africa

International mercenarism in Africa must be seen in the context of commercial engagement in warfare in Africa. IPMCs can be seen as one end of a spectrum. In a number of African countries we see what may be called a 'military-commercial complex'. This is a variant on 'military-industrial complex' of some western states. The military-industrial complex ties arms manufacturers, armies and politicians together in a web of common economic interest. In the military-commercial complex we are not concerned with the production of armaments, but other economically profitable spin-offs from war and militarism. It is a symptom of the way in which war has become a means of livelihood and profit in some parts of Africa. Even in some countries at peace, military establishments have become deeply enmeshed with commercial activities, with detrimental effects on democratic life. Components of the military-commercial complex include the following:

1. Military involvement in commerce. In many military-run states and some

civilian ones, generals have a close engagement in commercial activity. This may be formalized, in the form of military-owned companies, or may be informal in nature. Secretive, corrupt or even criminal links between military establishments and the private sector may be an important factor in military governments hanging on to power, and the terms on which they are ready to hand over government to civilians. In 1978, Zairean President Mobutu Sese Seko encouraged military officers to become involved in commerce. In 1982, Sudanese President Jaafar Nimeiri set up the Military Economic Board, and brought a wide range of private sector companies under military control. Although the Board was dissolved (at the insistence of the World Bank) two years later, military officers' control of leading companies remained in place (de Waal, 1994). In Nigeria, the military's control over huge areas of the country's economy is legendary. For some Nigerian officers, service with ECOMOG in Liberia was a golden opportunity for making windfall profits through the export of vehicles and other saleable commodities. ('Every Car Or Movable Object Gone', quipped Liberians.) (Ellis, 1999: 163, 170-7).

2. Self-reliance by armies in the field. Faced with the financial and logistical problems of sustaining themselves in the field, some armed forces turn to income-generating activities. These range from extracting tolls at checkpoints, to looting livestock for sale, to trading in items such as hardwoods, gold, diamonds and even arms. Requisitioning food, accommodation, transport and domestic servants from local communities is a variant of this. These activities may have the immediate aim of keeping army units fed and well-supplied with fuel and ammunition, and they can also enrich commanders personally. In Somalia, the addiction of many militiamen to the narcotic leaf *khat*, and the readiness of *khat* traders to pay tolls in bundles of leaves has led to a self-sustaining cycle of mutual dependence.

3. Joint military-commercial operations. It is a short step from 'self-reliance' and self-enrichment to actually allowing military operations to be dictated by commercial considerations. A particular operation may be financed or supplied by businessmen who are interested in gaining or regaining control of a particular location where they have investments or where they see opportunities. Much of the Liberian civil war, following the killing of Samuel Doe and the initial failure of Charles Taylor to secure the presidency, appears to have been dictated by such considerations. For long periods, government operations in the Sudanese civil war have been determined by which merchants are ready to provide fuel and incentives for the officers. Similarly,

garrison commanders will be tempted to second their troops to serve to protect local commercial property, if local businessmen are ready to assist with salary incentives and equipment.

A variant phenomenon is connivance between commanders in opposing armies to sustain profits. For example, military officers in a besieged garrison town can have a vested interest in food shortages because they can gain windfall profits from their monopolistic control over food deliveries. Or they can make small fortunes by shipping out goods brought at knock-down prices from impoverished residents, desperate to buy essential goods or to escape. A protracted siege can lead to tacit or even explicit cooperation and profit-sharing between the respective commanders, at the expense of the civilian population.

4. Commercial construction of dual-use infrastructure. Private companies may assist in the conduct of military operations by building roads and airstrips, providing communications facilities and other essential infrastructure, and helping with the provision of employment and services to populations that are forcibly resettled during counter-insurgency operations. International aid agencies may also become engaged in a similar way, providing food, health care and shelter to destitute people who have been displaced by armies. A leading example of dual use infrastructure is the role of the oil companies in Sudan in building roads and airstrips that allow the Sudanese army to operate rapidly and effectively against the SPLA in the oil-producing areas and their environs.

5. A special variant of military profiteering has emerged in some armies in which the officer corps suffers from a high rate of HIV seropositivity. Army officers on regular salaries cannot possibly afford expensive anti-retroviral treatments that can prolong their lives, while army social services cannot afford to cater for their dependants after they die. But involvement in military operations, especially in mineral-rich localities, can provide a chance for buying essential drugs and also putting aside resources for their families.

6. Mobilization of militias. Faced with resource problems, it is tempting for senior government officials and military commanders to encourage self-armed militias as auxiliary forces. Tribal, clan or regional militias will usually support themselves through livestock raiding, looting and other activities. An extreme case is the Interahamwe in Rwanda. Many of them are in fact down-market mercenaries.

7. Buying in support and technical services. With the declining capacity of many African governments to deliver government services, including the basic

logistical backup for the army, and the trend towards privatization of service provision across the board, it is inevitable that the private sector will become more closely engaged in auxiliary services to the military. These services may range from provisioning troops to servicing equipment to supplying transport aircraft. Militaries also use commercial communications systems and may buy satellite images and other intelligence information from private sources.

8. At an individual level, many soldiers in African armies join up because of sheer poverty and the absence of an alternative source of income. For them, what matters most is obtaining a basic income, rather than loyalty to a state or a cause. Subsequently, conscripts may be drilled into a sense of loyalty and commitment, but economic motives are often basic. It is notable that many soldiers in one army have previously served in another: the RPA has recruited former members of the former Rwandese army, and some SPLA soldiers have defected to the Government of Sudan (and back again).

Across many war in the African continent, one can therefore talk about the 'mercenarization' of conflict. The engagement of IPMCs is therefore a logical extension of this approach to maintaining armies and conducting operations.

A variant of the military commercial complex is the phenomenon whereby a government sends troops to another country, by invitation, and one of that army's tasks is to engage in or guarantee commercial enterprises. One clear example is the deployment of Zimbabwean troops in the D.R. Congo, which is part of a package that ensures that Zimbabwean leaders can profit from the commercial exploitation of Congolese mineral wealth.

The extreme case is the emergence of warlords, itself a phenomenon brought about by the multiple causes including globalization and the decay of African governmental structures.

This has spawned local military forces that, either individually or under warlord instructions, engage in illegitimate resource appropriation and aspire to political power as a means of legitimising their leaders' economic enterprises.

Private Security Companies in Africa

Many African countries have seen the rapid expansion of private security companies. While mercenaries themselves may have an uncertain future, private security companies seem to have an assured market. These have a number of characteristics:

1. Poor personal security in many African cities has led to elites, middle class people, expatriates and companies treating their houses and offices as fortresses. Gated communities, surrounded by high walls and barbed wire, with uniformed security officers on patrol and checking the gates, are increasingly common. The market in private security is legitimate but easily abused. For politicians wishing to develop their own party militias or commercial protection forces, it is attractive to enter this market, which will generate revenue that can cover overheads. A private security company can thus merge into a politico-military force. Those who are 'protected' by such forces can also become hostages to their 'guards.' Also in some instances there is powerful collusion between police, private security guards and criminals.

2. Commercial enterprises in rural areas also tend to employ such companies, or to pay special incentives to local police or army to do the job. This is common for both domestic and international companies, and includes the protection of commercial farms and plantations, rural industrial complexes, oil extraction and mining. At what point does the engagement of private security to protect an oil installation cross over into actively supporting the counter-insurgency operations of an army? Many will claim that oil companies in Nigeria and Sudan, among others, have crossed this line.

3. In countries where the state has collapsed, notably Somalia, there is no alternative but the engagement of militia forces for protecting property, vehicles, etc.

4. The private security boom is linked to the demobilization of armies and special security forces after the Cold War, the end of Apartheid and the adoption of austerity measures by governments. There are many trained soldiers and security officers looking for employment. These individuals do not lost their personal contacts in military establishments when they are demobilized. They will use their personal networks with military and intelligence sources to evaluate job offers that come. If they decide to take on the contract, they will use whatever sources they can, calling in personal favours, to help them carry it out. Thus the line between private security and

governmental military and intelligence functions can become blurred.

Private security companies need regulation. There is high demand and legitimate supply. But in the context of poor personal security, decline of law enforcement institutions and the militarization of politics, it is important that their legitimate functions be separated from their illegitimate ones.

These considerations compel us to ask, what is different about IPMCs? Is it simply that they are international? Is it that they have a continuity of institutions and personnel with the mercenaries engaged by colonial powers and international commercial interests in the 1960s and '70s? And can we develop a strategy for the problem of IPMCs without also addressing these wider challenges posed by the military-commercial complexes of Africa and the 'mercenarization' of warfare?

IPMCs and Trans-National Corporations

This growing influence of corporate and sub-state armies is occurring at a particular point in Africa's history. Mercenary forces were used widely by the colonising powers in the 19th century and afterwards when European powers and their proxies invaded the interior of the continent. There are clear parallels in the way in which IPMCs are being used again now, as some countries' mineral resources are extracted on the cheap by transnational companies (TNCs). International commercial interest in Africa is focused on a few resource-rich enclaves, which can be serviced and protected in isolation from the poverty and instability of the rest of the continent. International PMCs are becoming part of the structure of corporate globalization. There are strong personal, financial and corporate connections between certain IPMCs. For example, some IPMCs are associated with TNCs, notably mining and oil interests.

The ethical issues are complex. It is important to identify the components of our discomfort, so as to be able to see which are legitimate, and which can be tackled. Among the ethical issues that colour our response to the TNC-PMC linkages are the following:

1. The implicit or explicit racism of the mercenary interventions. International PMCs often have a continuity of personnel and attitudes with earlier generations of mercenaries who were employed by colonial interests. The attitudes expressed and practices followed by their white officers may be racist. Some even revel in racism and in the obvious

parallels with their imperialist forerunners.

2.   Mercenaries often escalate the level of violence, especially through the introduction of high-tech weaponry such as helicopter gunships. They add an additional twist to the intensification of a war. They bring in more arms, and may prompt their adversaries to do the same, often in contravention of international arms embargoes. Hence they are a contributor to the militarization of Africa and the escalation of armed conflict.

3.   The excessively high profits garnered by both the IPMCs and (especially) the mineral companies that contract them (because only high profits would make it worthwhile to run the risks that such operations entail). IPMCs may make deals that include direct access to minerals such as diamonds, or shares in oil concessions. This is especially in cases where a bankrupt government cannot guarantee cash payment. There is a powerful commercial nexus between arms companies, mineral companies and mercenaries.

4.   The fact that revenues accruing to the host government are probably mainly spent on buying weapons and prosecuting war.

5.   The prevalence of corruption in the nexus between transnational companies, governments at war, and IPMCs, which mean that little if any of the benefits of the natural resources will ever reach the inhabitants of the locality.

6.   The fact that TNC operations may also be associated with violations of workers' rights, displacement of local communities, environmental damage, and other exploitative or abusive relationships with the local population.

Each of these elements is, in itself, a problem, and justifiable grounds for criticism. The tendency is clear. There is no question that the combination of TNC and IPMC activities, through their very nature, and because they will occur in the context of instability and violence, will tend towards raising one or more of these unpleasant ethical questions. But, is IPMC activity intrinsically wrong? Or are these problems just side-effects, and should IPMC activity be regulated so as to minimise or eliminate them?

Ideological Mercenaries

The common image of a mercenary is an individual motivated by money alone. However, there are also ideological mercenaries, who fight for an international ideology, and intermediate cases. We can distinguish three main strands of ideological mercenarism. The first is the familiar right wing variant. Many of the white mercenaries who fought in Africa in the 1960s—and some who fight today—were motivated not only by payment, but also by a particular cult of machismo and violence, and by right-wing racist ideology.

The second is the Islamist variant. During the Afghanistan war, the CIA funded and trained substantial 'international brigades' of fighters against the Soviet forces. Famously, one of these was Osama bin Laden, who has since become one of America's betes noires. Since the Soviet withdrawal, these Islamist brigades have scattered across the Arab and Islamic world. They have contributed to the conflict in Kashmir, to the terrorism in Algeria, and to the wars in Somalia and Sudan.

Finally, and controversially, there is the left-wing variant. For the sake of consistency, the left-wing 'international brigades' must also be fitted into this category, although they may be 'soldiers of conscience' rather than 'soldiers of fortune'. Che Guevara's expedition to the Congo in the 1960s and the Pan Africanist liberation fighters who joined Frelimo may have been motivated by the highest ideals, and may have taken no pay— but they *do* fit the definition of 'ideological mercenaries.' More recently we can identify the Pan African battalion that fought with the SPLA (including Ethiopians and Ugandans among others) in the late 1980s and early 1990s, and—arguably—some of the Ghanaians, Guineans, Burkinabes and others who joined Charles Taylor's National Patriotic Front of Liberia.

IPMCs and International Intervention

The last decade has witnessed a much more interventionist international agenda in Africa. There is a readiness for the international community, usually but not always under the auspices of the UN Security Council, to authorise military interventions. At the same time, there is a reluctance on the part of western countries to contemplate casualties among the members of its forces. The killing of eighteen American soldiers in combat in Mogadishu and the capture of one more in October 1993, and the murder of thirteen Belgian troops in Kigali in April 1994 was, in both cases, enough for those countries to pull out their forces as quickly as they could. But the public outcry in the west if mercenaries are killed will be muted, if there is any at all. Another reason is that the proliferation of low-intensity conflicts around the world has stretched multilateral peacekeeping resources to the limit; supplementary sources of intervention have therefore become a necessity, hence the hiring of the corporate dogs of war. Finally, supporters of private military companies see multilateral peacekeeping as too costly, slow, incompetent and ineffective. This, they claim, is because it is premised on principles of neutrality, consent of warring factions and intervening forces, factors that put too many bureaucratic hurdles in the way of effective intervention.

In the light of the above, some scholars see mercenary outfits and private armies as the peace-enforcer *par excellence* in the post-Cold War era, particularly in weak, resource-rich states that have been stripped of superpower protection and are threatened by collapse from within. For Howe, for example, 'private forces can start up and deploy faster than multinational forces, and may carry less political baggage, especially concerning casualties.... They have clearer chain of command, more readily compatible military equipment and training, and greater experience of working together than do *ad hoc* multinational forces. [In addition,] they may be financially less expensive than other foreign forces' (Howe, 1998: 308-9). Shearer, in pointing out the readiness to take sides in internal conflicts as an advantage IPMCs have over multilateral forces, insists that 'the growth of [private] military companies is a private sector response in part related to the shortcomings of negotiations in resolving [conflicts]' (Shearer, 1997: 859).

Private security has increasingly become an element in humanitarian operations in complex emergencies. In Africa, the turning point was Somalia in 1991-2. The few NGOs that remained in Somalia after the collapse of the Siad Barre government in 1991, could function only by employing private armed guards for their operations. Even the ICRC, for the first time in its history, decided that it would do so—on the grounds that the only alternative was withdrawal, and that would have contributed to a humanitarian disaster. The ICRC argued that Somalia in 1991-2 was an exceptional case demanding exceptional measures. But, it can be claimed that this was merely an extreme case of a common dilemma.

In many instances, humanitarian organizations find themselves paying, directly or indirectly, for 'security' provided by armies, security forces or guerrillas. It is rare for any armed forces to provide protection for humanitarian compounds, staff, commodities or vehicles without some form of pay-off. More widely, humanitarian agencies have found it necessary to employ security advisers who can provide detailed risk assessments for operations, train staff in how to respond to security emergencies, and where necessary negotiate for protection. This is a short step from employing IPMCs for advice on strategy and physical protection in extreme circumstances.

One of the outcomes of this debate is that IPMCs gain legitimacy. For obvious reasons they will tend to focus their public relations efforts on how they can play a role in humanitarian operations and as protectors of legitimate democratic governments. IPMCs obviously have an eye on this market. However, the TNC market is likely to be larger and more reliable. Hence, from the IPMC point of view, perhaps the greatest advantage of involvement in humanitarian operations, and even the debate about it, is that it provides them with cover for their standard and more lucrative enterprises. If IPMCs are being considered as UN subcontractors, then it will be difficult to enact legal measures to ban them.

The debate about the role of IPMCs in humanitarian emergencies has arisen simply because of the failure of most other mechanisms for resolving these problems, and the unwillingness of western countries to risk casualties. Aspects of this debate have not been fully aired, including the following:

1. An exaggeration of the capacities of IPMCs, to the extent that they are given an unwarranted mystique. Up against disciplined and determined forces, even the most fearsome mercenaries are no use. The way in which the Serbian mercenaries in Kisangani, Zaire, ran away when the city was attacked by Rwandese-AFDL forces in early 1997 is a case in point.

2. A misapprehension about the causes of multilateral failures. The U.S. and UN did not fail in Somalia because of lack of military hardware or unwillingness to fight. They failed because the strategy adopted was flawed. If the political rationale and strategy for an intervention is fundamentally wrong, it does not matter whether it is implemented by UN forces or by IPMCs. The main difference is the political fallout in the event of casualties.

3. A stress on the technical aspects of intervention and humanitarian operations, rather than the social and political. While there are clear areas in which current models of multilateral intervention and humanitarian require better technical expertise, the main requirements are for greater social and political sensitivity. It seems highly unlikely that an IPMC will be more socially and politically sensitive than a multilateral intervention force or a humanitarian agency. A 'can-do', operations-oriented, militaristic mentality is more of an obstacle than an asset in complex emergencies. Linked to this is the assumption that IPMCs are apolitical: they are merely a technical service like a transport contractor. Experience suggests that

this is a dubious assumption to make.

4.   The last decade of research and analysis into humanitarian intervention has concluded that one of the main priorities is for greater accountability and transparency, among all aspects of the operation including the military. The introduction of IPMCs would represent a retreat from this principle.

5.   It is true that neutrality can be an obstacle to effective multilateral enforcement actions, and in some cases (e.g. Rwanda in 1994), the unwillingness of the UN to take sides contributed to a disaster. However, do IPMCs represent an improvement in this respect? If IPMCs are ready to take sides, how do we know that they will take the side of democracy and human rights, and not the side of profit alone? How are IPMCs to operate where they have simultaneous commercial and 'humanitarian' interests which may not coincide?

While it is conceivable that some immediate, short term security dilemmas could be resolved by the use of private security forces, it is clear that they do not contribute to long-term solutions. In fact, it is virtually certain that they will cause more problems than they solve. The worst-case scenario is that some of the characteristics of IPMC-TNC operations will become reproduced in IPMC's so-called 'humanitarian' operations.

The IPMC issue is in fact a distraction from the main debate about humanitarian intervention and complex emergencies. Instead, the main focus for the debate should be on how to find solutions to the political crises in African countries.

Legislative Attempts to Combat Mercenaries

In a world of sovereign states, each of which has (or aspires to have) a monopoly of legitimate violence within its domestic jurisdiction, mercenaries are an anomaly. The concept of private security companies to provide protection against crime is acceptable, but the idea of private *military* organizations that practice warfare (a manifestation of political violence) is not. The consensus of international humanitarian law (IHL) has always been hostile to the idea that mercenaries could be legitimate combatants. Thus the 1949 Geneva Conventions restrict the rights awarded to mercenaries, and the 1977 Additional Protocols emphasis the differences between members of belligerent parties in internal conflicts and mercenaries.

133

International law has also been hard on mercenaries. Africa has led the way, with a series of resolutions against mercenaries and the world's first international convention specifically targeting mercenaries. The 1977 OAU Convention for the Elimination of Mercenarism in Africa was adopted in the aftermath of the use of mercenaries by former colonial powers, especially in Congo. Many African countries have signed this Convention. Although this is the strongest piece of international legislation of its kind, it suffers from a number of shortcomings related to its genesis at the height of the Cold War and the liberation struggles in Southern Africa (Kofi Oteng, 2000). It was adopted specifically to deal with the threat of mercenaries hired by colonial or racist regimes to combat independent governments, and did not envisage independent governments doing the same to pursue internal wars. The Convention therefore reflects the OAU principle of non-interference in the domestic affairs of member states. Hence it permits a recognised independent African government to utilize foreign military forces, including both the invited forces of another government and private military forces. In addition, the Convention's definition of mercenarism is limited to those who seek financial gain from their activities and does not include those who fight for ideological reasons.

Commentators have argued that the OAU Convention against mercenaries is in urgent need of review to cope with today's realities. An improved definition is 'the practice of professional soldiers freelancing in external circumstances away from their countries of origin or residence' (Fayemi, 2000: 16).

Subsequently the UN has adopted the International Convention against the Recruitment, Use, Financing and Training of Mercenaries. But this has attracted only 27 signatories and 17 ratifications, a number described as 'derisory' (Robertson, 1999: 200). Most western countries, including the U.S., Britain and France, have been strongly opposed to any general prohibition on mercenaries. They argue that they cannot restrict the freedom of their nationals to risk their lives in foreign wars, should they so desire, and that there are certain circumstances in which the use of mercenaries cannot be ruled as unacceptable. For example, it has been argued that it may be acceptable for a state to employ mercenaries when defending itself against an external aggressor. Instead, some opponents of a general ban argue that mercenaries should be prohibited only in specific cases, for example when a country is under UN sanctions, or is an aggressor, or when the employer is a criminal syndicate.

Domestic law in many states also restricts mercenary activities. In response to the international outcry against the operations of EO, South Africa passed a law restricting mercenary activities abroad. Following public interest in and criticism of British engagement in Sierra Leone, including the role of Sandline, the British government is also examining the issue.

There are clear cases in which mercenaries have been involved in initiating or escalating conflict. Historic cases include attempted coups in the Comoros initiated and implemented by mercenaries in partnership with opportunistic politicians. But, such cases are less common than the scenario in which IPMCs are brought in because of an already-existing conflict.

There are important ambiguities running through both IHL and international law concerning IPMCs.

1. International law provides wide discretion for governments to respond to insurgencies and rebellions. It is common practice for armies to have non-nationals in advisory or training roles. Where does the employment of advisers and trainers stop and the engagement of mercenaries begin?

2. IHL is applicable where the government's adversary is a belligerent that has a recognisable command structure and exercises some basic political and administrative functions. IHL does not, for example, extend to fighting organized crime, and there is no restriction on the use of private security companies in this regard. Where does crime fighting stop and counter-insurgency begin?

3. International law is premized on the existence of a state that is capable of discharging its basic obligations, including the maintenance of law and order. IHL is premized on the existence of a belligerent party that can fulfil the minimum function of maintaining discipline and administering a civilian population. What is to be done where these preconditions are not met? Strong arguments can be made that no commercial companies should enter a conflict zone where there is this level of disorder. However, if a company is already in place, and these conditions develop, is it entitled to stay and employ an IPMC? Arguably, it would be abrogating its obligations to its employees and others who depend on it in the local community, if it simply left. The same applies, with more force, to humanitarian organizations (as in Somalia in 1991-2).

Clearly, governments that employ IPMCs will try to push the loopholes and ambiguities that exist in their favour as much as they can. We may also find companies with legitimate commercial activities and humanitarian agencies making the argument that they are obliged to employ private security or even IPMCs, as the lesser of two evils.

This suggests that it may be both impossible and inadvisable to try to ban IPMCs outright. Might it be more appropriate to prioritize the restriction of the 'side-effects' of mercenary activities? This is an intrinsically difficult activity: of necessity, mercenaries will operate in the most violent, secretive, corrupt and dangerous environments. Instead, the final section of this chapter will suggest a multi-faceted approach, operating at different levels, with both short and long-term goals.

Implications

This chapter has argued that the phenomenon of mercenaries is a complex one, embedded in the current political and economic crisis in Africa. The engagement of IPMCs by TNCs, and the debate over their roles in humanitarian emergencies, is symptomatic of wider crises in Africa including the mercenarization of conflict and the need for mechanisms for intervention in complex emergencies.

There are existing legal prohibitions on mercenaries, such as the OAU Convention and domestic legislation in some countries such as South Africa. As this chapter has outlined, these need to be revisited to ensure that the appropriate enforcement mechanisms are established. As a matter of principle, mercenaries should be outlawed. The UN, regional and subregional organizations, and humanitarian agencies, should be bound by international conventions on mercenaries. Their ethical standards should be as high as, or higher than, states. This will also have the effect of eliminating the prospects of IPMCs gaining spurious legitimacy through selling themselves as humanitarian workers who happen to have guns. If the UN and other international organizations clearly indicate that IPMC activity is in principle unacceptable, then it will be easier to utilize legal measures and mobilize public opinion against them and their activities.

Meanwhile, it is perhaps even more important that the particularly deleterious 'side-effects' of mercenary activity should be prohibited and penalized. These include the following:

1. The escalation of conflict, especially through the introduction of new weaponry.
2. The breaking of arms embargoes.
3. The extraction of hyper-profits, including payment in kind, for both IPMCs and TNCs operating in conflict zones.
4. Corruption and lack of transparency in their dealings with TNCs and governments.
5. Human rights violations, perpetrated either directly or indirectly, through their logistical contribution to governments' war efforts.
6. Forced displacement of local communities.

7. Environmental destruction.

These abuses are, for the most part, already criminalized and the challenge is to find ways of enforcing the existing laws and conventions, rather than introducing new legislation. This is a campaigning issue for advocacy groups, including civil society in the affected countries and those who are in solidarity with them. A particular focus for advocacy can be the strength of the links between IPMC activities and these 'side effects': the idea of a 'good mercenary' is based on myth rather than reality.

More widely, this chapter has demonstrated how the phenomenon of mercenaries needs to be analysed—and responded to—in the wider context of how wars are conducted on the continent. African governments have a responsibility to reverse the 'mercenarization' of conflict and undo the 'military commercial complexes' that exist in Africa. A fundamental principle of good government and democracy should be the separation of the military from commercial activities, a linkage that leads inevitably towards corruption, meddling in politics, and conflict.

Alternatives need to be found for responding to the situations in which IPMCs appear to be a 'necessary evil', such as the protection of humanitarian operations and the defence of elected governments. The search for these solutions lies beyond the scope of this chapter, but we can mention, first, the need for *political* strategies for effective intervention, and second, the need for finding the right regulatory and legal framework for humanitarian operations in conflict (cf. de Waal, 2000). We cannot rule out completely the option of seeking exceptional measures in truly exceptional cases. In Somalia in 1991-2, for example, the ICRC decision to employ armed guards was undoubtedly correct. But we must recognise that few humanitarian emergencies qualify for this exceptionalism.

Finally, the prevalence of mercenaries reflects and sustains the belief that the only way of achieving political change in Africa is through the use of force. The militarization of society and politics in Africa has been a recurring theme throughout the chapters of this book. It is through long-term, comprehensive demilitarization that the continent of Africa will be able to achieve a political normality, and begin to meet the aspirations of Africans.

---

[1] This chapter draws heavily on Musah and Fayemi, 2000.

7

POST-CONFLICT DEMILITARIZA-TION

This chapter is concerned with what happens after a peace agreement is concluded, or there is a military conclusion to a civil war with one party emerging victorious. The management of the transition to a peaceful, de-militarized country poses even greater challenges to the former belliger-ent parties and the international community than the earlier phases of war-fighting and peace negotiations.

This chapter is particularly concerned with the challenge of demilita-rization. This is arguably the most important component of any post-con-flict transition. But it is also one for which the parties are often least pre-pared. Demilitarization is an extraordinarily complicated task, involving a wide range of tasks from actually removing arms from former combat-ants to ensuring that former combatants can be absorbed into civilian life to promoting a change in political culture to render political violence ille-gitimate. Demilitarization is not helped by the multiple difficulties of post-conflict transitions themselves.

The Complexity of Transitions

The management of post-conflict transitions is one of the most complex challenges for contemporary Africa. It is compounded by the fact that most post-conflict countries are expected to undertake several transitions at the same time, including some or all of the following: from war to peace, from authoritarianism to democracy, from subjugation to self-determination, from command economies to free markets, and from relief to development. Some transitions have been successful, but most have been fraught with problems, and some have collapsed back into war and even genocide.

International organizations and donors have usually sought to handle transitions on a case-by-case basis, in two respects: one country at a time; and each element of a multiple transition without full reference to the others. This approach has shortcomings, and a strong case can be made that transitions require support in a much more strategic, patient and regional manner. Many countries have been called upon to make transitions to peace and democracy in a regional context that is unfavorable. For example, the post-1991 transitions in Eritrea and Ethiopia had to take place in the context of civil wars in neighboring Sudan and Somalia, both of which had a destabilizing effect. The attempted transition in Rwanda negotiated at Arusha in 1993 was undermined within a few months by the coup and subsequent massacres in Burundi. It is very likely that no successful transition would have been possible in Namibia and Mozambique had there not been simultaneously the beginnings of a transition to democracy in South Africa. Few countries are immune to destabilization by a neighbor at war. South Africa and Nigeria are possibly the only such cases in sub-Saharan Africa, simply by virtue of their size. A basic lesson is that most countries will not have a successful transition if it is handled in isolation.

In several cases, countries have suffered from 'transition overload', being called upon to make several stressful transitions at the same time. The case of Rwanda in 1993-4 is instructive: the country was undergoing a major economic 'adjustment', a transition from war to peace, and also a transition from one party to multi-party system, all at the same time. The multiple stresses would have required a combination of extremely skillful national political leadership combined with a sympathetic but forceful international support to avoid the transition collapsing. In the event, the stresses were too much for the country's political system and the extremist political leadership relaunched the genocide that the peace agreement was designed to halt. Another failed transition occurred in the Democratic Republic of Congo in 1997-8, and again much of the blame can be attributed to the fact that the country had to undergo simultaneous military, political and economic transitions without a facilitative international environment. The basic lesson from these experiences is the necessity of careful linking and sequencing of elements of transitions.

Transitions fall into a spectrum between defeated transitions and negotiated transitions. Ethiopia and Eritrea after 1991 and D.R. Congo are examples of the former; Zimbabwe in 1979 and South Africa in 1994 are examples of the latter. However, this is not a simple dichotomy: most cases are a mix. Victorious forces usually have to negotiate with others. Even in Eritrea, in which a single armed force enjoyed a position of total and undisputed dominance and did not permit any other political organizations, the ruling party negotiated with some individuals for their return on a case by case basis. It is difficult to say which kind of transition is more viable. There are cases of successes and failures for both kinds.

Transitions vary as to their speed of implementation. At the outset, expectations are high and enthusiasm is great. But patience is important. There are always setbacks and risks, and it is important to anticipate these and not to let them derail the process. Usually, immediately after a peace agreement or an outright military victory, there is a honeymoon period of quiet, followed by an upsurge in insecurity, perhaps related to the banditry of frustrated demobilized soldiers or the insurrection of armed groups that suddenly realize that their expectations will not be met. Handling such threats in a restrained manner, and avoiding panic or overreaction, is important, for national governments, neighbors and international actors.

Political transitions also vary as to the degree of external involvement. This can be very high, as with Namibia, or minimal, as with Ethiopia and Eritrea. However, donor financial involvement in economic transitions is always high, with corresponding impact on political transitions. External involvement, including mediation and peacekeeping forces, can be central to the success of some transitions. For example, persuading Renamo to engage in the peace process and democratization in Mozambique depended heavily on external guarantees. In Sierra Leone, the survival of the elected government is wholly dependent on the ECOMOG forces (initially) and the UN (and increasingly the British) military intervention.

But a high degree of external involvement in negotiation can also bring limitations. For example if the parties are seeking a creative approach to conflict resolution such as self-determination, the concerns of foreign mediators can be a problem. The fact that the self-declared Republic of Somaliland, formerly north-west Somalia, which has been consistently far more stable than southern Somalia, has not been recognized, reflects this. The United Nations and other facilitators are more concerned with maintaining a unitary state of Somalia than with exploring the arguably more practical solution of multiple states. By contrast, Eritrean independence was achieved by force of arms in the context of a long term unwillingness that grew into a readiness to recognize this reality by both Ethiopia and the wider international community. The U.S. convened the May 1991 London peace talks in part with the agenda of maintaining Eritrea as a region of Ethiopia, but was faced with a *fait accompli*. Ethiopia's federal constitution was negotiated purely internally—with the EPRDF in a dominant position—which allowed for a high degree of innovation. No international mediator would have been so ready to accept this.

Transitions are extremely complex and place great demands on governments. The normal requirements of managing government are magnified. These challenges are compounded by the shortage of trained people in African countries, a problem particularly acute in war-torn countries because many are killed or flee abroad.

From War to Peace

A post-war period is always dangerous. There are forces with an interest in renewed war, disgruntled individuals, and no shortage of soldiers and weapons. One of the major tasks of a post-conflict transition is the merging of armies, disarmament, demobilization and the reintegration of former combatants. Commonly, the security aspects of a peace agreement demand the most protracted and complex negotiations.

Failure to address the security aspects of a transition can lead to disastrous failure. In Angola there were high hopes of simultaneous transitions to peace and democracy in 1991. But the failure to ensure effective disarmament and demobilization of forces before elections were held undermined the entire process, resulting in a renewed war even more bloody and destructive than its predecessor. Subsequent 'transitions' in Angola have proved to be no more than truces, during which the billigerents took the opportunity to rearm and reorganize their forces.

There is a need for a comparative study of the success or otherwise of transitions. While there has been academic and policy-related attention to the prospects of success in peace negotiations, the question of whether a peace agreement or negotiated transition will actually stick has been less investigated. Is it possible to generate simple empirical correlations between factors that influence the success or failure of transitions? What incentives and disincentives are crucial to preventing the return to conflict? One hypothesis to be tested is that it is the financial incentives for the belligerent parties' leaders that are key: the more economically comfortable they become with peace and power-sharing the less likely they are to resume a war.

Cases such as Angola lend support to the argument for cutting a deal between the elites behind the different parties, dividing the top jobs, and settling all the outstanding security issues, before moving towards elections. But this makes a mockery of democratization and frustrates the basic and most legitimate demands of the people. If there is to be peace with democracy, then all aspects of disarmament, demobilization and integration need to be planned and implemented very carefully. The following sections examine components of this.

The Creation of a New Army

A new national army should be one of the main outcomes of any transition. This is always an exceptionally sensitive and complicated issue. In the case of a merging of former adversaries, it raises the following questions, among others:

1. Size, composition and mix of new national army; proportion of officers and men to be drawn from different existing groups.
2. Compatibility of ranks between different armed forces, and equivalences of qualifications (e.g. how are long-serving rebel commanders who have not gone to any staff college or military academy to be recognized).
3. Integration of forces and command structures (at what level different armed forces should maintain separate units or be merged).
4. Standardization of disciplinary procedures.
5. Accountability for past abuses.
6. Pensions, widows' allowances and disability benefits.
7. Procedures for new recruitment.

In cases where the merging of forces is not an issue, the challenges will be fewer. This may be where the opposition is purely civil (e.g. military rule has been brought down by civil protest), or where an insurrection has been militarily crushed but there is still a need for a political settlement. Alongside these practical issues, there are the political and cultural issues of ensuring that a new national army stays out of politics, and does not engage in political violence (mutinies, attempted coups, or threats of these). The armed forces will need to have the size, posture, training and orientation appropriate for the preservation of national security.

Each country will need to find its own path. The foundation for this should be coherent national security doctrine, appropriate to each country.

To date, there has been a remarkable lack of public debate on national security issues across Africa. Conducting such debates and trying to establish consensuses on the basic elements of national security is a task for the immediate future.

Problem of Dealing with Multiple Armies

In many cases, the war-peace transition involves multiple armed forces. As well as the different kinds of armed forces aligned with the main billigerents, there may be others. For example in Ethiopia in 1991, there were literally dozens of small liberation fronts, some of which had no more than a handful of members. Some were virtually defunct, having at one time waged a real struggle. Others were created in the final weeks of the struggle against Mengistu, or even formed after his defeat. Some had a real base among a certain constituency, others did not. In Sudan today there are many different armed forces, some members of the opposition National Democratic Alliance, some aligned with the government, and others that are mainly self-armed in defence of the interests of a particular group.

In such situations, questions of political pluralism, recognition of parties, devolution of power, and distribution of seats in a national assembly and posts in national and regional governments, are inseparable from the decision whether or not to recognize a certain armed group as legitimate, or not. There are difficult judgements to make as to whether a certain group requires a political response (a negotiated agreement) or a security one (confrontation, arrest and detention).

Disarmament and Demobilization

Disarmament deals with the problem of getting armaments out of the hands of private individuals, especially demobilized combatants and former members of militias and security forces, so that the state can reassert its monopoly on the legitimate use of force. Experience suggests that the more voluntary the process of disarmament, the quicker, cheaper and less dangerous it will be. However, it is likely that any disarmament process will have to involve some non-voluntary components, because some individuals or groups will always be reluctant to surrender their weapons which they see as a guarantee of their position and security. Linked to disarmament are two other issues, namely controlling the market in arms, in particular the private market in small arms, and the clearance and destruction of land mines.

Demobilization deals with how the excess number of combatants, who cannot be absorbed into the new structure of the national armed forces, are to be dealt with. The combatants in question include various categories:

1. Members of national armed forces.
2. Members of specialized security forces.
3. Former anti-government guerrillas.
4. Militiamen in organized forces aligned with one of the major parties.
5. Those who have taken arms in self-defence, independent of any major party.
6. Child soldiers.
7. War veterans.

Each category needs to be treated differently. A basic rule is that the more the problems are understood and planned for, the greater the possibility of obtaining cooperation. For example, if all those in category 5—the self-armed—are treated as illegal-armed bandits, and their arms are forcibly confiscated, then serious problems may ensue. Instead it is far better to link their disarmament with a parallel process of addressing the problems that caused them to become armed in the first place, which may be a problem of local crime, or local ethnic disputes. It is also important to bear in mind that the early stages of demobilization may see an increase in crime, as some demobbees prefer to retain their weapons and turn to armed banditry to gain a livelihood.

Child soldiers have a special status and special needs that are increasingly given special attention by national and international agencies. There is a growing literature on this subject and their needs will not be discussed in detail here. However, it is important to mention that the definition of a child soldier as any combatant under age eighteen can create difficulties. While we can be confident that a child of, say eight or ten years old, is solely a victim in need of demobilization, rehabilitation and education, the same is not necessarily true of youth in their mid-teens. In all societies, teenagers are a politically aware and active group. In most African societies, 15- and 16-year-olds are traditionally considered old enough to fight. In some African wars, teenagers have been among the most ready volunteers to join insurgencies. For example, this was the case in Uganda in the 1980s and in Sudan. These young people may be highly motivated and unwilling to be demobilized, and they may particularly resent the condescending attitudes of those who seek to infantilize their status and ignore their motivations for taking up arms. It is indicative that some recent attempts to demobilize 'child' soldiers from the SPLA have met with threats of resistance from teenage soldiers.

Veterans—those already retired or demobilized from the armed forces when the peace agreement is signed—are easily overlooked but are an important category. They have legitimate claims and grievances. They are likely to be experienced soldiers who have status and influence among their comrades.

It is very likely that the parties will try to trick their adversaries and any independent disarmament commission, by holding some forces in reserve, or 'demobilizing' soldiers into newly-created paramilitary units.

Spontaneous demobilization occurs when combatants simply desert and return to their families. Many combatants who have been unwillingly conscripted will do this at the end of a war, particularly if they have only recently been recruited. Others have developed parallel business interests to which they can turn their attention. Organized demobilization usually involves the encampment of combatants, followed by their registration and disarmament, which is then followed by their rehabilitation or retraining and release. The longer soldiers have served, and the fewer non-military skills they have, the longer and more difficult the process of demobilization will be. Demobilization must include a comprehensive socio-economic settlement and sustainable lives outside of uniform and guns.

It is tempting to place demobilized soldiers into the police and various other uniformed forces. This is fraught with problems. The skills and attitude needed among civilian police are very different to those need for soldiers. In addition, placing demobbees in forces such as wildlife scouts or demining units, or creating new units for them, runs the risk of creating paramilitary units that may become autonomous or aligned with a political party.

It is certain that security problems will arise during any demobilization. The question is not *if* there will be incidents of violence, perhaps even including mutinies, but *when* they will occur and how serious they will be. There are several categories of violence:

1. Crimes carried out by ex-combatants, and armed banditry in rural areas, purely for economic gain.
2. Acts of terror or punishment by ex-combatants to draw attention to their plight. (The most likely targets are their former political leaders who they believe have neglected them.)
3. Destabilization and sabotage by former security officers still serving in official specialist security services.
4. Mutinies or rebellions by units that think they are being treated unfairly, who resist orders to demobilize or transfer. This is the most

serious threat to any transition.

5. Continuing armed rebellion inside the country or attacks from neighboring countries.

How should a transitional government respond to these threats? Each approach has its advantages and drawbacks. A 'law and order' approach that suppresses resistance with force is most governments' preferred option. If successful this will deter future resistance and reinforce the authority of the government. But if the grievances are deep, suppression will merely intensify them. And if suppression is not successful, then there is serious danger that the war will re-ignite. The alternative is negotiation with the resistors. If the mutinous groups are sufficiently well-armed and mobilized this may be the only option. The danger with this approach is that it lends legitimacy to violent resistance as a political strategy. It may encourage others to follow the same path in order to have their grievances addressed.

Clearly, a government faced with violent resistance to its disarmament and demobilization programme is in a no-win situation. The solution is to identify the dangers in advance as much as possible, so that violent resistance can be minimized (eliminating it altogether is probably impossible). Overall it will be helpful if the demobilization process is made as voluntary and participatory as possible, with good information passed to all involved to allay their fears.

However, the approach of early and complete consultation with the potential demobbees also has its problems. In particular, it is possible that if soldiers (on any side) are made aware of the likelihood that they will be demobilized, with rather limited prospects of employment, it is possible that they will resist making peace altogether. In some cases it is possible that achieving a negotiated peace depends on the unrealistic expectations of combatants that they will gain personal rewards.

Re-integration

The most substantive part of demobilization is re-integration: what will former combatants do *after* they are demobilized? Will they go 'back' to rural life? Or will they be unemployed, with the risk of becoming criminals and future rebels? How should their re-entry into civilian life be facilitated? What education, employment, training, incentives etc., should they be given? There are various possibilities in terms of development and welfare programmes aimed specifically at ex-combatants, or the provision of special rights and incentives for ex-combatants (such as quotas for employers whereby a set percentage of people employed are former combatants).

These considerations alone make it important that demobilization is correctly sequenced with any economic adjustments that need to be made. Successful reintegration is incompatible with austerity measures and public sector lay-offs. In many cases civilians will have negative attitudes towards former soldiers, therefore making former combatants socially accepted may be as important as providing economic opportunities.

Experience shows that few former combatants prefer to 'return' to rural life. Commonly they joined the army in order to escape from what they saw as an unacceptable existence. Many see themselves as future commanders or leaders, or as acquiring a good education, or as becoming entrepreneurs. It is important not to make untested assumptions about soldiers' aspirations. Reintegration programmes should follow careful surveys of the background, motivations and aspirations of the soldiers. During wartime and also during peace negotiations, it is very difficult to obtain this sort of information, as it is potentially a sensitive security issue. However, as soon as a peace agreement is signed, such research should begin without delay. The practice of settling the claims of rebel leaders and hoping they will deliver their troops has not often worked rather new 'leaders' are reproduced ready to go back to the bush or remain there.

Reintegration programmes tend to focus on providing economic skills and opportunities for former soldiers. But providing them with political training is also needed. Many soldiers have political ambitions, but may lack the political skills required to seek office under a civilian electoral system. Training former soldiers in the political skills necessary for fighting an election campaign may be a positive investment in civilianizing a country as it emerges from war.

Disabled or chronically sick former combatants pose a particular challenge. Their rights need to be carefully considered. There is a temptation to put them in special hostels or discharge them and quietly forget about them, but, quite apart from considerations of fair treatment, the potential for violence will remain. The disabled may feel they have nothing to lose and become ruthless and fearless, and they do not forget how to handle weapons. Disabled former soldiers in Zimbabwe and Somalia have caused serious disruption when their needs have not been met.

The re-integration of *civilian* members of guerrilla regimes is just as important as the re-integration of combatants. In cases of protracted struggle, rebel armies build up substantial civilian infrastructure, including administrators, teachers, health personnel, judges and law enforcement officers, etc. If a former liberation front sets up a new government from scratch (as in Eritrea) the problems are minimized. But if these personnel need to be absorbed into an existing national bureaucracy, there can be difficulties. For example, special measures will need to be taken to ensure that certificates and ranks awarded by the rebel movement are where possible, respected and integrated into the existing government system.

Rehabilitation

For individuals who have spent most or all of their youth and adult lives as combatants, entering civilian life can be a traumatic experience. Former soldiers have life experiences that are shared solely by their surviving comrades in arms. They may find themselves isolated, despised, misunderstood and frustrated. They may suffer personal or psychological problems associated with their experiences during wartime, problems that may be compounded by the lack of acknowledgment they receive from society, and their isolation from former comrades.

Post-conflict societies need to find a means of recognizing former soldiers and rewarding them, without reproducing a culture of militarism. This is a difficult line to tread. One element may be formal monuments and days to honor those who have died during the wars. Former soldiers retain great loyalty to their former comrades, and nothing is more likely to anger them than disrespect for the dead. War memorials and days of mourning are means of formalizing this respect for the dead, and also honoring those who survive.

Veterans' associations are an important means of providing social and psychological support and comradeship to former soldiers. They can also provide an essential means whereby former soldiers can organize in a non-violent and democratic manner to express their frustrations and press for their demands on governments. Without such channels, some may turn to violence. It is also important to develop appropriate mechanisms for counselling. Many soldiers are afflicted by post-traumatic stress disorder and other psychological problems arising from their experiences.

Sequencing Disarmament and Demobilization

Negotiating the right sequence for disarmament and demobilization, and then ensuring that the parties respect this, is an essential component of a transition. Forces with little political clout such as tribal militias may be disarmed and demobilized first; elite and politically-aligned forces are likely to be disarmed late or not at all.

There are very serious questions about how demilitarization should be sequenced with other transitional processes. For example, belligerent parties may insist that they retain an autonomous command to guarantee their basic interests during a transition to democracy. But then their politically-partisan forces may be in a position to intimidate voters or, as occurred in Angola, launch renewed war if the electoral results are not to their liking. Also, if demobilization occurs at a time of austerity and lack of employment opportunities, disturbances and mutinies are far more likely.

From Military to Civilian Politics

Transitions to democracy invariably begin with high hopes. The highest hopes are always disappointed; sometimes even the most modest ambitions are disappointed too. The case of Sudan in 1985 is instructive: the transitional government failed to resolve the fundamental political and economic problems of the country, and the successor elected government inherited a country in a deepening civil war and suspended from the IMF. It is little wonder that the elected government lasted barely three years.

Creating a pluralist political system with respect for basic civil and political rights is a hugely complex business, usually slow, and detailed discussion of it lies outside the remit of this chapter. The chief concern here is how civil politics is linked to demilitarization.

Introduction of Pluralism

Democracy is usually taken to mean a multiparty system. A transition to pluralism will be facilitated by peace. In fact, no democracy can survive if a war is continuing. Even apparently-vibrant democratic systems are undermined by conflict, as for example occurred during the parliamentary regime in Sudan from 1986-9. The likelihood of a successful transition is also helped if there is a strong tradition of civilian government, civil society, free expression, and tolerance of different viewpoints. This 'democratic culture' is important. Where it exists—such as in Senegal and Northern Sudan—it appears to persist even when there are systematic attempts to uproot it. Thus, for example, Sudan was able to organize very free and fair parliamentary elections just twelve months after the overthrow of the sixteen-year dictatorship of Jaafar Nimeiri. The main political parties in Sudan, which had formally been banned during this entire period, immediately revived themselves almost as though they had never been suppressed. But where such traditions do not exist, establishing them is a slow task.

The economic factor is important. Prosperity facilitates pluralism. If there is an expanding public and private sector, and there are real economic options to be put to a popular vote, then citizens are more confident in civilian politics and that elections are meaningful. Where the only economic future is austerity, whoever wins, then electing a government is not about defining policies but solely about personalities.

The most important factor of all is the demilitarization of politics. Multi-party politics can, under some circumstances, become the division of a country into territories controlled by paramilitaries associated with ostensibly 'civilian' parties. There is a tendency in many countries for political parties to adopt paramilitary models of organization. This is manifest both in the structures of command and hierarchy within the parties, and in how they conduct business and persuade voters. In many countries, political parties have had paramilitary wings, open or disguised. Intimidation of voters is rife by such 'youth wings', 'Youth for President X or Y', party thugs or similar para-military groups. In Rwanda, these armed wings were responsible for genocide. Democracy cannot be fully established until these paramilitaries are demobilized, and party politics is fully civilian, conducted without intimidation. In some circumstances, supposedly 'civilian' politics can be just as militarized as politics under a military regime.

Other elements include freedom of expression, an independent judiciary, and the existence of trade unions, professional associations, etc. But political parties are the making or unmaking of democracy. One of the main challenges in a transition to democracy in Africa, especially in the aftermath of conflict, will be creating the right conditions for truly civilian and democratic political parties.

Even in democratic systems, public discussion of national security issues is usually very limited, if it is not banned altogether. This removes some of the most crucial questions of national policy from any democratic forum. One of the most significant steps that can be taken to promote civil rule is to open public debate on key questions of national security, including the correct size and posture of the armed forces, the priorities for a national security doctrine, and the nature of relations with neighboring countries.

How quickly should political competition be introduced? And should that competition be completely free, or should it be managed in some way? In some transitions, there is little choice, because multiple parties have engaged in overthrowing the former regime. This is particularly the case for civilian uprisings, as in Sudan in 1985. However, where there is a military victory by one part, political competition can be managed, or suppressed altogether. This in turn leads to a number of questions. Should the government have a veto on any stage of the transition? Or is there a sequence that the government is locked into? International engagement tends to prefer the latter: the international community is impatient for results and does not want to be committed to lengthy political processes.

There are advantages to either arrangement. Centralization of power means that state institutions can be consolidated and stabilized before any transition is initiated. Where transitions are attempted without achieving institutional stability or the consolidation of power, as in Sierra Leone, they can easily be undermined. Where they are attempted without grave national questions being resolved first, they are doomed to failure. However, there is also a serious danger of a transition becoming so protracted that in effect the transitional government becomes a permanent force in power, endlessly procrastinating and saying that the country is not 'ready' for democracy or civilian rule. Nigerian military rulers have become adept at manipulating and prolonging transitions, ensuring that the outcome is favorable to the continuation of a powerful military presence in politics.

Abuse to Rule of Law

Countries emerging from dictatorship and civil war have taken one or a mixture of three different approaches to accountability for the past. Each has its advantages and problems.

The first is the amnesty or forgiveness approach. This is the traditional way to end an internal conflict or to encourage a dictator to yield power without bloodshed. In fact it may be the only way to get armed forces to lay down their arms, and especially security forces to submit to civilian rule. For this reason alone it may be the only option. Trials can be destabilizing—military officers who feel under threat may be tempted to mutiny or launch a coup. But an amnesty runs the risk of institutionalizing impunity, and in the long term, of encouraging abuse. In the context of a state-awarded amnesty, reconciliation between abused and abuser, or between communities that were in conflict, may be more difficult. In addition, even if a country wishes to grant impunity, the creation of an international criminal court, and the adoption by many countries of legislation that gives their courts extra-territorial jurisdiction for crimes such as genocide or torture, means that such impunity will only be effective within national boundaries. There is no statute of limitation for crimes against humanity, and the legality of amnesties for the most heinous crimes is always open to challenge, so that impunity can never be guaranteed.

A second option is a truth commission and its variants. Telling the truth is the basic requirement of justice. It is therapeutic for victims and shaming for perpetrators. It is an important exercise in human rights education and can also be a process of nation-building, as citizens learn what they have in common, and how many people from different walks of life suffered under a dictatorship. Truth commissions are often underrated, dismissed as toothless. But the very process of painstakingly and publicly documenting the past can have very important implications.

A third approach is the judicial one: conducting trials of abusers. The victims of abuses have a real and legitimate demand that wrongs be righted. Trials can be a way of purging the political system. But often the number of criminals is simply far too great for a judicial system to manage, and the lesser criminals will be let free, or merely given a token punishment. Questions of resources and speed will dictate that a smaller number be prosecuted properly, rather than a larger number poorly or slowly. The need to respect for prior amnesties will also limit those who can be prosecuted.

In the case of genocide, the judicial approach is essential, and the other approaches are possible only in the context of prosecution of the architects of genocide.

If the judicial approach is adopted—or if individual pursuit of cases is permitted—it is important that it is coordinated and not ad hoc. There is nothing more certain to induce cynicism among the populace than to see elite people pursuing claims for restitution of confiscated property through the courts, while those responsible for large scale rural massacres remain unpunished.

Finally, it is important that any procedures taken against members of a former regime are matched by the creation of a judicial system that is independent and effective, so that there is a credible mechanism for preventing such abuses being perpetrated again.

We should note that 'justice' and 'truth' can be made a fetish to serve particular political purposes. One way to silence critics of a new government is to accuse them of wanting to cover up the truth or obstruct justice, with the implication that the critic has something to hide in his or her own past. In some cases the accusation may be justified, while in others it may not be. It is important to stress that none of the three approaches outlined above can be truly politically neutral. All are influenced by political agendas, and in particular by the need to build a new national political narrative which will give legitimacy to a certain set of political forces and processes, and exclude others. All concepts of 'truth' and 'justice' are politically contested by the parties.

We should also note that the opportunities for pursuing the different options are narrowing. The creation of the International Criminal Court and the precedent set by the President Pinochet case mean that the international community is moving in the direction of the judicial approach. It follows that if a war-affected country decides for an amnesty approach, then it may lost international standing, and its leaders may run the risk of arrest and prosecution for past crimes if they travel abroad. The case of President Charles Taylor of Liberia may be the first instance in which an elected African head of state is likely to be detained if he visits Europe or North America, or perhaps certain African countries. The implications for local peacemaking are complex: we may be faced with warlords who can obstruct peace, who have nothing to lose because they can never gain international respectability.

What Becomes of a Liberation Front?

A liberation army is commonly run like a one-party state. The armed forces and political movement are under centralized control, which rules through a de facto state of emergency in the area it controls. I.e. army, party and government functions are not separate. At the level of the highest leadership, the roles are fused together. Individuals within the struggle may move between military, political and civil or administrative posts. There is no independent judiciary.

The outcome of a transition to peace should be the separation of these roles and institutions. But a former rebel movement that has enjoyed an effective unified political-military command will see many reasons against dismantling this.

1. If it is a victorious transition, those newly in power will be under little pressure to separate institutions and disperse powers. Those holding power usually try to accumulate more power, not give it away.

2. In a negotiated transition, the parties will be sharing power, but not fully trusting one another. There is always an incentive to cheat on the disarmament and demobilization process, and hold some forces in reserve as a guarantee. Or they may form a partisan paramilitary force, perhaps as a 'youth wing' or local militia. This is to be expected, but should also be minimized.

3. A former rebel movement will be reluctant to abandon the separate command of its own forces until the basic political objectives enshrined in an agreement have been achieved. For example, a regional force demanding self-determination is unlikely to abandon a unified political-military command until after a referendum has been successfully conducted.

4. A liberation front may lack the personnel, skills and organization to function effectively as a civilian political party. It may fear that its most talented political cadres will defect to form their independent parties, or that rival civilian parties that have not made the sacrifices of armed struggle will snatch their constituencies

154

away. There is likely to be an abiding fear that the 'revolution', for which so many sacrifices were made, will be lost to a party that is merely opportunistic and well-financed.

5. The conditions that gave rise to the formation of the liberation front may still exist, in part. Left-wing liberation fronts are usually committed to an ambitious agenda of social transformation in addition to taking political power. Having taken power, the programme of revolutionary social transformation becomes a priority. This is a long and challenging process, and leftist parties tend towards militarized mobilization of society in order to achieve the objectives of post-war reconstruction, development and social transformation. The liberation army is also envisaged as a progressive social force with a wider agenda than military victory: its energies may now be devoted to these tasks. Widespread demobilization after military victory would leave these socio-political aims unmet, and the front will be tempted to remain mobilized—or even undertake further mobilization—in pursuit of these objectives. However, this model of pursuing development and change will tend towards a militaristic mode of governance, dominated by a ruling party, and stand in the way of civilianising politics.

A negotiated transition to peace will therefore be a balancing act between giving the leaders of a liberation front the privileges and positions they have won through armed struggle, and ensuring that they cannot subvert the democratic wishes of the people through intimidation or resort to force.

'Demilitarizing the Mind'

As long as the strategies of coup, mutiny or 'people's war' remain perceived as a legitimate political option, any civilian political system will remain precarious. A fundamental challenge is to render illegitimate any form of violence intended to transfer political power from an elected government. This section discusses the culture of war and militarism in Africa and the challenge of changing it.

War is about gaining and exercising power. Combat is the manifestation of power at its most brutal and uncompromising. Certain forms of power relations are intrinsic to war, including authoritarianism, militarism, secrecy, obedience, hierarchy and of course violence. In 18th century Europe, some liberal political philosophers went so far as to say that war between monarchical states was no more than a conspiracy to maintain despotism on all sides. The conduct of war leaves little room for voluntary consensus, dissent, or democracy. Different kinds of political system ensure that different kinds of people rise to the top. During wartime it is most likely that militaristic leaders will emerge, who may be reluctant to introduce civilian politics.

Demilitarization is not an agenda of completely dismantling armies and despising soldiers and their values. The military cannot and should not be eliminated physically and their attitudes and values are an important component of any society. The problem is the military in excess: in excessive numbers and elevated status, and a militaristic mode of conducting political and social affairs.

Demilitarization is also a challenge for wider society. The values of militarization affect not just soldiers but all members of society. Military attitudes and practices can be reproduced at all levels of society: in party politics, in business, in religious organizations, in civil society, in schools, in the family. A particular challenge is the legacy of left-wing militarism, and specifically the idea that the unfinished agenda of revolutionary sociopolitical transformation should be achieved by continuing military-style mobilization of all sectors of society. This idea still exercises a powerful grip on many African intellectuals and political leaders, who therefore lend academic and political credibility to the idea of a militaristic mode of politics and governance. Militarist mobilization easily lends itself to metaphor for facing all kinds of challenges. For example, the ongoing attempts to contain the HIV/AIDS pandemic are commonly described by Africa's political leaders as requiring 'mobilization for a war.'

Understanding the culture of militarism that afflicts many parts of Africa is a challenge for scholars and activists. Why is violence so deeply embedded in so many of Africa's political cultures? One task is to study the legacy of slavery, imperialism and racist rule in Africa, and the hegemonic violence introduced into the continent during these centuries. Is there a continuity between this historical violence and what occurs today? And if so, what? But it is also important to analyze more recent cultures of violence, including studying the political philosophy of violence developed by, among others, Nasserites, Fanon, and 'people's war' theorists. Why have these been so influential? Why do they remain so strong even despite the practical failures of their advocates in government? A counterpart of this is looking at African advocates of peaceful political struggle, studying the political philosophies of non-violence espoused (for a while) by, among others, Nkrumah and Kaunda. Why were these abandoned? Can they be revived? Do they have continuities with the civilian, pluralistic, civil society-oriented notions of governance that are now increasingly accepted in Africa and globally? And how can specifically African traditions of non-violent struggle and social change be reinvigorated within this context? A final component is developing the feminist critique of violence, built around concepts such as 'hegemonic masculinity' (Connell, 1987). What resonance does it have in Africa? Does it speak to the experience of African women? Can such a political philosophy be introduced into the mainstream of political debate in Africa?

From various quarters, the pressure for civil politics is growing. Internationally, it is no longer acceptable for a government to claim a civil war as purely a domestic affair of no concern to neighbors or the international community. All wars now attract the attention of international peacemakers. Domestically, civil society organizations are more and more vocal in their demands for peace and civil politics. In the economic arena, civil war spells economic disaster, and militaristic political organization is notably inefficient as a basis for organizing an economy. Unfortunately these pressures have not yet translated into a lessening of the number of wars in Africa.

Implications

Each transition is unique and has its own dynamics and constraints. But the brief analysis of this chapter suggests several general lessons that can be drawn about the prospects for demilitarization during a transition.

First, transitions involve turmoil. Demobilization can rarely be carried out without some resistance and violence. Those negotiating transitional arrangements and entering transitions must be aware of these likely problems, and plan for them in advance. This point cannot be overstressed.

Second, far too little is known about demilitarization during transitions. There is an immense need for studying and understanding the security requirements of disarmament, demobilization, reintegration and the creation of new national armies. This agenda is so large, and the wish-list so long, and the resources needed so great, that it is tempting simply to conclude that demilitarization is either an impossibility, or requires such remarkable conditions of economic growth and democratization, that it cannot be tackled in a practical manner. It is true that the agenda is ambitious: this is the reason why it must be studied carefully.

Transitions are multiple and need to be carefully coordinated and sequenced. 'Transition overload' should be avoided. The most stressful periods of political transitions, such as demobilization, should not coincide with periods of austerity or economic crisis. This is particularly the case because countries engaging in political transitions are taking risks.

There is a need for some tangible benefits to accrue—and be seen to accrue—for transitions to stay on track. Donor generosity is needed, which could take the form of special post-conflict trust funds, debt relief, 'conditionality holidays', or similar measures.

Finally, demilitarization is more than the removal of armed men from the political scene. It also entails a profound change in African political culture, so that violence is delegitimized. In particular it involves ensuring that political programmes, on left and right, are pursued using civilian and non-violent means. Those on the left must recognize that abandoning violence and militarism does not entail abandoning struggle for social justice and human dignity.

BIBLIOGRAPHY

Adler, Emanuel and Michael Barnett (eds.), 1998, *Security Communities*, Cambridge, Cambridge University Press.

Bach, Daniel C. (ed.), 1999, *Regionalization in Africa: Integration and Disintegration*, Oxford, James Currey.

Chapleau, Philippe, 1998, *Mercenaries SA*, Paris, Desclee de Brouver.

Clough, Michael, 1992, *Free at Last? U.S. policy toward Africa and the end of the Cold War*, New York, Council on Foreign Relations.

Connell, R. W., 1987, *Gender and Power*, London, Polity Press.

Davidson, Basil, 1992, *The Black Man's Burden: Africa and the Curse of the Nation-State*, London, James Currey.

Deutsch, Karl, 1957, *Political Community and the North Atlantic Area*, Princeton, Princeton University Press.

de Waal, Alex, 1994, 'Starving out the South,' in M. Daly and A. Alsikainga (eds.) *Civil War in the Sudan*, London, I.B. Tauris.

de Waal, Alex, (ed.) 2000 *Who Fights, Who Cares? War and Humanitarian Action in Africa,* Trenton, NJ, Africa World Press.

Ellis, Stephen, 1999, *The Mask of Anarchy, The destruction of Liberia and the religious dimension of an African civil war*, London, Hurst, 1999.

Fanon, Frantz, *The Wretched of the Earth, Harmondsworth, Penguin, 1967.*

Fawcett, Louise, and Andrew Hurrell (eds.), 1995, *Regionalism in World Politics*, Oxford, Oxford University Press.

Fayemi, J. 'Kayode, 2000, 'Africa in Search of Security,' in Abdel-Fatau Musah and J. 'Kayode Fayemi (eds.) *Mercenaries: An African Security*

Dilemma, London: Pluto Press.

Gilpin, Robert, 2000, *The Challenge of Global Capitalism: The World Economy in the 21st Century*, Princeton University Press.

Grossman, Dave, 1995, *On Killing: The Psychological Cost of Learning to Kill in War and Society*, Boston, Backbay Books.

Howe, Herbert M., 1998, 'Private security forces and African stability: the case of Executive Outcomes', *Journal of Modern African Studies*, 36.

Hurrell, Andrew, 1995, 'Regionalism in Theoretical Perspective,' in Fawcett and Hurrell (eds.) 1995.

Hutton, Pat, and Jonathan Block, 2001, 'Dirty War, Part II—the CIA in Africa', *New Africa*, February.

Ignatieff, Michael, 1997, *The Warrior's Honor: Ethnic War and the Modern Conscience,* New York: Metropolitan Books.

Kofi Oteng Kufuor, 2000, 'The OAU Convention for the Elimination of Mercenarism and Civil Conflict,' in Abdel-Fatau Musah and J. 'Kayode Fayemi (eds.) *Mercenaries: An African Security Dilemma*, London: Pluto Press.

Magaga Alot, 2000, 'Regional Peace and Security: The EAC Model,' Paper contributed to Justice Africa consultation on peace and security in Africa, Dar es Salaam, Tanzania, 10-13 November.

McKinley, R. D., 1984, *Aid and Arms to the Third World*, London, Frances Pinter.

Moore, Mick and James Putzel, 1999, 'Thinking Strategically about Politics and Poverty,' IDS Working Paper no. 101, October.

Musah, Abdel-Fatau, and J. 'Kayode Fayemi (eds.) 2000, *Mercenaries: An African Security Dilemma*, London: Pluto Press.

Robertson, Geoffrey, 1999, *Crimes Against Humanity: The Struggle for Global Justice*, Harmondsworth, Penguin.

Seekings, Jeremy, 1993, *Heroes or Villains? Youth Politics in the 1980s*, Johannesburg, Raven Press.

Shearer, David, 1997, 'Exploring the Limits of Consent: Conflict Resolution in Sierra Leone', *Millennium: Journal of International Studies*, 3.26.

Walker, Martin, 1994 *The Cold War*, London, Verso.

Index